deliver us
from evil

ALSO BY DAVID BALDACCI

The Camel Club series

The Camel Club
The Collectors
Stone Cold
Divine Justice

Sean King and Michelle Maxwell series

Split Second
Hour Game
Simple Genius
First Family

Shaw series

The Whole Truth

Other novels

True Blue
Absolute Power
Total Control
The Winner
The Simple Truth
Saving Faith
Wish You Well
Last Man Standing
The Christmas Train

David Baldacci

deliver us
from evil

MACMILLAN

First published 2010 by Grand Central Publishing, USA

This edition published 2010 by Macmillan
an imprint of Pan Macmillan, a division of Macmillan Publishers Limited
Pan Macmillan, 20 New Wharf Road, London N1 9RR
Basingstoke and Oxford
Associated companies throughout the world
www.panmacmillan.com

ISBN: 978-0-230-74668-8

3 5 7 9 8 6 4

A CIP catalogue record for this book is available
from the British Library.

Printed in Great Britain by CPI Mackays, Chatham ME5 8TD

Visit **www.panmacmillan.com** to read more about all our books
and to buy them. You will also find features, author interviews and
news of any author events, and you can sign up for e-newsletters
so that you're always first to hear about our new releases.

To Alli and Anshu,
Catherine and David,
Marilyn and Bob,
Amy and Craig:

Great friends all

deliver us
from evil

CHAPTER

1

THE NINETY-SIX-YEAR-OLD MAN sat in his comfy armchair enjoying a book on Joseph Stalin. No mainstream publisher would touch the delusion-filled manuscript since the author had been unfailingly complimentary about the sadistic Soviet leader. Yet the self-published book's positive opinion of Stalin appealed greatly to the old man. He'd purchased it directly from the writer not long before the latter was committed to a mental institution.

No stars could be seen hovering over the elderly man's large estate because of a storm moving inland from the nearby ocean. Though he was wealthy and living in great luxury, his personal needs were relatively simple. He wore a decades-old faded sweater, his shirt collar secured all the way to his fleshy neck, which was thick with wattles. His cheap pants lay loose over his skeletal and useless legs. The hypnotic drum of rain on the roof had begun and he settled farther back in his chair, content to delve into the mind and career of a madman who had killed tens of millions of people unlucky enough to live under his cruel fist.

The old man occasionally laughed at something he read, at least the particularly gruesome parts, and nodded his head in agreement over passages where disciples of Stalin explained his graphic methods for the destruction of all civil liberties. In the Soviet dictator he clearly saw the leadership qualities necessary to drive a country to greatness while also causing the world to shake with terror. He tilted down his thick spectacles and glanced at his watch. Nearly eleven o'clock. The security system went on promptly at nine, with every door and window professionally monitored. His fortress was secure.

A crack of thunder seemed to cause the lights to flicker. They sputtered twice more and fluttered out. In the lower-level electronics room the battery backup in the security system had been removed, causing it to cease functioning when the power supply was interrupted. Each door and window was instantly disarmed. Ten seconds later the massive backup generators kicked in and brought the electrical flow back to full power, returning the security system to online status. However, within that ten-second span a window had opened and a hand had darted out and caught the digital camera that had been tossed from ground level. The window closed and was locked a second before the system armed once more.

Oblivious to this, the old man idly rubbed his hairless head; it was mottled over with scabs and patches of sun-damaged skin. His face had collapsed long ago into a pile of gravity-ravaged tissue that pulled his eyes, nose, and mouth downward into a permanent scowl. His body, what was left of it, had followed a similar route of degradation. He relied on others to help him perform the simplest tasks now. But at least he was still alive, when so many of his brothers in arms, indeed perhaps all of them, were dead, many by violent means. This made him angry. History showed that inferiors were perpetually jealous of those greater than them.

He finally put down his book. At his age three or four hours' sleep at a time was all that was required, but it was now that he required it. He called for his attendant by pushing the blue button on the small circular device he always wore around his neck. It had three buttons, one for the attendant, one for his doctor, and one for security. He had enemies and ailments, but the attendant was mostly for pleasure.

The woman entered. Barbara had blonde hair and was dressed in a hip-hugging white miniskirt and tank-top blouse that allowed him a liberal view of her breasts as she bent down to help him up into his wheelchair. He had insisted on her wearing revealing clothing as a condition of employment. Old, rich, perverted men could do what they pleased. His wrinkled face nestled against her soft cleavage and lingered there. As her strong arms slid him onto the wide seat, his hand slipped under her skirt. His fingers glided along the backs of her firm thighs until they touched her buttocks. Then he gave each cheek a hard squeeze. He let out a small moan of appreciation. Barbara made no reaction because she was well paid to endure his groping.

She wheeled him to the elevator and they rode in the car together to his bedroom. She helped him undress, averting her eyes from his collapsed body. Even with all his fortune he could not force her to look at his nakedness. Decades ago she would have certainly looked at him, and also done so much more for him. If she wanted to live. Now he was simply helped on with his pajamas like an infant. In the morning he would be washed and fed, again like a baby instead of a man. The cycle was complete. From cradle back to cradle and then the grave.

"Sit with me, Barbara," he commanded. "I want to look at you." He said all this in German. That was the other reason he had hired her; she spoke his native language. There were few left around here who could.

She sat, crossed her long, tanned legs, and kept her hands in her lap, occasionally smiling at him because she was paid to. She should be thankful to him, he felt, because she could either work for him in this grand house where the tasks were easy and the time in between long, or else go whore herself on the streets of nearby Buenos Aires for what amounted to pennies a day.

He finally waved his hand and she immediately rose and closed the door behind her. He leaned back on the pillows. She would probably go to her room, strip off her clothes, leap in the shower, and scrub hard enough to rub the filth of his touch off her. He quietly chuckled at this image. Even as a shrunken old man he could have *some* effect on people.

He vividly remembered the glorious days when he would walk into a room, the heels of his knee-high officer's boots clicking on the concrete floor. That sound alone would send ripples of terror throughout the entire camp. Now *that* was power. Every day he was given the privilege of feeling that sense of invincibility. His every command was carried out with no hesitation. His men would line up the vermin, long columns of them in their filthy clothes, their heads bowed, but still they eyed the shine of his magnificent boots, the power of his uniform. Playing God, he would decide which ones would die and which ones would live. The living hardly got the better of it, for their reward was a hell on earth, as painful and miserable and degrading as he could possibly make it.

He shifted to the left and pushed against a rectangle of paneling on his headboard. The piece of wood swung outward and his hand shakily punched in the combination on the safe door revealed there. He slid his hand in and pulled out the photo, then settled back on his pillow and looked down at it. He calculated that it was taken sixty-eight years ago to the day. His mind was still all there, even if his body had deserted him.

He was only in his late twenties in the picture, but he'd been given great responsibility because of his brains and ruthlessness. Tall and slender, he had light blond hair that was striking against his tanned, square-jawed face. He looked so fine in his full uniform with all his medals, though he had to concede that hardly any of them were actually earned. He had never seen combat since he had never been able to muster much personal courage. The talentless masses could fire the guns and die in the trenches. His skills had allowed him to seek safer ground. His eyes filled with tears at the sight of what he had once been; and next to him of course stood the man himself. He was small in stature, but colossal in every other way. His black mustache was frozen for all time over the expressive mouth.

He kissed his younger self in the photo and then did the same to the cheek of his magnificent Führer, completing his nighttime ritual. He returned the photo to its hiding place and thought about the years since he'd fled Germany months before the Allies marched in and Berlin fell. He'd come here by prearrangement because he'd seen the inevitable outcome of the war, perhaps before his superiors had. He'd spent decades in hiding but once more used his "talents" to build an empire of wealth from mineral and timber exports in his new homeland, ruthlessly crushing all competition. Yet he longed for the old days, when the life and death of another human being was solely in his hands.

He would sleep comfortably tonight as he did every night, his conscience clear. He felt his eyelids growing heavy when he was surprised to hear the door opening again. He looked across the gloom of the chamber. She stood there silhouetted against the darkness.

"Barbara?"

CHAPTER

2

SHE CAME FORWARD after locking the door behind her. As she drew closer to the bed he could see that she was wearing only a cotton robe that barely covered her thighs and dipped low around the chest. Her tanned skin peeked out at him from several angles, except at the flap of the robe. There he could see the paleness of her revealed hip. She had loosened her hair and now it swept around her shoulders. She was also barefoot.

She slipped onto the bed next to him.

"Barbara?" he said, his heart beginning to beat faster. "What are you doing here?"

"I know you want me," she said in German. "I can see it in your eyes."

He whimpered as she took his hand and drew it inside the folds of her robe, near her breasts. "But I'm an old man, I can't satisfy you. I . . . I can't."

"I will help you. We'll take it nice and slow."

"But the guard? He's outside the door. I don't want him to . . ."

She gently stroked his head. "I told him it was your birthday and I was your present." She smiled. "I told him to give us two hours, at least."

"But my birthday isn't for another month."

"I couldn't wait."

"But I can't do it. I *do* want you, Barbara, but I am too old. Too damn old."

She drew closer, touched him where he hadn't been touched for decades. He moaned. "Don't do this to me. I tell you it won't work."

"I'm patient."

"But why would you want me?"

"You're a very rich and powerful man. And I can see that you were once very handsome."

He seized on this statement. "I was. I was. I have a picture."

"Show me," she said. "Show me," she moaned into his ear as she moved his hand up and down inside her robe.

He pressed the panel, extracted the photo, and handed it to her.

Her gaze lingered over the image of him and Adolf Hitler. "You look like a hero. Were you a hero?"

"I did my job," he said dutifully. "I did what was asked of me."

"I'm sure you were very good at it."

"I've never shown that picture to anyone else. No one."

"I am flattered. Now lie back."

He did so and she straddled him, unloosening her robe so he could see her body more fully. She also removed the call device from around his neck.

He started to protest.

"We don't want the buttons to be pushed accidentally," she said, holding it away from him. She bent down so her breasts were close to his face. "We don't want to be interrupted."

"Yes, you are right. No interruptions."

She reached in her pocket and held up a pill. "I brought you this to take. It will help with *that*." She motioned to his crotch.

"But I don't know if I should. My other medications—"

Her voice dipped still lower. "You will last for hours. You will make me scream."

"God, if I only could."

"All you have to do is swallow this." She held up the small pill. "And then take me."

"Will the pill really work?" In his excitement a bit of spittle appeared on his lips.

"It has never let me down before. Now take it."

She handed it to him, poured out a glass of water from a carafe on the nightstand, and watched as he swallowed the pill and greedily slurped down the water.

"Is it getting bigger?" he asked eagerly.

"Patience. And in the meantime I have something to show *you*." From the pocket of her robe she pulled out a slim camera. It was the one that had been tossed to and caught by Barbara at her window when the power had gone off and the security system had disarmed.

"Barbara, I feel funny."

"It is nothing to worry about."

"Call the doctor to come in. Press the button for him. Do it now."

"It is fine. It's merely the effects of the pill."

"But I can't feel my body. And my tongue—"

"It feels large? My goodness. The pill must be working on your *tongue* and not on your other part. I will have to register a complaint with the manufacturer."

The old man gurgled loudly. He tried to point to his mouth but his limbs wouldn't work anymore. "Push the but—"

She moved the call device farther away and pulled her robe tight, cinching it up. She settled next to him. "Now, here are the pictures I want you to see."

She turned on the camera. On the small screen an old black-and-white photo of a face appeared.

"This young boy was David Rosenberg," she explained, pointing to the youthful but gaunt face on the screen; the hollow cheeks and glassy eyes indicated that death was not far away. "He never made it to his bar mitzvah. Did you know that before you ordered his death, *Herr Colonel Huber*? He was already past thirteen, but of course in the camps Jewish rites of passage were not observed."

The old man continued to quietly gurgle, his terrified gaze still on the photo.

Barbara pressed a button and a young woman's face appeared on the camera screen. She said, "This is Frau Helen Koch. She was killed by a rifle bullet to the belly fired by you before your first cigarette of the morning. By all accounts she only suffered for a mere three hours before expiring while your men kept back all attempts at aid by her fellow Jews. In fact, you killed two people that morning, since Frau Koch was pregnant."

While the rest of his body remained immobile, the old man's fingers started to claw the covers. His gaze was on the call device, but though it was only two feet away, he couldn't reach it. She tilted his chin back and held it there so he had to gaze at the screen.

"You have to focus, Colonel. You remember Frau Koch, don't you? Don't you? And David Rosenberg? Don't you!"

He finally blinked his assent.

"I would show you the pictures of the other people you condemned to death, but since there are over a hundred thousand of them, we don't have time." She pulled a photo from the pocket of her robe. "I took this from the frame on the piano in your beautiful library." She held the picture in front of his face. "We found your son and daughter and your grandchildren and your great-grandchildren. All these innocent people. You see their faces. Just like David Rosenberg and Helen Koch and all the others. If I had time I'd tell you in exact detail how each will die tonight. In fact, seven of them already have been butchered simply because of their connection to you. You see, Herr Colonel, we wanted to make certain that there were no monsters left to reproduce."

He started to cry, his mouth making little mewing sounds.

"Good, good, tears of joy, Herr Colonel, I'm sure. Maybe they will think our sex is so good you cry. Now it's time to go to sleep, but keep your eyes on the picture. Don't look away. It is your family after all." When he closed his eyes, she slapped his face, forcing his eyes open. She leaned down and whispered into his ear in another language.

His eyes widened.

"Do you recognize it, Herr Huber? It's Yiddish. You heard that phrase often in the camps, I'm sure. But in case you never knew the translation, it means, 'Rot in hell.'"

She placed a pillow over his nose and mouth but did not cover his eyes, so he could see his doomed family as his last image during life. She pushed down with considerable strength. The old man could do nothing as his oxygen vanished. "This is a far easier way to die than you deserve," she said as the pump of his lungs quickened, seeking air that wasn't there.

After his chest lurched one final time, she removed the pillow and placed the picture of Huber in his uniform in the pocket of her robe, along with the small camera. They had not killed his family and had no intention of doing so. They did not murder innocent people. But they had wanted him to believe, with his final dying breath, that he had precipitated the destruction of his loved ones. They knew his death could never match the horror of the slaughter carried out on his orders, but this was the best they could do.

She crossed herself and whispered, "May God understand why I do this."

Later, she passed the guard, a cocky young Argentine, on the way back to her room. He eyed her with obvious lust. She smiled back at him as she playfully twitched her hips, letting him glimpse some pale skin under her thin robe. "Let me know when it's *your* birthday," she teased.

"Tomorrow," he said quickly, making a grab for her, but she darted out of the way.

That is very good, because I won't be here.

She walked directly to the library and returned the photo to its frame. An hour later the lights flickered once more and then went out. The same ten-second gap occurred before the generator kicked on. Barbara's window opened and then closed. Dressed all in black with a knit cap over her hair, she climbed down a drainpipe, skirted the perimeter security, clambered over the high wall around the estate, and was picked up by a waiting car. It was not that difficult since the security measures at the estate were chiefly designed to keep people out, not in. The driver, Dominic, a slender young man with dark curly hair and wide, sad eyes, looked relieved.

"Brilliant job, Dom," she said in a British accent. "The timing on the power going out was spot-on."

"At least the forecasters were right about the storm. Provided a good cover for my engineering sleight of hand. What did he say?"

"He spoke with his eyes. He knew."

"Congratulations, it's the last one, Reggie."

Regina Campion, Reggie to her intimates, sat back against her seat and pulled off the cap, freeing her dyed blonde hair. "You're wrong. It's not the last one."

"What do you mean? There are no Nazis like him left alive. Huber was the final bastard."

She pulled the photo of Huber and Adolf Hitler from her pocket and gazed at it as the car raced along the dark roads outside Buenos Aires.

"But there will always be monsters. And we have to hunt down every one of them."

CHAPTER

3

SHAW WAS HOPING the man would try to kill him, and he wasn't disappointed. Seeing your freedom about to end with the distinct possibility of an execution date in your future just made some people a bit peeved. A few moments later the fellow was lying unconscious on the floor, the imprint of Shaw's knuckles on his crushed cheek. Shaw's backup appeared a minute later to take the man into custody. Shaw mentally crossed off his to-do list a heartless zealot who used unwitting children to blow up people who didn't believe in the same god he did.

Ten minutes later he was in a car going to the airport in Vienna. Sitting next to him was his boss, Frank Wells. Frank looked like the meanest son of a bitch you would ever run into, principally because he was. He had the chest of a mastiff along with the beast's growl. He favored cheap suits that were perpetually rumpled from the moment he put them on, and a sharp-edged hat that took one back several decades. Shaw believed that Frank was a man who'd been born in the wrong era. He would have done well in the 1920s and 1930s chasing criminals like Al Capone and John Dillinger with a tommy gun and not a search warrant or Miranda warning card in sight. His face was unshaven and his second chin lapped against his thick neck. He was in his fifties and looked older, with about eighty years of acid and anger built up in his psyche. He and Shaw had a love-hate relationship that, at least judging from the foul expression on the man's face, had just swung back to hate.

A part of Shaw could understand that. One reason Frank favored wearing his hat inside cars and indoors was not simply to cover his egg-shaped bald head, but also to hide the dent in his skull where a pistol round fired by Shaw had penetrated. It was not an ideal way to begin a healthy friendship. And yet that nearly lethal confrontation was the only reason they were together now.

"You were a little slow on picking up Benny's movements back there," said Frank as he chewed on an unlit cigar.

"Considering 'Benny' bin Alamen is the holder of the number three slot on the Most Wanted Terrorists list, I'll just take a moment to pat myself on the back."

"Just saying is all, Shaw. Never know if it might come in useful next time."

Shaw didn't answer, primarily because he was tired. He looked out the window at the beautiful avenues of Vienna. He'd been many times to the Austrian capital, home to some of history's greatest musical talent. Unfortunately, his travels here were always for work, and his most vivid memory of the town was not a moving concerto but rather almost dying from a large-caliber round that had come uncomfortably close to his head.

He rubbed at his hair, which had finally grown back. He'd had to scalp himself for a recent mission. He was only in his early forties, six and a half feet tall and in rock-hard shape, but when his hair had come back there'd been a sprinkle of gray at the temples and a dab at his sharp widow's peak. Even for him the last six months had been, well, difficult.

As if reading his mind, Frank said, "So what happened with you and Katie James?"

"She went back to being a journalist and I went back to doing what I do."

Frank rolled down the window, lit his cigar, and let the smoke drift out the opening. "That's that, huh?"

"Why would there be any more than *that*?"

"You two went through some serious stuff together. Tends to draw people closer."

"Well, it didn't."

"She called me, you know."

"When?"

"While back. Said you left without saying good-bye. Just walked off into the sunrise."

"Didn't realize there was a law against that. And why didn't she just call me?"

"Said she tried, but you'd changed your number."

"Okay, so maybe I did."

"Why's that?"

"Because I felt like it. Any other personal questions?"

"Were you two sleeping together?"

This comment made Shaw noticeably stiffen. Frank, perhaps sensing he'd gone too far, looked down at the folder in his lap and said quickly, "Okay, we'll be wheels up in thirty minutes. We can go over the next job on the wings."

"Great," said Shaw dully. He rolled down his window and breathed in the morning air. He did most of his work in the middle of the night and many of his "jobs" ended in the early morning hours.

I work for something loosely called an agency that doesn't officially exist doing things around the world that none will ever know I did.

"Agency" policy allowed its operatives to go right up to the line of legality, often crossing it, sometimes obliterating it. The countries financially and logistically supporting Shaw's agency were part of the old G8 vanguard and thus technically constituted the most "civilized" societies in the world. They could never employ brutal and sometimes lethal tactics through their own official channels. So they circumvented that problem by secretly creating and feeding a hybrid beast that was only graded on results achieved through any means possible. Typically, neither personal rights nor the benefit of legal counsel entered the equation.

Frank studied him for a moment. "I sent some flowers to Anna's grave."

Surprised, Shaw turned to him. "Why?"

"She was a fine woman. And for some reason she was head over heels for your sorry ass. That was the only flaw I could find in the lady, her poor judgment in men."

Shaw turned to look back out the window.

"You'll never find anybody that good ever again."

"That's why I'm not even bothering to look, Frank."

"I was married once."

Shaw closed the window and sat back. "What happened?"

"She's not living anymore. She was sort of like Anna. I married way above my pay grade. That stuff never strikes twice."

"At least you made it down the aisle. I never got that chance."

Frank looked like he was going to say something else, but lapsed into silence. The two men rode the rest of the way to the airport without speaking.

CHAPTER

4

The Gulfstream rode into the air on smooth winds. Once they'd leveled off, Frank brought out the usual file: photos, background reports, analyses, and action recommendations.

"Evan Waller," began Frank. "Canadian. Sixty-three years old."

Shaw picked up a cup of black coffee with one hand and a photo with the other. He was staring at a man whose head was shaved down to the scalp. He looked fit and strong and his facial features were sharp and angular, like an image on a high-def LCD screen with megahertz levels. Even from the photo the eyes seemed to house a current of electricity that looked capable of shooting straight out at Shaw, delivering a mortal wound. The man's long nose appeared as though it started mid-forehead and ran arrow straight to the top of his mouth. It was a cruel mouth if there ever was such a thing, thought Shaw. And this man was no doubt cruel and evil and dangerous. If he weren't all of those things, Shaw wouldn't be looking at his photo. He never went after saints, only violent sinners.

"Looks good for his age," said Shaw, dropping the photo onto the small table.

"For the last two decades at least he's been into anything that makes lots of money. On the surface he's golden. Legit businesses, keeps a low profile, gives to charities, is into helping third world countries build infrastructure."

"But?"

"But we've discovered that his underlying wealth is built on human trafficking, mostly young Asian and African teens mass-kidnapped by Waller's people and then sold into prostitution in the Western

Hemisphere. That's why he's so into third world development. It's his pipeline. He uses that as a way to get the product he needs. And his legit businesses launder the cash from those activities."

"Okay, that qualifies him for a well-deserved visit from me."

Frank stood and poured himself a Bloody Mary from the small bar set up against one wall of the aircraft and dropped a celery stalk in the glass. He sat back down, jiggling the ice with a long spoon. "Waller hid the details well. It took us time to get the goods on him, and even then it may not hold up in a court of law. The guy's bad, no doubt about it, but proving it is another thing."

"So why are we even bothering to go after him if we can't put him away? That'll just warn him off."

Frank shook his head. "This is not a snatch-and-prosecute. It's a snatch-and-rat. We take him and convince him it's in his best interests to enlighten us about a new line of business for him that we just found out about."

"Which is?"

"Nuclear materials trafficking with Islamic fundamentalists on the worldwide watch list. He rats them out, he gets a deal."

"What kind of deal?"

"Basically he walks."

"To keep enslaving young girls?"

"We're talking avoiding nuclear holocaust here, Shaw. It's a trade-off the higher-ups are willing to make. At least we'll put his operation out of business for a while. But he gets his freedom and all the money he's no doubt hidden around the world."

"So he'll just open for business again. You know, sometimes I get confused about which devil we're actually dealing with."

"We deal with them all, just in different ways."

"Okay, so what's the plan?"

"We found out that he's heading to the south of France for a little holiday in between planning nuclear holocausts. He's rented a villa in Gordes. You ever been there?" Shaw shook his head. "It's really beautiful, so I hear."

"So is Vienna, at least so I hear. All I usually get to see are the sewer pits, emergency rooms, and the morgue."

"He travels with heavy security."

"They always do. How do you see the extraction?"

"Quick and clean, of course. But the French are totally outside the loop on this. We can expect no help from them. If you go down, your ass is cooked."

"Why would I expect anything less?"

"The timing will be tight."

"The timing is always tight."

"That's true," Frank conceded.

"So we kidnap him, work on him, and hope he breaks?"

"Our job is just to get him. Others will break him."

"Right, and then let him walk?" Shaw said in disgust.

"The suits make the rules."

"*You're* wearing a suit."

"Correction. The guys wearing the *expensive* suits make the rules."

"Okay, but if you recall, the last time I was in France things didn't go very well."

Frank shrugged. "So let's get down to the details."

Shaw drained his coffee cup. "It's all in the details, Frank. Plus a hell of a lot of luck."

CHAPTER

5

REGGIE CAMPION drove her ten-year-old dented Smart Car City-Coupé from her flat in London past Leavesden to the north and continued on for a few more kilometers. After meandering through narrow country roads she turned off onto a one-car-wide dirt lane, eventually passing through lichen-covered stone columns that bore the name "Harrowsfield," which was the property she was now on. Her gaze then carried, as it usually did, up the twisty crushed gravel drive toward the old crumbling mansion.

Some claimed Rudyard Kipling had once leased the estate. Reggie doubted that, although she believed it would have appealed to an author who had created such marvelous, intrigue-laden adventure stories. It was a vast place, jury-rigged in parts, with secret doors and passages, stone turrets with cold chambers, an enormous library, corridors that ended in solid walls, an attic filled with equal parts museum-quality artifacts and junk, a rabbit warren of a cellar with musty bottles of mostly undrinkable wine, an antiquated kitchen with a leaky roof and exposed, sparking wiring, and enough outbuildings to house several army battalions on over a hundred hectares of neglected grounds. It was ancient, falling apart, smelly, mostly uninhabitable, and she loved it. If she'd had the money she would have purchased it. But Reggie would never have enough money for that.

She often stayed overnight here. A hopeless insomniac, she would wander the dark mansion for hours. It was then that she thought she could feel the presence of others who also called Harrowsfield home though they were no longer among the living. She would have preferred to stay out here full-time. Her flat was small, basic, in an undesirable part of the city, and was still more than she could afford. She had cut back on luxuries such as food and clothing in order to get by. She had certainly not chosen this career path for the income potential.

She parked the car in front of the old carriage house now turned into garages and a workshop and saw that several people were there ahead of her. She used her key to open the door into the mudroom of the mansion and a little chime was heard. An instant later a broad-shouldered muscular man a little under six feet and in his thirties emerged from an inner room. He was holding a cup of tea in one hand and a customized nine-millimeter pistol in the other, and that was pointed at Reggie's chest. He was dressed in tight-fitting, snake-hipped corduroy pants, a white button-down shirt with the sleeves rolled up, and slim black leather loafers with no socks despite the damp chill that was normal for Harrowsfield even in the heat of summer. His fierce dark eyebrows nearly met in the middle of his forehead and his shaggy brown hair hung down to them.

On seeing her he slipped the gun in his shoulder holster, grinned, and took a sip of his tea. Whit Beckham said, "Eh, Reg, you shoulda rung up when you hit the gateposts. Almost shot you. Be in a funk for weeks if I did that." His robust Irish accent had softened over the last few years to where Regina could understand almost all of what he said without the services of a translator.

She slipped off her jacket and hung it on a wooden peg on the wall. She was dressed in faded jeans, a burgundy lightweight turtle-neck sweater with the collar turned up, and black ankle boots. Her hair was returned to its original shade of rich dark brown and was secured at the nape of her neck with a tortoiseshell clip. She wore no makeup, and as she stepped into the light thrown through the windows, one could see, though she was only twenty-eight, the beginnings of a fine web of lines around her wide, intense eyes.

"My mobile never manages to work round here, Whit."

"I reckon it's time to get a new mobile service then," he advised. "Tea?"

"Coffee, the stronger the better. It was a long flight and I didn't sleep much."

"Coming up."

"Brilliant, thanks. Dom here? Didn't see his motorbike."

"I think he parked it in one of the garages. And it's not a motor-bike."

"What then?"

"It's a crotch rocket. Has to do with horsepower and such, see?"

"Right, interesting stuff, male toys."

He gave her a look. "You doing okay?"

She feigned a smile. "Smashing. Never better. You do it once, it gets easier each time."

His face creased into a frown. "That's a crock of shit and you know it."

"Do I?"

"Keep in mind that Huber killed a few hundred thousand people and got away with it for over sixty years."

"I read the same briefing papers you did, Whit."

He looked put off. "Well, maybe you need to take some time off then. Recharge."

"I am recharged. Only took that long flight and a couple of drinks to do it. Colonel Huber is extinguished from my memory."

Whit grinned. "You sure you're not going mental on me?"

"No, but thanks for asking. So who's here?"

"Usual suspects."

She checked her watch. "Early start?"

"New job, everyone gets a bit giddy."

"Including me."

"You really sure about that?"

"Don't be a prat. Just get me the damn coffee."

CHAPTER

6

Reggie walked through passages smelling of mildew until she reached a set of wooden double doors with lavish burned-in engravings of books on each. She tugged one door open and passed through into the library. It had three walls of books and sliding ladders running on tarnished brass rails to reach them. A fourth wall was lined with old photos and portraits of men and women long dead. The room was anchored by a floor-to-ceiling stone fireplace, one of the few in the house that worked properly. And even this one tended to belch smoke into the room with regularity. She took a moment to warm herself in front of the flames before turning to look at the people seated around the large Spanish-style table with turned legs that sat in the center of the room.

Reggie nodded to each of them, all older than she except for Dominic, who looked well-rested at the other end of the table. Her gaze then settled on the elderly man who sat at the head of the table. Miles Mallory's outfit was tweed on tweed with elbow patches, crooked bow tie, a wrinkled shirt with one edge of a collar pointing to the ceiling, sensible blunt-toed shoes, and socks that failed to cover the man's chubby, hairless shins. He had a massive head circled by a rim of grizzled gray hair that had not seen the barber's shears in months. His beard, however, was neatly trimmed and matched the color of his hair except for a creamy patch the size of a penny near his chin. The eyes were green and probing, the spectacles covering them thick and black, the jowls heavy, the mouth small and petulant, the teeth tobacco-stained and uniformly leaning on their neighbors. He held a small curved pipe in his right hand and was busily packing it with his most noxious tobacco concoction, which would soon permeate the room and forcibly remove most of the oxygen.

"You look excited, Professor Mallory," said Reggie pleasantly.

"I have already done so with young Dominic, but may I be the first to congratulate you on your excellent work in Argentina?"

"You could be, but I beat you to it, Prof," said Whit as he came into the room and handed Reggie a cup of coffee so hot the vapors were still visible though the kitchen was about a mile from the library.

"Ah, well," said Mallory good-naturedly. "Let me be the second, then."

Reggie took a sip of the coffee. She never felt comfortable talking about what she had done, even with people who'd helped her do it. Yet killing someone who had slaughtered so many did not draw the typical human emotions. To her and everyone sitting at the table their targets had forfeited any rights they had by their heinous acts. They might as well have been discussing the killing of a rabid dog. But perhaps, Reggie thought, that would be an unfair comparison.

For the dog.

"Thank you. But unfortunately, I'm sure Herr Huber will still rest in peace."

Mallory said stiffly, "I doubt very much if the colonel is resting comfortably at this moment. The flames, I'm very certain, *do* hurt."

"If you say so; theology was never my strong point." She settled in a chair. "But Huber is now history. So we move on."

"Yes," said Mallory eagerly. "Yes. Exactly. Now we move on."

Whit grinned wryly. "Then let's see if we can ride the monster one more time without getting our bloody selves trampled."

Mallory nodded at the slim, fair-haired woman seated to his immediate right. "Liza, if you would be so kind." She passed around manila folders bulging with copies of documents and held together with multiple blood-red rubber bands.

"You know, Prof," said Whit. "All this can go on a portable USB stick and from there onto our laptops. It's a lot more convenient than toting all this around in my car."

"Laptops can be lost or compromised. Or even stolen. 'Hacked,' I believe, is the precise term," replied Mallory with a trace of indignation, but also with the slightly insecure look of someone to whom computers remained an enigma.

Whit held up the folder. "Well, bloody paper can be nicked pretty easily too, particularly ten kilos of the stuff."

"Now, let's get down to business," said Mallory brusquely, ignoring this comment. He held up a photo of an older man in his sixties with a long nose, a shaved head, and an expression that summoned only one reaction: fear.

"Evan Waller," said Mallory. "Believed to be born in Canada sixty-three years ago, but that is incorrect. His public reputation is that of a legitimate businessman. But—"

Whit spoke up. "But his private rep is what?" He took the pistol from its holster and laid it on the table.

If Mallory was annoyed that Whit had interrupted him or placed the gun within view, he didn't show it. In fact his eyes gleamed as he said, "Evan Waller is actually Fedir Kuchin."

As he looked around the room and there was no discernible reaction from the group, disappointment replaced his glee. "Ukrainian born, he served in the military and then in the national secret police that reported directly to the KGB." When even this revelation did not generate any comment he added sharply, "Have none of you heard of the Holodomor?" He looked at the opposite end of the table. "Dominic, surely at university you must have," he said imploringly.

Dominic shook his head, his expression pained at having failed the older man.

Reggie spoke up. "*Holodomor* is Ukrainian for 'death by hunger.' Stalin killed nearly ten million Ukrainians in the early 1930s through mass starvation. That included nearly a third of the nation's children."

"How the hell did he manage that?" asked a disgusted Whit.

Mallory answered. "Stalin sent in troops and secret police and they took all livestock, poultry, food, seeds, and tools, with particular emphasis on the Dnieper River region, long known as the breadbasket of Europe. Then he sealed the borders to prevent escape and replenishment of the stolen articles, and also to stop the news from getting out to the rest of the world. No Internet back then, of course. Entire towns starved to death; nearly a quarter of the rural population of the country perished in less than two years."

"Stalin rivaled Hitler in the atrocity department," said Liza Kent pointedly. In her late forties, she looked very old-fashioned in her long skirt, clunky shoes, and white blouse with a frilly collar. Her light blonde hair, interlaced with strands of silver, was very fine and cut to her shoulders, but she wore it back in a tight bun. Her face had no memorable features and she kept a penetrating pair of amber eyes mostly hidden behind thick lenses housed in very conservative frames. She would blend nicely into virtually any crowd. In reality, she had served with British intelligence for a dozen years, ran high-level counterintelligence ops on three continents, and had a Romanian-manufactured rifle bullet perilously near her spine. This injury had forced her premature retirement on a modest government pension. She'd quickly tired of puttering around her small garden before joining the professor.

"Why did he do it?" asked Dominic.

"You ask why Stalin killed?" snapped Mallory. "Why does a snake bite? Or why does a great white shark devour its prey with nearly inconceivable savagery? It was simply what he did, on a larger scale than almost anyone before or since. A madman."

"But Stalin was also a madman with a motive," interjected Reggie. She looked around the table. "He was trying to wipe out Ukrainian nationalism. And also to prevent the farmers from resisting collectivization of agriculture. It is said that there is not one Ukrainian living today who did not lose a family member through the Holodomor."

Mallory smiled appreciatively. "You are an excellent student of history, Reggie."

She gave him a stony gaze. "Not history, Professor. *Horror*."

Whit looked confused. "Am I missing something? Because all that happened as you said in the 1930s. If he's only sixty-three, Waller, or this Fedir Kuchin bloke, wasn't even alive back then."

Mallory made a steeple with his hands. "Do you think simply because Stalin died that the genocide stopped, Beckham? The communist regime persisted for several more decades after the monster breathed his last."

"And that's where Fedir Kuchin comes in?" said Reggie quietly.

Mallory leaned back, nodding. "He joined the army at a young age and rose relatively quickly. Being uncommonly bright and unflinchingly ruthless, he was fast-tracked early on for intelligence work, ending up in the secret police, where he rose to a position of despotic power. This was around when the Red Army was meeting both its match and downfall in Afghanistan. In addition, other Soviet satellite countries, like Poland, were making a hard push for liberation and would continue to do so up until the fall of the communists. Kuchin received orders directly from the Kremlin to do all in his power to crush any opposition. While his superiors largely reaped the historical credit, he became, in essence, the man in the field who would keep Kiev in line with Moscow. And he very nearly succeeded."

"How?" asked Whit.

In answer Mallory opened his file folder and motioned for the others to do the same. "Read the first report and then look at the series of pictures accompanying it. If that doesn't answer your query I'm afraid nothing will suffice."

For several long minutes the room was silent, except for a few gasps whenever someone encountered the photos. Reggie finally closed the folder, her hand shaking a bit as she did so. She had faced many monsters that stood on two legs, and yet their depth of pure evil still managed to astonish and even unnerve her at times. She was afraid that if the day came when it didn't, she would have lost all trace of her humanity. Some days she worried she already had.

"His own version of the Holodomor," commented Whit in a subdued voice. "Only he used aerial poisons, toxins placed into water supplies, and thousands of people at a time forced into pits where they were burned alive. The foul bastard."

"And Kuchin carried out the sterilization of thousands of young girls," added Reggie in a hushed tone, the spiderweb of lines around her eyes deepening as she said this. "So they could never bear males who might fight against the Soviets."

Mallory tapped the file. "On top of a hundred other such atrocities. As is often the case with cunning men like this, Kuchin saw the fall coming long before his superiors. He falsified his death and fled to Asia, from there to Australia, and then on to Canada, where he built a new life with forged documents and a charisma that managed to conceal his underlying sadistic nature. The world thinks he's a legitimate and highly successful businessman, instead of the mass murderer and war criminal that he actually is. It took three full years to piece this file together."

"And where is he now?" asked Reggie, her gaze holding on one photo she'd slipped from the file. It depicted the remains of an unearthed mass grave where the skeletons were small because they were all children.

Mallory puffed his pipe to life and a pungent cloud of smoke rose above his head. "This summer he will be traveling on holiday to Provence—to the village of Gordes, to be more specific."

"Then I wonder what it will feel like," said Reggie to no one in particular.

"What will what feel like, Reg?" asked Whit curiously.

She looked once more at the photo of the small bones. "To die in such a beautiful place as Provence, of course."

7

THE LONG MEETING had ended, the morning had given way to dusk, but Reggie still had work to do. She slipped outside of the dilapidated mansion and took a few moments to study the grounds in the dwindling light. Ever since the headquarters of Miles Mallory's organization had been established here, Reggie had read up on the history of the place. Originally a feudal castle had stood on the footprint where the mansion did now. The surrounding lands had been the fiefdom of the wealthy lord of the manor, who ruled his people encased in a suit of armor, ready at a moment's notice to cleave in a skull or two if necessary with his battle-axe.

Later, the castle had fallen and in its place the mansion had risen. The fiefdoms had dissolved and the squires had replaced armor and mace with the threat of debtor's prison if the farmers renting their lands did not pay their bills. The property had remained in the same family for many generations, finally descending to distant cousins of the original owners whose income had never approached the level necessary to maintain the estate. During the two world wars Harrowsfield—Reggie had never discovered a definitive account of where the name came from—was used as a hospital for wounded soldiers. After that it lay abandoned for several decades until the government had been compelled to take it over and make minimal repairs. Mallory had discovered the place and finagled the use of it. To the outside world it was merely an informal gathering place for eccentric academics whose work was as esoteric as it was innocuous.

Reggie passed by columns of ragged English boxwoods, their urine odor sweeping over her. Even though it was very late in the spring, a chilly breeze nudged at her back as she trudged along. She zipped up her worn leather jacket, which had belonged to her older brother. Though he'd only been twelve at the time of his death, he had been over six feet tall and the jacket enveloped her, even as his death had shattered her. She still felt emotionally brittle, like a pane of cracked glass that would disintegrate with the very next impact.

After a walk of a quarter mile she pushed open the door of what had once been the estate's greenhouse. The smell of peat and mulch and rotting plants still drifted into her nostrils even though there had been no gardener or gardening here for decades. She passed by broken glass and loose boards that had dropped from the ceiling. Shadows were cast in all directions as the sun continued its descent into the English countryside. The chilly breeze turned still colder as it was funneled through the small openings in the windows and the walls, fluttering spiderwebs and rustling the disintegrating remnants of a horticulturist's paradise.

Reggie reached the set of double doors set at an angle into the corner of the structure. She inserted her key in the heavy padlock, tugged open the doors, and pulled the chain on the bare light bulb set just inside the revealed space. A moment later the passage she stepped down into became dimly illuminated and smelled strongly of damp soil, making her feel slightly sick. She touched dirt, walked downward at a twenty-degree angle for another fifteen paces where the tunnel leveled out. She had no idea who'd carved it out of the earth or why, but it did come in handy now.

She reached the end of the passage where a number of mattresses had been placed on end and positioned front-to-back. A small table was set against a dirt sidewall. On the table was a stack of paper and a small battery-powered fan. She picked up the top sheet and, using a clip, fastened it to a cord that hung between the two sidewalls of the tunnel. Next to the stack were a number of ear mufflers and safety goggles. She slipped a pair of mufflers around her neck, where they dangled loosely, and put on the protective eyewear.

On the sheet of paper was the blackened image of a man with black rings running around it. She paced off thirty feet, turned, took out her pistol from its belt holster, checked the load, slipped the ear mufflers on, assumed her preferred firing stance, took aim, and triggered off her full mag. There was very little ventilation down here and the acrid burn of the ordnance was immediately absorbed into her nostrils. Bits of dirt dislodged by the gun's discharge fell from between cracks in the weathered boards forming the tunnel's beamed ceiling. She coughed, whipped the air with her hand to clear the smoke and dust, and walked forward to examine her marksmanship, pausing for a moment to turn on the fan. It lazily oscillated back and forth, but took its time in clearing away the haze. So much for first-class shooting facilities.

Seven of her eleven rounds were placed where she wanted them, in the torso. All would have hit vital organs if the target had been real. Two shots were in the head, also where she had aimed. One round had fallen outside a proper kill zone by a millimeter. The last shot had missed by an unacceptable margin.

She replaced the target with a fresh one, reloaded, and did it again. Ten out of eleven. She did it again. Eleven for eleven. She did it once more. Nine out of eleven. Despite the efforts of the fan, the tunnel was now heavy with the smoke and her lungs felt congested.

"Bloody hell," she barked, as she hacked and whipped the murky haze with her hand. Reggie figured she could blame the last few misses on not being able to actually breathe or even see the damn target. She trudged back down the tunnel wishing that they could have a proper gun range, but the tunnel was the only place where the sound of the shots wouldn't carry to a pair of ears that might in turn contact the local constabulary. Doddering academics were not supposed to have penchants for firearms. She was surprised to see Whit standing by the doors leading back into the greenhouse.

"Reckoned you'd be down here. How's your aim?" he said.

"Bloody awful." She closed the double doors and locked them.

He leaned against a glass-topped storage cabinet that had once been used to hold seedlings. In the deepening chill his breath came out as small vapor. "Well, don't get your knickers in a knot. Your choice of weapon isn't often a gun. You're more the knife and pillow gal. I'm the nine-millimeter man."

She frowned at his bluntness. "You really can be an idiot sometimes, Whit."

"I'm not making light of it. But you're wound tighter than anyone I've ever met."

"Then you need to get out more. I'm actually pretty laid-back."

"So what do you think about this Fedir Kuchin bloke?"

"I think we'll be seeing him in Provence soon enough."

"Little close on the planning end. I'd prefer some more time."

She shrugged. "The way the professor tells it, the viper doesn't come out in the open very often. This may be our only chance."

"Your cover has to be top-notch. This guy has the resources to check deep."

"Our people have always come through before." She waited, sensing that he had more to say.

"I want in on this on the ground," he said suddenly, then paused, probably to study her reaction to these words. "Maybe you can nip over to the prof and talk to him?"

Reggie slipped her pistol into its belt holster and wiped her hands off on a rag she drew from a workbench. "The plan's still preliminary. There's time for that."

"You know how Mallory thinks. He fancies you as always the first choice for the tip of the spear."

"You've had your share of mission leads, Whit," she said firmly.

"I *did*, before you came along. Don't get me wrong. I'm not blaming you. You're excellent, really brilliant at this stuff. And since it's mostly old blokes we go after, having a lady in the lead makes sense for getting their guards down. But I'm not bad either. And the thing is, I didn't sign on for this job to carry the bags all the time. I'd like to get me whacks in too."

She considered this for a few moments. "I'll talk to the professor. Kuchin isn't a nonagenarian Nazi who'll get duped by a pretty face and a glimpse of thigh, now is he?"

Whit grinned and moved closer, running his gaze over her. "Don't sell yourself short, Reg. That stuff works for most men. Young and old."

She smiled and lightly smacked him on the cheek. "Thanks for the offer, but shove off." Before he could take another step toward her, Reggie passed by him and set off back toward the mansion. She made only one other stop: the estate's graveyard. It was situated a respectful distance from the main house, past a stand of birch and nearly surrounded by a hedge of stout English yew. The headstones were darkened by the passage of time, and it seemed even colder here, as though the corpses below could somehow extend their chilly influence to the surface.

She stood in front of one grave and, as she usually did, read off the ancient marker.

"Laura R. Campion, Born 1779, Died 1804. An angel sent on to Heaven." She had no idea if she was related to Laura R. Campion, or whether the woman's middle name was Regina. She'd only been twenty-five when she'd passed, not so unusual back then. Perhaps she'd perished in childbirth as so many women from those times did. On discovering this grave marker one morning while walking around the estate, she'd eagerly set out to find other Campions buried here. There were none, though other family names were repeated across the burial plots. She'd researched Laura R. Campion on the Internet and at the library but found nothing. Thomas Campion had been a poet born in the 1500s, and one of his best-known works had referred to a woman named Laura, but there was no connection that Reggie could see.

Walking back to the house she thought of her family, at least the one she used to have. She was the only one left, that she knew of, anyway. Her family tree was a bit complicated. Because of that there was a hole in her chest through which nothing could pass. It was a total dead zone. Each time she tried to come to grips with what was motivating her to travel the world in pursuit of evil, the zone repelled her, never allowing her closure, never allowing her a free breath.

After fetching her things from the house she began the drive back to London. More meetings at Harrowsfield would come. Intelligence and background briefs digested down to the smallest detail. A plan would finally evolve and they would refine it, attempting to massage out all possible errors. Then when preparations were complete she would travel to Provence and attempt to kill another monster. In that simple equation Regina Campion would have to find all the solace she was ever likely to possess.

CHAPTER

8

SHAW WAS IN PARIS, just having finished an intense day of prep work. He changed into long shorts and a loose-fitting white T-shirt and went for a run along the Seine, passing the Jardin des Tuileries, the Orangerie Museum, and the Grand Palais. His feet pounded along the Avenue de New-York before he cut across a bridge, passed over the famous river that bisected Paris, and a few minutes later ran underneath the wide base of the Eiffel Tower. He slowed, jogging through the green space before picking up his pace again. Eventually he ended up in the Saint-Germain section of Paris, on the Left Bank where his small hotel was situated. He normally preferred the adjacent Latin Quarter while in the city, but Frank had made other arrangements.

He showered, changed his clothes, and met Frank for dinner at a restaurant near the Orsay Museum. They sat in the rear corner of the outside eating area, which was cordoned off from the sidewalk by rectangular flower planters set on tall wrought iron stands. Before leaving Frank gave him a slip of paper.

"What's this?"

"A phone number."

"For who?"

"Just call it."

Frank wedged his hat down on his head and walked off. Shaw could see him pause at the doorway to light one of his favored small cigars before quickly disappearing into the mass of people threading their way along the crowded street.

Shaw walked back to his hotel, trying to lift his spirits by absorbing the magic of one of the most enchanting cities on earth, but the effect was exactly the opposite. It was in a hospital in Paris, where he was fighting for his life after having his arm nearly hacked off by a neo-Nazi, that he'd learned of Anna's death. It was shortly after he'd asked her to marry him, and she'd said yes. She was a gifted linguist and had actually said yes in multiple languages. Shaw had even gone to the little town in Germany where her parents lived to formally seek her father's permission for his daughter's hand in marriage.

And then she was dead.

Shaw's path took him along the river. He crossed over to the island where Notre Dame Cathedral stood. It had been recently cleaned, centuries of grime scraped off with pressurized water. For some reason Shaw had preferred it dirty. He checked his watch. It was nearly nine and the church shut down at 6:45 on weekdays. Tourists still roamed around taking shots of the famed exterior and themselves in front of it. He was not a particularly religious man and he wasn't sure why he was even here.

For prayer? Well, he was out of luck. God apparently was closed for the night.

Shaw walked back to his hotel, unlocked the door to his room, and sat at a small desk chair, pulling out the slip of paper. He picked up his cell phone and punched in the number.

"Hello?"

Shaw hadn't heard that voice in months. Unprepared for it, his finger hit the disconnect button. *Damn you, Frank.* Shaw had thought the phone number had something to do with the current mission. But it hadn't.

That was Katie James's voice.

He lay back on the bed and stared at the pale blue ceiling.

Their last day together had not worked out exactly as Shaw had wanted it to. Well, maybe it had, since at the crack of dawn he'd left the hotel in Zurich where they'd been staying, grabbed a shuttle to the airport, and took the next flight out; he didn't really care where it was going. She'd woken up, gone down to breakfast to meet him, as they had planned, and probably become frantic when he didn't show. She'd tried to call him, but he'd never called her back. He'd changed his number. He didn't really know why he'd done all this.

He'd never run from anything or anyone before. But he'd woken up in Switzerland on a chilly morning and just knew that he had to be alone.

So I just ran.

He stared at the slip of paper again. He should at least give her a chance to bitch at him for what he'd done. Yet an hour went by and he didn't move.

Then he sat up and punched in the number.

"Hello, Shaw," she said.

"How did you know it was me?"

"You called over an hour ago and then hung up."

"You couldn't know that. I've got caller block."

"I still knew it was you."

"How? You don't get other calls?"

"Not on this phone. The only person I gave the number to was Frank so he could give it to you."

"Okay," he said slowly. "So why didn't you try to call back? You just had to hit redial on my number."

"I figured I'd let you work it out. How have you been?"

"Don't you want to scream at me?"

"Why, would that be productive?"

That didn't sound like the Katie James he knew. She was all emotion, wearing her heart on her sleeve and in her news stories. The lady was impulsive, something that Shaw both objected to and admired about her because it was so different from who he was. Or at least who he'd thought he was. As it turned out, around her he could be pretty spontaneous.

Shaw got up and walked over to the window overlooking the cobblestone courtyard of the hotel as night fell solidly over Paris. "I'm okay. How have you been?"

"Back doing freelance. I got some permanent job offers but none of them really interested me."

"Bunch of rags?"

"*New York Times. Der Spiegel* in Germany, even *Rolling Stone*, real bottom dwellers."

"I thought you wanted to get back in the game."

"I guess I was wrong. How's Frank?"

"The same."

"So you're back in *your* game, apparently."

"I guess so," he mumbled.

"Where are you?"

"Working."

"I'm in San Fran for now. So when do you think you'll get a break from work?"

"I'm not sure."

"Not sure if you'll survive the next job, or something else?"

He didn't answer.

"Well, if you ever want to talk you have my number."

"Katie?"

"Yes?" Shaw could hear her breaths coming a little more quickly.

"It was good to hear your voice."

"Take care of yourself. And remember, you don't have to do everything Frank tells you to."

She clicked off and Shaw tossed the phone on the bed.

CHAPTER

9

DOMINIC LOWERED his glass of beer and tapped Reggie on the arm.

"I'm sorry, Dom, what were you saying?" she asked sheepishly.

They were at a restaurant a few blocks from her London flat and her mind had drifted to other things while he'd been speaking.

"That I knew Whit talked to you about what was coming up."

"He stopped me outside the shooting range. Did he tell you he was going to?"

"I was actually the one who suggested he go to you."

"Why me? He could have gone directly to the professor."

"He and Whit don't always get on."

Reggie frowned. "None of us get on all the time. It's the nature of the beast."

She swallowed some tea and played with a biscuit on her plate. It was gray and drizzly outside, and a sharp wind smacked against the window, apparently trying to force its way inside. Across from them an ill-nourished fire sputtered in the soot-caked fireplace. Reggie knew if the weather stayed like this through the summer, half of London would become suicidal and the other half would seriously contemplate it. Ordinarily, a trip to warm, sunny Provence would be a godsend. *Ordinarily.*

"You know he wanted a frontline place with Huber but the professor objected?"

She leaned forward and lowered her voice. "That was Huber. Whit going in guns blazing wasn't going to work in that situation. The old Nazi wanted boobs and ass, not a touchy Irishman with tats and a Glock."

Dominic raised an eyebrow. "Whit has tattoos?"

Reggie sighed wearily. "Get on with it, Dom. I'm tired."

"But perhaps with Kuchin Whit can participate?"

"I told Whit I'd talk to Mallory, and I will." She eyed him over her cup. "What about you? What part do you want to play?"

Dominic shrugged. "I've been reading up on the Holodomor ever since our first meeting. I really want to get this bastard."

"Just don't let your emotions run away with you. That makes you lose your focus, and that's where mistakes come in."

"How do you turn it off? How do you not feel?"

She leaned still closer and her lovely eyes grew wide and her smile seductive. "I'll tell you how. Every time Huber put his hand on my ass I pretended it was you, Dom, feeling me up. And that got me through it." She tongued a piece of biscuit into her mouth.

Dominic blinked and looked confused, his cheeks tinged red.

Reggie laughed. "I'm just kidding. I'm taking Whit's advice to lighten up more. Seriously, when he did that he wasn't touching me, he was grabbing Barbara, his German bimbo. I had to play the role in order to take him down. One step at a time. It was just a role. That's how I got through it. I get emotional and lose it, he walks. That's the best motivation not to ever lose it. Because then they win."

Dominic swallowed the rest of his beer. "What was it like?"

She stared dully at him. "What, when he had his bloody hand up my skirt?"

"No, I meant when you, you know?"

"I really didn't think about it, to tell you the truth. I just did it."

"I've never had to do it yet. I was just wondering."

"When the time comes you'll deal with it, Dom. Everyone does it differently, but you'll finish the job. I have no doubt."

He was silent for a moment and then said in a low voice, "The other Nazi hunters turned them over to the police and they were tried in court. Why don't we do it that way?"

Reggie leaned forward and said in a near whisper, "Those are just the cases you read about in the newspapers. And do you really think there aren't groups that turned the Germans directly over to the Israelis? And do you think the Jews gave them their day in court? And people are losing interest. The Americans have a division at their Justice Department devoted to the Nazis. Funding and personnel have been slashed because everyone believes the old Hitler lovers are mostly dead. As if the bloody Third Reich had a monopoly on evil. I've seen genocide in Africa, Asia, and Eastern Europe that would bugger the imagination. Evil has no geographic boundaries. Anyone who thinks otherwise is barmy."

After a few moments of silence Dominic changed subjects. "So how do you see the plan formulating?"

She gave him a stern look. "In a way that I don't want to discuss in a public place."

"Sorry. I'm heading out to Harrowsfield tonight."

Reggie relaxed. "So am I. The professor wants to start early. And the couple in the flat above mine are screwing their brains out every hour. All I hear is 'Oh God, oh God, yes, do me!' I turn my wireless up all the way, but it's still driving me mad. Do you want to ride out together?"

"No, I'll take my motorbike."

"You mean your crotch rocket?" she said wryly.

"What? Oh, you've been talking to Whit about more than missions."

"Pretty rainy to be doing the two-wheeler, isn't it?"

"I've got all-weather gear." He added wistfully, "I like it better at Harrowsfield than I do my place in Richmond."

"I like it that I'll be able to get a good night's sleep."

"I'll see you there then. I have to stop for some petrol first. Cheers."

As they got up to leave she put a hand on his shoulder. "Dom, when the moment comes all you need to focus on is that justice is finally being done. That's all. And you'll be fine. I promise."

CHAPTER

10

THE NEXT MORNING Reggie woke early. She sat up in her bedroom on the third floor of Harrowsfield and shivered. This part of the house was never heated. She looked out the window. The rain had passed and she thought she could actually see some sunlight breaking through the cloud cover. She washed her face with water from the tap, changed into sweats and sneakers, left the mansion through the rear, and started her run. Five miles later, sweaty and her lungs percolating nicely, she returned to the house. The smells of coffee brewing and bacon and eggs cooking drifted out from the kitchen. She quickly showered, enduring the last minute of rinsing with only cold water as the old pipes muttered and clanked in protest of their usage. She changed into jeans, flats, and a black V-neck sweater with a white tee underneath and headed downstairs.

There sometimes could be as many as twenty people at Harrowsfield, though today she knew the number was closer to ten, some of them historians doing research in the library or in a set of offices set up on both the main and second floors. Their one goal was to identify the next monster the team would go after. There were linguists immersing themselves in some language from lands where new evil lurked. Still other researchers were poring over old cable communications, pilfered diplomatic records, and handwritten accounts of atrocities smuggled out of third world countries. The task was harder now, she knew. The Nazis had been meticulous record-keepers. Subsequent sadists, operating in many different places, weren't nearly as accommodating in leaving a trail of their pervasive wickedness.

Mallory had used great care in vetting all of the people who worked here. There was no formal recruitment, of course. One couldn't put an advertisement in the paper seeking justice-minded vigilantes comfortable with killing folks who desperately deserved it.

In her case, Mallory had sought Reggie out at university where he was a visiting scholar. After a months-long courtship of sorts, he'd broached the subject of bringing to justice Nazis who'd fled Germany before the fall. When she'd enthusiastically agreed with the goal, he'd gone a bit further, finally ending with the theoretical possibility of saving the world the price of a trial by also playing the roles of judge, jury, and executioner.

More months had passed while he allowed her to stew on that. When she'd voluntarily returned to him with more questions, he'd answered them, to a certain extent. When he could sense her commitment deepening he'd let her meet with some other folks. Whit was one and Liza another. Another month passed and then Mallory brought her some news clippings of an old man who'd been found slain in his lavish home in Hong Kong. Though it had never been made public, Mallory told her that the fellow had been identified as a former concentration camp commander and one of Heinrich Himmler's right-hand men. They had talked long into the night of the ethics involved in such an action. It was never explicitly said, but Reggie suspected that the professor and other people she'd met through him had been behind the killing. By then she desperately wanted to be part of it.

It was only then that he had brought her to Harrowsfield. She went through an array of tests to determine if she had the psychological makeup to be a member of the group. She passed that barrier easily enough, demonstrating a rigid coldness that surprised even her. Next was physical fitness. A fine athlete, she was pressed to levels of strength and endurance she never knew she possessed. Her lungs near collapse, she willed her battered body over treacherous terrain she didn't realize existed in the bucolic English countryside. To his credit, Whit Beckham was next to her every step of the way, though he'd already endured this when he first signed up. After that was the specialized training: weapons, martial arts, and survival skills in myriad challenging conditions.

In the classroom she learned how to research a target and study their background to gain valuable intelligence. She was taught foreign languages and how to lie with aplomb; how to act out roles and discern when other people were doing the same. She came to learn how to trail someone so stealthily that they would only know they were being followed when she walked up to them. These and dozens of other skills were drilled into her to such an extent that she no longer had to think about them.

After her training was complete she'd acted as support on three missions, two where Whit was the lead and another where Richard Dyson, an experienced Nazi exterminator and since retired, had completed the final act. Her first mission in the lead had involved an elderly Austrian living in Asia who'd helped Hitler kill hundreds of thousands of people simply because they worshipped under the Star of David. She'd gotten into his circle by becoming a nanny to his young wife's child. The monster had been married five times. He had enough wealth obtained through the theft of antiquities during the war that he could keep divorcing and remarrying and still live in great luxury. They had one child, a five-year-old boy conceived through artificial insemination using donated sperm. Reggie suspected that the old Nazi had selected the sperm donor based on the color of his skin, hair, and height—namely, white, blond, and tall.

She'd worked with them for one month, and in that time the husband had made a half dozen passes at her. From what he'd told her once while he was in a drunken stupor, she could easily become wife number six if she played her cards right. One night she came by prearrangement to visit him in his bedroom—by his choice he and his wife kept separate boudoirs. He was again drunk and easily handled by Reggie. When he was tightly bound and his mouth gagged, she pulled the pictures from a hiding place and showed him the faces of some of his victims, a strict requirement of all the missions. At the end of their lives the monsters had to know that justice had finally caught up to them.

The fear he showed had amused her at first. But when the time came to finish the job, Reggie had hesitated. She'd never told anyone this. Not Whit and certainly not the professor. Her encouraging words to Dominic had also left out this piece of personal history. The monster had looked at her with pleading eyes. His gaze begged her not to do it. During her training she'd been told that this moment would come. And she'd also been instructed that no training in the world could fully prepare her for it.

And they'd been right.

Her resolve seemed to pour out of her with each tear shed by what was now a harmless old man. As she lowered the knife, she saw the relief in his eyes. She could just say that her cover had been blown and the mission was a failure. No one would ever know.

There were two things that prevented that from happening. One was the mocking sneer that emerged in the man's eyes as he saw her weaken. The second was the picture of Daniel Abramowitz, age two, with a bullet hole in his small head. The photo had come from the monster's own archives, which he'd lovingly assembled over the years he ran the camp.

She had plunged the knife into his chest until the hilt smacked his sternum. She gave the blade first an upward and then a downward jerk, and performed the same motion horizontally, severing arteries and destroying heart chambers, as she'd been taught to do. The sneer was gone from the old man now. For one long second, while life still remained, she saw in his countenance hatred, fear, rage, fear again, and then simply the flat, glassy stare of death.

"May God understand why I do this," she whispered, the words that had become a ritual for her at the end of each mission.

Reggie had never hesitated again.

11

FROM THE KITCHEN Reggie grabbed some buttered toast and put it on a plate with fried sausages and a sliced apple. Also juggling a cup of hot tea, she carried it all to the library. As she entered, Professor Mallory looked up from a large book written in Polish, took out his pipe, and smiled. "I thought I heard you come in last night. Your car has a distinctive sound."

"It's called a wretched exhaust pipe." She sat down next to him, lined her toast with the sausages, bit into it, and drank her tea. "Where's Whit?"

"I don't believe he's here yet. But I expect him shortly."

"I wanted to talk to you about the personnel for the Kuchin job."

Mallory laid aside his book. His bow tie was still askew, but this morning his shirt-collar points were both directed to where they should be and it looked like he'd actually combed his hair.

"Do you have thoughts?" he asked.

"I believe Whit should play a prominent role."

"Did he ask you to talk to me?"

"Not in so many words."

"It's difficult for you, I know. And him."

"How do you mean?"

"Well, you've supplanted him as the leader in the field, Regina."

The professor was the only one among them who referred to her by her proper name.

"I don't see it exactly that way."

"But it *is* exactly that way."

"You know, Professor, quite frankly, you could use a bit more tact."

He smiled at this mild reproach. "If you try to gloss over the truth or massage the facts all you're doing is heightening your chances of arriving at an erroneous conclusion."

"Whit is a good asset."

"I completely agree with you. And if it were women we were going after we would probably have greater use of him in the lead role. Unfortunately, our targets trend to the male and heterosexual side."

"He's gone after men. Successfully."

"Successful to the extent that they were terminated, yes. But we like to handle our work under the radar. For example, if we left evidence behind of why we had ended the lives of these people and that became public, you know what would happen?"

"The remaining ones would hide even deeper. But there are no more Nazis."

"It doesn't disprove the point. And let me correct you. There are no more Nazis of which we are aware. New intelligence may lead to more work in that arena. But take Kuchin. We dispose of him and word leaks out, other Eastern European mass murderers with new lives—and there are at least a dozen we're researching at present— would be forewarned."

"But we don't broadcast why we're killing them. It's never made public."

"But that's not the only way to warn someone."

"I'm not getting what you mean."

Mallory said, "Your first lead target was the old Austrian married five times. You tied him up and did your job, but you ransacked the house and busted a door lock, so it looked like a robbery. And you didn't do a bunk and scamper away but rather stayed on during the investigation so no one suspected you of anything. Now, let's take Whit. This was before your time, but in one lead assignment he killed a former Gestapo chieftain by shooting him in the genitalia. He was supposed to inject the fellow with a poison that dissolves in the body in two minutes and is untraceable. He claims that the bottle the poison was in broke. It doesn't take a genius to figure out that putting a bullet in a man's private region and letting him bleed out is a revenge-style killing. In fact, it could well have jeopardized future targets."

"Maybe the bottle did break. Everything doesn't go smoothly in the field."

The genial look faded from Mallory's face. "Oh, I'm sorry, I left out one piece of critical information, didn't I? Whit painted a *bloody* swastika on the man's *bloody* forehead and had the effrontery to ask me if I thought that was too *subtle*."

Reggie suppressed a smile. "Oh."

"Quite right, *oh*. The international press had a positive field day and made our future work that much more difficult. Mr. Beckham and I had a row about that one."

"I'm sure."

"In Huber's case we already know that they believe he died after attempting to have sex with the beautiful Barbara, and that she fled in fear of retribution. No one is pursuing it, because the man was ninety-six years old and apparently died extremely happy." The professor could not resist a smile at this remark.

"But we do have an advantage in this case. The world has no idea Evan Waller is Fedir Kuchin. Even if he is killed under mysterious circumstances, other men in hiding like Kuchin will probably take no note."

The professor shook his head. "No, no. We can't count on that. There will be press. There will be inquiries. Someone somewhere may recognize the man. He has kept a very low profile for decades. Even with his so-called philanthropic work, no one gets to see him. It's all done through intermediaries. But still we can't draw unnecessary attention to the matter."

"Well, I can't fake having sex with the man and then have him conveniently die like I did with Huber. There are limits to what I can do. Perhaps a businessman like him has other enemies and we can foist the blame there. What do we know about other dealings he might have had?"

Mallory shrugged. "Not that much. Our people had other priorities. They were looking for Kuchin, not a possibly dishonest entrepreneur. I agree he might have other interests that would satisfy his evil nature, but I don't know what they are and we have no time to look for them now."

Reggie sat back. "I still think Whit should be in on this one.

Kuchin looks well capable of taking care of himself. I won't be able to single-handedly overpower him. It needs to be a total team effort at the end."

"It's true, our prey are getting younger and stronger, aren't they?" He tugged absently at his beard. "I largely agree with you. You will need muscle on this. And whilst he has some shortcomings, Whit certainly has that. You can tell him I said so."

Reggie looked irritated. "Why don't you tell him yourself?"

Mallory looked bemused. "We don't get on that well. Now, let's get down to some details before the meeting officially starts."

"Why do you do this, Professor?" she said suddenly.

"Do what? You mean smoke this foul-smelling pipe?"

"You're not Jewish. You've never mentioned that anyone you loved ever suffered at the hands of any of these vile creatures. So why?"

He eyed her steadily. "Does a man need a reason to pursue justice?"

"Indulge me."

"Not today. Perhaps another time. I can tell you one thing. You'll enjoy your little abode in Provence."

"Really? And why is that?"

"It's a five-level villa with extraordinary vistas of the Luberon valley, and you can walk to the quaint village of Gordes in under five minutes. Horribly expensive, the lease payments are more than I paid for my cottage. And that's not the best part."

"What's the best part?"

Mallory's bushy eyebrows twitched in delight. "It's right next to where our Fedir Kuchin will be staying."

CHAPTER

12

Evan Waller sat back in his desk chair and read the spreadsheet for the fifth time. He loved numbers; his nimble mind grasped their complexities easily, massaging data into precise conclusions. He made his decision, rose, poured himself a slender finger of Macallan's, and drank it. He put the glass down, picked up a pistol, and faced the man bound to the chair.

"Anwar, what am I to do with you? Tell me." His voice was deep, cultured, and overlaid with traces of his Eastern European origins. His tone was that of a disappointed father to a misbehaving child.

Anwar was a short man with a thickened, soft body who slumped in his chair, his arms and legs tightly bound. His face was round and his skin would normally have been a light brown color, but now yellow and purplish bruises clustered on his cheeks, forehead, and jawline. A knife cut traveled from his left cheek to his split nostril. The blood there had congealed and blackened. His dark hair was slicked back solely with the sweat of fear.

"Please, Mr. Waller, please. It will never happen again, sir, I swear."

"But how can I trust you now? Tell me. I want to find a way. I value your services, but I need to know I can trust you."

"It was her. She put me up to this."

"Her? Tell me."

Anwar let a trickle of blood drop from his mouth and onto his pants leg before answering. "My wife. The bitch spends money like it is water. You pay me well but it is never enough for her. Never!"

Waller sat down in a chair across from the captive. He put the gun down and looked intrigued. "So Gisele put you up to this? To steal from me to cover her spending?" He clapped his hands together.

The sound was like a gunshot and Anwar flinched. "I had my doubts about her from the beginning, Anwar, I told you this, did I not?"

"I know, sir, I know. And as usual you were right. But for her I never would have done this terrible thing. It made me sick to do it. Sick because you have been so good to me. Like a father. Better than a father."

"But you're a man. And a Muslim. You should be able to control your woman. It is part of your culture. Your faith."

"But she is *Brazilian*," exclaimed Anwar, as though that would explain everything. "She is a she-devil. A wicked, wicked slut. No one can control her. I have tried, but she beats me. Me! Her own husband. You have seen the marks yourself."

Waller nodded. "Well, she *is* much larger than you. But you are still a man, and I despise weakness in men."

"And she cheats on me with other men. And *women*!"

"Repulsive," said Waller in an indifferent tone. "So you know where she is?"

Anwar shook his head. "I have seen nothing of her for a week."

Waller sat back and spread his hands. "If we find her, what do you suggest?"

Anwar spit on the concrete floor. "That you kill her, that is what I suggest."

"So you trade her life for yours, in effect?"

"I swear to you, Mr. Waller, I never would have thought of betraying you. It was that bitch. She made me do it. She drove me crazy. You must believe me. You must!"

"I do, Anwar, I do." Waller stood, walked over, made a fist, and drove it into Anwar's already swollen face. The little man slumped to the side, his dead weight kept in the chair only by the bindings. Waller grabbed him up by his slicked hair. "Now you have been suitably punished. You are valuable to me. Very valuable. I cannot afford to lose you. But this is your only forgiveness, do you understand?"

Anwar, the blood trickling from his mouth, mumbled, "I understand. I swear that I do. Thank you. I do not deserve such mercy." He started sobbing.

"Crying is not manly, Anwar, so stop it, now!"

Anwar choked back his last sob and looked up, his right eye puffy, his left one nearly closed.

Waller smiled. "I must reveal something to you. You will find it of interest I'm sure. We located your wife. We have Gisele."

"You have her?" said an astonished Anwar.

"And I agree with you, she is a she-devil. A woman designed by God to drive men insane. Would you like to see her, tell her what you think of her before we kill her?"

"It would give me great pleasure," muttered Anwar unenthusiastically.

"Or perhaps you would like to do the honors? A bullet to the brain of the evil woman? It may do you much good. A catharsis. A character builder."

Anwar flinched. "I am an accountant. I have no courage for that."

"Fine, fine. I just thought I would extend the offer." Waller turned to one of his men. "Pascal, bring the woman in to face her wronged husband."

Pascal, a small, trim man in his thirties, passed through another door. A few moments later the door opened again and Anwar could see his wife's head peering around the doorframe. Normally her skin was even darker than her husband's. But now she looked terribly pale, her eyes wide in stark terror.

"You miserable bitch. You devil. See what you have caused. You have . . . you have . . . ." Anwar faltered as the door opened farther and Pascal marched in holding the severed head by the dark strands. Pascal didn't smile at the horror on the husband's face. He just clutched the back of the head and held it up, as he had earlier been instructed to do by his employer.

"Oh God. Oh God. No, no, it cannot be." Anwar looked at Waller, then back to his wife's head. "It cannot be."

"It is, Anwar. It is. But now you can return to work a happy man."

Anwar sobbed for a few more moments before lifting up his head and letting out a tortured yet relieved breath. "Thank you, Mr. Waller. Allah thanks you."

"I have no need of your Allah's blessings, Anwar." Waller raised his pistol and aimed it at the man's head, his eyes first focused on the metal nub of the sightline on the end of the muzzle and then onto the ultimate target.

Anwar jerked back. "But you said—"

"I lied." The bullet torpedoed into Anwar's brain. Waller relaxed and then triggered another round, tattooing the skin just to the left of the first entry wound. He placed the fired gun on the table and took a few moments to pour one more finger of scotch. Drinking this down slowly as he walked across the room to reach the door, he turned back and glanced at two of his other men.

In an admonishing tone he said, "Just remember this time that a two-hundred-pound man needs twice that weight to hold the body properly underwater."

"Yes sir, Mr. Waller," said one of the men nervously.

"And melt down the damn gun."

"Right away, sir."

"And Pascal, get rid of *that*," he added, pointing at the woman's head. "Cheers." Waller disappeared through the door and settled into a black armored Hummer that sped off the moment he buckled his seat belt. An Escalade followed with another Hummer in front of Waller's ride.

He'd discovered that his "trusted" accountant had a slush pile siphoned from Waller's substantial cash flow. It was minor skimming, less than a tenth of one percent, and had done Waller no financial damage, but it was an unforgivable act. To let it go would have been a sign of weakness. In Waller's business your competitors and people who worked for you were constantly looking for any signs of frailty. If they thought they'd found it, your mortality rate went up a thousand percent. He understood that lesson well, since it was how he'd come into the business many years ago. His mentor had let a minor slight go by with no consequences. Three months later he was being eaten by wolves in the Pacific Northwest and Waller was in charge. Over the next two decades, there had always been consequences whenever someone had betrayed him. He had no desire to be devoured by wolves. He would much prefer to do the eating.

He looked at the person sitting next to him. Alan Rice was thirty-nine, a graduate of a prestigious university in England, who'd traded the halls of academia to help Waller run his empire. Some men were just drawn to the dark side because that's where they could thrive properly.

Rice was slender, his hair prematurely white. Though his features were delicate, his mind was muscular, brilliant. Men like Rice were seldom content to be second-in-commands. But he'd also helped triple the size of Waller's business in a short period of time, and Waller had given him additional responsibilities commensurate with his talents. Waller was the only indispensable one in his business, but it was close to the point where he could not run it without Rice.

Waller flexed his gloved hand.

Rice noted this movement and said, "Recoil on the pistol bad?"

"No. I was just thinking about the last time I'd killed someone."

"Albert Clements," said Rice promptly. "Your Australian point man."

"Exactly. It makes me wonder. I pay them extraordinarily well, and yet it never seems to be enough."

"You have thousands, you want hundreds of thousands. You have millions, you want tens of millions."

"And they must think I'm a fool to let them get away with it."

"No. They just think they're smarter."

"Do you think you're smarter than me, Alan?"

Rice looked over his shoulder at the building they'd just left. "I'm more intelligent than the man you just killed, if for no other reason than I have no wish to die at your hands. And I would if I tried to fool you."

Waller nodded, but his expression wasn't quite as convincing.

Rice cleared his throat and added, "I understand that Provence is beautiful this time of year."

"There are few times when Provence isn't beautiful."

"You've spent much time there?"

"My mother was French, from a little town called Roussillon. It's the site of some of the largest ochre deposits in the world. Many famous painters, like Van Gogh, traveled there to obtain the earthy pigments for their palette. And unlike many other villages in Provence, the buildings are not white or gray stone but wild reds, oranges, browns, and yellows. If I were a painter I would move to

Roussillon and capture its images using only its colors. We had happy times there, my mother and I."

"Have you been back as an adult?"

"Not to Roussillon, no."

"Why not?"

"My father died there when I was twelve."

"What happened?"

"He fell down the stairs and broke his neck."

"An accident?"

"So *they* believe, yes."

Rice looked startled. "So it wasn't an accident?"

"Anything is possible."

"Then your mother . . . ?"

Waller placed a large hand on Rice's narrow shoulder and squeezed a little. "I didn't say my mother, did I? She was sweet and good. Such an act would've been unthinkable to the purity of her soul."

"Yes, I'm sure. Yes, I understand."

The orbital ridges around Waller's eyes seemed to deepen. "*Do you understand, Alan?*" He removed his hand and pulled a note from his pocket. "I see that a young American woman is leasing the villa next to mine."

"We just found that out. However, I doubt she poses a threat."

"No, no, Alan. We don't know what she poses yet, do we? The proximity alone is enough, is it not, to raise questions?"

"You're right. I will find out all that I can. So will you visit this Roussillon? Is it far?"

"Nothing in Provence is really that far."

"Then you will go?"

"Perhaps I will."

"Just don't become a victim of some accident yourself."

"Please do not concern yourself for me. My father was careless and weak. His son is not."

CHAPTER

13

Y<small>OU TALKED</small> to her, didn't you?" asked Frank.

Shaw looked up from the papers he was studying. "Who?"

"Don't play stupid. Katie!"

"How'd you know?"

"Because your head has been in your ass the last few days. If I'd known you'd be like this I never would've given you the damn number. So how did she sound?"

"Fine."

"What'd you two talk about?"

"What the hell is it to you?"

"Nothing. Whatever. Excuse me for giving a shit. Okay, back to Evan Waller."

"I don't like the plan. It has too many holes."

Surprisingly, Frank nodded. "I agree with you. What do you suggest?"

"Simplifying it. Events on the ground tend to complicate things anyway. Start simple, then if things get hairy they're still manageable. You start out complicated and things go to hell, it's not good because there are too many pieces that can go wrong."

"We know where he lives in Montreal, but taking him there has never gotten authorization from higher up. Too public, too much collateral damage potential, and the guy never keeps to a schedule there. He moves like a ghost, always varying his route and routine."

Shaw said, "Then we have to find one moment in time in Provence where he does keep to a schedule and the collateral damage is minimal."

The two men looked at the floor plan of the villa where the

human trafficker would be staying. On the wall was a plasma screen containing more data, including all roads in and out of the target area.

Frank clicked a button on a control pad on the table in front of him and a set of pictures came up on the large screen. "He always travels with these guys, all major kick-ass types. And that's the ones we know about. There may be more as backup."

"He'll advance-team the site, lock it down, and then sit on it," added Shaw as he studied the bodyguards, each one looking tougher, meaner, and more capable than the last. "How reliable is the intel on his travel itinerary?"

"Very. We got it off phone chatter, email, and company credit card transactions."

Shaw looked up. "Americans? They've got the best hard- and software for that."

"Let's put it this way, I owe the heads of NSA and CIA a really nice meal."

Frank pulled out some docs and read over them. "His flight plan was filed. He's flying from Montreal to Paris in his private wings. Refuel and then on to the airport at Avignon. Short hop in the bird. He typically travels in a three-vehicle motorcade. He's got car rentals reserved in Avignon."

Shaw pushed a button on the laptop and another picture came up, an exterior shot of the street where Waller's rental was located. "There's a villa next door."

"Already leased to someone."

"Who?"

"Did a prelim. Tourist. Looks absolutely clean."

"Right next door, though?"

"Gordes is a very popular destination and those villas are in high demand. We couldn't exactly stop them from being leased without raising a big red flag. But it doesn't matter. We're not doing the snatch in Gordes. Too much collateral damage possibility."

Shaw looked at another computer screen that gave a partial itinerary for Evan Waller. He sat up straighter. "How do you know he's going to the caves at Les Baux-de-Provence?"

"He had to get special permission for the tour and we accessed that data."

"Why? Isn't it open to the public?"

"Well, our Mr. Waller wanted a very private tour. Closed off to the public. To make that happen he paid big bucks. The place is in private hands. They can do what they want. When we saw the payment going to them we hacked their computer system and found the schedule. So we know the exact date he'll be there."

Shaw swiveled in his chair to face another computer whose hard drive was clean except for factory-loaded software, including a browser. They used it to connect to the Internet. He hit some keys and read over the results. "Okay, I've actually heard of this place. It's a photo-exhibition gallery; light show on the rock walls, a narrated tour, recorded documentary, yada yada. They choose a different artist each year." He sat, mulling this new information over. "I think we have our extraction location."

He spun the laptop around and let Frank look at the screen. It was information about the exhibition venue. "The caves have one entrance, lots of rooms, and few attendants, so it's easy to get lost or disoriented. We cut the power source and the extraction team is already in place with optics and one-shot-and-drop tranquilizer guns. We separate the boss from the muscle and off we go."

Frank thought about this. "Limits collateral damage too. We'll need eyes on the ground ahead of time to confirm all the details."

"No argument there. But what better place to take a rat than in a hole?"

"But if the hit misses at the caves the guy's going to be on his private wings out of France."

Shaw sat back. "It's not perfect, but it's the best we can do under the circumstances. His trip to the caves is the only time we'll know for sure where he'll be going. And I really don't see how we can miss."

CHAPTER

14

THE EXTRACTION PLAN was in place. The caves had been gone over thoroughly by assets on the ground in Provence. Shaw would also visit the caves when he got there. In the meantime he had studied detailed plans of the caves' exterior and interior until he could draw them out on paper from memory. Waller was scheduled to travel there less than a week after his arrival; his private tour began at 10 a.m. sharp.

After each long day of work, which included handpicking the members of the hit team and prepping them, Shaw would go to his hotel, change, do his run, and then wander the streets of Paris alone until the darkness thickened and his energy waned. One night he was eating alone at a café across from the Jardin du Luxembourg, a place Anna Schmidt had loved. They'd walk through the gardens, hand in hand, watch the children sail their wooden boats in the large central fountain, and then sit and observe people drift by. He couldn't go back there now because for him it was hallowed ground that could not be trod on again. But he had ventured close enough to see some of the flowers from a distance. That was the best he could do before his chest started to tighten and his eyes moistened.

He'd just ordered his food when he looked around the restaurant, checking each table. A decades-long habit, it was as natural to him as drawing breath. He drew a quick one when he saw her standing there in the doorway that separated one dining area from another.

Katie James didn't look as thin as the last time he'd seen her, which was good because she'd needed to put on some weight. Her naturally blonde hair, spiky and dark the last time they'd been together, had grown out and now nearly touched her shoulders. She had on a white skirt, two-inch heels, no hose, and a dark blue long-sleeved blouse. He'd never known her to wear a sleeveless shirt, primarily because of the bullet wound on her upper left arm.

As she walked toward him he could see that her makeup did not quite cover the darkened circles under her eyes. She was a beautiful woman; many men in the room turned their heads to stare, incurring the wrath of the ladies with whom they were dining. Yet apparently a glimpse of Katie James walking across the room was worth the risk.

She didn't wait for him to extend an invitation; she simply sat down across from him. "You look good," she said. She eyed his hair. "A little gray?"

"A little. You look all the way back. Put on a few needed pounds. Although I kind of liked the dark, spiky hairdo." He paused. "How did you know where I was?" He answered his own question before she could. "Frank. What's his interest? I've never known him to care one way or another about my personal life."

"I don't think he did until Anna was killed."

"He told me you called him."

"I wouldn't have had to if you'd ever called me back."

"I'm sorry I walked out on you."

"There were no ties. You're a big boy, I'm a big girl. My only problem with that was I wasn't sure you were alive. That's why I called Frank. To make sure you were okay."

This made Shaw feel even guiltier. "Well, I'm fine. Back working. Everything's okay. I told you that on the phone."

"I wanted to see for myself."

He looked down at the table. "Have you eaten dinner?"

"I'm not hungry."

This surprised him, her turning down his invitation to dine with him, and his face showed it. "Katie."

She rose. Their gazes locked for an extended moment. "Good luck, Shaw."

She hesitated for another second, long enough for him to say something to keep her there. Yet he remained quiet.

She turned and left.

Shaw sat there for several beats, a massive struggle going on inside his mind. Finally, he threw some euros on the table, hustled from the restaurant, and looked up and down the crowded street.

But Katie was already gone.

CHAPTER

15

It was after midnight as Reggie crept down to the library at Harrowsfield. The rain was beating against the windows and a cold wind was catapulting down the chimney, feeding a burst of oxygen onto a fading fire. She closed the door behind her, sat at the long table, and picked up a file. Under the light of a single table lamp she went over the murderous career of Fedir Kuchin for probably the hundredth time. The atrocities hadn't changed, of course, but if anything they had become more firmly embedded in her mind. She could recite the statistics from memory; she could see the faces of the victims, pages and pages of them. The images of the mass graves, unearthed long after the man had fled the locations of his brutal handiwork, appeared to be seared onto her corneas.

She picked up a grainy picture—they were all grainy pictures, as though violent death could never have any fragment of color—and stared down at the face there. Colonel Huber had had his David Rosenbergs and his Frau Koches, photos Reggie had selected from countless others to show the man at the moment of his death. Well, Fedir Kuchin had his own testaments to a level of insane cruelty that all these men seemed to possess.

The photo she was looking at now was that of a man with an unpronounceable surname. He'd been neither wealthy nor well connected. He'd lived nearly a thousand kilometers from the capital city of Kiev. He was a simple farmer with a large family, one that he worked long hours to support. His crime against the state had amounted to his refusal to turn in his friends to the KGB, to Fedir Kuchin specifically. His punishment had been to be doused with petrol and set on fire in front of his wife and children. He had been burned to bone and cinder while they were forced to watch and listen to his screams.

She picked up another document. Originally written in Ukrainian, it had been translated for her on another piece of paper. It was the order condemning the doomed farmer to death by fire. Fedir Kuchin's signature appeared large and bold at the bottom of the page, as though he wanted no doubt as to who was the instigator of the man's horrible murder.

Finally, she gingerly picked up another old photo. It was Fedir Kuchin himself. She held the paper only by the edges, as though afraid to actually touch the image of the man. He was wearing a uniform with the collar undone. In one hand was a pistol, in the other a bottle. It was obviously a staged photo. Back then he had dark hair, slicked back with a severe widow's peak. His face had not changed all that much over time. Yet the eyes were what drew one in. Reggie felt as though she were traveling down a dark path to the very center of them, losing herself in shadows from which meaningful escape seemed unlikely. She righted herself and slowly put the photo back down, covering it with a stack of paper.

Over the next thirty minutes she went through dozens of other pictures of the dead, Kuchin's bloody fingerprints on each one. The paperwork was in some ways mechanical; it could have been purchase orders for equipment or food. Yet it was written commands to kill other human beings, done in old-fashioned triplicate complete with carbon copies. Death by bullet. Death by fire. Death by gas. Death by the blade. Death by the noose. All neat and nice. Thank God for those carbon copies, thought Reggie. Without them it would have been nearly impossible to track down and then administer justice to men like Kuchin.

"Extra reading, my dear?"

Startled, Reggie looked around.

Professor Mallory stood in the doorway in an old, tattered checked robe, holding a book and staring at her.

"I never heard you come in," she said, obviously unsettled that the old man could have gotten this close without her knowing.

"Well, I am light on my feet, despite my size and rheumatism, and you were very much engrossed in what you were doing." He stepped forward and glanced down at the papers and photos with an inquiring look.

"I couldn't sleep," she said. "I often can't sleep," she admitted.

He sat down in a worn leather chair near the fireplace. "A fact of which I am aware."

"What are you doing up? Do you have insomnia too?"

"No, Regina, not insomnia." He winced in pain as he settled himself farther into the cracked leather. "An enlarged prostate, I'm afraid. Given a choice I'd gladly take the insomnia."

"I'm sorry."

He eyed the file she was holding. "So what do you think? Any brilliant insights?"

"He's a man without remorse. He signed off on a thousand death warrants like he would a damn pub bill."

"Well, I agree with you, but that's something we already knew."

He rose, placed another small log on the fire, sat back down in his armchair, and opened his book.

"What are you reading?" Reggie asked.

"On a wild night like this? Agatha Christie, of course. I still feel compelled to see if Hercule Poirot's 'little gray cells' will do their job one more time. It seems to often inspire my own brain, however inferior it might be to the diminutive Belgian's."

Reggie rose and stood in front of the fire. Before coming downstairs she'd pulled on jeans and a sweatshirt, but her feet were bare and a chill had worked into her. "There *was* one thing, Professor."

He looked up from his pages as the storm threw rain at the old leaded window with nearly the force of an errant hose. A scream from the angry wind came down the chimney and Reggie backed away from the sound and sat on a small hassock near him.

"What thing?" he asked.

"Kuchin is a religious man."

Mallory closed his book and nodded. He pulled his pipe from his pocket and began to stuff it with tobacco.

"Professor, if you don't mind, that smell actually makes me sick."

He looked surprised. "Why didn't you say so?"

"I guess I didn't want to hurt your feelings." She gave a hollow laugh. "I guess after the things I've done that seems a bit odd."

His expression remained serious. "What's odd? That you have enormous compassion? I would imagine that facet of your personality is one major reason you do this job."

Reggie hurried on. "Anyway, I read over the case notes. And it says that Kuchin goes to church every Sunday and gives large sums for religious purposes."

Mallory slipped the pipe back in his pocket. "It's true enough. I've seen it before with men like him. Seeking redemption, solace, hedging one's bets, even. It's madness, of course, for such men to believe that any 'god' of goodness would have anything to do with the likes of them after death."

"Mass killers, you mean?"

Mallory interpreted the intent behind her words immediately. "You are nothing like the Fedir Kuchins of the world, Regina."

"Funny, some days it's hard for me to tell the difference, really."

Mallory stood so fast that he dropped his novel. He strode over to the table, picked up a piece of paper, and came back to her, thrusting it in her hands.

It was the photo of the remains of the incinerated farmer. "*There* is the difference, Regina. Right there." He took her hand, gripped it firmly, and looked directly into her eyes. "And now tell me about the church."

CHAPTER

16

They were sitting in a car outside Charles de Gaulle Airport. Shortly, a turboprop plane would be taking Shaw to Avignon. The plan was for him to stay there a few days before venturing on to Gordes, which was less than an hour's drive away.

Frank said, "Amy Crawford is already in Provence."

"I've worked with her before. She's a top-notch field agent."

"Got the plan down pat?"

"In my head it's perfect. We'll see how it flies on the ground."

Frank made to light one of his little cigars, but Shaw stopped him. "Give it a rest until I'm twenty thousand feet up. I need the extra oxygen right now."

Frank put his cigar away. "Nervous? Not like you."

"I saw Katie the other night."

"The hell you say. Where?"

"Right here in Paris. You telling me you didn't know?"

"Scout's Honor. First I heard of it."

"Come on, Frank. She showed up at the restaurant where I was having dinner. How do you think she managed that?"

"You ever stop and think that the lady is a world-class journalist? She finds stuff out."

"Right." Shaw clearly did not believe this.

"What'd she want?"

Shaw didn't answer right away because he didn't really have an answer. *What did she want? Was it really just to see for herself that I was okay? But I told her that on the phone.*

"Shaw?"

He noticed that Frank was staring at him and didn't look happy.

"You just zoned out on me. You're heading out on a mission against one very scary guy and you're already zoning? Not good."

"She didn't really say what she wanted. And she only stayed a minute."

Frank gripped his arm. "What, you telling me you didn't invite her to join you for dinner? She traveled all that way and—"

"How do you know how far she traveled?"

Frank made a face and slumped back in his seat.

"Why are you doing this?"

"Doing what?" said Frank grumpily.

"Half the time you act like you don't give a crap if I live or die. The other half it feels like you're trying to play matchmaker."

"My mother was the same way with me. Must be genetic."

"We're not family, Frank."

"Hell, in some ways we're closer than family. And who else do you have?"

Shaw looked away, tapped his travel documents against his thigh. Who else did he have? Just Frank? God, that was a depressing thought. "So why do you think she came to see me?"

"Ask me a hard one. She wanted you to tell her, face-to-face, to stay."

"You know that for a fact?"

"It doesn't take a brilliant deduction. And no, she didn't tell me that, if that's what you're really asking."

"Nothing can happen between her and me, Frank."

"Well, something already has, apparently."

"Anna's grave isn't even cold and—"

"It doesn't have to be about that. You think a smart lady like Katie doesn't know what you're feeling about Anna? She knows you're not going to jump into bed with her. She knows you may never jump into bed with her. And I don't think she even wants that. At least not now."

"So now you're a shrink?"

"I'm just a guy making a reasoned observation."

"So what does she really want?"

"You two shared a lot. Went through hell together. Both came out of it emotional wrecks. I think she just wants to be your friend."

"Well, here's a news update for you, my line of work doesn't allow for friends."

Shaw slammed the door shut behind him and walked off to grab his wings to Avignon.

Frank stared after him until the tall man disappeared into the masses entering the airport. He told the driver to head on. He pulled out his cigar, started to light up, and then stuck it back in his jacket pocket.

"Sometimes you don't know how lucky you are, Shaw," he muttered to nobody.

CHAPTER

17

FEDIR KUCHIN was a very smart man, smarter than all of them had thought. Not only had he outwitted Professor Mallory, but he'd outmaneuvered Reggie and her team on the ground in Provence. The penalty for this failure was steep. Reggie stared over at the bodies of Whit and Dominic. Whit's head was gone; Dominic no longer had a face.

Reggie had been forced to kneel in the center of the freezing room while Kuchin and his men encircled her. There really was no escape this time. She looked up into the long, cruel face as he stroked her chin with one of his hands. She would have attacked him, but her hands and legs were bound. She focused on the bodies of her dead colleagues so she wouldn't feel the touch of the monster against her skin.

Kuchin laughed, a smug, deep laugh that seemed to go on for minutes. Did you think it would be that easy? he said to her. Did you really? After all those years of guarding myself against this very thing, you really thought someone like you could get to me? You're an amateur sent in to do a professional's job.

The stroking changed to a hard slap and Reggie fell backwards, hitting her head on the concrete floor. He immediately pulled her back up by the hair. His face nearly touching hers, he said, Tell me your name. Your real name.

Why? she mumbled.

Because I like to know these things.

No, I won't.

He hit her in the mouth with his gun, loosening two teeth and breaking a third. She tasted blood and pieces of her gum and swallowed part of one shattered molar.

No.

He hit her again in the stomach and she doubled over. He stomped on her right hand, snapping two fingers. He crushed her left knee with another blow.

Now!

Reggie, she muttered as the blood trickled down her face.

Reggie, what?

Reggie Campion.

Well, Reggie Campion, now you'll know.

Know what?

What it feels like to die in beautiful Provence.

He motioned to one of his men, who came forward with the canister. A moment later Reggie could taste the petrol as it poured over her, clogging her nostrils, stinging her eyes.

She wanted to be brave. But she heard herself scream, No, please. Don't. Like a child. Pathetic. Weak.

Kuchin smiled, took the match from his pocket, struck it against the heel of his shoe, and held it up for her to see.

No, no, she cried out.

I actually thought you'd be a worthier foe, Reggie, said Kuchin.

No, please, don't kill me.

This time the monster wins, Reggie Campion, he said.

He dropped the match on her head and she burst into flames.

With a scream muffled only by the covers over her face, Reggie threw herself out of the bed and landed on the floor, her body twisting and turning, grinding itself into the floor as she fought the imaginary flames. Then, coming to her senses, she stopped and lay still for several minutes. She managed to crawl to the bathroom before emptying her stomach in the toilet, and then collapsed on her back on the cool tile floor.

She lay there breathing hard, waiting for the waves of sickness to fade. Finally she struggled up, stumbled to the window, and looked out onto the grounds of Harrowsfield. As the time to leave on the mission grew closer she usually liked to spend less time at the estate and more at her flat. However, the sexually energetic couple in the room above her had still not satisfied themselves. So she'd come here.

Yet as she had driven away from London she'd also felt a pang of envy. *When's the last time I had sex? Pretty pathetic when I can't even remember.*

The rain had passed but the air had not lost its chill. Reggie lifted the window and leaned out, taking deep breaths as the nightmare's sickening effects faded.

I'm having night terrors about the bloke and I haven't even faced him yet. Not good, Reggie. Not good.

The worst part had been the vision of Whit and Dominic lying dead. Her fears could not be a reason for them to die. She had to get her head straight.

She dressed in jeans, sneakers, and a frayed hooded sweatshirt with "Oxford" stenciled on the front and slipped out the rear kitchen door. She wasn't sure if Whit had gone back home or stayed over. She didn't want him, or anyone, to see her like this. It only took her a few minutes to reach the old cemetery and, even in the dark, mere seconds after that to locate the old tombstone of Laura R. Campion. She stood in front of it, hands in her pockets.

In a completely irrational way, since she had no family left alive, Reggie had come to think of this dead woman as representing a touchstone for her, to visit in times of stress and uncertainty. It was madness, though, she knew, to try to escape the terror she was feeling by coming to a cemetery in the middle of the night and staring at the grave of a woman dead for over two hundred years who as far as she knew had no connection to her at all.

"Yet I must be a bit mad," she said softly, "to do what I do."

And yet it *was* perfectly sane, she told herself, to be afraid of a man like Fedir Kuchin, who burned children alive without a second thought. A man who'd slaughtered thousands of people at a time in horrific ways. It would be madness *not* to be afraid.

On the other side of the graveyard was a small private chapel that had fallen into ruin. Its stone-block walls were blackened with age, the roof was partially fallen in, and the thick arched wooden doors had grown frail from termites and rot.

Reggie passed inside and walked up near the altar. She would come here on occasion to get away from the demands of her "career" and to listen to the birds that had taken up roost in the old joists of the structure. There were no stained glass windows, simply lead ones that had been broken or merely disintegrated. Through these openings the sounds of the surrounding woods poured inside.

Apparently unlike Fedir Kuchin she had long since given up notions of a higher power guiding them all. She had done so for a simple reason. An all-knowing, all-powerful, benevolent god would never allow the monsters to roam the earth, killing whomever they desired. So for her, their mere presence in the world ruled out any possibility of a benign supreme being. Others would argue that point, and many had with her. She listened patiently to their reasoned statements and then simply disagreed with their conclusions.

They would have two more days to finalize everything, and then she was leaving for Provence. Before that happened she and the professor would make the exact decision on how to do it. Whether Fedir Kuchin lived or died would depend on their making the right decision.

Finally, realizing all that was riding on this, and despite her own personal misgivings, Reggie knelt down at the altar, put her hands together, and started to pray, that good would defeat evil one more time.

She figured it couldn't hurt.

CHAPTER

18

THE VILLA that Evan Waller would be staying at cost over twenty thousand euros per week and he'd leased it for a month, paying in advance, or so the leasing agent had told Shaw. The house was parked next to the cliffs of Gordes and rose five levels high, reachable inside only by a single spiral limestone staircase. The place had six bedrooms and a saltwater pool in the rear grounds where there was also an al fresco dining area under a wooden pergola, along with an outdoor kitchen and propane grill. The villa's owner had recently renovated it, and all the appliances, including the Wolf gas stovetop in the spacious kitchen, were new.

Shaw knew all of this because he was meeting with the leasing agent at her office in Gordes in the guise of being a potential renter for next year. The agent was polite and informative.

"Don't take too much time," she'd warned him in efficient French. She was a Brit transplant but her French was very good. "Just yesterday there was another person here who wants to lease for next year too."

"Really," said Shaw. "Who might that be?"

The woman arched her eyebrows. "That is confidential. But she is young, American, and quite lovely. And obviously quite well-to-do. These villas are the best in the area and beyond the purse of most. The same builder did the renovation on the villa next door. They're not exactly alike inside, but there are many similarities, including the limestone spiral stairs connecting all floors."

So much for confidences, thought Shaw. "But if the place is leased now as you said, where's the tenant? The villa is empty."

The woman appeared uncertain. "It's true he's leased it for the month. Paid in advance."

"So it is a *man*, then?" Shaw said.

She looked upset with herself. "Yes, but his name is confidential."

"Of course."

"Anyway, he's not here yet. It was quite unusual, actually. I mean, to pay thousands of euros for something you're not even using? Well, it's not for me to say, I suppose. Rich people are peculiar that way, aren't they? But you yourself must be rich, if you're looking at renting such a villa."

"I've done well in life," Shaw said modestly. "And we can speak in English if you prefer, though your French is far better than mine."

She looked both pleased and relieved by this. Her demeanor and tone instantly changed, and her British accent rang loud and clear. "Well, that's sweet of you to say. I've been doing these lessons for a month to get that gurgling thing going in my throat, but I can't say I've quite got the hang of it. These French, though, they speak so beautifully, so brilliantly, don't they? But it just about wrecks my poor esophagus."

"Mine too."

"Anyway, since the place is empty I could've taken you up for a quick peek, but we don't want to barge in and find Mr. Waller in his underpants, now do we?" She chuckled.

"So it's Mr. Waller?"

The woman looked chagrined. "Now look what I've gone and done. Okay, that's the man's name, but don't bandy it about. Our work *is* confidential."

"Of course. Not a word. Thank you."

He left her and walked to the place in Gordes where he was staying, a small hotel that also had a spa. Situated on the precipice of the Vaucluse plateau with the Luberon valley and hills beyond, Gordes could be reached almost faster on foot from the villas below by a series of steps cut into the rock. A car ride was quite circuitous and involved a number of switchbacks. The village of white and gray stone structures clung to the rock sides like bees to a honeycomb. The village itself was twice crowned: by the Catholic church with its soaring bell tower and by a medieval castle that now housed part of the town's government.

He called Frank and filled him in. Ever since he'd arrived here Shaw had methodically reconnoitered each building of note in the town. He probably knew Gordes better than many of its longtime residents. He and Amy Crawford were due to meet tomorrow, but Shaw had been in contact with her since he'd landed in Provence.

There were a number of possibilities in the village for lunch, so he took his time reading menus printed on crisp white paper and tacked onto exterior walls. He selected L'Estaminet Café near the town center and had his meal, supplementing it with a glass of Rhone, which was of course quite popular around these parts. On the other hand, Italian wine was almost impossible to find, Shaw thought with a grin. His smile faded when she walked in. Though the place was teeming with tourists, for some reason he knew this must be the American of whom the real estate agent had spoken; young, lovely, and so well off.

She was in her late twenties, with streaked blonde hair that he sensed wasn't her natural color. Her skin was tanned to almond with a few freckles on her shoulders the size and color of coffee beans. She was wearing a sundress with a scalloped front allowing a glimpse of her cleavage; leather sandals covered her long, narrow feet. Shaw could only see her in profile as she was escorted to her seat. But as she put her bag in the chair next to her she momentarily turned his way.

It seemed that Shaw's eyes and brain were disturbingly out of sync, as though his mind had expected his pupils to signal something other than what they had just seen. Yet he didn't know exactly why he had any expectation at all. Her face was not perfect. Her nose was a bit long and thin and a little too sharply angled; the eyes were a tad large for symmetry when aligned against her face, the cheeks somewhat flat. Yet somehow all put together these elements made her far more memorable than if her features had been flawless. Beautiful women, especially in the south of France, were not so rare, but someone who did not fit neatly into a category was often unforgettable.

Her body was athletic; the shoulders well-developed, her legs long and defined, the calves particularly muscular as though she had walked uphill a great deal in her life. Because of her leanness she looked taller than what he approximated was about five-seven, but she also seemed small to him. Yet since he stood six foot six in his bare feet, just about everyone other than basketball players seemed diminutive to Shaw.

As he continued to think about it, Shaw realized that what had startled him was that though she was obviously young, she seemed old, not physically, of course.

She seems far too serious for someone that young.

Though he'd finished his meal, a curious Shaw chose to stay and have a café and a cup of strawberry sorbet. Once or twice he thought he saw her glance his way, but it might have been his imagination. He finally paid his bill, rose, and left. If he'd turned around, he would have seen definitive proof that she had noticed him, her gaze lingering long after he'd closed the door.

He walked down the uneven cobblestone streets but kept the front of the restaurant in sight. Twenty minutes later she stepped out the door, looked around, and started down the path that would carry her to the villas below. That included one shortcut, down a short flight of worn stone steps that would eliminate about a minute out of the trip by subtracting a switchback from the route.

Shaw followed her, wondering where she was staying. He was surprised to see her approach and then unlock the front door to the villa next to where Waller would be staying. And she'd made inquiries about the other villa too. Despite Frank's finding nothing on the woman, she would still bear watching. Surprises were never good especially if Shaw was on the receiving end of one.

CHAPTER

19

THE NEXT DAY Shaw traveled fifteen kilometers and met up with Amy Crawford near the ruins of an old fort set high on top of a hill, as old forts often were for strategic reasons. Crawford was petite, barely up to Shaw's chest. But he knew she was proficient in several martial arts, was a marathon runner, and could kill or disable with either her hands or her feet. Yet while her physical prowess was superb, it was her coolness in the field that had attracted Shaw's attention and caused him to select her for the team.

They drove separately to the old quarry where the caves at Les Baux were located and took the tour. Shaw had a pinhole camera in his shirt and videotaped everything for later analysis.

Walking back to their cars, Crawford said, "Good to be working with you again."

"Same here."

"Based on the floor plan in there, extraction should go smoothly. Guy couldn't have picked a more convenient place for us to do it."

"And he probably knows that too. So he and his guards will be on high alert. We'll have two seconds of surprise. It's incredibly rare we have this sort of detailed intel on a target. We have to hit our marks perfectly."

"Understood."

Shaw motioned for her to get in her car, a two-door Audi. He climbed in the passenger seat. "Give me the extract from A to Z; make sure we're on the same page."

Crawford fingered the steering wheel. "Private tour starts at oh-ten hundred. His past experience shows he'll travel with a minimum of four and a max of six muscle, holsters and Glocks. They hit the entrance. The tour guide is our plant. He's got hair-follicle audio feed and a pinhole video on his guide badge that'll give us their movements in real time. He'll make sure the flow matches the timetable as close as possible. All attendants have been previously removed from the scene. Five minutes to read the orientation materials on the walls, plus listening to the recorded introductory spot, puts us at oh ten-ten tops. First room goes in five minutes. Second in two. Third in four. That puts our time mark at twenty-one minutes past oh-ten hundred. Fourth room is ground zero. Sixty meters by sixty meters, good cover on front and left sidewalls. Extraction team is already in position. Power is scheduled to be yanked sixty seconds after they hit ground zero. Seven shooters with flex optics and laser-guided dart rifles. Aim points are neck, arm, or thigh in case of body armor. Our guy in the power room commences his five-second countdown as soon as the video feed shows the last muscle in the party cross Room Four threshold. Code word 'red' comes over our headsets one second before power is cut. Fire to commence on that one-second mark to prevent any reaction that might foul the shots. You take out main target while I drop the guy on his hip, with the other shooters dropping the man in their prescribed sectors, flowing outward from main target. All muscle and main target down in two seconds."

"Exit?"

"Two passages branch off east and west from that cave. West circles back to the entrance. East passage is two hundred meters long and empties to an emergency exit that takes us to the other side of the quarry. There's an egress road at that point. Wheels waiting in the form of an ambulance. Gurney is stowed in the east passage. Target loaded on; that'll take no more than thirty seconds. The same to get him down the passage. Wheels roll as soon as the ambulance doors clunk shut. Private airstrip is forty minutes south of here. Wheels up as soon as the aircraft door closes. Target and extraction team are out of French airspace before his muscle wakes up in a dark cave and wonders what the hell just happened."

He nodded appreciatively. "Then on to the next job," said Shaw.

"Story of my life too." She hesitated, glancing at him.

"What?" he asked, noting her trepidation.

"Just scuttlebutt. Always wondered if it was true."

Shaw looked at her inquiringly. "What?" he said again.

"Did you really shoot Mr. Wells in the head?"

"We had a little misunderstanding."

She smiled. "I like your style."

"Frank's actually not a bad guy once you get past the two hundred pounds of anger and dysfunction."

"Really?"

"No, not really."

CHAPTER

20

THE NEXT DAY Shaw watched with interest as the mystery lady did her shopping in Gordes. Men of all ages stared as she walked by in a sunhat and knee-length skirt that the sneaky breeze would occasionally catch and pitch upward around her thighs. Then the men would stare with even greater focus. While seeming to window shop along the street, Shaw watched as men approached her speaking French, Italian, Greek, and English, at least by his count. They were offering to help her with her shopping, the language, or perhaps assisting her off with her clothes in the privacy of their room. She politely declined all offers. She in fact needed no help. She spoke fluent French and she knew the prices of things. And she could bargain. Shaw had watched her haggle over a blouse, a decorative blue-and-yellow plate, a bottle of wine, and a dozen zucchini flowers presumably to later fry up, until arriving at the prices she wanted.

That night, he was sitting at an outdoor café in Gordes contemplating what to have for dinner when he was surprised by her walking up to his table.

"*Parlez-vous français?*"

"*Oui, je parle français.*" But he added, "*Mais mon anglais est meilleur.*"

She smiled warmly. "My English is much better than my French too. Do you mind if I join you? I've eaten alone the last few times, and while it started out kind of fun, it grows old fast."

He indicated for her to take a seat. "Please."

She took off her hat and set it on the seat next to her before picking up a menu.

"What looks good?" she asked, lifting up her Maui Jims though the setting sun was dropping a bucket of glare right at her.

"Chicken puttanesca, or you can never go wrong with the old steak and pommes frites with salad."

"Shall we order wine?"

"We're in Provence. I think it's the law."

They gave their orders to the waiter, who promptly brought the selected bottle of red and two glasses. He poured and left them alone.

"I'm sure this seems very forward of me," she said. "Coming over to you like this."

"I'm not sure there is such a thing as 'forward' anymore for men or women."

"First things first, I'm Jane Collins. But Janie to my friends." She held out her hand. With an amused look Shaw shook it.

"Bill."

"American?"

He nodded. "You?"

"What it says on my passport."

"I'm from D.C."

"And what do you do in our nation's capital?"

"As little as possible. I was a lobbyist, but I sold my practice and decided to see a little bit of the world beyond Capitol Hill."

"Do you have a family?"

"Let me play the proud dad." He took out his wallet and handed her the picture of a girl and a boy, that Frank had provided him. "Michael and Alli. They're back in the States."

She handed the photo back. "Beautiful. So your wife's not with you?"

"We're divorced." He slipped the photo in his shirt pocket. "The picture's a little old. They're both teenagers now."

"You must have started early, you don't look that old."

"Keep drinking wine, I like the effect on your vision. How about you? What's your story?"

"Nothing very exciting. My dad made huge amounts of money. He and my mom died way too early and I was the only child."

"Sorry to hear that. I guess the money doesn't make up for it."

"I never thought it could, and I turned out to be right. I was young when they passed away, but I still miss them."

"I can understand that."

"But life goes on," she said, staring off for a moment before looking back at him and managing a weak smile. "I'm rich, I like to travel, see different places. It's so beautiful here. So how long have you been in town?"

"A few days."

"And after this?"

"Italy and then Greece. But I'm taking my time. My whole life has been run on a tight plan. I'm sort of into winging things now."

"Where are you staying?"

Shaw shifted uncomfortably in his seat. "Well, maybe there is such a thing as forward after all."

Her cheeks reddened. "Okay, I guess I deserved that. I tend to ask too many questions and volunteer too much about myself to complete strangers."

"I would agree with that. The part about you being rich is not something you want to blab about. Too many lowlifes who'd take advantage of that information."

She looked like she'd been scolded. "I guess you're right."

"How come you're solo? Don't you have any friends who'd like to travel with you? I'm sure you go first-class."

"Friends have jobs. That's the downside to not having to work for a living."

"I think most people would be able to cope with the trade-off," he said kindly.

"Well, *we* could hang out."

"You don't even know me."

"Sure I do. You're um . . ."

"Bill," he said helpfully.

She playfully punched his arm. "From D.C. Ex-lobbyist guy and divorced with two beautiful teenagers. See, my memory's not that bad."

"Okay, Jane—"

"Janie to my friends."

"All right, Janie, but just take it slow with people."

She said sheepishly, "I'm nearly thirty; you would've thought I'd have gotten that lesson by now."

"Some people never get it."

"So where'd you learn to speak French?"

"How do you know I really can? The few words I spoke aren't exactly going to get me a job at the UN. Your French sounded pretty authentic. Where'd you learn?"

"I took an immersion class for six months before I came here. It's amazing what you can fit in your day when you don't have a job."

Shaw lifted his glass of wine and clinked it against hers. "I'm really looking forward to finding that out."

Their food came and they continued to talk through dinner. They split the check using cash. Afterwards they walked through the street. Most of the shops were closed at this hour, but the warm breeze was nice, there were many people strolling about just as they were, and music could be heard coming from a bar past the town center.

She looked up at him. "How tall are you?"

"About six-six."

"You must've been the tallest lobbyist in D.C."

"Nope, they have some ex-NBA players trolling for dollars there. One of them is seven feet. Poor guy has to duck through doorways when he's pressing the flesh and begging for his supper."

"Well, I'm down this way," she said.

Shaw hooked a finger over his shoulder. "I'm that way."

"Maybe we'll run into each other again."

"Small town, the odds are good."

She smiled. "I'll be far more reticent next time."

He returned the smile. "And I'll be far less critical."

Reggie Campion immediately returned to her villa, where she made a call. She explained her meeting with Bill to Professor Mallory and gave him a detailed description of the man. "Find out what you can. There's something about him."

"All right, Regina. But it may be nothing."

"And it may be everything. I trust my instincts. Word on Waller?"

"On schedule."

"Then I have my work cut out for me if this new development turns into a mess. You're certain everything is a go on my cover?"

"It has been for quite some time. One of our benefactors owns a technology company with elite-level programs and access to numerous core databases. He allowed us in through a back door to do all we needed to do. All the information you've memorized is backed up in all the places anyone might look. Vital records in the U.S., an American Social Security number, bank accounts, educational backgrounds, degrees conferred, parents' history. Oh, did you like your Facebook page?"

"Brilliant. Nice chums I have. And I must say, Professor, you certainly know more about computers than you let on."

"I'm just an old duffer. Merely regurgitating what I'm told."

"If you say so."

"Don't push yourself too hard."

"It's the only way I stay alive."

Barely a half mile away Shaw was sitting on his bed lifting a nice set of prints off the special coating on the photo of the fake kids he'd handed "Janie." Using a handheld computing device he scanned them in, emailed them to Frank, and then called him.

"Sounds like a hottie," said Frank after Shaw finished filling him in.

"I don't like 'hotties' showing up when I have a job to do, especially if they're staying at the villa next door to my target. And she made inquiries about Waller's place earlier too."

"But from what you said, she's a bit of a ditz."

"We don't know that for sure. Could be an act."

"I told you our prelim gave off no warning bells. You going paranoid on me?"

"No, Frank, I've *been* paranoid for a long time."

21

D<small>O YOU</small> believe in God?" Waller asked Alan Rice.

They had just gotten off Waller's plane after a long flight. Now the two men were riding in the back of a rental Escalade on the way to a meeting. Rice had his gaze on the laptop screen where numbers flew across. If he was surprised by his employer's question he didn't show it. "I haven't thought about it since I was a child, really."

Waller looked interested. "And if you thought about it now?"

"I would come down on the side that says one should hedge his bets, though I must admit I haven't exactly been doing that very well."

Waller looked disappointed. "Really?"

"But with the caveat that one should still count on individual efforts in getting what one wants in life rather than praying to something one can't see."

Waller looked pleased by this answer.

"I take it you are not a practitioner of a faith, Evan?"

"On the contrary, I pray every morning and night and go to church every week. I believe in God with all my heart, as did my mother and her mother before her. The French love the good life, but are very pious about their faith, you know."

"But I don't understand—"

Waller waved him off. "I don't condemn others for not believing or, as you say, 'hedging your bets.' They must deal with God at some point." He stared at Alan. "*You* must deal with God at some point."

Rice was quick to glance back at the computer screen before an unfortunate choice of words or telling facial expression escaped from him. *Then you must deal with God too. And I don't believe praying twice a day and going to church will save you from hell.* Those words would have cost him his life. "So tonight?" he prompted.

Waller nodded slowly and rolled down the window a bit to let in some air. "Another religious vexation, actually. The men we are meeting believe that whoever they kill in life will serve them in death. They also believe that virgins await them in paradise. I'm surprised more men have not converted to Islam based on that concept alone."

"They might have except for the fact of wives' putting their feet down on their husbands' necks."

"Alan, you are in rare form tonight."

Rice said in a serious tone, "This is quite a different sideline for you. Dealing with Islamic terrorists?"

"Are you not tired of the Asian whores? How many *units* does it take to fill the crotches of Western male civilization?"

"Apparently more than we can obtain. But the money is colossal and steady. It's the cash flow engine for all our other endeavors."

"A man needs fresh challenges."

"But highly enriched uranium? To make a nuclear device? It could as easily go off in Montreal as New York. I would not put great faith in their aim."

"The world needs to be shaken up a bit, don't you think? Too staid. Too predictable. Those on top have been there a long time. Perhaps too long."

"I didn't know you had an interest in geopolitics."

"There are many things you don't know about me. But I think we are here."

Rice looked out the window and saw the building come into view. The plane ride had been very turbulent in the final twenty minutes as they had landed at the tail end of a passing thunderstorm, and the thirty-mile ride out into a rural part of the country had done nothing to settle his stomach. The people they were meeting with were making his belly uneasy for another reason. His boss, of course, had been undisturbed by the storm, or, apparently, by the upcoming meeting.

Anyone who was looking for the parts to a nuclear weapon so that they could detonate it and kill as many people as possible was of course insane. Rice could accept that his employer was at least partially insane, but he had learned how to survive around the man. The folks tonight were an unknown entity. He'd wished that Waller had not insisted that he come.

When he'd attempted to decline the request, Waller was predictably blunt in his response. "The right-hand man cannot select his encounters. And the squeamish cannot be the right-hand man. And, unfortunately for you, I have no use at all for any other body part you possess, Alan."

The words were jesting, the tone in which they were said was not. Thus Rice had gotten on the plane and flown across numerous time zones to help his boss negotiate the deaths of thousands.

"How do you want to open the meeting?" Rice asked him.

"We will greet, we will smile. If they want us to eat and drink we will. Then we will negotiate. By the way, do not show them the bottom of your shoe, a great insult."

"Anything else I should know?"

"Yes, the most important of all."

Rice looked at him expectantly.

"If the need arises to run, make sure you run fast."

Rice looked shaken. "Do you think the need might arise?"

"I cannot tell. But one thing I do know is I don't trust desert men in *hattahs* who want to blow up the world."

"Then for God's sake why are we here?"

"I spoke of a man needing a challenge."

"Do you really think we may need to run?"

"Perhaps. If so, just make sure I am in front of you."

"And if you're not?"

"I will shoot you and then run over your dead body."

CHAPTER

22

THE HOME was large, contemporary, and miles from any other dwelling. They were met at the front gate by a man in a dark British-tailored suit and wearing a turban. He searched Waller and Rice, and Waller's gun was confiscated. "That's a customized Heckler and Koch nine-millimeter," he told the Arab. "I expect it back in the same pristine condition."

If the man understood this he made no sign of it.

"And my men?" Waller indicated behind him at the six burly fellows who had held on to their hardware. He'd asked the question and thought he knew the answer. In halting English the Arab said that they were free to come inside and could also keep their weapons. Waller frowned at this directive but said nothing.

Rice looked up at the face of the darkened structure. "Doesn't look like anyone's home," he said hopefully.

As they walked up the front drive, Waller said, "Oh, they're home. I'm sure we'll be very welcome."

"Why don't you sound too certain of that?"

"I am certain. It must be your nerves running away with you."

"I wonder why," the other man said under his breath.

The interior illumination was weak enough that Rice had to squint to make out things in the farthest corners of the large rooms. The bodyguards trailing them, Waller and Rice followed the turbaned man deeper into the house.

The man paused at a pair of large double doors that appeared to be made of stainless steel. He opened them and motioned the others through. When they passed into the room, they saw one man sitting at a round table in the center, the space lit only by a single table lamp. The man was dressed in a loose-fitting robe known in the Muslim world as a *thobe*. He was boxy through the middle though his face was drawn. His beard was trimmed short and he wore no headdress.

"Sit," he said, motioning to the chairs set around the table.

Waller took his time looking around the room gauging tactical positions and then motioned his men to take up posts in various spots. He eased into a chair and studied the man.

"I was expecting more people," he said.

"I am authorized," said the man in clear English.

Waller noted the sheen of perspiration on his face, the way his eyes wandered the room. And then the Arab snapped his attention back to Waller and Rice.

"HEU," said the man.

"Highly enriched uranium," said Waller.

"How can you get it?"

Waller looked puzzled. "This has already been explained."

"Explain again."

"The HEU Purchase Agreement between Russia and the United States signed in 1993," began Waller in a monotone as though set to lecture a class. "It's a way for the Russians to dismantle their stockpile of nuclear weapons, reduce the uranium to a form that can be used in nuclear reactors and other nonweapon processes. I can bore you with terms like uranium hexafluoride, depleted uranium tails, blendstock, and the like, but the bottom line is the Russians had five hundred tons of HEU they agreed to sell to the Americans. Thus far the Yanks have received about four hundred tons, averaging thirty tons per year. The entire process is monitored by both sides except for the initial dismantling and separation of the HEU metal weapons component from the rest of the nuclear weapon. The Russians perform this initial step on their own. In so doing, it allows certain people with contacts inside this process to help themselves to a bit of nuclear gold."

"And you have such contacts?" asked the man.

Again, Waller looked perplexed. "If I didn't I can't think of a reason why I would be here negotiating with you." He held up his cell phone. "One call can verify that I do."

"How much are we talking about?"

"For the weapons or the quantity of HEU?"

"HEU."

Waller noted that the man was rubbing his fingers together a bit too fiercely. He caught Waller looking at this movement, and the hand disappeared under the table.

"Five hundred tons of the material can be used to arm roughly thirty thousand nuclear warheads, or about as many as the Soviets possessed at the height of the cold war. My contacts can smuggle me two hundred pounds of HEU. That's enough for two warheads that could devastate a large city or be used to arm a number of smaller improvised devices that can be deployed against multiple targets."

"So it is very valuable?"

"Let's put it this way. Iran is spending billions of dollars as we speak to build the facilities, technology, and processes to ultimately achieve what I'm offering to sell to you tonight. The only thing more valuable on earth might be plutonium, but that is impossible to get."

The Muslim sat forward abruptly. "So the price?"

Waller looked at Rice once more and then back at the man. "And you say you're authorized to make an agreement?"

"To paraphrase you, I wouldn't be here if I was not."

"And your name?"

"Unimportant. The price?"

"Two hundred million British pounds wired to my account."

Waller was about to say something else when the man said, "Agreed."

Waller glanced down at the Muslim's midsection and then sniffed the air. He dropped his cell phone and bent down to pick it up. The next moment Rice fell backward as Waller lifted up the table and pushed it on top of the Muslim. He grabbed Rice's arm and screamed to his men, "Run!"

The next instant Rice felt himself being flung through a window. A jagged edge caught him on the leg, tore his pants, and then bit into his thigh. Something landed on top of him, driving the wind from him. Then he was jerked up and pulled along, his breath coming in gasps, his injured leg bleeding badly.

The concussive force of the house exploding hurled him ass over head. Debris poured down, even as he felt Waller covering him with his own body, the older man breathing in strained bursts. Once the boards, bricks, shattered glass, and the odd piece of furniture stopped falling, Waller and Rice slowly sat up.

"What the hell," began Rice as he clutched his injured leg.

Waller rose and dusted off his clothes. "The idiot was a suicide bomber."

"How did you know?"

"The *thobe* is designed to be loose-fitting; his clothes were too tight because dynamite sticks are bulky. His eyes were unfocused and he was looking at us but not looking at us. He was hiding something, and it's human nature to feel that if you don't look at someone, they can't see you. You'll also note that same instinct in dogs."

"Unfocused eyes?"

"He was probably drugged to get through his mission, because really who wants to blow themselves up, even for virgins in paradise? And then there was the smell."

"Smell?"

"Dynamite is contained in water-soaked wooden sticks. It has a distinctive odor. And I also got a whiff of metal. Probably shrapnel balls contained in the canvas pack he had wrapped around his belly. That provides for maximum carnage at the point of origin. I dropped my phone so I could look under the table. There was a bag next to him. It held the battery with wires connected to the explosive that would detonate the bomb pack sewn around his body. Sewn so he couldn't easily remove it. That's why he put his hand under the table, to hold the detonator. And the man didn't rise to greet us. Very unlike a Muslim. But dynamite packs are heavy, and he was probably afraid we might glimpse something suspicious if he exposed himself in that way." Waller shrugged resignedly. "I should have seen it far earlier. Now let's take a look at your leg."

He squatted down and tore open Rice's pants leg and examined the wound more closely. "Sorry I had to push you through the window."

"My God, Evan, you saved my life."

"It's bleeding, but it's not deep enough to have hit an artery."

"You're sure?"

"I've seen such wounds before. If it were an arterial wound you wouldn't be conscious because you would have nearly bled out by now." He used strips from Rice's pants to fashion a rough bandage. "We'll get you medical attention as soon as possible."

He looked over at the house and saw one of his men staggering toward him. He hurried over to the fellow, took him by the arm.

"Pascal, are you hurt?"

"No, just got my bell rung."

Pascal was Greek and his skin was dark, his hair darker still and curly. He was five-nine and wiry with a motor that never quit. He could run all day, shoot straight, possessed nerves of iron, never moved fast when caution was called for, and no one moved faster if the situation demanded ultimate speed. He was the smallest of Waller's men and also the toughest. Since Pascal had come to stay with him when he was only ten years old, Waller had groomed him to rise to the top of his security chain. He did not possess the mind to run the actual business, not like he or Alan Rice. But still the man was an invaluable piece of Waller's security team. "What about the others?"

"Tanner and Dimitri are dead. Dimitri's head got blown off. It landed in a damn flowerpot. The rest of the guys are okay, just bumps and bruises. Explosion knocked out one of the trucks, though."

Waller eyed the smoky mass near the front door. The Escalade had taken the brunt of the blast, fortunately shielding the other vehicles from damage. Screams came from their left and Waller and Pascal started running in that direction. From out of the darkness three people emerged; two struggling with one.

Before Waller and Pascal could reach them the two finally won. The captive was the man in the fine suit who'd led them into the house.

"Son of a bitch was trying to get away, Mr. Waller," said one of the men holding the captive's arms behind his back.

Waller reached out and gripped the turbaned man's throat.

"You want me to shoot him, Mr. Waller?" asked Pascal.

"No, no, Pascal. I need to talk to him first."

Waller looked into the man's eyes. "You are a little fish. The man who blew himself up? He too was a little fish that you throw back because it is not worth your time. But you *are* worth my time. I need to know who authorized this. You understand me?"

The man shook his head and started speaking rapidly in his native language.

Waller answered him, in his native tongue. He looked delighted at the shock in the fellow's eyes before ordering his men to collect Tanner's and Dimitri's remains.

"One more thing," said Waller. He reached into the captive's pocket and pulled out the customized nine-millimeter pistol that had been confiscated earlier. "I'm quite fond of this gun. So fond, in fact, that I will use it to kill you after you've told me what I need to know."

Riding back to the plane, Waller sat next to Rice. "A doctor will meet us at the airfield and fix your leg," he said.

"Why would they invite us down here and then try to blow us up?"

"I don't know why yet. But I will find out and then hit them back far harder than they just hit me."

Rice shook his head and gave a hollow laugh. Waller shot him a glance.

"What?"

"I was just thinking that after all this you're going to really need that holiday in Provence."

CHAPTER

23

SHAW STRETCHED HIMSELF out along the top of the flat rock set at the far end of Gordes and checked his watch. It was one o'clock in the morning. Tourist buses came all during the day, disgorging their passengers, who would stand where Shaw was now, prone, and snap their digital pictures of the breathtaking views. Shaw was also here because of the views, only his were of the twin villas, Waller's and Janie Collins's. His electronic night glass turned solid masses, such as people, cars, and potted plants, into firm heightened outlines with many discernible features, while casting the background into a liquid green. There was one light on in the woman's place, while Waller's was dark. Not surprising since the man was not there yet.

He had not seen Janie Collins for a couple of days, but his interest in her had only increased. Shaw moved his torso a bit to provide relief against the sharp rock digging into his shoulder. The movement from below brought him back to alert. He focused his glass and watched as she emerged from light into darkness that his optics ate through with enviable clarity. Janie was barefoot and wearing a robe. As she slipped it off he saw she was wearing a one-piece bathing suit underneath. She slipped on swim goggles, tied her hair back, and dove in, breaking the surface of the water cleanly.

She cut through the water with sharp strokes. She reached one side, did a flip turn, and proceeded back the other way. After five laps, Shaw knew she was counting her strokes. There was little ambient light, no moon, and the light from the house lost all potency before it reached the poolside, so there was no way she could see the walls to know when to turn. Thirty laps later she'd not diminished her speed. Shaw had to keep rubbing his eyes because her methodical movements were hypnotic, like watching a metronome whisk back and forth.

The light coming on caused Shaw to leave the woman and focus on the villa next door. As the man came into view Shaw saw that it wasn't Waller. He couldn't see his features that clearly, but the man was bigger and far bulkier than the Canadian. Shaw assumed that he was part of an advance security team. As Shaw had predicted to Frank previously, Waller's men would search the place and then lock it down, probably posting sentry perimeters until the boss arrived. It was the same protocol the United States Secret Service used.

Shaw watched as the burly man dressed all in black expertly searched the outdoor space, his pistol out and ready as it pointed into darkened corners. Shaw saw the man flinch and then look over his shoulder. In a few seconds he'd passed by the pool in Waller's rear grounds, gained hand- and footholds on the dividing wall between the properties, and scrambled upward to peer over it.

Shaw's glass shot back to Janie. Finished with her swim, she was walking up the steps of the pool. As he continued to stare, she stripped off her wet bathing suit and let it fall to the pool deck. She picked up the towel and dried off before wrapping it around her. Shaw swiveled his gaze to the man at the wall. Even with his electronics he couldn't see the man's features clearly enough, but he assumed the guy was pleased with this show of female nudity. He was certain the man would report back to Waller with this juicy bit of intelligence. "Janie" might have inadvertently made a very serious blunder.

An hour later the Waller villa went dark and Shaw let his night glass swivel back to Janie's house. He stiffened a bit. In the darkest corner, by an alcove, he thought he saw movement. Was it Janie? Or had one of Waller's men gotten into the rear grounds from the other direction while Shaw was focused on the villa next door?

Shaw's mind raced ahead. Had the woman locked the rear sliding glass door? Shaw decided that she probably hadn't. She was too trusting, too ready to give out personal information. For the time being he forgot about any vague suspicions he might have had of her. She was probably a young, naïve heiress vacationing next door to a psychopath who sold young women into sexual slavery.

Shaw jumped to his feet and ran. He had a Vespa he'd been get-ting around on, but the little engine's whine would be problematic at this hour of the night. He pounded down the empty cobblestone streets of Gordes, past the town square, down a shortcut by the church, around an alley, and down another set of aged steps that cut still more time off the trip. Passing an amphitheater that hosted concerts during the warmer months, he skipped down the final set of stone risers that would deliver him to within ten meters of the two villas. He peered around a corner of stone jutting out from the otherwise sheer face of the cliff. Janie's villa was on the right, Waller's on the left.

There was a silver Citroën van in the small park-off directly in front of Waller's villa. By Janie's entrance was her small two-door crimson Renault with its rear hatch a bare foot from the front door. Shaw could see that the Renault was empty but the Citroën wasn't. Two men sat in the front, one of them probably the guy he'd seen doing the earlier recon, but he couldn't be sure about that. He calcu-lated that their line of sight had one blind spot. Proceeding along this path slowly, he tested the validity of this assumption. The two sen-tries remained right where they were. Shaw turned a corner and was now at a point where he could gain access to Janie's rear grounds.

The wall was six feet high, but unlike the common wall between the two villas, on top it had long stones mortared in vertically that added another eighteen inches to the height. That was probably be-cause this wall was next to a public walking path. That would make peering over the wall impossible and climbing over it painful. Shaw found this to be true on his first attempt to mount the barrier. He let go, dropped to the street, slipped off his jacket, covered his scraped hands with it, and tried again. He was up and over the wall in a matter of seconds, dropping noiselessly to the other side in the soft grass. He crouched, getting his bearings. He was in the side yard whose border was planted with climbing roses and luscious bougainvillea. The pool area was up a short flight of flagstone steps to his left. He put his windbreaker back on, his small night scope in one of the pockets.

He tried not to think about what Frank would say if he could see him right now. He was jeopardizing the entire mission by being here. He knew that. Yet he also knew that he wasn't going to let one of Waller's hired thugs have a free go at the young woman either. He crossed the short patch of grass and scrambled up the stack of steps.

Shaw felt the muzzle of the gun against his head a millisecond before he heard the click of the hammer being pulled back.

CHAPTER

24

THAT WAS the first mistake. The person was too close, mere inches away, which allowed no adequate buffer to ward off a sudden counterattack. The second mistake was not pulling the trigger and killing him. Shaw's thumb jammed behind the trigger, making discharge impossible. His other four fingers closed on the muzzle, jerking it downward so it pointed at the ground. The final mistake was not letting go of the pistol. He pulled hard, bent his body forward, and the figure sailed over him, landing hard in the grass. He ripped the gun free, straddled the body, and pointed the weapon at the person's head.

"Janie?"

She was lying under him, her cotton robe askew and her hair in her face. She was breathing hard, probably from the impact with the ground. She had on a pair of tennis shoes, a robe, and not much else that he could see.

Her knee slamming into his left kidney sent a jarring pain up his back. He fell sideways and lay hunched over in the grass next to her. The two rose slowly, nursing their bumps and bruises. Shaw kept the gun in his hand.

"What the hell are you doing here?" she demanded, her gaze flitting from the gun to his face.

"I saw lights on in the villa next door. Then I thought I saw a guy coming over the wall into your grounds."

She looked around. "From *where* did you see all this?"

Shaw pointed at the cliffs. "I was taking a stroll. From up there it's a clear line to your villa."

"How did you know where I was staying?" she said sharply.

He looked sheepish. "Okay, I confess, I followed you home the night we had dinner, but just to make sure you got here okay. You know, rich woman traveling alone? I was worried about you." He held up the gun. "I'm a little surprised you have one of these."

"Like you said, I'm rich and traveling alone. And I have a permit for it."

"Really?" He handed it back to her. "I thought France was pretty strict about guns."

"Money solves many problems," she said coolly.

He rubbed his back. "Let me guess, in addition to foreign-language immersion classes, you also have time for martial arts."

She fingered the gun before releasing the hammer and placing it in the pocket of her robe, which she cinched up tightly. "I heard something in the rear yard, but I didn't see a man come over the wall. Well, that is, except for *you*."

"But you must've seen the lights come on next door. And there's a van out front with two men in it."

She gazed at the wall separating the two villas. "Maybe I did. I . . . I can't be sure." She looked back at him. "So you can see my villa from the cliffs?"

"Yeah. The tourist buses come there every day and take photos of the villas, the valley, and the mountains." For some reason Shaw could tell that she knew all of this. That along with her having a gun now rekindled his suspicions. "Your pool is the only one directly visible from that vantage point. The pool next door is mostly hidden by a garage and some trees."

She glanced at the dark waters. "The pool?" She shot him an accusatory look. "Could you see me swimming then? And afterwards?"

Shaw didn't hesitate. "All I saw was the guy. That's why I came down here, to make sure you were okay. I would've knocked on the front door, but again there were the dudes next door and I wasn't sure what was going on. And it is after one in the morning."

"Yes, it is. I'm surprised you're still up."

"Yeah, I was surprised to see you too. Guess I'm still on U.S. time. You sure you didn't see anyone?"

"No one, and the doors are all locked." She paused. "I didn't know lobbyists were so good with defensive maneuvers and guns."

Shaw managed a chuckle. "Hell, it was all luck. When I felt the muzzle against my head I just sort of freaked. Last time I fired a gun I was thirteen. It was a .22 caliber rifle and the targets were tin cans stuck on a fencepost. But where did you learn to sneak up on people like that? I never even heard you."

Shaw had thought it impossible for anyone to do that to him.

"I took ballet. I'm light on my feet."

When she didn't say anything else, he lightly touched her arm and said, "I'm just glad you're okay. I better get going now."

"Maybe we can see if the men are still out there," she said, turning toward the villa.

Shaw mutely followed her, noting the grass stain on the backside of her cotton robe from where he'd thrown the woman. The house was dark and she didn't turn on any lights as they moved through the space, Shaw following her lead. He could tell that she had excellent night vision. They reached the front room, where Shaw could see the oak double doors leading outside. The room was barrel-vaulted, supported by visible curved wooden trusses in a style often seen in older European homes. The interior walls were thick, with a stucco veneer. They kept the cool or heat in as needed. The furnishings were eclectic, costly, and plentiful to the point of the large room feeling slightly cluttered but cozy. To his left he noted the corkscrew limestone staircase that provided access to the interior five floors. A lot of space for one person.

They drew close to the door and he watched as Janie eased back a curtain of the sidelight next to the doorway. Shaw peered over her shoulder. He breathed an inaudible sigh of relief when he saw the Citroën van still there with the dark shadows in the front indicating the men were also still present and accounted for.

She closed the curtain and took a step back, turning to him. "Thanks for your concern, Bill."

"Anytime. You have any idea who those guys are?"

She shook her head. "Maybe we should report this to the police."

"Maybe we should," said Shaw. He had no intention of doing any such thing, and something made him suspect that she wasn't going to call them either. "Well, I better get going. Do you mind if I go out the way I came in? Those guys look a little rough for my tastes."

She nodded absently, her gaze on his face. "I'm sure you could handle yourself just fine."

She followed him out to the rear, where he used his jacket as protective cover while he hoisted himself back up on the wall. While he perched there momentarily, she said, "Maybe we can get together soon?"

"Okay. I feel after tonight we've really bonded."

She seemed to force a smile. "I think so too."

"Look, I'm planning to grab some coffee and a croissant at the little village bakery around nine tomorrow morning. Why don't we meet there?"

As soon as he disappeared over the wall, Reggie stripped off her robe to reveal dark shorts and a navy blue tube top underneath. She waited for a few beats before going back in the villa and exiting through a door on the lower level that emptied out onto the public path. Finding the same blind spot in the observation lanes of the men in the van that Shaw had earlier, she started following him. He took the shortcut up to the village and wound his way slowly back to his hotel through the silent streets. If he knew he was being followed he gave no indication of it.

Reggie broke off her tail when he entered the hotel's front doors. At least she knew now where he was staying. She made her way slowly back down to the villa, skirted the men in the van, and re-entered her villa the same way she had left it. She retrieved her robe where she'd dropped it on a table and carefully lifted out the gun. She put it in a plastic baggie. It had Bill's prints on the muzzle.

She searched the place from top to bottom after locking all the doors. Satisfied, she put on a long T-shirt, climbed into bed, and made a call.

Whit answered on the second ring. His voice did not sound sleepy. He and Dominic were staying at an isolated cottage barely fifteen kilometers away. She filled him in on the night's events.

"I don't like this guy," Whit said.

"There *were* two men out front," she pointed out.

"Yeah, but you still don't know what his angle is. I think we can safely assume that he's not some bloody lobbyist from the States. The whole mission could be compromised now."

"I don't see him working for Waller, if that's what you're getting at. He wouldn't have pointed out the man's advance team to me and then warned me about the man watching me."

"So if he's not with Waller, what then?"

"I don't know. I've got his prints on my gun that I'll send along to you. I want to see if we get a hit somewhere."

"Okay, I can pick it up tomorrow. But look, Reg, it's hard enough going up against Kuchin. We don't need any unknown shit on top of it."

She put the phone down and lifted the sheet over her. But she couldn't sleep. She rose, padded over to the window, opened it, and stared out. She was on the top floor of the villa with excellent views of Gordes. Up there was a tall man who'd just manhandled her. He could have killed her tonight but he hadn't. She'd never seen anyone move that fast, that fluidly. Not Dominic or even Whit. Or even her.

Who is he?

"Damn," she muttered before closing her window and flopping on the bed with a long groan. This complication was the last thing she needed right now, if it somehow caused them to miss getting Kuchin. It took another hour for her to fall asleep.

In his room Shaw had just finished talking to Frank, reporting in what had happened. He stripped down to his skivvies, but couldn't sleep. Lying down he sometimes found it hard to breathe because of a recent nasty attack on his windpipe by a fellow named Caesar. Shaw's muscles were long and ropy and he was actually stronger than he looked. Yet the giant Caesar had been more physically formidable. However, Shaw had gotten a little help in their confrontation from unexpected sources. Love. Hate. Rage. But mostly hate and rage. The result was he was here and Caesar wasn't.

He rose and opened his window to let in some fresh air. His window didn't have a view of the villas below, but he could see them clearly in his mind.

So who was the woman and why was she really here? She might be simply who she said she was. Rich and traveling alone, a woman might carry a weapon—it was not unreasonable. And the database search on her fingerprints had produced no hits. Then an image drove into his mind that he tried but could not get rid of. Her bathing suit coming off and revealing the long, tanned torso sliding down into the smooth, shapely, and naked backside. Massive waves of guilt poured over him. He got back into bed and finally fell asleep.

CHAPTER

25

Evan Waller closed his eyes and let his mind wander back twenty, thirty years. In his mind's eye the trappings of the legitimate Canadian businessman with the underlying criminal enterprise fell away and the soul of Ukrainian Fedir Kuchin emerged like a serpent discarding an old faded skin for a supple new one. His gaze wandered over his bare arm, searching for a spot to do it. He made a bicep, the clench tightening the rubber strap around the muscle. The veins in his forearm swelled. His eye lit on one tunnel of blood and he pushed the needle in and forced down the plunger. The customized cocktail flowed into him, some steroids, some purified drugs, a bit of his own expensively purchased elixir from the Far East. It was totally unique, what he was shooting in himself. As it should be, he felt. What was good enough for everyone else was not good enough for him.

He took a deep breath and let the fire rain over him, from the inside out. He smiled, sat back, then the adrenaline hit. He jumped up, did some jacks, then some rat-a-tat push-ups, then more jacks, and then he snagged the pull-up bar and did a quick ten, grinning with each one.

He dropped back to the matted floor, breathing hard. He looked in the mirror. For sixty-three he was in extraordinary shape. For sixty-three, fifty-three, hell, probably even thirty-three, at least by softened Western standards. He had small wedges of love handles and the rock abs were no longer there, but the belly was flat and when he clenched it the muscle underneath was hard. His thighs were a little thinner than before, but his arms and shoulders still bulged. He rubbed his bald head, checked the gray mat of hair on his chest. It didn't really matter anymore what he took, how much he exercised, how far he ran, he was still getting old. A part of him was grateful about this, grateful that no one had managed to kill him yet. The other part, well, he was just getting old. And he didn't like it.

He showered, rubbing the sting out of his arm around the injection site. Wrapped in a robe, he walked through the confines of his Montreal penthouse. He had fabulous views through the latest generation of ordnance-proof material. He knew this because the U.S. president had similar materials on his limo and at the White House. Also laced into the thickened window glass was a membrane that distorted the image portrayed to the outside world. He was now standing in the middle of the room, but the image projected through the glass wall had him seven inches to the right. Five minutes later and at another spot in the room, his image would be nearly a foot to the left. It constantly changed so no one could draw a perfect bead on him. At least in theory.

As he stood looking out into a cool summer night he glanced down at his chest for the telltale red dot from the sniper scope. There could be something out there that could calibrate the image illusion and shatter the whiz-bang barrier he'd put up between himself and his enemies. Yet he didn't step back into the shadows. If they wanted him badly enough they could try. They had better take him down with the first shot, though, because they wouldn't get a second chance. In his world whoever killed harder survived.

The Muslims would soon find that out. The man they'd captured had not lasted long. After thirty minutes alone with Waller and his little toolbox the fellow had told him everything he'd needed to know. Well, almost everything. He knew the names of the men who'd ordered his death and their locations. And there was one more fellow, Abdul-Majeed. He had been Waller's initial point of contact, leading him down the road that had nearly resulted in his death. Waller was not easily fooled, and yet Abdul-Majeed had managed it.

What the captured Muslim could not tell him was why they had attempted to kill Waller, because he didn't know. At least he'd sworn that with his last dying squeal. That was the most perplexing question of all. Was there some other force out there targeting him?

He changed into dark slacks and a white silk shirt, then rode the private elevator down to the garage where his men met him. He allowed no one in his apartment, not even cleaning personnel. Not even tough, faithful Pascal. It was his private sanctuary. They climbed in their caravan of SUVs and rode out from under the cover of the parking garage.

Their route was north and the metropolis quickly fell away to more open spaces. Waller tapped his fingers on the glass, watching the large trees pass by in the darkness. He thought he saw a moose near the roadway and then it was gone. His father had hunted animals for food back in the rural part of Ukraine where he'd grown up. Now his son hunted human beings for pleasure and profit. This was one of those excursions.

The building was drafty, cold. Because of the poor insulation, condensation clung to the windows like a fungus. Waller slipped on a warm coat and walked through the door opened by one of his men. The room was large, warehouse-size, with girder ceilings that disappeared into darkness. Six people stood lined up in the center of the space. They wore black jumpsuits and hoods covered their heads. Their feet were shackled, their hands bound behind them. The tallest one barely came up to Waller's pecs.

"How's the leg?" he asked the slender man who appeared out of the shadows.

Alan Rice had apparently recovered from nearly being blown up, though even in the dark his skin seemed paler than normal and he was limping a bit. "Nothing a handful of Advil can't fix."

"How many do we have tonight?"

Rice opened his mini-laptop and the light from the screen burned like a small fire in the dark. "In this shipment, ninety-eight. Sixty percent from China, twenty percent from Malaysia, ten percent from Vietnam, four percent from South Korea, and the remainder a hodgepodge from Myanmar, Turkmenistan, Kazakhstan, and Singapore."

"What are we currently getting per unit?"

Rice clicked some computer keys. "Twenty thousand U.S. dollars.

It's up five percent from last year, even though the economy tanking affected some of our downstream buyers. That's an average. We get more for the Malaysians and Koreans and less for the Stans women."

"International tastes?" said Waller as he walked around the hooded figures. He clicked his finger and a spotlight hit the small group. "Prejudice against the ladies of the former Soviet Union?" he said with disapproval.

"Well, the ones we're getting from there *are* pretty scrawny," noted Rice. "And you have the exotic factor still with the Far East Asians."

"Actually I've always found Eastern European women the most beautiful in the world."

Waller looked over where Pascal stood, hands clasped in front of him, not behind, so the gun pull from the holster would be faster if necessary. Seeing Pascal always gave him a measure of comfort, and not just because of the man's protection skills.

Pascal was his *son*.

His bastard son conceived with a Greek woman Waller had met on holiday. Pascal of course did not know this. He had no emotional attachment to the younger man, nothing that approached love or devotion. Yet Waller had felt some obligation to the boy, particularly since he had done nothing to support the mother. She'd died in extreme poverty, leaving only her orphaned son behind. He had allowed this to happen for no other reason than he'd lost interest in the woman, who'd been lovely to look at but really was only a simple, uneducated peasant. He'd taken Pascal, at age ten, trained him up, and now the boy turned fierce warrior worked for him, protected him from all harm. Yes, Pascal had well earned his rank in Waller's little army.

"Pascal," he said. "What sort of women do you like? Eastern Europeans or the Asians?"

Pascal did not hesitate. "Greek women are the most sensual things God ever created. I would take Greek over anything else."

Waller smiled, lifted one of the hoods, and looked down at the revealed girl, whose facial features evidenced her Chinese origins. She was barely fourteen and blindfolded and shivering from equal parts cold and fright. Her mouth was taped over so her whimpers were muffled even though there was no one around to hear her scream who would care.

Waller did the calculation in his head. "So one million nine hundred and sixty thousand for the current shipment?"

"Correct. Minus expenses. The net is still north of one point six million. All in U.S. dollars, so far still the currency standard-bearer. Although I've been hedging our cash flow reserves in Chinese RMBs and Indian rupees just in case."

Waller turned to look at him. "The margins have softened. Why?"

"Fuel costs on the ships primarily. They don't travel on the *QE II*. We go on the cheap, transporting them in cargo containers, but it's still expensive. And we have to use two boats for one shipment because of the logistics and to avoid detection. That alone doubles the fuel costs. We have to provide basics like food and water and bribing crewmen to let in oxygen on a regular basis. But it's really the only way. Air transport is too problematic and they've yet to invent the car that can travel over the Pacific. But it's still an enviable net profit."

Waller nodded as he continued to circle the women. "How many shipments are we receiving?"

"Four a month, roughly the same number of units in each. We've discovered that figure fills the containers quite nicely, and we find we only lose two to three percent on the trip over due to starvation, dehydration, and sickness among other factors. That's well below industry standard for human trafficking, which averages about a twelve percent loss factor."

"Why did you select these six?"

Rice shrugged. "The best. In looks, in health. Your choice, of course. But we did a thorough prescreening."

"I respect your efforts."

Rice drew closer. "It beats dealing with maniacs in turbans."

"You think so?" asked Waller in amusement. "I found it quite exhilarating. And it's given me a new goal in life. To exterminate every last one of them."

Rice spoke in a voice so low only Waller could hear him. "Do you think that's wise, Evan? These people are truly insane. They'll kill us, themselves, anybody."

"But therein lies the challenge. I want Abdul-Majeed in particular. He was the frontman and he wasn't there. That means he was the one who betrayed me. And his betrayal cost me two of my best men, may God watch over their souls."

Since Dimitri and Tanner had killed at least six people that Rice had personally witnessed, he doubted God was doing anything with them.

"But why would they do that? You had what they wanted."

"I intend to ask that very question when I find dear Abdul." Pascal's BlackBerry chirped and he glanced at the message.

Waller had not missed this. "Yes, Pascal?"

Pascal came forward and whispered into his boss's ear. Waller smiled. "The Muslims have come home to roost."

"Progress?" asked Rice.

"It seems," Waller said curtly.

Waller stared at each of his men who stood silently in the darkness, hands clasped in front of them. He had drawn most of his associates from the military ranks of various countries, and they had retained their discipline and protocols. This pleased Waller, since he had worn the uniform as well. His gaze settled on Rice. "It would be disappointing to learn that I had a traitor within my own ranks."

Rice managed to find some courage under the withering gaze and said, "Don't look at me. Why would I betray you only to get myself blown up?"

"An adequate response. For now."

Waller lifted the hoods off the rest of the ladies, scrutinized them as he would cattle in an auction, and finally settled on one, the smallest. He gripped her skinny arm and pulled her along, her feet stumbling with the shackles.

"We've soundproofed a room upstairs," said Rice. "New carpeting and furniture too. Do you want the shackles and cuffs off?"

"No. Give me two hours and then send someone to clean up."

As soon as Waller was outside of earshot one of the guards edged over to Rice and said in a low voice, "Isn't Mr. Waller worried about stuff?"

"Like what?" asked Rice sharply.

The big man looked embarrassed. "You know, like AIDS, STDs, stuff like that."

"These women are all virgins. That's sort of the point, Manuel."

"But still, third world shit. Man never knows."

Rice gazed up the rickety set of stairs where his boss had disappeared with the girl. "I don't believe he actually has sex with them."

"What, then?"

"I don't really want to know."

CHAPTER

26

Reggie was waiting at the bakery by the time Shaw got there. They ordered and ate their pastries and drank their fresh coffee outside on bistro chairs. Reggie's hair was swept up under a Red Sox baseball cap. She had on jean shorts, a pale blue T-shirt, and Saucony running shoes. Shaw was dressed in slacks, loafers, and a white long-sleeved shirt.

Reggie sipped her coffee, ran an eye over him, and said playfully, "You still dress like a lobbyist, even in Provence."

Shaw smiled and eased back on the little chair. Behind them a workman was washing down the streets using a fire hose. The rush of water would follow the laws of gravity and work its way over the cobblestone streets, down worn stone steps, and eventually snake down the cliffs in diminished rivulets.

"Old habits die hard." He took a bite of croissant. "But I left the ties and jackets in the closet."

"Where are you staying? I think it's only fair since you know where I am."

He hooked a finger over his head. "Hotel and spa down that way. It's nice. I'm thinking about getting a massage later today." He drank his coffee, wadded up the paper his pastry had come in, and tossed it in a nearby trash can. "Those guys still around?"

"The Citroën was there this morning, but only one man was inside. Whether they stayed there all night I don't know. It does seem sort of mysterious," she added innocently.

"How's your back where I threw you?"

"Fine, how's your left kidney?"

"Not that great, actually. That's why I'm thinking about the massage."

"Next time remember to phone before you scale my wall."

"Funny, these villas are usually rented out fully during the summer. But the one next to yours has been empty since I got here."

She forced a smile. "You're a nosy one. Are you obsessing about villas now?"

You were nosy enough yourself. He said, "No, just curious. I was thinking about renting one, but it was way too much money for me."

"I thought all lobbyists were rich."

"Except for the divorce, I'd be a very wealthy man. Now I'm still well off, but just by half."

"I doubt I'll ever get married."

"Why's that? Not intending to sound crass, but you'd be quite a catch for some young guy."

"Why young?"

"Well, you're young. Most people marry folks close to their own age."

"How old are you?" she asked, smiling.

"Too old for you."

"You're flattering and disparaging yourself at the same time. I'm impressed."

"It's a talent I've burnished over the years. I hope you have your gun in a safe place. The cleaning help around here come across it you'll have some questions to answer from the local cops."

"It's in a very safe place, thank you for your concern."

"So dinner tomorrow night?"

"I can't do it tomorrow night. How about the next?"

"Okay. Here in town?"

"No, there's a village nearby with a little restaurant that overlooks the valley. Do you kayak?"

He looked surprised by the sudden change in topics. "I've done it. Why?"

"I have a spot reserved today with a kayak company in Fontaine de Vaucluse. I hear the river there is really beautiful. I was wondering if you'd care to join me? We'd have to leave in about an hour."

Shaw finished his coffee, thinking quickly. "Okay. I'll just have to change into something more appropriate."

"A bathing suit would be fine."

"Well, my goal is to stay *in* the boat. Even in summer I bet that water is cold."

"You never know, you have to be prepared for the unexpected."

As they parted company, Shaw watched her walk down the street. When he saw the man coming toward him he ducked down an alley. It was the thug he'd seen last night spying on Janie. Whether he was following Janie or not Shaw couldn't be sure.

He had yet to make up his mind about the lady. And that bothered him. Despite a well-crafted plan he had no idea how things would play out. He could sense his rear flank was exposed and he wasn't sure what to do about it.

For now, apparently he was going to go kayaking. And he meant to heed the woman's advice and be prepared for the unexpected.

27

I DON'T THINK I've ever seen water this clear," said Reggie as they paddled along.

She was in front and Shaw was in the rear of the red kayak. He'd changed into long bathing trunks and a loose-fitting T-shirt with a life jacket worn over it. Reggie had on a striped bikini top under her life jacket and a pair of white cotton butt-huggers, thin enough for the striped bikini bottom to be visible through them. She had the same Red Sox baseball cap on, only now it was turned backwards.

"You're good at this," said Shaw as he watched her muscled delts work, dipping the paddle in and out of the water. He'd synchronized his movements with hers except when he had to use his paddle as a rudder to navigate them around the curves of the river, whose current was deceptively fast. In large masses under the otherwise clear water were bright green and purple vegetation and long strands of what looked like kelp. Shaw felt like he was in a large aquarium.

"I like the water. When I lived in Boston I crewed on the Charles River every chance I got."

He said, "Okay, so you're a ringer. Now I don't feel so bad about not being able to keep up with you."

"You're doing fine."

He dipped his hand in the water. It *was* very cold. He was definitely staying in the boat.

There were five other kayaks in their party, but Shaw and Reggie had quickly outdistanced all except for one. In that kayak Whit and Dominic, dressed as tourists and loudly speaking French, were acting out having a go at paddling. While Dominic held a camera and pretended to shoot video of Whit doing something funny, he was able to record about two minutes' worth of close-ups of Shaw.

They had to stop at various small dams and the guides helped them transport the kayaks over them. There was one "surprise" rapid that they easily navigated before ending their river run and climbing in the kayak company's van for transport back to their point of origin. Shaw and Reggie rode near the front, Whit and Dominic in the rear. The van rocked back and forth over winding and rutted dirt roads before they reached asphalt once more. Only once did Reggie glance back and flash Whit a signal by blinking her right eye. He answered by lightly squeezing the bag he was holding. Inside was the gun with Shaw's prints on it. By prearrangement he'd snagged it out of her car while the others were getting their kayak gear together.

They climbed out of the van and into Reggie's red Renault. Shaw had to bend his long torso and legs to awkward degrees to accommodate the small space.

"Euro cars are definitely not for tall people," Reggie said sympathetically.

"I'll survive."

The drive back to Gordes took less than twenty minutes.

"You can just head to your villa," he said. "I can walk back up to my place."

"How about a swim and some lunch first?" she said. "You're already dressed for it."

He hesitated, mentally going through all that this might entail. "All right. Sure."

They parked in front of her villa. Shaw glanced at the entrance to the villa next door. "Don't see the Citroën."

"I know. It was gone when I left to pick you up."

"Interesting. I saw one of the guys walking through town this morning."

"Really? Did you talk to him?"

He looked at her strangely. "Uh, no, he looked pretty tough. Sort of like a mobster."

She unlocked the door, disarmed the security system, and led him into the back. She passed him a towel and some sun block, pointing to his forearms that were already a bit red from the kayak ride.

"Yeah, all those years spent indoors," he lamented.

They went out to the pool area. She slid off her shorts and stepped out of her sneakers while he pulled off his T-shirt and kicked off his sandals.

Behind his sunglasses he took a moment to assess her physical condition and came away impressed. There wasn't an ounce of fat on the woman and her muscles were lean and defined; her midsection was a hard pack, her calves as defined as a professional sprinter's.

She dove in the pool and then came back up treading water with easy motions of her arms and legs. She nodded to her right. "That's the deep end. Twelve feet. Don't want you to hit your head, six-six."

He dove in and came up next to her.

"I'm going to swim some laps," she said.

And she did for the next twenty minutes, back and forth, flip-turning at the precise moment. He swam a few laps with her and then climbed out of the pool, toweled off, lay under the beautiful Provençal sun, and watched her.

When she came out later, she wrung out her hair, grabbed a towel, and looked up.

"What the hell are you doing?"

Shaw was standing on top of the stone-tiled dining table under a wooden pergola next to the wall separating her villa from its neighbor. The wall was high, but the table plus his own considerable height enabled him to easily peer over.

"Checking out the next-door thugs."

She crossed the tiled surface in a flash and forcibly pulled him off his perch.

He feigned amusement. "What's wrong?"

Her face was pink underneath the tan, her eyebrows knitted together in anger. "Just don't do it again."

"Why, aren't you curious?"

"You were the one who saw the creep spying on me. You said the guy you saw in the village this morning was tough-looking. Like a mobster. I don't want them mad at me. I'm on vacation."

"Fine, fine. That's reasonable enough. How about some lunch? I'm starving."

She regained her composure and continued to towel off. "I was thinking a shrimp salad, some bread to dip in olive oil, and a bottle of white wine? I got some tomatoes, cucumbers, and artichoke hearts from the market."

"Sounds great. Put me to work. I know my way around a kitchen. I can sous-chef with the best of them. Well, I can't really, but I can slice vegetables."

"I *will* put you to work." She slipped on her shorts, but did not cover up her bikini top. She twisted her hair back and secured it with a red scrunchie. She'd looked more voluptuous in her sundress, Shaw noted. And yet he was really thinking that she'd failed his little test. He'd stood on the table—a spot he'd calculated could not be seen from next door unless someone were standing in the rear grounds— simply to gauge her reaction. She'd said all the right things, exhibited normal concern about getting mixed up with "tough" people. Yet Shaw had been doing this a long time, and his instincts told him that her emotional underpinnings accompanying these words were off the mark just enough. She *was* fearful, but not for the obvious reason.

He helped her fix lunch and they ate outside; their talk was innocuous for the most part and neither mentioned the developing plot next door. Later he walked back up to his hotel. He immediately checked the three little traps he always set to see if someone had been there. They were located such that a cleaning person would not disturb them while performing their regular duties—his desk drawer, his closet, and on one of his bags.

He sat back on his bed. Of the three traps, two had been sprung. While he'd been out cavorting with "Janie" someone had searched his room.

CHAPTER

28

WALLER SHOWERED and used a razor to slice a few errant hairs off his head. He was not naturally bald, but had begun shaving his head as an act of disguise when he'd fled Ukraine. He knew that almost nothing changed a man's appearance more than hair added or subtracted.

After giving himself another injection of his special elixir he strode through his penthouse, reaching the end of a corridor and a built-in cabinet. He twisted in a counterclockwise motion the pull knob on the right-side cabinet door and a piece of wood slid aside, revealing a digital pad. He punched in a four-digit code. There was a click and the cabinet front moved forward on smooth hydraulics. Waller passed through, and the door, operating on a motion sensor, automatically closed behind him. It was a nifty piece of craftsmanship.

Waller's penthouse was over ten thousand square feet, not including the "hidden" space located here, in the center of his home. This was the primary reason why he allowed no one else in his apartment. He couldn't chance anyone discovering it. The space was a bare concrete shell, part of the original bones of the penthouse. The man who'd constructed this "safe room" for him was of Ukrainian descent, loyal to Waller, and now dead, of natural causes. Waller rarely if ever killed his true friends.

He'd decorated the safe room himself. Stainless steel boxes with electronic locks had been delivered via a secure courier and Waller had unpacked them alone in this sanctuary. He stood in front of an old metal locker with "Fedir Kuchin" engraved on a small plate affixed to its door. He took out his officer's parade uniform. It still fit rather well, he thought, though it was tight in places where gravity had bested him. He secured his gun belt around his middle, in which was holstered a vintage Russian 9x18 Makarov PM-53. This had been the Soviet Union's standard military sidearm for forty years, ending its run in 1991 when the Soviet empire collapsed completely. He placed the bright blue cap with gold piping on his head with the red Soviet star in the middle and turned and looked at himself in the mirror bolted to one wall. The material was scratchy and the fabric did not breathe very well, but to him it was the finest silk.

In his full KGB dress regalia he was propelled back to a time in his life that even then he had realized would be the high point of his existence. He touched the medals, ribbons, and badges riding on the left side of the jacket. Three Irreproachable KGB Service Medals, Distinguished Worker of State Security, graduate of Leningrad University badge, and another badge indicating that he had attended the prestigious Andropov Red Banner Institute. He also had medals for combat service, which he'd earned with his blood in Afghanistan among other places. There were many terrible things his enemies could truthfully call him, but a coward was not one of them.

Though born in a rural fishing village only six hundred kilometers from Kiev, Waller had always considered himself a Soviet and not a Ukrainian. His mentor in the KGB had been a three-star colonel general with the reputation of being the "Butcher of Kiev." This man was also Ukrainian-born but had sworn his allegiance to Moscow. Everything Waller knew about counterintelligence, crushing insurgencies, and ensuring the security of the Soviet way of life had come from this man. Waller had a picture of him on the wall next to the red Soviet flag with its golden hammer crossed with a golden sickle and the star denoting the Communist Party residing in the upper canton.

He marched to the center of the room, came to rigid attention, and saluted this great Soviet, who was now dead, having been unceremoniously shot for his glorious service. Then Waller, feeling slightly foolish at this attention given to a man long in his grave, seated himself at an old 1950s-era metal desk that he had used when with the KGB in his home country. Old papers and forms in triplicate with cumbersome carbon copies were stacked neatly on his desk. Scarred metal filing cabinets were lined against one wall. Inside those plain depositories were as many of the records of his decades-long service to his adopted country as he had managed to smuggle out. He would come here from time to time to go over these "accomplishments" and allow himself to relive past glories.

In truth, he cared little for his current life. He was rich, but money had never been a primary goal. He had been born poor, grown up in poverty, and joined the ranks of those defending his way of life. Yet even those in the highest levels of the Communist Party typically only had "luxuries" such as a flat with its own bath and a car. It did not pay nearly as well as capitalism.

Yet now that is what I am. A capitalist. The same thing I fought against all those years. Well, I have to admit, the Americans probably had it right.

The trafficking of young girls for prostitution bored him. He had entered into negotiations with the Muslims to sell them nuclear weapons capability principally because it allowed him to recapture a little of his past, when what he did, what he ordered, affected thousands. Now he was just a businessman, like so many others. He made a lot of money, he lived in great luxury, but if he were gone tomorrow who would care? No history book would hold his name. His superiors in the KGB had earned much of the credit for his work. They were immortal. By comparison, he was quite ordinary. Yet there were those who knew what he had done. And that was why he'd had to run, hide like a mouse in a wall. He'd had little choice if he wanted to live. He had seen what happened to comrades who were not so nimble. Some were torn apart by hordes of angry people who had spent their entire lives imprisoned while living in their own country. He understood the emotion perfectly; he just didn't want to suffer the consequences of it.

He opened another drawer, pulled out an old book, and leafed through it, revealing page after page of drawings, in his own hand. He had always been a good sketch artist, having learned the skill from his mother, who had earned her living as a street artist first in France and then in Kiev before ending up in a fishing village that was icebound five months of the year, married to a man who did not love her. Even now Waller did not know the full history of the pair and what had drawn them together. Reproduced in this book were many of the people he'd killed, their dead or dying faces done in charcoal, black ink, or pencil only. There was no color in this book. The dead did not require it.

The next book he slid out of his desk might have surprised some people who had known the old Fedir Kuchin. He hefted the Bible in his hand. The Soviet Union of course had been vehemently opposed to organized religion of any kind. "The opium of the masses," as Marx had pointed out. Yet Waller's mother had been French and a devout Catholic. And she had raised her son in her religious beliefs even though it was a very dangerous thing to do. She read the Bible to him every night while his usually drunk father slept.

What had first appealed to Waller about the readings was how much violence was contained in a book purportedly espousing peace and love. Many people were slaughtered in ways even the grown Fedir Kuchin would not have employed. Reciting the Lord's Prayer with his mother each night, she had always emphasized one phrase above all others, lingering over it as though giving it its due.

"And lead us not into temptation, but deliver us from evil."

Waller well knew the evil she was referring to: her husband.

His poor mother, good to the last. Yet what she didn't understand about evil, her son clearly did. Given the proper motivation anyone was capable of terrible cruelty, baseless savagery, horrific violence. A mother would kill to protect her child or a child his mother. A soldier kills to protect his country. Waller had killed to protect both his mother and his country. He was good at it, understood quite clearly the mind-set required. He was not desensitized to violence; he respected it. He did not use it cavalierly. Yet when he did employ it, he couldn't say that he didn't enjoy the process, because he did. Did that make him evil? Perhaps. Would his mother have considered him evil? Clearly not. He killed for his country, his mother, and his own survival. When people struck him he struck back. There could be no fairer set of rules ever conceived. He was who he was. He was true to himself, while most people lived their lives as a façade only, their real selves buried under a platform of lies. They would smile at their friend before thrusting the knife into his back. Under those parameters who was truly the evil one?

The lion roared before it attacked, while the snake slithered in silence before sinking its fangs into unsuspecting flesh.

I am a lion. Or at least I used to be.

From a storage locker he pulled an old projection camera, set it on his desk, and plugged the power cord into an outlet. He opened his desk drawer and took out a projection reel with film wrapped around it. He snapped it into place on the camera, fed the film through the machine, pointed the camera at a blank concrete wall, turned down the lights, and flicked on the projector switch. On the wall appeared black-and-white images from over thirty years ago. Striding into view was a young Fedir Kuchin in full uniform. The present-day Kuchin smiled proudly when he saw his younger self.

On the wall the young Kuchin marched to the center of a compound with high fences of concertina wire and guard towers visible all around. He said something and armed men drove a dozen people forward into view, forcing them to kneel in front of Kuchin with thrusts from their gun barrels. There were four men, three women, and the rest children. Kuchin bent down and said something to each of them. Sitting in his desk chair, Waller mouthed these same words. This was one of his favorite memories. On the wall the black-and-white Kuchin led the children off to the side, away from the adults. From his pocket he took out candy and gave it to the frightened kids with rags for clothes, even patting one little girl on the head. From the pocket of his uniform the present-day Waller withdrew a decades-old disc of stale chocolate from that very occasion.

As the starving kids hungrily ate their treats, Kuchin walked back over to the adults, pulled his pistol, and executed each one of them with a bullet to the back of the head. When the screaming children rushed forward to hold their dead parents, Kuchin shot them too, sending his last bullet into the spine of a little girl who was cradling her dead mother's head. The final image was Kuchin taking a half-eaten piece of candy from the dead fingers of a boy lying sprawled in the mud and devouring it himself. When the film reel finished playing and the wall became light again, Waller sat back with a level of pride and satisfaction that had once been his on a daily basis. That had been his job, and he had done it so well. No one in Ukraine had done it better.

He took off his uniform and hung it carefully back in his locker, smoothing out a few wrinkles in the fabric. Before turning out the lights and exiting, he glanced back at the flag and the photo of his mentor.

I just want something worthy of me again. Something that really matters.

He turned out the light, secured the door, and returned to the only life he had left. He was leaving for France shortly. Maybe he would find something there to make him care again.

CHAPTER

29

REGGIE HEARD the horn toot from outside. She checked her watch. She was running late. She peered out her window and looked down on the street below. Shaw was sitting on his Vespa near her front door. He was dressed in khaki pants and a white cotton shirt he wore untucked. Loafers minus socks were on his feet. She tapped on the window, got his attention, and held up two fingers.

She hurriedly finished dressing and clipped on her earrings. Next she tidied her hair in the mirror, though it wouldn't make much difference after the ride on the scooter. She smoothed down the front of her dress. She'd chosen a formfitting one because of their mode of transportation. She didn't need a skirt billowing over her head as they raced along the rural roads of southern France.

Finishing with her lipstick, she hurried down the stairs. She locked the front door and waved to Shaw.

"You look terrific," he said.

"That was the goal," she shot back. "You look very handsome in a carefree sort of way. So unlike a lobbyist. I'm duly impressed."

"Good, because that was *my* goal."

She climbed on the back and took the helmet he handed her, strapping it on.

"Pretty scooter," she said, stroking the pale blue metal.

"Best way to get around here. Hold on."

She gripped him around the waist and leaned into his back. With her hands around his middle Shaw felt a burst of electricity rush down his spine. He even jerked a bit, it was so visceral.

"You okay?" she said.

"Fine. Just sore from all that rowing." He hit the throttle and they sped off going about twenty kilometers an hour. When they reached the main road he accelerated to double that.

"Okay, where to?" he called over his shoulder.

"I'll tap your back left or right," she answered. He nodded to show he got that.

Fifteen minutes later they were chugging up a steep hill, the Vespa's 125cc engine whining in protest. Shaw found a parking space and they lifted off their helmets and Shaw attached them to the bike. They walked up to the restaurant, which was only a half block away, and sat outside on a terrace overlooking the valley.

"Nice pick," said Shaw as they eyed the vistas.

"The food is wonderful too," she said.

They placed their orders and, from habit, each took a few moments to observe the tables around them. When they'd finished, their gazes settled on each other.

"So you're divorced with two kids? Are they with their mother?"

"For now, but we share custody."

Shaw broke off a bit of bread, soaked it in fresh olive oil, and then drank some of his wine. "How about you? All I know is you're rich."

She wrinkled up her nose. "That's pretty much it. I'm involved in a few charities. Mostly I travel, looking for something, I guess. Just not sure what." She took a sip of wine and tugged her hair behind her ear. She didn't look at Shaw—her gaze eased past him. For some reason Reggie was having a hard time staying in character.

He said, "You look like you're thinking way too hard. Just chill. You're on holiday."

She ran her finger around the rim of her wineglass. "So who do you think the people are renting the villa next to me?"

He shrugged. "I have an idea."

She sat slightly forward, looking at him expectantly.

He noticed this and grinned. "Hey, no grand revelations, okay? I did check with the real estate office in town, but they don't handle that listing and didn't know anything." Shaw wasn't about to admit that he'd talked to the agent controlling the listing or that he knew she had too.

"Okay," Reggie prompted. "And?"

"And I think it might be some political type. You know. They have an entourage. They send in security ahead of time. Stuff like that. I saw it all the time in D.C."

Reggie sat back, trying not to look disappointed. "Or it might be somebody quite rich, even richer than me."

"Right, right. Like Bill Gates or Warren Buffett."

"Or a mobster. You said the one guy looked really tough."

"Well, even Bill Gates probably doesn't hire wimpy-looking security. You want to look tough as a deterrent. Goes with the job."

"I suppose you're right."

"We'll just have to wait and see who shows up."

Their food came and as they ate the conversation turned to other subjects. They drove back to Gordes two hours later when the daylight was just beginning to run out completely. When Shaw turned onto the small side street leading to Reggie's villa a man dressed in a black suit and a white T-shirt stepped in front of them, blocking the way. Shaw had to stop so abruptly that Reggie bumped against him and almost slid off the scooter before righting herself.

Shaw lifted his visor and eyed the guy. He was only a couple of inches taller than Janie, but even through the suit Shaw could see the guy was wiry, not a gram of fat. The hair was curly, the chin jutting, the eyes focused and missing nothing, the hands strong and nimble-looking. Shaw knew he was right-handed because the shoulder holster was on the left side under a little bump-out built into his jacket just for that purpose.

"Where you folks going?" Pascal asked pleasantly.

"I'm taking this lady home," said Shaw. "And since this is a public street, I'm not sure why we're even having this discussion."

Behind him Shaw could see Reggie squirming slightly. He felt one of her fingernails digging into his side.

Pascal turned around and stared at the two villas. "Ma'am, are you the one leasing that villa?" He pointed to the one on the right.

Reggie didn't lift her visor. "Yes."

The man gazed at her, his eyes running up and down, from the helmet to her long bare legs.

"So you're Jane Collins?"

Now Reggie snapped up her visor. "How did you know that?"

"The real estate agent was very helpful."

"That's an invasion of privacy."

"No," Pascal said calmly. "It's just part of my job."

"What job would that be?" asked Shaw.

"Let's just say I'm in safety management."

"Can we go now?" asked Reggie.

"Sure, I'll just follow you on up and make sure you get in okay."

"I don't think the lady needs any help," said Shaw.

Reggie said hastily, "No, it's all right."

Shaw puttered up to the villa, the Vespa's single headlight illuminating the way, while the man followed behind. They could see that not only was the Citroën van back but there were two large SUVs that had somehow made their way up the narrow streets off the main road heading into Gordes without shearing off their side mirrors. The villa also had all the lights on inside. Shaw could see shadows pass back and forth in front of one window.

They slipped off the Vespa and Reggie opened the door. The *beep-beep* of the security system sounded.

Pascal had stopped near the scooter and he nodded appreciatively. "Good thinking, ma'am, using your security system. Can never be too safe."

"Do you want me to come in, Janie?" Shaw asked as Pascal stood there watching.

She hesitated before eyeing the other man. "No, that's okay. I'm tired. Thanks for dinner."

She closed the door and Shaw got back on the scooter.

"Foxy woman," said Pascal.

Shaw had known men in special forces units around the world who looked just like this guy. They could run circles around the tall, bench-press-muscled jocks. In that line of work the essential wasn't strength or even speed, it was endurance. The tortoise definitely won in that world. These guys could kick ass with the best, shoot the wings off bees at four hundred yards, change plans in midstream, read complicated maps on the fly, employ stealth when it was called for, and steamroll the other side when stealth was all played out. But in the end it was all about survival. That's why Shaw had never lifted many weights but had instead run the soles off his sneakers up one side of a mountain and down the other. That

and a good, true aim and stout nerves made all the difference between going home safe or getting wedged in a box for all eternity.

He broke free from these thoughts when Pascal stepped next to
him and said, "You need anything else? If not, I'd appreciate you
moving on so I can secure this area."

No overt threat, very professional, Shaw thought. The guy was
good. But then a man like Waller could afford the best. Shaw rode
back to his room and phoned Frank.

"Okay," Frank said after Shaw briefed him. "Game on. Keep me
posted."

Shaw changed his clothes, waited another three hours, and then
headed back out again on foot, after retrieving his night optics—
which looked like an ordinary camera—from the hotel's safe deposit
room. He slipped through the dark streets of Gordes. Normally he
would be pleased that the target was in town and on schedule. Even
though the villa had been rented and the private tour at Les Baux arranged, plans changed and there was never any guarantee that Waller
would actually show up in Provence. Yet Shaw was not pleased. The
target was here, but so was Janie Collins. Shaw suspected nothing
good could come out of that.

CHAPTER

30

Reggie looked in the bathroom mirror as she washed away her makeup with a damp cloth. She had on a long green T-shirt and white bikini panties, and her hair hung straight to her shoulders. She turned off the light and moved to the window overlooking the street in front. The van and one SUV were still there. The second truck had left about twenty minutes ago; Reggie had heard it start up but had been too late getting to the window to see who'd been in it.

She'd texted the professor and Whit and told them that Kuchin's men were here. The message had gone out over a secure line, but would still seem innocuous to anyone who might intercept it. It had read simply, "Dear Carol, the views here are even more beautiful than I thought. I'm going to get up early to see the sunrise."

She walked into her bedroom and edged open the window, which swung out like a door. From here she could see a portion of the rear grounds of the next-door property. She was startled to see the silhouette of a man sitting in a chair near the end of the pool smoking what looked like a cigar. There were no lights on in the back, but the moon was bright.

It's him. It's Fedir Kuchin.

If Reggie had had a gun, she could have ended the man's life right then. But that was not the way they did things.

She saw the man flinch. Had he seen her watching? That would have been virtually impossible. She was not in his line of sight and there was no light at her back. Still, she eased back into the room but left the window open, figuring if she tried to close it that would alert him that someone was watching.

She drew a deep breath, pulled off her T-shirt and panties, slipped into her bikini, and walked down the stairs. She slid open the rear door and stepped to the darkened pool.

"Okay," she said quietly, "here we go."

She slipped into the warm water, kicked off, and started doing her laps.

From the cliffs Shaw watched the two villas through his night glass. He saw Reggie standing at the window and then leaning out to peer next door. His gaze next swung to the man in the other villa's rear grounds. Evan Waller sat there smoking a cigar while two of his security men stood nearby. Shaw zoomed in on the man. His optics gave off no signature, so he wasn't overly concerned that anyone could spot him. And even if they had night-vision equipment, he was looking through a crevice formed between two boulders. The odds that they could "make" him under those conditions were too small to worry about.

Waller's movements were leisurely. He was talking on a cell phone. A few minutes passed and Shaw was about to give up his surveillance when he saw Reggie emerge from the back sliding door in her bikini, a towel in one hand.

"Oh, come on," Shaw said to himself. "You know the creep was already spying on you."

As though he had heard Reggie come outside, Waller rose and walked over to the wall that separated the two villas. One of his men joined him there and was pointing at Reggie's villa. Shaw zoomed in some more. It was the same muscle that had peeped on the lady earlier. He was probably giving Waller a blow-by-blow account of the incident. The resolution on Shaw's optics was good, but not quite good enough to show someone smiling. However, even without the confirming picture, he was convinced the man was grinning about whatever he was thinking right now.

Shaw flinched when the muscle bent down and formed a stirrup with his hands. A moment later Waller was boosted up and peering over the wall. Shaw swung his surveillance in the other direction. Reggie was still doing her strokes. Shaw hoped she would keep doing them until the two men went inside. His hopes were dashed as she stopped swimming and walked up the steps and grabbed her towel.

Shaw swung back around to look at Waller, who was still peering over the wall. The son of a bitch was probably drooling by now. Or maybe wondering if the lady would be a good recruit for his prostitution business.

He looked back at her. *Don't strip, Janie. Don't.*

Now it appeared as though she'd heard him. At least she kept her bikini on, toweled off, wrapped it around her, and walked into the house. No one watching her could see the waterproof bud in her right ear where she had been receiving communications from Dominic. Shaw wasn't the only one watching them from the cliffs tonight.

Waller quickly climbed down from his perch and the two men went inside. Shaw left his observation post and walked back to his room. There was sweat under his armpits though the night was cool. He called Frank and told him what he'd just seen. His boss wasn't nearly as concerned as he was.

"I don't care about the chick. All I care is that he goes to Les Baux on schedule." He added ominously, "And that better be all you care about too, Shaw."

Shaw slowly put the phone down. He was a pro, been doing this forever. The only time he'd really lost it was when he'd allowed himself to care about something other than the mission. Well, when he'd found himself caring about *someone*.

CHAPTER

31

WEARING HER SUNDRESS, sandals, and a bright blue kerchief around her hair, Reggie unlocked the door to her villa, stepped through, and nearly bumped into him. She looked up at the man and confirmed for herself that he looked even more intimidating in person than he had in the old photos. He was dressed in black slacks and a white short-sleeved shirt that he wore tucked in and that showed off his trim waist. Though in his sixties he had retained a great deal of the muscle of his youth. His shoulders were broad, his arms sinewy, and his thighs hard under the black fabric. And yet what drew her attention were the eyes.

She'd beheld the gaze of many mass killers, but the power in Fedir Kuchin's eyes was something at a different level. They seemed capable of snatching every secret she'd ever kept right out of her soul. Compared to him the old Nazis were scared children.

He put out a hand. "I appear to be your neighbor," he said. "Evan Waller."

His Ukrainian accent was gone now, buried under decades of a homespun Canadian cadence.

She shook hands, his long fingers enveloping hers. "Jane Collins."

He stood uncomfortably close. He was four inches shorter than Shaw but still towered over her.

"I understand you had a little misunderstanding with one of my men last night. The fault is entirely mine. Rest assured it will not happen again. I would like to make it up to you. Perhaps dinner tonight? At my villa or in the charming little village up the cliff?"

His big body seemed to press in on her while she thought this through. She gazed for a moment over his shoulder and saw two of his men staring at them. One had a little smile glazed onto his mouth. He was probably the one who had seen her naked by the pool, she thought. Male lust was as easy to read as alphabet blocks. And then there was the smaller man from the night before. For some reason she was more leery of him than the bigger man.

"Well, that's very nice of you, but—"

He smiled disarmingly as he interrupted her. "No, no, before you reject me, think about it. I didn't even allow you to lock your door before pouncing. My apologies. I will await your answer later." He eyed her straw basket. "You are going to do some shopping, I see?"

She nodded. "They have a wonderful market twice a week in the center of town. Everything from clothes to vegetables."

"Well, I must investigate this market for myself. Would you mind if I walked with you? It's a lovely morning and I would like to stretch my legs."

"Did you just get in?"

He slipped an arm through hers and she was forced to walk next to him. His action was gentle, seemed natural, and yet Reggie found no viable option of resistance without ripping her limb free.

"A long flight, yes. I live in Canada, my homeland. Before that I was in Hong Kong. Another even longer flight. Have you ever been there?"

Reggie shook her head.

"A city more full of energy than any other." He smiled and added, "And a place where one can get anything one wants. But you are American, correct? You're used to getting what you want."

"Why do you think I'm American?" she said, feigning suspicion.

"Merely a reasoned deduction based on your accent and appearance factors. Am I not correct?"

"No, I am American."

"Then we are neighbors in that way too. Our two countries. I see providence at work here."

"When I came home last night your men knew my name."

Kuchin waved his free hand carelessly. "Standard security procedures, I'm afraid. You see, I am a very wealthy man. I live a very boring life and I have no enemies of which I'm aware. But the company I head up, they insist on these precautions." He laughed. "I'm Canadian after all; a peaceful hardworking people." He patted her arm. "I can assure you that there will be no more intrusions into your privacy."

Really, thought Reggie. *Does that include spying on me while I'm swimming?* She hadn't the benefit of Shaw's night optics, but from the corner of her eye she had observed him watching her last night from over the wall. And Dominic had confirmed this through her ear bud. Alerted by Shaw's information of the peeping guard, they had set up an observation post barely a half kilometer from where Shaw had been watching from the cliffs. However, Dominic and Shaw had been totally unaware of each other's presence.

"Are you really sure about that?" asked Reggie. "Your security person seemed very persistent."

Kuchin was beaming as he rubbed her arm. "I am quite sure. He works for me. And I can see that you are a delightful young woman whom I feel quite safe with."

I look forward to proving you wrong on that, Fedir, thought Reggie.

"And I understand that you were with a man last night? Please tell me he is only a casual acquaintance so that I have some hope of seeing you on occasion while I'm here."

"I just met him recently."

"Wonderful. So no husband or longtime beau then?"

"No." She looked up at him in feigned perplexity.

He seemed to interpret her look in just the way she desired. "No, no. I am single but I could have children your age, my dear. Just indulge an old man who desires the innocent company of a beautiful young woman and nothing more."

She said playfully, "You don't look that old."

"You just made my day far happier."

"And you're sure nothing more?"

"You're playing with me, is that right?"

"Maybe a little."

"Good, that is a good first step. Have you been to Provence before?"

"Once."

"I have been here often. If you would permit I would take it upon myself to show you some of the beautiful sites near here. The Palais des Papes, or Popes' Palace, in Avignon, the finest example of a Roman aqueduct in all of France at Pont du Gard, the photo exhibition caves at Les Baux-de-Provence, the beauty of Roussillon, and the wine country to the north. In fact, I know a café in Gigondas where the pastries alone are worth the trip."

"My goodness, you certainly don't waste any time, Mr. Waller."

"And why live if one desires to waste time? For me life is precious. I go, go, go because I know one day it will be over. And no matter how much money one has, or fine houses, or anything else, it will all be gone when you breathe your last. And please, it is Evan. You embarrass me by using my surname."

"Well, Evan, let's start with the market and go from there, how does that sound?"

"Perfectly logical." He squeezed her arm in a way that indicated his insistence on "nothing more" was a lie. "Off to market we go."

Reggie could now understand what the professor had meant by the charm of the man. If she didn't know of his past, she could find him intriguing, fascinating even. But she did know of his past and this allowed her a way around the charm. And from there it was but a small step to ending the man's life.

CHAPTER

32

Shaw was making his way around the crowds that had already gathered at the market. There were hundreds of vendors, some with simple baskets pulled from their old, tiny cars and set up on rickety tables, while others had row after row of stacked goods on professional-grade display racks. Idly killing time, he had been here an hour, had two cups of coffee and an almond croissant, and was about to make his way down a long narrow street where still more sellers had migrated when he saw them approaching.

He acted on his first impulse and took cover behind a rack of cotton dresses and ladies' hats. He crouched down, as though he was examining a pair of leather boots on one counter, but his eyes behind the sunglasses were focused on two people.

Janie Collins and Evan Waller were walking arm in arm up the street to his left. She had a basket in one hand and Shaw could see that she had already purchased some things. Two steps behind them were the muscle. One was the runt from the night before, the other one was six-five and about two-eighty. Shaw scanned the other streets, doorways, and even the rooftops to see if any additional guards were around. He didn't see any, and he would have if they were there.

What the hell is she doing with him? The guy must not have wasted a moment.

He fell in behind them, but keeping well back and using the cover of people and goods for sale whenever they looked around and might've spotted him. This was one of the few times when his height was a drawback. Taking refuge next to a stand selling hand-cranked music boxes and T-shirts, Shaw stopped to take a good, hard look at Evan Waller. He came away impressed, at both the man's obvious physical fitness and his confident manner. He was clearly regaling the lady with amusing anecdotes, and for some reason Shaw's gut clenched every time he saw her laugh at one of the man's remarks.

For a moment Shaw thought Waller had looked in his direction when he was exposed in front of a stand selling leather jackets, but then the man had looked away and guided his companion to another destination. Shaw watched as Waller purchased a handcrafted necklace for her and then placed it around her neck, his fingers lightly touching Janie's skin. Twenty minutes later, her basket full, the pair, followed by the silent sentries, slowly made their way back down to their villas, leaving Shaw standing there undertaking a swift analysis that led to nothing helpful.

He hurried back to his room and called Frank.

"The lady's playing with fire and might just get burned," Shaw said. "There must be a way to protect her from this guy."

"Whoa, Shaw, whoa. I thought we had this conversation. We didn't send your butt to Provence to protect some rich chick from the States. You're there to bring in Waller, that's all."

"We can't just let this guy . . ."

"What? Have his way with her?" Frank chuckled. "Geez, you're a piece of work."

Shaw sat on his bed and rubbed his thumb against his index finger so hard it made a squeaking sound. "He could kill her. Or kidnap her and make her a prostitute."

"Yeah, right. He kills or snatches a wealthy young American staying in the place next to his just so the police will come and investigate? I don't think so. And why would he do that when he can get as many fourteen-year-old orphans from Asia as he needs for his business? The guy's on holiday. He finds out there's a goodlooking chick next door that swims in the nude. He probably just wants to get laid."

"And that's okay with you?"

"It's none of my business. Do you see it differently?"

Shaw hesitated. He wasn't exactly sure how he saw it. No, maybe he did, but was afraid to voice it, at least to Frank.

"What if she screws up the op?"

"How so?"

"I don't know. But how about we just pull the plug on the whole thing?"

"Are you nuts?" barked Frank. "We don't get him this time, he might not surface again until London or New York goes boom with a mushroom-cloud chaser. Now focus on the op, Shaw, and cut this other crap out."

Shaw put down the phone and let out a small groan. After this was over he was never, ever coming back to France.

CHAPTER

33

Reggie bent low to snap a picture of a bee on a stalk of lavender. She rose, slipped the camera in the back pocket of her white jeans, and walked toward the Abbaye de Sénanque. Founded by Cistercian monks in the twelfth century, it was located about thirty kilometers from Gordes along a winding drive through the mountains on roads that were ostensibly two lanes but practically only had room for one car.

She walked toward the ancient building where for centuries men had come to learn the intricacies of their faith. Now it housed a chapel, a bookstore and gift shop, and other event space. Monks still lived there and produced a variety of items for sale, including honey and liqueurs. The grounds were covered in the lavender fields for which Provence was known, although Reggie had passed equally impressive swaths of sunflowers on her way here. However, she had not come for the horticultural aspects of the abbey. She was here for a meeting. She'd chosen this rendezvous spot chiefly because it would have been impossible for anyone to follow her here. One-lane death traps did that for you.

She strolled along with a tour group, breaking off toward the gift shop when they veered into the chapel. The room was warm and a single fan puttered overhead, managing only to move pockets of warm, stale air from one place to another. A machine in the small foyer sold both Cokes and cappuccino. She headed to the section of the shop housing large picture books on Provence, many of which of course had lavender fields on the cover.

As she stood browsing a book on the abbey's history, her cell phone buzzed. She checked the text message. It read, "six o'clock."

She put the book down, picked up another, and turned casually around.

Whit was standing behind her checking out a small wooden carving of the abbey building you could purchase for fifteen euros. He wore a baseball cap, shades, raggedy jeans, a week's worth of beard, and had his iPod ear buds in. He put the book back and strolled outside. She waited a minute and then followed after buying the book she'd been looking at.

She saw him standing over by a low stone wall that stretched in front of the building. He was holding his camera and looking through the lens. He glanced up and saw her.

"Would you mind taking my picture in front of the abbey?" he asked.

She smiled. "Only if you'll do the same for me."

They alternated taking shots of the other and then strolled along together.

"Any results on my friend Bill?" she said in a low voice.

"Negative. No hits on prints. And we scored a zero on his picture too. He must be a good little boy. His full name, by the way, is William A. Young."

"What does the A stand for?"

"We could never find that out."

"Do you think he'll realize you two went through his room?"

"We were very thorough in putting everything back exactly. His passport is American, the address checked out. There are lots of lobbyists named William Young registered in America. We can't crank through them all in the time we have. Probably a waste anyway. I don't see any dirt there."

"Or his back cover could be as good as mine."

"*Or* the bloke could be who he says he is, Reg."

"He scaled a wall and then disarmed me. A lobbyist?"

Whit looked troubled by this. "Well, he is a big guy. But I guess I see your point. So what do you want to do?"

"I'm not sure. What does the professor think?"

"The brilliant one has deferred to your expertise in the field."

"Great. So what do *you* think?"

"I reckon we have to nail Kuchin and changing plans willy-nilly now based on flimsy intelligence could screw everything up. So we go with the original plan and if something solid does come up, we work around it."

"How's Dom?"

"Fired up and ready to go. So what're your first impressions of old Fedir?"

"The same as my original ones. He fills up every bit of space he's in and then some."

He glanced at her skeptically. "Not getting swept off your feet, are you?"

"With the monster? Hardly."

"Actually I'm not talking about Kuchin."

She gave him a hard stare.

Whit grinned maliciously. "Tall, mysterious, and the scaler of walls?"

"I'll pretend you didn't say that," she answered coldly.

"I'm not trying to tell you what to do—"

"Then *don't*, Whit."

"Just watch yourself."

"Look who's talking."

"What's that supposed to mean?"

She gave him a sideways glance. "Did you really paint a swastika on a target's forehead using his blood after shooting him in the balls?"

"What can I say? I'm an artiste."

"Right. I'm heading back."

"So dinner with our Ukrainian friend tonight?"

"Yes."

"I wonder if tall and mysterious will be hovering."

"It's a small village."

"Well, just don't get yourself in the middle of a ménage à trois. They can be messy. And before you ask, yes, I speak from experience."

"Whit, I don't know how I tolerate you some days."

"It's bound to be my charm."

"How do you know you even have any?"

He looked offended by the question. "Jesus, woman, I'm Irish. It's in our DNA."

34

R<small>EGGIE HAD INSISTED</small> that they eat at one of the restaurants in Gordes instead of at his villa, and Waller had finally relented.

"You are tenacious," he had said in a mildly scolding tone.

"No, I'm just exercising common sense. I don't really know you. And my parents wouldn't have wanted me to go unescorted to your house, even just for dinner."

"Wise people, your parents."

"They *were*, yes."

"I see. I am sorry."

"So am I," Reggie had said firmly.

They had walked up together to the village and taken a table outside that was wrapped by a three-foot-high wrought iron fence. As usual, Waller's men hovered at a nearby table. However, Pascal was not part of the security team tonight.

"Do they always go where you go?" Reggie asked as she observed the armed men.

"One of the prices that must be paid for success," Waller said, spreading his arms in mock helplessness. He was dressed in a blue blazer with a white pocket kerchief, khaki slacks, white silk shirt, and royal blue deck shoes that showed his bare pale ankles. The air had not yet cooled from the day's heat and there was a line of perspiration across his brow. She was sure there would be curves of sweat under his armpits too. Reggie had opted for a pale blue skort, yellow blouse, and white sandals, with a matching yellow scarf around her hair. There was no sweat on her face.

"It would be hard to imagine anyone trying to hurt anyone around here," said Reggie as she finished her last bite of beef.

Waller sipped his wine and eyed her appraisingly. "It is serene here, bucolic. Beautiful." He smiled. "Just as you are."

At a wave from Waller the waiter brought a second bottle of the same wine and poured it out. Reggie picked up her full wineglass and began to swirl the liquid around, absently checking its color against the flame of the lighted candle set in a bowl in the middle of the table. "You mentioned that you might have children my age. *Do* you have children?"

He waved a hand carelessly. "No, I was merely speaking hypothetically. I suppose I was always too busy for children."

"Wife?"

"If I had one now, she would be with me on this trip."

"Had one now? So you were married?"

"Yes."

"Did she pass away, or were you divorced?"

"Questions, questions," he said in a casual tone, but his look was sterner.

"I'm sorry," Reggie said. "I was just curious."

"Both."

"What?"

"The first one died and the second one divorced me." He patted her hand. "You remind me a little of my first wife. She was beautiful too. And stubborn."

"What was her name?"

Waller started to say something and then seemed to catch himself. "That is the past. I don't dwell on the past. I live for the present and look to the future. Let's finish this wonderful Bordeaux and then take a stroll and admire all things French."

Later, he guided her back to the street where they set off, his arm through hers. She once more eyed the bodyguards. Waller followed her gaze.

She said, "I suppose for you it's necessary, but I wouldn't want to have to live my life that way."

"But you yourself are obviously well off. You travel in style; you rent luxurious villas in one of the most beautiful places on earth.

Are you not worried about being kidnapped? Or even killed for your money?"

"I have no money with me unless you count a few euros. If they want my credit cards, they hardly have to kill me for that. And if they kidnap me there won't be anyone to pay the ransom. So you see, I would be a very inadequate target for a criminal."

"Perhaps you are right. Now, the man you've been seeing, he looks like he would make a competent bodyguard."

"Bill *does* look like he can take care of himself."

"Ah, so it's Bill. His last name?"

"He didn't tell me his last name," she said truthfully. Whit had found it out for her.

This ignorance seemed to brighten Waller's spirits. "Then you are not that friendly with him. I have only been here a short time and already you know *my* last name."

"It's not a competition, Evan."

"Of course not," he said in an unconvincing tone.

"And you are old enough to be my father, like you said."

"In truth, I am actually old enough to be your grandfather, well almost." He let go of her arm and pointed across at the church. "There is one of those in every village you will travel to here."

"A church? Yes, I suppose so."

"People use religion for much, mostly to explain their own short-comings."

"That's an unusual theory."

"Books filled up by foolish people who don't want to take control of their own lives. So they look for some divine providence to explain their desires."

"You mean to guide them?"

"No, I mean for excuses. The people who actually do something with their lives do so from here." He tapped his chest. "They don't need men in collars telling them what to think and who to pray to. And most importantly who to give their money to."

"I take it you're not a regular churchgoer."

He smiled. "Oh, but I am. Every week I am there. And I give much money to the church."

"Why, if you think it's a bunch of crap?"

He took her arm once more. "No, I do so because it's in my heart. I believe. And there is much good with faith. Much good. My mother would have been in a convent if she'd had her way. Fortunately she did not, otherwise I would not be here. I loved my mother very much."

Reggie turned to see him staring directly at her.

"I am going on a private tour of the Les Baux photographic exhibit this week. Have you heard of it?"

"I read about it, yes."

"Goya is the selected artist this year."

"Goya? Not a very uplifting choice."

"It is true that many of his masterpieces are bleak, but they have such power, such insight into the human soul."

"They depict evil," Reggie said, before looking away from the man she considered one of the most evil she had ever pursued.

"Yet evil is a large component of the soul. Its potential inhabits everyone."

"I don't believe that," Reggie said breathlessly. "I refuse to believe that."

"You may refuse if you choose to, but that does not mean that you are right." He paused. "I would like for you to accompany me on this tour. We can debate further this point then."

Reggie didn't answer right away. "I'll think about it and let you know."

He smiled through this mild reproach, bent down and kissed the back of her hand. "I enjoyed our dinner, Janie. And now, as I have business to attend to, I wish you good night."

He turned and walked off, his men following him.

Reggie just stood there in the middle of the street, desperately trying to divine what that last look had truly meant.

"Troubled?"

She turned around.

Shaw was leaning against a pillar in front of the church.

35

E<small>VAN</small> W<small>ALLER</small> climbed into the black SUV and his three-vehicle motorcade roared off, throwing road dust on an older couple slowly making their way up the hill to Gordes. Waller sat back and studied the screen on his phone. The email was brief, which he liked, and to the point, which he liked even better.

"How long?" he called up to the driver.

"GPS says fifty minutes, Mr. Waller. Crappy roads."

"Make it forty."

The man punched the gas and spoke into his headset. "Roll harder." The other two vehicles in the column immediately gunned it.

Thirty-nine minutes later the three vehicles transitioned from a two-lane to a one-lane road and eventually wound their way far back to a small stone house wedged in among a stand of leafy trees. The yard was dirt, the roof in disrepair, and the stone crumbling. It was clear no one had lived here for a long time. And there was no other house for miles.

Waller popped open the SUV's door and stepped out, waiting only a few seconds for his men to clear the area by sight, though he already had a man posted there who had come out of the house when the trucks had arrived. Waller marched into the house, his men bringing up the rear, with two left outside on perimeter watch.

The room was small, dark, and smelled of feces and mildew. It had no effect on Waller. He'd experienced much worse. There was one narrow table in the middle of the room, seven feet long and turned on one end so it reached nearly to the low ceiling. Two of the legs had been sawn off and the table edge rested against the floor. The remaining two legs were wedged against a wall for support. A naked man with dark hair and a beard was tied spread-eagled to the table-top. Waller looked over at Pascal, who stood in one darkened corner, his gaze on the man with no clothes.

"You did well in organizing his capture, Pascal."

"He tried to run, Mr. Waller, but he didn't know how to."

Waller walked up to the captive. From the light thrown by a couple of battery-powered lanterns, he could see the ambivalence in the man's features. This angered Waller. Either fear him or hate him, but feel something. He slapped the man across his bloodied face.

"Are you awake, Abdul-Majeed? You do not seem to be all here."

"I am awake. I see you. So what?" Waller knew that the man's casual attitude was meant to embolden the Muslim and deflate his own expectation, as though Waller were the captive instead of the other way around. In actuality, it probably achieved neither. Fat Anwar the accountant had been westernized. Abdul-Majeed was still hard, a man of the desert for whom extreme privation was the norm. Waller had to respect such a man, but only to a certain degree.

"Do you miss Kandahar, Abdul-Majeed? Or do you like the beauty of Provence better?"

The man shrugged. "I like this room. It is actually better than what I have in Kandahar. But, again, so what?"

Waller took a step back and smiled. He had to admire at least the man's courage.

"I do not like to be betrayed."

"You do not understand the ways of the Muslim world, then. It was not betrayal. It was negotiation. It was caution. And all of Islam has been betrayed by the West many times. So why should you be any different?"

"I am here on holiday and yet I have to take time away from pleasantries because you tried to cut me out of the deal."

"It is simply business. Do not take it personally."

"Forgive me, but I always take it personally when someone tries to blow me up."

"Then you are too sensitive."

"Why did you do it?"

"You lied to us," Abdul said simply.

"I do not lie when it comes to business."

The Muslim scoffed. "A Canadian? You have enriched uranium? I do not think so. You are most likely a spy. *That* is why we tried to kill you."

"Actually, I have *highly* enriched uranium. It is a critical difference. And if you did not believe it, why bother to deal with me at all?"

"I meant that *I* did not believe it. But others of my group did. They made the mistake and I was left with the mess to clean up."

"But they were right and you were wrong."

"Again, so you say. The Americans own your country. Everyone knows that. Canada is a satellite of the great Satan. A dog does not leave its master's side."

Waller turned to his men and flicked a hand at the door. They obediently left and shut the door behind them with Pascal being the last one out. Before closing the door he pointed to a metal case sitting on the floor in one corner of the room. He and his employer exchanged a look of mutual understanding.

Waller turned back to the captive and grabbed a handful of the man's filthy hair. "This is simply because you think I'm Canadian? Can you truly be that stupid?"

Abdul-Majeed's eyes flashed interest for the first time. "*Think* you are Canadian? You mean you are not?"

"No, Abdul-Majeed, I am not." He slipped off his jacket and pulled up his shirtsleeve, revealing a mark on the inside of his upper arm, where it could not be easily seen when his shirt was off. He held it up in front of the Muslim. "Do you see that? Do you know what it means?"

Abdul-Majeed shook his head. "I do not know of such marks."

Waller pointed to them one by one. "They are alphabet letters."

"That is not English," said Abdul-Majeed. "My English is good. I don't know what that is."

"It is Ukrainian. It is a variation of the Cyrillic alphabet. It stands for the Fifth Chief Directorate. Tasked to provide internal security against the enemies of the Soviet Union. I loved my job. So much that I burned it into my skin."

Abdul-Majeed's eyes widened. "You are Ukrainian?"

Waller rolled his shirtsleeve back down and put his jacket back on. "Actually, I always considered myself a Soviet citizen first and foremost. But perhaps that is simply splitting hairs. And since Ukraine was the repository for a good deal of the nuclear arsenal of the former Soviet Union, do you now understand? I still have many contacts there."

"Why did you not tell us this?" spat out Abdul-Majeed.

Waller pulled up a chair and sat down. "It's not my responsibility to provide you with my personal history, simply enough HEU— highly enriched uranium—to blow up a large part of a major American city. Do you even know what HEU really is, Abdul-Majeed?"

"It is Allah's weapon."

"No, it has nothing to do with *Allah*," Waller said derisively. "Uranium is a naturally occurring mineral found all over the world in trace quantities. It took the Germans during Hitler's reign to realize its peculiar potential through precise fission, namely to destroy people and property in vast quantities. Did you know that one can actually hold *highly enriched* uranium in his hand and not feel any adverse effects until years later? I have done so myself. Stupid of me, of course, but to hold that much power? The temptation was too great when I was a young and foolish man, though the toxic effects will probably kill me before my time.

"It takes fifty kilos, or nearly a hundred and ten pounds, of the substance to create a nuclear detonation. Whereas one would need nearly one ton, or twenty times that amount, of *low-enriched* uranium to produce a single nuclear bomb. It takes far less plutonium, about twenty pounds or so, to do the same thing. But unlike HEU, plutonium has to come from the reprocessing of nuclear material from reactors. And no country would allow terrorists to obtain that because, like a fingerprint, the device possesses the chemical signature of that country."

"You promised enough material for a suitcase nuke," Abdul-Majeed said.

Waller shook his head in disappointment. "You know, if you're going to be in the nuclear terrorist business, you should take the time to really understand the science. Suitcase nukes are bullshit, the stuff of Hollywood films and paranoid politicians. It's more like an SUV nuke. It can be done perhaps in a smaller footprint, but the smaller the device, counterintuitively perhaps, the greater its maintenance costs. And it would take a very strong man to carry around a suitcase weighing hundreds of kilos and the nuclear core would not last long. No, what I promised you was enough highly enriched uranium processed through second-generation gas centrifuge techniques to provide the core of a nuclear explosive device. That is fissile uranium containing in excess of eighty-five percent uranium 235. That means it is weapons-grade. I can also offer you, for a reduced price, weapons-*usable* grade, which only has twenty percent U-235. The boom will be far less, but you will still get a damn big boom with radiation fallout."

Waller stood and moved around the room, but his gaze remained on the Muslim.

"I can also offer technical assistance. For instance, wrapping the weapon's fissile core in a neutron reflector because it will dramatically lessen the critical mass, which is a good thing when you want as much explosive power as possible. It's a tricky balance. A bit too much U-238 isotope and the chain reaction that gives the substance its ability to mass-fission is rendered unworkable. Then, no boom and no burn."

For the first time Abdul-Majeed looked impressed. "You know much about this."

"Yes, *I know much about this*," mocked Waller. "I lived in Ukraine when it was one large atomic weapon waiting to be deployed. I have worked in nuclear facilities." He added ominously, "And I have tortured scientists suspected of selling out their country to the Americans and their allies. It was a most valuable classroom for me on many levels."

"Then we were wrong about you. We can go through with our deal."

Waller looked amused. "Oh, you think so? After you tried to kill me?"

"Why not? You did not die. Things are explained. You will make much money."

"Well, it's not always about money, is it? And not everything is explained. For instance, I know you didn't make the decision to kill me, because you aren't important enough to do so. But I want the names of those who did."

Abdul-Majeed smiled grimly. "That you will never know."

"Have you ever been tortured, Abdul-Majeed? Forgive me if I refuse to use the ridiculous term 'enhanced interrogation.' I prefer to cut to the chase."

The Afghan looked bored. "Sleep deprivation, waterboarding, cattle prods, loud music."

"No, you misunderstood me. I asked if you'd been *tortured,* not *coddled* by what passes for torture these days."

Waller walked over, opened the metal suitcase, and pulled out various instruments. "It is said that the Germans knew how to torture people, and indeed they were good at it. Today, the Israelis have the reputation of being the best interrogators, and they claim to not torture at all, but instead to use psychological means. As for me, I believe the Soviets stood alone when it came to such things. We had the best snipers and also the best interrogators. And I am old-fashioned. I have no patience for the latest technological gadgets. I use tried-and-true methods of extracting what I want based on one fact."

"What fact?" the Muslim said in a hollow tone.

Waller turned to him. "That people are soft shits. Are you a soft shit, Abdul-Majeed? We will find out tonight, I think."

CHAPTER

36

WHY WOULD I be troubled?" asked Reggie.

She made no move toward Shaw, so he came to her.

"Sorry, guess I was wrong about that. How was dinner?"

"It was fine. He knows his wines very well. Good conversationalist."

"I'm sure."

"Is there a problem?"

"I told you one of his guys was spying on you. Then they block off the street like they own it—"

"Evan apologized for that," she said, interrupting him.

"Oh, it's Evan?"

"That *is* his name. In fact he told me his last name too. Unlike you. It's Waller."

"Young. Bill Young." He paused. "Someone searched my room the day we went kayaking."

Reggie looked genuinely startled by this news and both her respect for and suspicion of Shaw increased. "Was anything taken?"

"Not that I can tell, no."

"Why would someone do that?"

He shrugged. "Gordes is certainly turning out to be more exciting than I thought it would be."

They started to walk along. Up ahead, near the village square, a band of teenagers were playing guitars and drums and a small crowd of people had stopped to listen and drop money in their basket.

"He asked about you," said Reggie.

"About me? Why?"

She smiled. "I think he wanted to know if you were serious competition for him."

"And what did you tell him?"

"That I hardly knew you. Which is true."

"You don't know him either," he pointed out.

"He seems nice enough. I mean, he's far too old for me." She playfully smacked his arm. "He's even older than you."

"For some reason I don't think age differences matter to a guy like that."

"Well, I think that's my decision to make, not his. If I tell him to back off, I'm sure he will."

"He doesn't look like a guy who takes no for an answer."

"But you don't know him. You've never even met him."

"Did he tell you what he did for a living?"

"A businessman."

"Well, that covers a lot of possibilities."

"I'm sure it'll be fine. This is Provence after all. What's he going to do?"

Shaw quickly looked away, his pulse hammering at a vein near his temple.

"Are you okay?"

"Dinner's not agreeing with me."

"You want to go back to your room? I can make my way back to the villa by myself."

"No, I'll walk you."

They took the shortcut and arrived at her villa a few minutes later. "Seems like our boy's out for the night," he said, looking at the empty parking spaces in front of Waller's villa.

"He did leave rather abruptly after dinner," she noted. "Said he had some business to take care of."

"Busy guy."

Her next words sent a cold dread down Shaw's back. "He's going to Les Baux, to see the Goya exhibit. He asked me to go with him."

"And what did you tell him?" Shaw asked, a bit too sharply.

She stared at him, perplexed. "I told him I'd think about it and get back to him."

Shaw thought swiftly and the words tumbled out of his mouth. "You don't have to do that."

"Why not?"

"Because you're going with me to Les Baux. Tomorrow. I've wanted to see the exhibit. I'd meant to ask you earlier."

"Really?" she said skeptically.

"We can make a day of it. Have some lunch in Saint-Rémy?"

"Why are you doing this? Are you thinking this is a competition too? I'm not a prize to be won."

"I know you're not, Janie. And if you'd rather go with him instead, I'll understand perfectly. It's just that . . ."

"Just what?"

"I just wanted to spend some more time with you. That's all. No fancy explanation. Just be with you."

Reggie's features softened and she grazed his arm with her hand. "Well, how can I turn you down since you asked so nicely." She smiled. "It's a date. Now the critical question is, Vespa or car?"

"It's a little far for the Vespa, so I think your Renault would work out far better. Let's say nine o'clock? I'll walk down to your place."

"Let me come up and get you."

Shaw looked at her curiously.

"I just think it'll be easier that way. We can drive straight out to the main road."

"And Waller won't know anything about it, you mean?"

"That's right."

"I can take care of myself."

"I'm sure you can, Bill." She paused. "And so can I."

CHAPTER

37

WALLER PLACED a sticky patch connected to a long thin cable against the side of Abdul-Majeed's neck. Then he connected the line to a small battery-powered monitor that he turned on.

"What is that?" asked Abdul-Majeed nervously.

"It is nothing to worry about. It just measures your pulse. I do not have enough electrical power here to shock the truth out of you, my Muslim friend. But there are other ways." Waller placed a cuff around the man's arm and then plugged the cord running from the cuff into the same device as he had for the pulse reading. "And that of course measures your blood pressure."

"Why do you need that?"

"Because I want to make sure I stop the pain before I kill you, of course."

Abdul-Majeed tensed and began to chant under his breath.

"So your god is great, Abdul-Majeed?" said Waller, translating the words. "We will see how great he is to you."

Abdul-Majeed did not answer, but kept up his chanting. Waller checked the readout of his vitals on the screen. "Your pulse is already at ninety-eight and your blood pressure is elevated, and I have not even started. You must relax your breathing; calm your nerves, my friend."

"You will not break me!" the captive said defiantly.

Waller took duct tape out of his box and wound it around the man's forehead, chin, and shoulders and around the table several times. The result was that Abdul-Majeed could not move his head or upper torso even an inch away from the wood.

"Do you know why I do this?" Waller asked. "It is so you will not be able to render yourself unconscious when the pain becomes too great. I have known men to crack their own skulls in order to escape it. I made that mistake once, but never again. Torture does not work if one cannot feel the pain."

Waller pulled more items from his box, placed one in his pocket, and came back over to the table. "They say that the agony of a single kidney stone passing through one's body is even greater than that experienced giving birth. I have never given birth, of course, but I have passed kidney stones and the pain is indeed severe." He slipped on latex gloves, looked down at Abdul's private parts, and then held up a thin glass tube twenty centimeters in length.

"This will have to serve as my kidney stone. Now take a deep breath. And then relax."

Instead the man's breathing accelerated and his cheeks bulged out as though he were tensing before the killing blow fell. "You will not break me!" he screamed over and over.

Waller methodically worked the glass tube up the man's penis, using a rubber hammer to finish tapping it in. Abdul shrieked in pain with every millimeter it was thrust inside him.

"It is no more than a catheter, really. Now, this, this is the painful part."

He slipped the vise grips from his pocket and looked at him. "All I require are names."

"Go to hell!" screamed Abdul.

"Of course, very original of you." Waller set the tension on the grips, lowered them into position, and snapped them into place, crushing the glass tube inside the man.

This time the scream was far louder than before. Waller's men, who were waiting outside but near the door, looked at each other and then nervously moved away from the sounds. Only Pascal stayed close to the doorway, ever alert.

"You are bleeding in a place you would not like, Abdul," said Waller, peering down at his work.

The response was a string of shouts in the man's native tongue.

"Yes, yes, my mother and father are already quite dead, thank you," said Waller.

The tears rolled down Abdul's strained face, his jaw muscles bulged and shook. His tethered neck was stretched tight in his ag-ony, every vein and artery visible. So great was his misery that if Waller had not bound it to the table, he would have indeed smashed his skull against the wood.

Waller continued on calmly. "I learned Pashto and a little Dari during the Soviets' disastrous intrusion into your country. They are hard languages to learn, but not as difficult as English, which has so many exceptions there are no rules left." He checked the monitor. "Pulse one-thirty-nine. I've seen far higher. When I run, in fact, I can get it up to over one-forty and I'm sixty-three. You are a young man, this is nothing. Now your blood pressure *is* one-fifty over ninety. A bit precarious. Well, let's see."

He snapped the grips on a new location and the man's pelvis jerked upward, pulling against his bindings as he roared in pain again.

"Pulse one-fifty-seven. Okay, now I believe that I have your at-tention. We were discussing names."

In gasps, Abdul said, "You will just kill me if I tell."

"Now that is progress. That is good. We are closer to negotia-tion. And yet if you tell me, do you want me to just let you go? But if I do then you could go and warn those who betrayed me. Hardly a worthy proposition."

"So I die then?"

"I did not say that."

Waller undid the grips and then locked them higher up, crushing a particularly sensitive part of the Muslim's anatomy.

Again, Abdul's shrieks slammed into every corner of the small room. He threatened to kill Waller, behead him, disembowel him, come back and haunt him, slaughter everyone he ever cared about.

"I understand your anger, my friend, but it gets us nowhere," said the Ukrainian. He looked down. "You are bleeding more heav-ily, Abdul, but it is not life-threatening so have no worries."

Waller went back to his box and pulled out a small scalpel. He held it up for the Muslim to see. "A surgeon's knife; it is very deli-cate, very effective. I make one incision here and here." He placed the blade against two spots on Abdul's neck. "And you bleed out in minutes. But I don't want that, so instead I do this."

Seconds later Abdul's right pupil had been slashed open. The Muslim writhed in agony, his screams again filling the small space.

Waller studied the monitor. "One-ninety-five on the pulse rate. That is unsustainable, my friend. And your blood pressure, yes, it too gives me trouble. You will assuredly suffer a stroke if you don't calm down. I truly fear for your health."

He looked down at the sobbing and now partially blinded man. "Would you like me to now employ sleep deprivation or play what they call the rap music?" He bent lower. "What do you say? You are begging me? What, to kill you, my friend? No, no. I am not a violent man. I am a fair man. And I do not kill. But instead I do the work piecemeal." The knife struck again and part of the captive's left ear fell to the dirty floor.

He checked the monitor readout. "Over two hundred is the pulse and the blood pressure is not good, not good at all. I tell you to calm and yet you do not. You are too stubborn." He turned back to the Muslim. "I will let you rest a bit. And then the *real* interrogation will begin. If you thought this was painful, Abdul, you will be disappointed, I think. This, this was merely the foreplay."

Waller withdrew from his case an instrument that looked somewhat like a large cheese grater, only its cutting edges were longer and looked lethal and were also on pivots, so they could turn at different angles. "I know you can see what I'm holding, but you may not realize what it is. So I will ask you a question. What is the largest organ in the body?" Waller pretended to wait for a response. "You say you do not know? Then I will tell you. It is the *skin*. Yes, the skin is the largest organ in the body. Many people do not realize this. Adults average two square yards of skin on their bodies, weighing up to nine pounds. Yes, nine pounds. Now, with this tool that I am holding I can shave all the skin off your body in less than one hour. I do not make empty boasts. I have done it before. It takes a firm hand and an efficient method. I start with the face and work my way down. It comes off in long strips, you see. Not counting the face and the arms, which are slightly problematic and require extra time, I once almost did a continuous roll of skin from the torso to the feet. Sadly, the procedure broke down near the knees. You see, the woman had very bony knees. I was disappointed of course, but still, I was proud of my accomplishment.

"Now, because I of course cannot have you thrashing around while I perform this task, I will inject you with this." He reached in his metal case and held up a small bottle of liquid and a syringe. "The Soviets came up with it back in the seventies. It paralyzes the body but allows the person to be fully conscious and aware of everything. You understand me? You will feel nothing when I peel off your skin, but you will be able to see it all. That is why I left you with one eye. So you would not miss a second of the procedure. The effects wear off in a few hours. And then, well, then you will feel a lot."

"Please, please," sobbed Abdul-Majeed.

Waller smiled down at him. "So you do not prefer the taking of the skin? Well, then did you know that if cut out of the body properly a man can hold his own intestines for hours? You would think that one would bleed out, but it's not true. You will surely die of something else, but not because of blood loss, because I know what I'm doing. Now, I will tell you that my practice is to stuff the intestines inside the mouth, at least as much as will fit. Perhaps I am too soft but I find it wicked to expect a dying man to *hold* his own bowels. You have twenty seconds to decide which you prefer, or I will make the decision for you. And, in the spirit of full disclosure, I am very partial to the skin."

Finally, in gasps interrupted only by sobs, Abdul-Majeed said, "I will tell you what you want to know."

Waller smiled. "Now that is ironic. Because I will tell you something first. I know who ordered my killing. They are already dead, in fact. I saved you for last."

"Then why did you do this to me?" the captive screamed.

"Because I could. And it is good for one to practice. Otherwise one's skills diminish. You said I could not break you. But I did." Waller's voice lost its casual tone. "And if someone hits you, my friend, you have to hit them back or else they will think you are weak. And I am many things, but weak is not one of them."

"Then kill me," roared the disfigured man. "Finish it."

Waller took his time pulling off the cuff and pulse monitor and vise grips and packing them away in the box. "You are not important enough for me to waste any more of my time. Tell Allah I said hello. And that I wondered what kept him from coming to your aid. Perhaps, like me, he also had better things to do." He raised the scalpel once more. "What I am about to do now is an act of mercy, Abdul-Majeed. You will understand why very shortly." He slashed the Muslim's good eye, fully blinding the man. "It would be the height of cruelty to allow you to see what is coming next."

The man's screams of terror followed Waller out the door. His men stiffened to attention when they saw him emerge from the cottage. Waller nodded. "I'm done."

Pascal along with another man hustled to an SUV that had pulled up within the last few minutes. They opened the back gate and hauled out two animals. They were burly pit bulls tethered to metal control poles. Leather muzzles were securely fastened over their snouts. Using the poles, the men, with difficulty, maneuvered the lunging beasts to the front door. Then they released the wire nooses connected to the poles, whipped off the muzzles, and pushed the animals through the opening, slamming the door behind them.

As Waller nimbly stepped into his ride, the snarls of the attacking dogs and the screams of Abdul-Majeed could be heard over the sound of the vehicle's engine. Waller slipped in his ear buds and selected a joyful song on his iPod even as his thoughts turned back to the beautiful young woman he'd had dinner with tonight. He looked forward to seeing her again.

Soon.

CHAPTER

38

THE AIR was cool, but oddly heavy. The darkness here was more intense than anything Reggie had experienced. She could only flash her penlight every few seconds to see where she was going. Twice she bumped into hard objects, skinning her arm and bruising a toe. She kept making her way down, pausing every few seconds to listen. After she passed through a door something grabbed her.

"Jesus Christ!"

"Shhh. You'll wake the bloody dead."

A light flashed on the face next to her, revealing a grinning Whit.

"What the hell were you thinking sneaking up on me like that? If I had a gun I would've shot you."

Whit turned the light away from his face. "Sorry, Reg, I guess this place does something to you. Makes you all silly."

"Is it *all clear* at least?" she said sternly, her breath returning to normal.

"Of all living things. See for yourself." He swept his light around. Reggie took in the revealed objects.

Crypts.

They were in the catacombs of Gordes's Catholic church. Since Reggie had articulated her plan to Professor Mallory back at Harrowsfield they'd used the church as the focal venue of their plans. Whit and Dominic had explored its interior and were thrilled to find it held all they needed to entrap their quarry.

"How many do you reckon?" she asked.

"Dunno. Didn't bother to count 'em. It's a lot, though."

"Now show me the pass-through you found. That's the critical piece."

He led her back the way she had come in to an intersection of two passages: the one they'd come through that led to the catacombs, and the second heading off to the left. They walked down this long passage that was dimly lit by a few flickering electric lights, then Whit hooked a left, led her down a long flight of aged steps, through another door, and they finally arrived farther down the cliffs and on the other side of Gordes, near the villas.

He said, "Brilliant on your part using the religion angle."

"It'll only be brilliant if it actually works. Where's Dom?"

"Back at our digs. He's got an itchy finger to get this guy."

"Then it's your job to calm him down. I already told him that's how mistakes happen. And with a guy like Kuchin we can't afford any errors."

They walked back to the catacombs.

"So where's *Bill*?" Whit asked.

"Why?"

"I saw you talking to him earlier tonight. Just wondering."

"You were spying on me?" Reggie said.

"No, just covering your back. Partners do that, you know."

"Okay, *partner*, we're going to Les Baux tomorrow to look at the Goya exhibit."

"You think that's wise?"

"Why wouldn't it be?"

"Because you could spend that time further ingratiating yourself to Kuchin, now couldn't you?"

That was true, thought Reggie. And yet she wanted to go to Les Baux. Or maybe she just wanted to go with Bill to Les Baux.

Whit seemed to be reading her mind. "You talk about focus, Reg? Then why don't you practice what you're bloody preaching?" he said heatedly.

She looked up at him angrily. "You worry about Dom and yourself. And you're the one who went off mission in your last lead."

"What, by shooting a Nazi in his nuts and painting Hitler's sign on his head? I told you before, I'm an artiste."

"No, you just made our job a lot harder."

"Oh, so you've bought into the professor's theory on keeping a low profile so the future bastards won't dig their hole deeper?"

"I don't consider it a mere *theory*."

"Well, consider this, love. You don't think these blokes we're hunting are dug in as deep as they can be? You don't think they know folks are coming after them? The prof wants a low profile? I say we scream our work to the heavens. I *want* these bastards to know we're coming. I want them to lie awake at night thinking about how grisly their deaths will be. I want them to piss in their pants with fear, just like the people they slaughtered had to. See, for me, that's all part of the fun."

"What we do *isn't* fun, Whit," she said, though by her expression his words had stung her, had uncomfortably reached a level in her mind she hadn't before visited.

"Well, maybe that's the principal difference between you and me."

The two stared at each other in the semidarkness until Reggie said, "Do you have the poison yet?"

"Enough to kill ten Fedir Kuchins." He looked around the room they were in. "I say right here is good. Tie him to that slab over there. Read him his life story and then do the drip-drip. You got down how you want to show the prick his terrible deeds? That's the last piece as far as I can see."

"Getting there. And after that?"

"Right, low-profile shit." Whit flashed his light on a crypt against the wall. "That one's top is very loose. Took a lot of elbow grease from Dom and me, but we got it done. Nothing but bones at the bottom, plenty of room. I checked around the village, they don't use the catacombs anymore. Doubt they'll ever find the guy till he's bones too. Work for you?"

"Yes. I'm sure the professor will be very pleased too."

"Not my job to please him."

She grabbed his arm. "We have to be on the same page here. There's too much at stake."

He firmly disengaged her fingers. "I may disagree with people over stuff, but when the time comes to do the job, I'll do the bloody job. That good enough for you?"

"Yes."

"In the meantime, enjoy Les Baux with your beau."

In another few seconds, Reggie was alone.

She waited a few more minutes and then made her way back out to the darkened streets. Even after midnight Gordes was lovely and felt safe. There was no one about as she made her way quietly back to the villa. She was aware that people would probably be watching her as she approached Kuchin's place. His men kept a 24/7 vigil around their boss. What Reggie hadn't counted on was someone watching her as she left the church.

And this time it wasn't Shaw.

CHAPTER

39

Because of the time difference it was one hour earlier back in England than in France. At Harrowsfield, Professor Mallory sat fully dressed at a desk in the small study adjacent to his bedroom. He was prepared to work through the night on a new project that would follow after the successful completion of the Fedir Kuchin matter. He puffed his pipe and sent acrid plumes of smoke to the stained ceiling. A light rain started falling as the professor finally set aside the journal in which he was making notations and sat back in his chair, lost in thought.

He heard a tap at the door.

"Yes?"

"It's me, Professor," said Liza.

He rose from the chair as she opened the door. She was dressed in a long nightgown with a beige wool robe over the top. Her hair hung down to her shoulders. Slippers covered her feet.

"Is everything all right?" he asked.

She sat down on a small worn leather couch across from him as he retook his seat. "I just heard from Whit. He and Reggie have confirmed the site and the details have been worked out for the final phase."

"That's excellent." He studied her. "But you look concerned."

"It was something in Whit's voice. He sounded upset. So I called Reggie and spoke to her. She also sounded upset, but when I pushed her on what was the matter, she refused to talk about it. When I tried ringing Whit back, he didn't answer."

"So you think they might have had a row?"

"It seems so. And it couldn't have come at a worse time."

Mallory put his pipe aside, wandered over to the window, and looked out past the rain-splattered glass. "Did you contact Dominic too?"

"No, he and Whit are rooming together, so I didn't think he could be candid. And I don't want to create even more tension."

Mallory clasped his hands behind his back and stared moodily out into the dark. "I should have anticipated this. I should have had Whit remain behind and sent either Caldwell or perhaps David Hamish with Dominic. Whit has resentment, a great deal more than I had thought, apparently."

"You don't think that will interfere with him performing his duties?"

"If I had the answer to that I wouldn't be worried, would I?"

She glanced over at his desk. "Burning the midnight oil again?"

"I seem to do my best thinking after dark."

"Any further word on funding?"

Surprised, he turned to her. "Why, what have you heard?"

"Folks know it takes a lot to keep this place functioning. It's not like we do this for money, but people are paid *some* wages. And the upkeep here. And then there's the mission expense. The rent on the villa where Reggie is staying is quite staggering. It all adds up."

Mallory remained silent for a few moments before sighing and sitting back down. "Things are a bit tight, I won't deny it. The villa lease is all right, though. A gentleman of considerable means with a Ukrainian background stepped up for those funds. And I have one or two other prospects. It must be done discreetly, of course."

"Of course." She added, "When was the last time you had a holiday, Miles?"

"A holiday?" He chuckled. "I could be incredibly saccharine and say that what I do here is a holiday, but I will refrain from doing so."

"Seriously, Miles, when was the last time?"

His eyes took on a faraway look. "I suppose while Margaret was still alive. Rome. And Florence. She always loved the statue of David. She would sit and stare at him for hours. Quite the fan of Michelangelo was my dear wife. It was a nice visit. She became ill after we returned. Six months later she was gone."

"If I recall that was eight years ago."

"Yes, yes, I suppose it was. Time does march on, Liza."

"Everyone here is under considerable strain, but some more than others. You are our leader. We cannot afford to lose you."

"I'm fine. Or as fit as an overweight and sedentary old professor can be." He looked around. "I do love it here, this old wreck of a place. Regina loves it here too. I hear her wandering around at all hours of the night."

"She visits the cemetery regularly. Did you know that?"

Mallory nodded. "In particular the grave of Laura R. Campion. No connection that I have ever been able to discern. Yet she does seem drawn to the woman."

Liza gave him a piercing stare. "Was there a particular reason you targeted Reggie for recruitment?"

He gave her a hard look before saying, "None different than any other. She passed all the hurdles. But it really starts off with a simple judgment call on my part. In that regard Regina Campion was hardly unique."

She eyed him for a few seconds before looking away.

"Now this American," Mallory began.

"Bill Young."

"Yes, it's not good. A distraction. Perhaps more. We have no real information on the man. Anyone can pose as a former lobbyist."

Liza ran a hand along the drawstring of her robe. "True enough. By the way, Whit also reported that Reggie will be traveling to Les Baux with him tomorrow."

Mallory looked startled. "Les Baux? For what purpose?"

"Whit didn't know why. He felt strongly that she should be working on Kuchin instead."

"As do I. I think I'll ring her right now."

"Don't do that, Miles."

"But—"

"She's under a lot of stress, but Reggie has the best instincts of anyone we have in the field. I think we can trust her. I think she's earned that, don't you?"

Mallory seemed frozen with indecision, but his features finally relaxed. "All right. I largely agree with that assessment," he added stiffly.

Liza rose and glanced at the desk once more. "I suppose you're working on the next one?"

"Never wise to let the grass grow, you know."

"Well, let's pray Reggie and the others come back alive so they can do it all again."

She closed the door softly behind her.

Mallory stared after her for a few moments, then went back to his desk, rummaged in a drawer, and pulled out the photo he'd received from Whit. He sat down and began studying the picture of Bill Young.

A troubling premonition was creeping up his spine. And something told him it had everything to do with this man. He did trust Reggie, but there was always a limit to trust in anyone. And nothing could interfere with their getting to Kuchin. It was too important. He debated for a bit and then decided to do it. He slipped a mobile phone out of his pocket and thumbed in a text message. The professor was not nearly as electronics-illiterate as he let on. He put the mobile away and sat back in his chair. He hoped he had done the right thing.

Sometimes in this line of work all you had were your instincts. When you were right all was well. When you turned out to be wrong, however? Well, innocent people sometimes died.

CHAPTER

40

REGGIE'S AND SHAW'S journey to see the Goya exhibit consisted of a winding ride over mountains and a series of stomach-churning switchbacks. The topography had changed completely as they ventured southwest. The area was dominated by calcium and limestone quarries. It reminded Shaw of the white cliffs of Dover in England.

"This really is quite extraordinary," said Reggie after they'd arrived at the exhibit and she peered around the rock walls. They were on the outskirts of Les Baux-de-Provence at the top of the Alpilles mountain range in an old stone quarry that had a bird's-eye view of the Val d'Enfer, or Valley of Hell. It was an unusual place for an art experience.

Every wall that she and Shaw could see was lighted up and the masterpieces of Spaniard Francisco José de Goya y Lucientes stared back at them in pixeled glory. There were typical portraits of Spanish royalty, but also the nude and clothed *Majas* that had created a public uproar when they were unveiled and were subsequently confiscated during the Spanish Inquisition for being obscene.

The works of the late Spaniard were also displayed on the floors. It was a little unnerving to be walking on acknowledged masterpieces, but after a few minutes one simply became entranced with the spectacle. Thematic music filtered across the darkened space, but there was no accompanying narrative audio. Prose was displayed along the walls, giving information about Goya's career. The images constantly changed as Shaw and Reggie walked along. One moment they were awash in brilliant colors, other times the hues darkened, casting a sobering feel over them. A few attendants in uniform were present, not to direct the patrons but only to admonish anyone attempting to touch the walls.

When Reggie and Shaw arrived at the section of the caves depicting Goya's later, far darker work, she fell silent. Shaw glanced over the brochure they'd been given at the entrance. However, it was bare-bones and did not tell what any of the paintings were.

"Pretty grim," he said to Reggie as a sad tune filled their ears.

"That's *The Third of May 1808*," she said, gesturing to the painting depicting French soldiers firing on defenseless Spaniards. "It commemorates Spanish resistance to Napoleon's invasion of their country."

"Were you an art history major?"

She shook her head. "No, just interested in it."

Reggie stared at the man in the white shirt in the portrait, his arms raised in either surrender or, more likely, defiance. His eyes captured the full horror of his situation. He and everyone around him were about to die. "When I told Waller that Goya was hardly an uplifting artist he said something strange."

"What was that?"

"Though he agreed the paintings were bleak, he said they were also powerful insights into the human soul. And he said something that really gave me a chill." She hesitated, as though she simply wanted to drop this thread of conversation.

"What did he say, Janie?" Shaw prompted.

"He said that the potential for evil lurks in everyone." She turned to Shaw. "I told him I didn't believe that. Do you?"

When Shaw didn't answer right away, she said, "Never mind. It doesn't matter." She looked over at the painting again. "This piece actually inspired later works by Manet and Picasso. People slaughtering other people. What an inspiration." Reggie wrapped her arms around herself and shivered. The temperature had dropped thirty degrees as soon as they passed through the entrance to the quarry and stepped inside the Cathédrale d'Images, as it was known.

The next section of the exhibition was from when an older Goya had become deaf and ill, reportedly suffering from a disease that was destroying his mind. The so-called *Black Paintings* were nightmarish in scope. A set of aquatint prints titled *The Disasters of War* were equally horrifying. After that came the piece titled *Saturn Devouring His Son*. It showed a monstrous, disfigured creature eating a headless, bloodied torso.

"I wonder if they give out free Valium when you exit this place," said Shaw, only half-jokingly.

"It's important to see this, Bill," said Reggie.

"Why's that?"

"If we don't we'll just keep repeating the same mistakes over and over. War, violent death, misery, all man-made and preventable."

"Well, we seem to keep making the same mistakes anyway."

"Were you ever in the military?" she asked suddenly.

"No." With a completely straight face he added, "The closest I ever came to battle was being in paintball fights in college."

"Lucky you."

"Yep, lucky me."

The last painting was *Courtyard with Lunatics*. As Reggie explained it, the piece portrayed the unfortunate inmates in a sixteenth-century asylum. She stood stock-still staring at the images. When Shaw glanced over at her, he saw a tear rolling down her cheek.

"Hey, Janie, maybe we should get back to daylight and have that nice lunch in Saint-Rémy."

She didn't appear to have heard him. When he touched her on the shoulder, though, she jumped and turned to him. Her eyes were reddened and moist.

Choosing his words carefully he said, "Do you know someone—I mean not in a place like that, of course—but someone who had some . . . issues?"

She didn't answer him, but turned and walked back through the space. After a moment he hurried after her. She stopped in front of the first painting on exhibit, *The Nude Maja*. The naked brunette was lounging on a chaise, her hands clasped behind her head.

"I have to say, that's more my taste in paintings," said Shaw. "At least over the flesh-eating monster back there."

"It's amazing how they're able to display these images on the walls." Reggie's eyes had dried and her voice had returned to normal.

"Well, they probably just use basic projection equipment, maybe even like a computer PowerPoint thing."

"So, pretty easy to do, actually?"

"I guess so, but I'm no expert." He smiled. "Why? You planning your own exhibition?"

She gave him a whimsical look. "You never know." She slipped her arm through his. "How about that lunch?"

On the way out they passed an old fortress that was carved out of the mountain. Reggie pointed up to it. "The King's Fortress. Built right out of the stone and placed perfectly for maximum defensive measures."

"Okay, were *you* ever in the military?" said Shaw.

"I just read a lot. And that French immersion class included a historical overview of Provence. The fort overlooked the King's Valley down there. The provincial crowns ruled their fiefdoms from up here."

"It's always rulers up top and everybody else down below. Separation is the key. Only thing that prevents anarchy, or democracy, depending if you're a ruler or the ruled."

"That was actually very philosophical, Bill."

"I have my moments."

They ate outside at a small café in Saint-Rémy. After that they toured the Popes' Palace in Avignon, getting caught in a sudden shower as they headed back to the car, which was parked in an adjacent underground garage. They ran laughing and soaked across the stone courtyard to the garage, Shaw using his jacket as an umbrella to cover them both.

"I guess that's why I like big guys," said Reggie, looking up at the large jacket over her.

By the time they returned to Gordes their hair and clothes had mostly dried. As they pulled up to Shaw's hotel Reggie's cell phone buzzed, indicating a text message had just arrived. She slipped it from her pocket and glanced at the screen, then put it away without commenting.

"Let me guess, Evan Waller wants to know where you've been all day?" said Shaw.

"Getting a bit jealous, are we?"

"No, I'm not the possessive type. But I don't think I can say the same for him."

"But like I said, you don't even know him."

"I've known lots of guys like him. And haven't we had this discussion?"

"Yes. But it's nice to know you care."

Shaw put a hand on her arm. "Seriously, Janie. Tread lightly with the guy. I've just got some weird vibes about him."

"I'll be careful. Would you like to get together for dinner later?"

"Not sick of me yet?" he said with a grin.

"Not *yet*, no," she said impishly.

"Okay, up in town or somewhere else?"

"How about I cook for you?"

He looked mildly surprised. "At your place? Sure. But only if you let me bring the wine."

"Deal. Say about eight?"

Shaw walked up to his room, unlocked his door, and froze.

The man sitting in the chair beside his desk stared back at him.

41

AFTER DROPPING Shaw off Reggie didn't return to her villa. She continued on out of Gordes again, passed her villa, turned onto the main road, and drove off. Twenty minutes later, after making certain she wasn't being followed, she reached her destination.

Dominic had seen her drive up and was waiting for her at the door.

When she walked in the cottage and saw the messy digs she said, "I see Whit has settled in quite nicely here. Where is he, by the way?"

"Out working on the job. Told me to hang here."

"I just got a text from the professor. That's why I'm here. He wanted to know if there are problems. Are there?"

Dominic tugged at the wrists of his sweatshirt. "I take it you and Whit had words."

Reggie sat down on the edge of a chair. "Why, what did he tell you?"

"You want his version straight or the cleaned-up copy?"

"What did he say, Dom!"

"Verbatim, that you've 'lost your bloody head over this bloke and you're possibly screwing everything up,' only he didn't use the word 'screwing.'"

"Is that what you think?"

"You went out with him today, right?"

"And I'm going to see him tonight too."

"Reg," he began.

She cut him off. "And do you know why?"

"Why don't you enlighten me?" he said sarcastically.

"I can see you've been hanging out with Whit too long. That tone doesn't become you, Dom."

"You may not agree with him on everything, but he's got good instincts in the field."

"No, he has *great* instincts in the field. But so do I. And this time he's just wrong."

"And why is that?"

They both whirled around to see Whit standing in the doorway that led to the small kitchen.

"I thought you were out," said Reggie.

Whit came forward and sank down on the couch next to Dominic. "I was and now I'm back. So keep talking. This is really informative."

"By the way, Bill knew someone had searched his room."

"Really? Guy's better than I thought. I'll have to keep that in mind." Whit continued to stare at her.

"Do that. At least for future missions."

"Back to *this* mission. And your relationship with little Billy?"

"Okay. I'll lay it out for you. I have a short time frame to get to Kuchin. The whole mission is predicated on him going where I want him to go at a certain time and day."

Whit tugged his jacket off and tossed it on a small table in one corner. "Just get to the part we don't know and are thinking the worst about, meaning you and bloody Bill!"

"Jealousy," said Reggie simply. "It's the fastest way to reel a man in. He thinks I'm spending too much time with Bill, Kuchin gets antsy. He's already reacted that way. That gives me the upper hand. He'll come at me hard: 'Janie, go to this beautiful place with me and that beautiful place and have this lovely dinner and drink that lovely wine.' And it'll come to the point that wherever *I* suggest that we go, he'll do it, without hesitation. So having Bill around actually made my job far easier. I don't have to overtly throw myself at Kuchin, which is very good, because a man like that will see through that sort of thing nine times out of ten. He believes he's coming after me, it's a whole different story. His defenses are down." She paused. "But if you two male-female experts have a better way, I'm listening."

Dominic looked over at Whit, who was still staring at Reggie. "So this is all tied to the mission?" Whit asked.

"It's always been tied to the mission, Whit. Everything I do in my bloody life has been tied to the mission. If you'd get your brains out of your crotch you might be able to see that. Or did I misinterpret your last remark back at Harrowsfield? What was it again?"

"A glimpse of thigh and a pretty face, more or less," said Whit with a smirk.

"What are you two talking about?" demanded Dominic as he stared between them.

"Nothing, Dom," she said.

"Are you two having an affair?" Dominic persisted.

Whit laughed. "Not for lack of trying, at least on my part, but Sister Reggie here's having nothing to do with it." The smile quickly faded from his lips. "Okay, Reg, what you just said makes sense. Jealousy."

"Jealousy," she repeated, staring him down. "It works with most men."

Whit looked away. "I'm hungry. You want anything?"

"No, but I do have a request."

He sat up, looking interested. "Shoot."

"I need some new equipment."

Dominic looked at her warily. "What sort of equipment?"

"Stuff that'll project pictures on a wall. Can you get it?"

"I don't see why not," said Dom. "There are big electronics stores in Avignon."

"Then get it, as fast as you can."

Whit looked confused. "What do you have in mind?"

She rose. "You'll see."

When she got back to her villa, Fedir Kuchin was standing in the middle of the narrow road, his arms open wide in welcome to her.

She wanted to place a bullet between his eyes. Instead she sighed, forced another smile, and climbed out of her car.

42

Shaw closed the door behind him and said angrily, "What the hell are you doing here, Frank? There's no face-to-face during an op, you know that."

Frank Wells remained sitting in the chair, his face looking slightly pinched. "You went out to Les Baux-de-Provence today."

"I know I did," snapped Shaw. "So?"

"Why'd you do that?"

"Because Waller had invited Janie to go with him on his private tour, and I couldn't let that happen." He held up a hand when Frank looked ready to say something. "It has nothing to do with her personally. It would've just been a logistical headache to have her in the way when we do the extraction."

"Yeah, well, I got bad news on that. It's why I'm here. Didn't want to tell you over the phone."

Shaw dropped his room key on the table and sank onto the bed. "What bad news?"

"They're pulling the op. Amy Crawford and the strike team are already wheels up and out of the country."

Shaw rose so fast he almost hit his head on the low ceiling. "What! Why?"

"Things have changed."

"Changed! How could they have changed? Waller's looking to sell nukes. Crazy people are trying to buy them from him so they can go and blow up a chunk of the world. How can that possibly change?"

"It does if he's no longer trying to sell them. And in fact he might very well have killed the people he was trying to do business with."

"How do you know that?"

"Found two bodies in a lake that match the descriptions of the Islamic guys who were dealing with Waller. They both exhibited signs of extreme torture. Plus we got chatter on the communication lines that indicates the Muslims are no longer working with our Canadian psycho and in fact have cut off all ties to him."

"How do you know he killed them?"

"We don't for sure, but we also just learned that a house where we believe Waller was meeting with a midlevel terrorist cell member was blown up. He might've lost a couple of guys, at least the entourage he has here is different from the one he normally travels with. We think maybe the Islamists double-crossed him, tried to kill him, and he retaliated. At least that's one theory, and probably the right one. It's not like I see the guy taking out the nuke freaks to save the world. He just cares about money."

"But, Frank, there's no reason to believe that he won't try again with a different group of buyers."

"Don't think so. This whole thing has drawn way too much attention now in places the guy doesn't want the spotlight. He's too smart to try anything now. He'll crawl back in his sex slavery ring hole for a few years. By then his access to the U-235 will have dried up too. We believed he was getting it from the stockpile the Russians were dismantling and sending to the Americans under a disarmament treaty. In a few years that supply will be all gone. That's why the higher-ups no longer consider the op worth doing."

"But it was a snatch-and-tell. He could still lead us to the terrorist cell."

"Not if he killed them all. The one guy we were really interested in, Abdul-Majeed, has fallen completely off the radar. Our intel concludes that Waller probably got to him too. Bottom line is there's no one left for him to rat on."

"But he's a bad guy. You just said he'll go back to his sex slavery business now. He has to be stopped."

Frank rose. "That's not our concern. We're officially pulling our tent on this one." He held out a packet of materials. "I got your new assignment here. Early morning flight out to Madrid, then on to wild Rio for a while. You'll get briefed on the way, but it has to do with Chinese ties to some violent antidemocratic leaders in that hemisphere. My counterpart in South America will be meeting you and going over more specifics." When Shaw didn't take the packet, Frank dropped it on the desk.

Shaw was shaking his head. "Tomorrow morning? That's not enough time for me to wind things up here."

Frank, who was heading to the door, stopped and turned back to him. "Wind things up? What the hell is there to wind up?"

"Give me an extra week here, Frank."

"A week! Forget it. Your orders are in that packet. You go to-morrow. It's all set."

"And if I don't?"

Frank drew closer to him. "Do you really want to go there?"

"I think I'm going to have to."

"Because of her? I thought you said there was nothing there."

"I said there was nothing *romantic* there. But I can't leave the lady alone with Waller. That'd be like signing her death warrant."

"Oh come on. We've had this discussion. The guy is not going to try anything with her. This is Provence. And the lady's not some abandoned young girl from a mud-hut town in Guangdong Prov-ince that nobody cares about. She's not in his wheelhouse at all."

"If the guy wants her, he'll take her. That I know. And I'm pretty sure he wants her. So just run some interference for me with the guys up top. Just buy me some time."

But Frank had already turned away. "Be on the flight tomorrow, Shaw. And stop playing guardian angel. The look doesn't wear well on you."

Shaw kicked the door shut behind the man.

CHAPTER

43

I MISSED YOU, Janie."

Waller took her hand.

"I'm sure you had plenty to keep you busy."

"If I may inquire, where did you go today?"

Reggie drew a shallow breath and said, "I went to Les Baux-de-Provence to look at the Goya exhibit."

His smile disappeared. "That is most unfortunate. As I explained, I was hoping to take you there myself."

"I'm sorry," she said curtly.

"And you went alone?"

"Evan—"

"I see. I'm sure you two had a wonderful time," he said with a trace of bitterness.

"Look, I'm sorry. It was just a spur-of-the-moment thing. There are lots of other sites we can visit around here."

This seemed to bolster his spirits. "You're right. Would you then join me for dinner tonight? At my home? I would be honored. I have engaged a local chef."

"I actually already have plans. Bill's coming over and we're going to cook at my place."

"So Bill is coming over. I see. I don't suppose you could cancel on *Bill*?"

"No, but I don't have any plans for tomorrow or the next day."

"Then let me claim that time right now and also every day after that. We can go to Roussillon in the morning, in fact."

Reggie pretended to think about this. "I guess that'll be fine, but let's take it one day at a time."

"Excellent." He bent to kiss her hand.

Reggie turned when she saw the slender man emerge from Kuchin's villa and start toward them. She noted he walked with a slight limp. He was dressed in blue slacks and a sleeveless yellow sweater over a white shirt.

Kuchin straightened. "Ah, Alan, let me introduce you to this lovely young lady. Alan Rice, Jane Collins."

They shook hands.

"Alan is my business associate. He works all the time, but I succeeded in convincing him to join me here for at least a brief time."

She said, "It was a good decision, Alan. There are few places like Provence."

"So Evan keeps telling me."

"Well, enjoy your time here."

"I plan to."

Later, Reggie was sitting on her bed and staring down at the tile floor. In a few days it would all happen. And during that intervening time she could make no mistakes, had to hit her marks to perfection, and still it might all go wrong. She knew that she had Fedir Kuchin where she wanted him. But she had been doing this long enough to know that not everything was always as it seemed to be. That he was cunning was without doubt, so she could not assume that she had deceived him fully. He was playing the role of the elder suitor quite admirably, but that was all it might be, a role.

She put her face in her hands. It was not easy, the career she had chosen. You literally couldn't trust anyone. And there was something else on her mind.

The potential for evil lurks in all of us.

Though she'd openly disagreed with Kuchin's opinion, in fact she could see some truth in it. Indeed, at a certain level what she did could be seen as evil. Judge, jury, executioner. Who was she to make those decisions? What gave her the right? And then there was the reason why she had chosen this life for herself. The image of her dead brother flashed across her mind. Only twelve, so innocent. A tragic loss.

She hurried to the bathroom, turned on the tap, and ran some water over her face. She had to stop thinking about such things. She had to focus.

She was playing Bill against Kuchin for the benefit of the mission. All the time she spent with either man was because of the mission, she told herself. Bill Young was merely a convenient piece on the game board, nothing more or less.

There was a momentary disconnect in her mind, like a flash of lightning's effect on a TV. When her synapses started operating again, the revelation almost made her sick.

If Kuchin thinks I'm really interested in Bill, he might . . .

A part of Reggie was cold and calculating. That part said collateral damage happened, but if the mission was successful the sacrifice was justified. Another part of her was repulsed by an innocent person's possibly dying just so she could claim her target. That, for her, was the epitome of the very evil she professed to be fighting against.

Reconcile that, Reggie.

Yet she had already set everything in motion. How could she possibly stop it now?

CHAPTER

44

Reggie stripped off her clothes and showered, scrubbing so hard it felt like her skin was peeling off her bones. Afterwards she dressed in jeans and a T-shirt, drifted downstairs, found her market basket, and headed up the hill to town. She left through a rear door that opened onto the cobblestone path so she would not have to deal with her neighbor.

An hour later she returned, her basket full of the ingredients for the meal. She prepped the kitchen, freshened up in the bathroom, and put on a white skirt and a light blue tank top. She remained barefoot, as she liked the coolness of the tile floor against her soles. She took time with her hair and face in the bathroom mirror, taking five whole minutes to decide on a bracelet and earrings.

She froze in the middle of this, staring at her made-up face and wide eyes made wider by the magic of eyeliner and mascara.

It's jealousy. Playing one against the other. That's all it is.

Whit's voice sparked across her brain. "So this is all tied to the mission?"

She kept staring at her image in the mirror. "It's always about the mission." One more monster ticked off the list. That was all she wanted. And however she got there it didn't matter.

The sound of the front doorbell almost made her collapse. She looked at her watch. Eight o'clock on the dot. She finished with her primping and rushed down the corkscrew stairs. When she opened the front door Shaw held up two bottles of wine. "The vintner in town swore these were the two best reds he had if my goal was to shamelessly impress a remarkably sophisticated lady of means."

Reggie took one of the bottles and glanced at the label. "He was right. I *am* impressed. These must have cost you a small fortune, even in Provence."

"I've never let money get in the way of fun. And as a lobbyist I'm used to negotiating folks down on things."

She rose up on her tiptoes and kissed him on the cheek. He followed her into the kitchen, his gaze running over the twitch of her hips.

"Do you miss the work?" she asked.

"Not really. I basically was paid an extravagant amount of money to make even more money for people who already had too much of it."

"I've got all the prep work assembled. Your instruments await you." She pointed to a serrated knife and a wooden chopping board set next to a pile of vegetables and tomatoes.

"Okay, but first a thirst quencher." He grabbed the corkscrew off the counter, worked the cork out, poured two glasses, and handed her one. They clinked and sipped. He put down the glass and picked up the knife. "So what are we having?" he asked as he started slicing.

"The main course is a stew with chicken, tomatoes, and vegetables and a few closely guarded secret spices. I've got a cheese platter and crackers with some stuffed olives to munch on beforehand. Then there's salad, some bread and olive oil, and a little creamy dessert that I bought at the bakery because I can't bake. The coffee of course will be from a French press."

"Sounds terrific."

"You know, as depressing as Goya can be, I really did enjoy today."

He glanced over at her as she was stirring the stew. "Me too. Must have been the company."

Reggie frowned. "Okay, in the interests of full disclosure, Evan asked me to go with him to Roussillon tomorrow."

Shaw finished dicing a tomato and started on the celery. "Are you going?"

"I told him I would, but I think I'll drive separately."

"Okay."

"You don't seem okay."

"If it were up to me you'd have nothing to do with the guy."

"But it's not up to you."

"I'm acutely aware of that."

"You really think he's a bad guy?"

"Let's put it like this, I don't want you to feel the brunt of my being correct on that issue."

She smiled. "Well, I take solace in the fact that you'll be here to protect me."

His thrusts at the vegetables became so fierce that she asked, "Is there something wrong?"

He dropped the knife and wiped his hands on a dishtowel. "I've had a change in plans. I have . . . I have to leave tomorrow. To go back home."

The color drained from her face. "Leave? Why?"

"Something's come up with my son."

"Oh, God, I'm sorry. Is it serious?"

"He's not sick or anything. It's more emotional than physical, but I'm his dad and it's important enough to cut short the wonderful time I'm having here."

"I can see why I like you. You have your priorities right."

Shaw looked away, ashamed at her unwittingly misplaced praise. "So I won't be here to protect you."

"I was just joking about that. It's not your job to protect me."

When he glanced at her again she'd turned her attention back to the stove. Shaw sensed something else in her features. Was it relief? Was she actually happy he was leaving?

They chatted about inconsequential things over dinner, and didn't linger over their coffee or dessert.

"I hope everything works out with your son," she said as he helped her clear the table.

"I hope everything works out okay for you too."

"Stop looking so worried. I'll be fine."

Shaw couldn't know that she was thinking, *And now so will you.*

Afterwards, at the front door, Reggie said, "Well, I guess this is it."

"Take care of yourself." He paused and added, "Our time together meant more to me than I think you can imagine."

"Oh, I don't know, I actually have a pretty good imagination."

He thought she was going to leave it at that, but then her arms slipped around him, and he hugged her back. Shaw thought he felt her grip him perhaps a beat too long and a bit too tightly. Yet perhaps she was thinking the same thing about him, he realized.

She kissed him uncomfortably close to the lips and Shaw felt himself maneuvering to reach her mouth on the next attempt. They heard a cough and both glanced over to see one of Waller's men watching them.

Reggie said in a voice loud enough for the man to hear, "Again, I'm sorry you have to leave tomorrow, Bill. Have a good flight back to America."

Then she closed the door. Shaw stared at the lion's head brass knocker for a long moment. Why the hell had she said that? He looked around and saw the muscleman's triumphant smile. The news of Shaw's imminent departure would no doubt be quickly reported to his boss.

"Nice night," the guy said.

Shaw walked back up the darkened path to Gordes. He took the shortcut, taking the ancient steps two at a time. The plane left from Avignon at eight in the morning. Avignon was about a fifty-minute drive, so he would have to leave Gordes early in the morning. And Janie Collins would be off to Roussillon with a man who made a fortune by selling girls into sexual slavery and who also wanted to sell nukes to fanatics.

He could opt not to go, but then Frank's men would come for him and he'd have to go on the run, which meant he would be no help to Janie. He could see no way out of this dilemma. But then again, as Frank had pointed out, he wasn't her guardian. He was here on a mission. That mission had been canceled and he was being deployed somewhere else. He had turned his back on Katie James, a woman who had risked her life for his. So what was making him want to stay and defend the honor and perhaps the life of a woman he barely knew? It was all irrational behavior, and if Shaw had always been one thing it was logical. But he also couldn't ignore what he was feeling.

And then in a burst of extreme lucidity it all came together. The villa next door, the gun, the kick to the kidneys, and continuing to swim in the pool when she knew people were watching. And, finally, playing him against Waller. For that, Shaw suddenly realized, was what she was doing. She was setting the guy up for some reason. But she'd let it be known to Waller's man that Shaw was leaving. The only explanation was that she was trying to make sure Waller would do nothing to harm Shaw. She was protecting *him*.

So engrossed was he in these new troubling thoughts that he never had time to block the descending blow. It connected squarely with the back of his head. His feet went out from under him and he struck the pavement, cutting his knees and elbows on the hard stone. He tried to rise but another blow sent him down face first. He felt himself being bound and then picked up and thrown into a small compartment.

Then for Shaw it all became black.

45

REGGIE ROSE EARLY; the night sky was still in the process of burning into dawn. She opened the window to her bedroom and gazed out. From habit she peered toward the villa next door but saw no activity. Still, she was sure his men would be on guard outside. Roussillon today and dinner at his place tonight and she dreaded all of it even though it could immeasurably aid in bringing Kuchin down. She was steadfastly counting the minutes to when they would end the man's life. It couldn't come soon enough for her.

She showered, dressed, and left her villa by the side door. She had something she wanted to do. No, something she *needed* to do. She walked up the hill to Gordes. There were a few people already about, including the man hosing down the streets. He nodded to her as she passed. Her feet carried her past the town square and around the curve of the road. The hotel was located on the left, through a set of double glass doors. She roused a sleepy-looking clerk at the front desk.

In French she said, "Can you ring Bill Young's room, please? Tell him it's Jane Collins."

The clerk, an older, thin man with puffy white hair and slack cheeks, looked a bit miffed and even suspicious. "It's very early, young lady. I doubt he's even up."

"He's expecting me," she lied.

"At this hour?"

"We're having breakfast together."

The clerk didn't look convinced but he rang the room.

"No answer," he said, putting the phone down.

"He might be in the shower," said Reggie.

"He might be," said the clerk defensively.

"Could you ring him again in a few minutes?"

"I suppose I could if it's necessary."

"It *is* necessary," Reggie said politely but firmly.

The clerk tried again five minutes later.

"Still no answer," he said in a tone that indicated their discussion was over.

"Did you see him go out?"

"No."

Reggie had a sudden thought. "He hasn't checked out, has he?"

"Why would he if he was going to have breakfast with you?"

"Plans sometimes change."

"He didn't check out. At least not while I've been on duty."

"Can you examine the register from before you came on duty?"

The man sighed but did so. "He didn't check out."

"Then can you go to his room?"

"Why?"

"To see if he's okay. He might be ill or he might've fallen."

"I seriously doubt that—"

"He's an American. They sue over everything. If he's sick or hurt and you don't check even though I asked you to it could open the hotel to enormous liability."

Her words had their intended effect. The man grabbed a key and headed up the stairs. Reggie started to follow.

"Where do you think you're going?" he asked.

"I have training in medicine. If he's hurt I can help."

They hurried up the stairs. The clerk knocked, then called out, and then knocked again.

"Unlock the door!" Reggie urged.

"This is very much against hotel policy."

"Oh for God's sake." She grabbed the key, shoved him out of the way, and unlocked the door. She stepped inside with the clerk right behind. It only took her a minute to see that the room was empty, yet all of Shaw's things were still there.

"The bed hasn't been slept in," she said, as she looked accusingly at the clerk.

"It is not my responsibility to determine that all guests are in and accounted for," he added with indignation.

Reggie thought quickly. The man had come on at midnight and Bill had left her home around eleven. It was a five-minute walk-up. What if he had never made it? But she'd made certain Waller's man heard that he was leaving town. He would have no reason to—

"Excuse me?" said the clerk.

Jolted from these thoughts, Reggie saw that he had his hand out for the key. She gave it to him.

"You should report this to the police," she advised.

"I do not think so. He might not have come back to the hotel last night because he had something better to do." He gave her a knowing look. "This *is* Provence after all."

"Can I search his room, then, for a clue to where he might have gone?"

"If *you* attempt that, rest assured that I *will* call the police."

Exasperated, Reggie pushed past him and raced back down the stairs.

She left the building and was hurrying back to her villa when she heard the screech of tires behind her. She turned and saw the car stop in front of the hotel. She flitted into the shadows and watched as three men, one wearing an old-fashioned hat, jumped out of the vehicle and raced into the hotel. She didn't venture closer because she could see that the driver was still in the car.

A few minutes later the men came out again, only now one of them was carrying something. Reggie instantly recognized it as the suitcase that was in Bill Young's room. As the car flew past where she was hiding she saw the man wearing the hat through the car's passenger window. He was on the phone, talking fast, and he didn't look happy at all.

Reggie hurried back to the hotel. The clerk sat mutely behind his desk.

"I saw the men come," Reggie began.

"This is the worst morning of my life," moaned the older man.

"What did they want?"

He stood. "What did they want? What did they want? The same thing you wanted. Who is this man you all want?"

"Did they say anything to you?"

"They said nothing."

"Then why did you let them take his things?"

In a tremulous voice he said, "Because they had guns. Now get out!"

46

Shaw awoke slowly and then tensed. He'd had a cracked skull once before and it felt like he had one now. He flexed his arms and legs but the bindings had been applied with skill. The more he pulled, the tighter they became. He finally sat motionless.

As his eyes adjusted to the darkness he sensed that the room he was in was small and, except for him, empty. There were no windows, so he must be in a cellar or maybe an old storage building. The floor was a concrete slab. The only light came from under the door that was directly in front of him.

With each beat of his heart there was an accompanying throb in his head. He deserved this, for letting someone sneak up on him that easily. Yet he'd let his guard down because he'd been thinking about things he shouldn't have.

Evan Waller could have two possible reasons for kidnapping him. First, he was jealous and wanted to take out his rival. Second, he'd discovered who Shaw really was. The first reason didn't seem so plausible, especially since Janie had let it be known that Shaw was removing himself from the field. But if Waller *had* found out who Shaw was, he wondered why he wasn't dead already. Maybe Waller wanted to gloat first. Maybe he wanted to torture Shaw like he had the terrorists before he'd killed them.

He raised his head slightly when the door opened and the man came in. Silhouetted against the partial darkness, the man said, "Are you awake?"

"Yes."

"Are you hungry or thirsty?"

"Yes."

Shaw figured if they untied him to eat and drink, he might have an opportunity to escape. The man came forward. Shaw didn't recognize him as one of Waller's men. The fellow held a bottle of water in one hand and another object in his other. He unscrewed the bottle top but he didn't untie Shaw. He just held the bottle to his lips and let Shaw drink.

"And just so you know, we have you in a clear firing line."

Shaw looked over the man's shoulder and sensed someone else in the darkness.

The man took the drink away and held out a chunk of bread.

"Bread and water?" asked Shaw.

"Better than nothing."

"Mind telling me why you caved in my skull and kidnapped me?"

"Basically for your own good."

"Why don't I believe that?"

"Doesn't matter to me what you believe."

"Okay, now what?"

"Now you just sit there and chill. We'll treat you well, food, water whenever you want it."

"All that water I'm going to have to take a piss at some point."

He pointed to his left. Shaw saw the toilet in the shadows. "Just let me know."

"Just like that?"

"Like I said, just chill and pretty soon you get out of here."

"Where's Waller?" Shaw said sharply.

"Who?"

"Now I don't believe you again."

The man locked the door behind him, leaving Shaw to puzzle all this over once more. He rocked back and forth in the chair and quickly found that it was bolted to the slab. These folks had put some thought into this. He wondered how far away from Gordes he was. He had no idea how long he'd been unconscious. He might not even be in France any longer.

If these guys weren't with Waller, who were they? No, of course they had to be with him despite his captor's feigned ignorance. He also wondered what Frank was thinking. When Shaw didn't show up at the airport Frank would go to his hotel room. Then he'd con-clude that Shaw had screwed him and gone AWOL.

He leaned back in the chair and took a deep breath. He was out of options. And Janie was probably with Waller right now. Or maybe dead.

47

YOU SEEM preoccupied."

Reggie looked over at Waller as they walked along the streets of Roussillon. They had driven separately, with her following the man's caravan of vehicles. Roussillon held all the charm of the typical Provençal village but with the added burst of ochre on most of the buildings.

"Just tired. I didn't get a lot of sleep last night."

"I hope nothing is troubling you so that you cannot sleep."

The man was dressed in ironed jeans, a white cotton shirt that he wore out, and leather sandals. A Panama hat covered his hairless head, protecting his pale skin from the sun. It gave him a jaunty, relaxed appearance that Reggie was having trouble discounting for some reason.

"Probably just delayed jet lag. This village really is beautiful. The colors are so different from anything I've seen."

"My mother was born here," he said proudly. "I remember it well from when I was a child."

Reggie paused to study a painting in a window, but she was really thinking of something else. She wondered how Fedir Kuchin had been able to escape from behind the Iron Curtain to come here as a young boy, or rather how his parents had with him in tow. Travel was severely restricted back then. His father must have been very high up in the Communist Party to be allowed such freedom. She also wondered how a Frenchwoman from a rural town in Provence had come to marry a Ukrainian communist. Yet perhaps he was telling her a lie. That was actually more likely.

"You like the painting?" Waller asked over her shoulder.

Reggie continued to study the peaceful harbor scene depicted on the canvas. "It's far more pleasant than Señor Goya's works."

"Ah, but this painter will never have the reputation of Goya. Goya did the world an important service."

She turned to him. "How so?"

"He lived during difficult times. War, poverty, cruelty. Thus he painted nightmares. As I told you before, using oils on canvas, he reminded the world that there is evil. That is an important lesson that we should never forget, but unfortunately we do all the time."

"Have you experienced such things?"

"I have read of such things, and they are to be avoided if at all possible."

"But sometimes I guess it's not possible."

"You are an American, so of course you would say such things. You are a superpower, you can do what you want."

Reggie wasn't sure if she saw a spark of envy in his eyes when he said this or if it was her imagination. He took her by the arm.

"I understand that dear Bill has left us."

Reggie almost pulled her arm away. "He had to go home. Some family issue."

"Then I will do what I can to fill any void."

She gave him a searching look and then forced a smile. "Don't make promises you can't keep."

"I never do that."

"So where did you and your family stay when you were here?"

"I will show you."

They walked on, through the center of town. A quarter of a kilometer past that, Waller led her down some worn steps and stopped at a small cottage with a wooden door and two windows in front.

"There," he said.

"It's very quaint."

"My father died in that cottage."

"God, I'm sorry to hear that."

"I'm sure he was too."

He took her arm again. "Now, for the lunch. Down this way. All is arranged. We must eat light because the meal tonight will be substantial."

"I take it you like to be in control."

"There are leaders and there are followers. It is the natural order of things. Would you want a follower leading or a leader following?"

"I guess it depends on where they wanted you to go."

"You are a strange young woman."

"I've heard worse."

"I meant that as a compliment."

His grip tightened on her arm. As they walked along Reggie found herself consumed with worry over what had happened to Bill Young. If Kuchin had harmed him? Then even killing the man would not be enough. Nothing would, if an innocent man had died because of her.

CHAPTER

48

I'VE GOT TO USE the john," Shaw called out into the darkness. "Now."

A minute went by and he thought that no one was going to respond. Then the door opened and the same man appeared. "I told you about the toilet in the corner over there."

"I don't think I can hit the bowl from here. Go figure."

The man stepped forward. "Then I guess I'll have to untie you."

"I guess you will."

"Firing line," the man reminded him.

"Right, got it." Shaw kept his gaze dead on the man as he approached, his muscles tensing, his mind burning through every possible angle and point of attack on the primary and secondary targets. He would put the man between him and the shooter and work his way out of here. It was as solid a plan as he could concoct under the circumstances.

Unfortunately, he never got a chance to execute it.

The man punched the syringe in his arm, right through his shirt.

When Shaw awoke, he was on the floor, his arms tucked under him. He slowly rose, flexing his limbs, trying to bleed circulation back into them. He did his business at the toilet and looked around. The room was empty except for the bolted-to-the-floor chair and a mattress lying in one corner and the toilet. He paced off the parameters of the square. Eight by eight. Sixty-four square feet with a ceiling that was not much higher than he was tall. Walls were stone and solid, no chinks in the mortar, slab floor. He lifted his hand up. The ceiling was plaster.

A rattling sound behind him made Shaw whirl around in time to see a tray of food come through a hinged slot in the lower part of the door that he hadn't noticed before.

He picked up the tray and carried it over to the mattress, sat down and ate, finishing off the bottle of water in a couple of long gulps. He examined the residue on the tray. No utensils, so no sharp edges. Styrofoam plate, plastic bottle.

A few minutes later a voice called out, "Slide it through."

He rose and passed the tray through the slot. It was barely three inches high and he had to lay the bottle of water down. He resumed his pacing, examining every square inch of his prison. His gaze returned to the toilet. He walked over, lifted the tank lid in back, and felt around. A minute later he'd worked free the long piece of metal. He walked over to the door and examined the lock.

Deadbolt. Made things problematic but maybe not impossible.

Plopping down in the chair, he began fashioning the metal into the instrument he needed to attack the lock. Well, actually two instruments since it was a deadbolt. He had no idea what time it was, day or night. They'd taken his watch. But he did start counting off the seconds in his head. He would work from the notion that the meal he'd been given was either lunch or dinner and time it out from there. It wasn't perfect, but it was better than nothing.

After he'd broken the metal in half and worked the pieces into proper shapes using the hard surface of the walls to bend them, he ventured quietly over to the door. He listened for a moment, his ear right against the two-inch-thick wood, at least judging by the width of the slot. The hinges were on the outside of the door, so they were no help to him. It was just him and the lock.

He got down on his hands and knees and edged open the slot a few centimeters. He listened for sounds of breathing, of movement, of a heart thudding too fast—other than his own, that is.

There it was. A foot grazing across the floor. He retreated to the chair and sat down, continuing to count the seconds. He needed to get out of here, fast. But that was obviously not going to happen.

Slow it down, take your time. Speed means mistakes.

His only problem with that philosophy was that Janie might not have a lot of time left. Even if Waller had nothing to do with his kidnapping, the guy was now free to do whatever he wanted to with her. And it sickened Shaw to think what the guy must want whenever he looked at the young woman.

Patience, Shaw, patience.

He fingered the pieces of metal and kept counting the seconds.

49

So how long have you worked with Evan?" asked Reggie.

She was standing on the terrace of Waller's villa looking at the descending sun. Alan Rice was next to her dressed in khaki pants and a loose-fitting shirt with a red kerchief around his neck. If he was looking for a debonair effect, he had missed the mark, she felt. He was sipping from a glass of wine while Reggie worked on some club soda. She'd selected a knee-length skirt and blouse with low heels for the dinner. Her hair was damp and hung to her shoulders. The trip to Roussillon had been relatively uneventful, and Waller had been charming and informative and treated her like a princess. She could see how an unsuspecting woman might be taken in. However, each time she looked at the man all she could see were the hopeless victims of his sick mind. And yet she smiled and was playful and even seducing to him at times, because she had to be.

"Nearly four years," said Rice, setting his glass down on a table and placing his arms on the chest-high stone wall enclosing the terrace. "He's a brilliant businessman."

"He seems quite accomplished at everything. Very worldly."

"That's the exact right word. Worldly."

"How did you two hook up?"

"I was working at a firm in New York. He came there on business. We met. He charmed me, like he does everyone else. One thing led to another. And I came to work for him."

"I assume it's challenging."

"Absolutely. Mr. Waller doesn't suffer fools or anyone else gladly. Makes for a lot of pressure to perform. But you learn a lot."

"Well, then you probably needed a little vacation. I see you're not limping as much. Were you injured?"

"Fell in the shower and messed up my knee awhile back. It's healing fine."

Waller came out a few moments later and Reggie noted that Alan Rice quickly disappeared back into the house. Waller took a sip of his cocktail and said, "I trust Alan was keeping you in good company."

"Absolutely. He really likes working for you."

He sat down on a sofa and motioned for Reggie to join him. "I am fortunate to have him."

She sat near him, their knees almost touching. "What kind of business are you in?"

"The kind that makes money."

"The profit motive drives you, I guess," she said coolly.

"When one grows up without money, yes, it can be a motivating force."

"But you came to Provence as a child. You must have not been in too desperate circumstances. Traveling here from Canada couldn't have been cheap, even back then."

He flashed a look that was inscrutable. Yet for one terrible instant Reggie thought she had gone too far.

"It's none of my business, of course," she added hastily.

"No, it's all right. As I mentioned, my mother was French. So we did not have to pay to stay anywhere. We had the family cottage. And back then we came by boat, third-class steerage. Followed by third-class steerage on a train. It was very cheap, if not very comfortable."

"Of course."

"And once one arrived in Provence, *how* one got there became irrelevant." He stood and looked out at the breathtaking view of the Luberon valley. "It is glorious."

She joined him. "It is." She added, "My mother would have said that God was in fine form when he created Provence."

"A religious woman, I take it?"

"A good Catholic, just like me."

"On her dying bed my mother said to me, 'Never forsake your

faith in God. It will keep you, in the good and especially in the bad.' She was a wise woman."

"And has it kept you, in good and bad?"

"No life is without pain. I am rich now, but once I was not. Once I . . ." He smiled. "I think dinner is ready. You will sit next to me. Alan is joining us as well. You should ask him about his theory on French versus California wines. It is most interesting. He is completely wrong, of course, but it is worth hearing nonetheless." He walked her into the dining room.

After the meal was done, they had more drinks and then dessert out on the lower patio next to the pool. Rice joined them for a few minutes but then abruptly left. Whether this was on a high sign from his employer or not, Reggie didn't know. Waller stared moodily at the water.

"You have a pool at your villa, correct?"

Reggie nodded. "I swim. In fact, after this meal I should probably swim a couple of miles to work it off."

He waved this comment away. "Ridiculous. You are in superb shape."

"You don't have much fat on you either."

"I do what I can," he said modestly. "Americans eat too much garbage, but you have obviously escaped that trap."

"Being wealthy gives me certain advantages many Americans don't have. I can afford to eat right, and I have the time to exercise."

"Here, a peasant can go to market and get the freshest ingredients for a few euros. And they walk to market and thus get their exercise." He paused and added, "But I judge no one."

Reggie felt her face flush uncontrollably at this statement. Fortunately, Waller was not looking at her. *You only judged hundreds of thousands of people to their deaths.*

She rose. "Thank you for a wonderful day."

He said, "You are not leaving."

She flinched for an instant, since it was not clear if that was a question or a command. "It's been a long day."

"But it is still early."

"Perhaps for you."

"I wish very much that you would stay."

"I'm sure I'll see you soon enough. And not everyone gets their wish."

He rose. "You will not reconsider? I would like to get to know you better."

"I need to swim."

"You can swim here."

"Good night, Evan. I can show myself out."

"There are few who would venture to disagree with me."

"I'm not disagreeing with you."

"But—"

She stood on tiptoes and pecked him on the cheek. "It's all in the timing, actually."

After she closed the door of her villa securely behind her, Reggie spit on the floor and then wiped off her mouth.

50

"Yes, Whit, I understand the situation quite clearly, perhaps better than you."

Professor Mallory sat at his desk in his study at Harrowsfield, attempting to light his pipe at the same time he was clenching the phone against his cheek with his left arm.

"I took the action that I deemed most prudent." Mallory paused as a string of words came over the line from the obviously upset Irishman.

Mallory finally got the pipe going and took a moment to suck greedily on the stem. He flicked the match out and dropped it on his desk, where it continued to smolder.

"I can't see where it's robbed you of any necessary manpower, but if you require reinforcements I can have them to you tomorrow. Yes, yes, well I can do the math too. You have four men for the out-side and then the three of you on the inside. If you think that's insuf-ficient?" He paused and listened some more. "Yes, I have talked to Regina, and no, she doesn't know about it. What really would be the point? Have the final details been worked out? I see. Projection equipment?" He listened some more. "Yes, I suppose that would come in rather handy. All right. Yes, just let me know."

Mallory put the phone down and puffed on his pipe. He looked up to see Liza standing by the doorway.

"Problems?" she asked.

Mallory cleared his throat. "Nothing unmanageable. Whit is a bit put out, but he'll get over it."

Liza frowned. "We're too close to D-day, aren't we, to have any-one *put out* over anything?"

"It'll be fine, Liza, don't worry."

"And you're telling me you're not concerned?"

"I'm always concerned until my people are back here safely. But they have everything under control and the plan is a sound one. In fact, Regina came up with a new wrinkle that I think will work out quite nicely."

"There *is* one flaw in your plan," pointed out Liza.

"No plan is perfect, and we had to put this one together rather on the fly."

"But they aren't even aware of the potential pitfall. You know I disagreed with you on that."

"Without that we wouldn't have gotten our shot at Kuchin."

"Yes, but that might be the difference between 'your people' coming home safely or not."

"I am quite aware of the risks," Mallory said a bit indignantly.

"You are, but they aren't, not fully."

"There is inherent risk in everything we do."

"Sometimes I wonder."

"Wonder what?"

"We sit here in our cozy old English country house and plan these things and then send them out to execute our plans."

"They participate in creating those plans."

"Good night, *Professor*."

She left Mallory to angrily puff on his pipe, until he knocked out the wedge of tobacco, stuffed the pipe in his jacket pocket, and sat there moodily in his old leather chair.

Whit sat gazing at the phone. Sometimes he just didn't get Mallory. No, that was wrong. He almost never understood the man. The professor had handed Whit another task at a critical time in their mission and the Irishman didn't appreciate it one bit. Babysitting Bill Young was not something he'd signed on for. He pocketed his phone and marched down the hallway.

"Give me the key, Niles," he said to the man stationed there, and he handed Whit the key.

Niles Jansen knocked on the door and called out, "Away!" Then he pulled his gun and pointed it at the door as Whit inserted the key. The door clicked open and Whit stood just inside the doorway.

Shaw stood against the far wall, staring back at him.

"Ready to let me go?"

"Sit," ordered Whit.

Shaw looked at the gun pointed at him and slowly walked to the chair and sat down. Whit moved forward a few inches.

"You know, you look familiar," said Shaw.

"I look like a lot of guys."

"So what can I do for you?"

"You can tell me what you're really doing in France."

"I'm on holiday. Why are you here?"

Whit leaned against the wall. "Lobbyist from D.C. who can scale walls and disarm people? You really think we're buying that?"

Shaw didn't say anything for a long moment. "I'm a *retired* lobbyist. And I was supposed to be returning to the States to be with my son. You obviously had a different idea."

"You look too young to be retired."

"I made my money and I wanted out. Is that a crime? Is that the reason you bashed me in the head and are holding me prisoner here?"

"Like you were told before, chill and you'll be fine."

"Yeah, but what about Janie Collins?"

"Who?"

Shaw crossed his arms and studied the other man. "What are you planning?"

"I don't know what you're talking about."

"But you're working together."

Whit shook his head slowly. "Again, don't know what you're talking about."

"Sure you do. I told Janie I was a retired lobbyist. I scaled her wall and disarmed her. No one else knew about that."

"Those things are easy enough to find out."

"No they're not. And why would you want to find them out?"

"So you're not going to tell me why you're here?"

"You first."

"Then you can just rot in here." Whit turned to leave.

Shaw hesitated and said, "Take care with Waller, he's not who you think he is."

Whit slowly turned back around. "What the hell do you know about it?"

"More than you, apparently. By the way, I just remembered where I saw you. Kayaking. You were tailing us. You're after Waller, aren't you?"

"Don't know what you're smoking."

"He's a dangerous guy."

"Really?"

Shaw knew he shouldn't do it, but his concern for Janie overrode his professional instincts for secrecy.

"Waller runs a global prostitution ring. He takes women from Asia and Africa and sells them into slavery in the West."

When this revelation only raised mild interest in Whit's features, he added, "He was also trying to sell uranium to some Islamic fundamentalists before he apparently killed them all after a disagreement."

"Terrorists?" exclaimed Whit.

"They probably screwed him somehow and he made them pay for it. He's a bad guy from top to bottom. And he has an eye for Janie, although I guess now I know that's not her real name. Whatever you guys have planned, you better account for Waller figuring some of it out beforehand. And you better start worrying that Janie doesn't disappear before you even get to your ground zero."

"And why are you telling me this?"

"I think you know why. If he gets Janie it's all over."

Whit slammed the door behind him and locked it. Shaw heard the two men outside talking fast. Then he heard footsteps as the men moved off.

He sat down in the chair. His initial instincts had been right and wrong. Janie Collins was not who she claimed to be. But she was not here to interfere with Shaw's mission; she hadn't even known about it, apparently. They'd gotten suspicious about Shaw, but didn't know why he was here. They had been working at cross-purposes.

So now the questions were clear. Why were they after Waller? And how were they planning to do it?

Shaw looked around at the four walls. He needed to get out of here more than ever. He had a sinking feeling that whatever plan they had, it would not be good enough. And chances were very good that Waller would kill them instead.

51

Reggie counted off her strokes, flipped, and headed back the other way. She was swimming faster than normal, so much faster, in fact, that she lost count and banged her head on the side of the pool. She floated to the top, rubbed her skull, and looked around. Waller's villa was dark. She eyed the wall separating the two properties but saw no spies there either. She treaded water for a bit and then swam to the steps and climbed out of the pool. She toweled off, grabbed her phone, and headed into the house. When she glanced down at the phone screen, she caught a quick breath. She had a text message. It was only one word. "NOW." It was their highest-level alert message.

She walked quickly inside and up to her bedroom, where she made the call.

"We have to meet," said Whit.

"Meet? When?"

"Right now."

"It's one o'clock in the morning."

"Now, Reg."

"What's wrong?"

"A new wrinkle you need to know about."

"Jesus, Whit—"

"Usual place." He clicked off.

She threw on some clothes and turned out all the lights as though she was going to bed. She went to the lower level of the villa, opened the rear door, made sure it was clear, and then hurried down the darkened path.

A few minutes later, taking great pains to make sure no one was following her, Reggie arrived at the rendezvous point. A hand on her shoulder almost made her scream.

Whit appeared from out of the darkness, his expression stony.

"What the hell is going on?" Reggie asked, clutching her chest. "Every time I have to sneak out it gives them an opportunity to become suspicious."

"It couldn't be avoided," said Whit as he sat down on the stone bench.

"Okay, it's obviously important, so tell me."

"We got new orders from the professor."

"What?"

"Let me rephrase that. *I* got new orders from the professor and already carried them out."

Reggie stared down at him in amazement. "What are you talking about?"

"He ordered us to take your boy out of the equation."

"My boy?"

"Bill Young."

"What! You didn't—"

"He's okay. We just did a snatch. He's resting comfortably."

"Are you crazy? He's—"

"It wasn't my call, okay? And the prof didn't want you to know. But I didn't like that. So I'm here telling you."

"Why would Mallory want you to kidnap Bill? He was leaving France."

Whit looked put out. "I didn't know that."

"I didn't have a chance to tell you."

"Probably wouldn't have mattered. The prof wanted him out of the way, and it was probably a good call considering what I just learned."

"What are you talking about?" Reggie said slowly.

"Your boy's not what he appeared to be." Whit paused. "I think he might be a cop or something. Maybe in counterintelligence, Interpol, something like that."

Now Reggie sat down on the stone bench next to him. "Why?"

"Things he said."

Reggie looked away.

"You don't seem shocked by this."

"I knew Bill had disappeared from his hotel. When I went to check, I saw some men go into his room and take his things. The clerk later told me they had guns."

"Well, thanks for telling me that."

"Tell me everything. From the moment you took him."

Whit laid it all out. He finished with, "He said to be careful whatever we were planning. He said Kuchin runs an international sex slavery ring. He snatches girls from Asia and Africa and sells them in the West. He also attempted to do a deal with some Islamic terrorists, sell them some nukes or something."

"Wait a minute. Does he know Waller is really Kuchin?"

"Don't think so, no. At least he never used that name. Anyway, Young said Kuchin ended up killing the Muslims. Guess they had a falling-out or something. But he said Kuchin definitely had an eye for you and to worry about you disappearing before we could make our move. He also said chances were pretty good that Kuchin would figure out at least partly what we were up to." Whit stopped talking and sat back. "I guess I misjudged the bloke. Turns out we were sort of working on the same side, but didn't know it."

"But if he doesn't know about Kuchin's past why is he after him?"

"Maybe the terrorist stuff, or the sex slavery ring."

"And Bill is okay?"

"Except for a little knot on his head, yeah, he's fine. Tough guy, but then we knew that, didn't we?"

"I appreciate you telling me, Whit."

"No secrets, right? But look, Reg, what Young said gave me an idea."

"What?"

"That Kuchin killed all those Muslims. We can use that to our advantage."

"How do we do that?"

He sat forward. "Here's how."

CHAPTER

52

Shaw leaned away from the door in frustration. Attempting to pick a deadbolt lock in near-total darkness using part of the guts of a toilet bowl tank could *only* lead to frustration, he told himself. There were over eighty-six thousand seconds in a day. Having counted over a hundred thousand seconds off in his head, and nearly driving himself mad in the process, the best Shaw could figure it was either the middle of the night or the middle of the day. He stepped forward and listened at the door. No steps, no breathing. And yet a solid door was between him and freedom. If he tried to break it down, they would be waiting for him with guns. He slumped back in the chair and tried to think of another way.

His motivation to get free had changed, but really only slightly. If these men were working with Janie Collins, that meant she wasn't alone in dealing with Waller. So if he tried to do anything to her at least she'd have backup. But he felt certain they weren't cops. The guy he'd talked with had seemed surprised about the sex slave trade and the nuclear terrorist pieces. So if they didn't know about his illegal activities, then what was their motivation to take the guy down? And if they weren't the authorities, why keep Shaw alive? A bullet to the head and a shallow grave in the middle of nowhere would've made more sense.

Thoroughly confused, Shaw sat in the chair and fiddled with the two pieces of metal he'd fashioned. Two useless pieces of metal from a toilet. If Frank could only see him now. As he glanced over at the commode, something occurred to him. He looked at the door and then glanced back at the toilet. Checking the jury-rigged tool in his hand, he thought it might just be possible.

* * *

"And how was your swim?" asked Waller. They were walking up to the village of Gordes the next afternoon.

"Refreshing. Did you enjoy watching?"

He looked taken aback. "Pardon?"

"I thought I saw someone peeking over the wall. I assumed it was you, but I guess it could have been one of your men." She glanced back at the pair of security guards trailing them.

"It was not me," said Waller stiffly. "And it was not one of my men."

"Perhaps I was mistaken then."

"Yes, you were."

Reggie wasn't sure why she'd made such a provocative statement to the man. No, maybe she did know. It was better than scratching his eyes out. Sex slaver. Nuclear terrorist. She drew a calming breath and managed a smile. "The big market is tomorrow. It's far larger than the one you saw before."

"I look forward to it," said Waller.

After finishing their shopping they passed by the church again. "Have you been in yet?" asked Reggie.

"Not yet. I will attend Mass on Sunday."

"I've been inside. It's quite lovely. Would you like to see it?"

Waller looked unsure, glancing back at the two guards. "All right. For a few minutes. Then we must eat. I am hungry. And after the market tomorrow I want to take you to Pont du Gard to see the aqueduct. Then we can have dinner near there at a truly delightful restaurant. Then the next day, Gigondas."

"You have it all planned out?"

"Of course I do." This blunt statement was softened by his smile.

They walked down the narrow alley and tugged open the church door. Inside it was noticeably cooler. They moved forward and saw the stairs leading up to the bell tower that was the highest point in Gordes. The two bodyguards, one of whom was Pascal, waited just inside the entrance.

As they approached the altar, Reggie genuflected and crossed herself; Waller did likewise. An elderly priest walked out and saw them. He spoke to them in French and Reggie answered before the priest moved on.

She said to Waller, "He just asked—"

"Yes, I know, my French is as good as my English, perhaps better. The church is closed, but we will only be a few minutes."

Reggie looked around. "Centuries of worshippers have passed through here. It's remarkable."

In a low voice Waller said, "It is glorifying to be in the presence of such power."

"Power for good," amended Reggie as she stared at the cross on the altar.

"In a church what else could there be?"

"I don't attend Mass as regularly as I should."

"We will go together Sunday."

"That's not possible, because I'm leaving on Saturday."

He looked stunned by this. "And going where?"

"Back home, to the States."

"Can you not change your plans?"

"Why?"

"Because I am asking you to. I want to spend more time with you here."

"But my villa lease will be up."

"I will take care of that. I will either extend it or you can stay at my villa."

"Evan, I don't think—"

He gripped her arm. "I will take care of it."

She winced at the pressure he was applying.

He slowly released her. "You have bewitched me. I am not in my right mind around you. I must watch myself."

"Perhaps I should watch myself too," she said, attempting a smile.

"But truthfully we must spend more time together. And when I go back to Canada it is a short trip to the United States. We can see each other there."

"You hardly know me."

"I am a quick judge of people. In fact, I can see right through them." He laughed in a way that made Reggie's throat go dry. But she had one more thing to do. It was the reason she'd brought him here.

"It's time to go back. I have a few errands to run in my car after lunch," she said.

Waller turned to head back the way they'd come.

"No," said Reggie. She looked mischievous and playful, a performance she'd worked on in the mirror at the villa. "I found a shortcut."

"What?"

"Follow me." She started off toward the stairs heading to the lower level.

"Where are you going?" he asked.

She turned back. "A shortcut, like I said." She glanced over at Pascal, who was watching her closely. "He can come too," she said with a laugh. "I'm not leading you into some ambush, come on." She skipped down the steps.

Waller nodded to Pascal and they followed. Reggie was waiting for them at the bottom. She led them farther into the bowels of the holy place. Reggie glanced once more at Pascal and saw that he had his hand near his gun. A minute later she pushed open the door and stepped out into daylight. She pointed to her left. "See? A shortcut down the cliffs. The passage was cut right through the stone. The villas are right down those steps."

Waller looked surprised and also impressed. "I passed by this door before and wondered where it led."

"Now you know," she said.

Now you know.

CHAPTER

53

I WANT TO SEE HIM," said Reggie.

"That is definitely not a good idea," replied Whit.

They were once more meeting at the Abbaye de Sénanque book-shop.

"I don't care if you don't think it's a good idea or not. I want you to take me to him."

"Does the professor know—"

"I'm not feeling that charitable toward the man right now. So take me to see Bill."

Shaw was sitting in the chair when the knock came.

"Away from the door!" called out a voice.

When it opened, Shaw blinked to adjust to the new level of light. Then he saw her standing there.

Reggie said, "I'm sorry about this. I had no idea what had happened to you."

"Then let me go."

"That won't be happening, Paddy," said Whit, stepping forward to stand next to Reggie.

Shaw noted the two other men at the doorway. They didn't have their guns out, probably her doing. But he assumed they were armed.

"Then tell me what's going on," said Shaw. "Maybe I can help you."

"Same answer as the last one," countered Whit.

Shaw shot him a glance. "Did you tell her about Waller, about his background?"

Reggie spoke up. "Yes, he did. And something you told us will actually help."

"What?"

"I can't say."

"Why are you after him?"

"Why were you after him?" replied Reggie.

Shaw didn't say anything.

"Nuclear terrorism?" she suggested.

"He's a bad guy," said Shaw. "He needed to be taken down. That's all I can tell you."

"So then why were you leaving town?" asked Reggie. "Before he was taken down?"

Shaw glanced over at Whit. "Who are you with? Interpol? Mossad? MI6 maybe? *Paddy.*"

Reggie started to say something, but Whit let out a loud grunt. "No one you would recognize," she finally said. "But why were you leaving town?"

"Op got pulled," said Shaw finally.

"Because he killed the terrorists? That doesn't mean he won't try again."

"I don't make the orders, I just follow them."

"And so do we," snapped Whit.

"How did you figure things out with me?" asked Reggie.

"Right before they caved in my skull it sort of all came together. The last piece was you tipping Waller's guy I was no longer an issue."

"I didn't want anything to happen to you."

"When are you going to do it?" Shaw asked.

"Okay, little visit's over," said Whit.

Shaw ignored him and kept his gaze on Reggie. "Why did you come to see me?"

"To tell you that I was sorry."

"Look, if Waller can get the drop on—"

She cut in. "He is very good, no doubt. But so are we. This is what we do."

"What is?" he shot back.

"As soon as it's over you'll be released unharmed," said Reggie.

She paused. "I saw some men leave your hotel with your things. One of them was wearing a hat and he didn't look happy."

"I'm sure he's not very happy with me."

"We can contact him, tell him you're all right. That this was not your fault."

"I'll take care of it. But let me ask you this. If you fail and Waller kills all of you, what then?"

Whit smirked. "Then it'll be up to you to get yourself out of here. Not too hard for a tough guy like you, right?"

Shaw wasn't giving up. "Tell me your plan and I'll point out the holes."

Whit shook his head. "And then maybe you escape and muck everything up? I don't think so."

"But—" began Reggie.

"No, Reg," snapped Whit, and then his face contorted because of this mistake.

Shaw looked at her. "Reg, for Reggie?"

"Thank you again," she said. She held out her hand. Whit moved to stop her, but Shaw was already clutching it. His fingers felt like they were on fire. When he looked at her he could sense she'd had a similar reaction.

Before the door closed Shaw called out, "I hope you get the son of a bitch."

His last image of the woman was her eyes staring at him before the door shut between them.

He rushed to the door and listened. He heard one word clearly. "Market."

Shaw groaned and slapped the door.

54

WHAT, Evan's not here with you?"

Reggie turned to see Alan Rice watching her. He walked across the main street in Gordes and joined her. "I thought his goal was to monopolize every minute of your time. And yet here you are, free and alone."

"I guess he had something better to do right now. Plus I had some errands to run. I just came here to pick up a few things."

"Do you have time for some coffee? With the sun behind the clouds it's gotten a bit nippy. I could use some java." He pointed behind her to a café on a side street near the Pol Para Museum situated in the village square.

They sat inside, ordered their drinks, and Rice didn't break his silence until each had their cups. "Evan is quite infatuated with you, I'm sure you know that."

"I enjoy his company. He's a nice man."

"No, he's really *not* a nice man, Ms. Collins."

"Pardon me?" Reggie said in surprise. "I thought you worked for him."

"I do, so I know him intimately. He is an enormously successful businessman. But nice does not enter the equation."

"And why are you telling me this?"

"I want to be sure that you know what you're getting into."

"I wasn't aware that I was *getting into* anything."

"I can assure you that Evan does not see it that way."

"So what do you suggest that I do about it?"

"You can leave Provence."

"I'm actually planning to leave on Saturday. If I do, you're saying this enormously successful businessman with a possessive nature would just let it drop?"

Rice sipped his coffee and then fiddled with his spoon. "Perhaps."

"So has this sort of thing happened before with Evan?"

"You mean with other women? Yes, it has."

"And what happened to the other women?"

"I don't really know."

"You're not being very convincing."

"That's ironic, considering I'm telling the truth."

"So who are you protecting here? Me or your boss?"

"I thought it was clear. I'm protecting Evan. I don't even really know you."

"I appreciate your frankness. So protecting him from himself?"

"That's one way of looking at it."

"Well, for me, it's the *only* way of looking at it."

"So will you leave? Now? Don't wait until Saturday."

Reggie rose and put down some euros for her coffee. "I don't think so, no. I've made plans to go with him to the market tomorrow, and I plan to follow through with it."

Rice stood. "Leaving now really would be the wisest thing you could do, trust me."

"That's the rub, Alan. I'm having a hard time trusting anyone right now."

A few minutes later Alan Rice stood next to a treadmill where his boss was performing his daily jog. Waller wiped his face with a towel and drank from a bottle of water as he increased the incline on the machine.

"You look troubled, Alan."

"I just had a chat with our little friend."

"Our little friend?"

"Jane Collins."

Waller slowed the machine and reduced the incline. "Why did you do that?"

"I'm worried."

"About what. We had the woman checked out, correct?"

"Absolutely, you saw the reports yourself."

"Then what is the problem?"

"I see how you look at her."

Waller slowed to a fast walk on the treadmill. "You see how I *look* at her?" he said questioningly.

"Please don't be upset, Evan. It's just that in the past you—"

The next instant Rice lay on the floor, blood flowing from his mouth. Waller stood over him, his hand cut from where it had struck the other man's tooth.

Waller bent down and pulled Rice to his feet. "Put some ice on that before it starts to swell," he said calmly.

"I was only trying to protect you," Rice stammered, clutching his jaw.

"If I were in need of protection that would be admirable. However, I am not." Waller stared fiercely at the other man. "You are my associate, Alan. You are my underling. Never forget your place. You are not and never will be my equal. Do you understand precisely what I am telling you?"

"I understand."

Waller put an arm around his shoulders. "Good, then we will speak of this no more."

Rice left to put ice on his injured jaw, leaving Waller alone to stare moodily out the window. He would never allow anyone to question his judgment or authority. Rice had come very close to doing both. Had there been anyone else in the room to hear this, Waller probably would have ordered his "right-hand man" put to death. However, he had displayed an alarming degree of independence just now, truly alarming.

And yet was there truth in his words? Did he need protection, essentially from himself? Yes, he was infatuated with Jane Collins; many men would be. Her close proximity aided in that infatuation. Yet it was much more than that. The woman was resisting him— now, that was the challenge. She was independent, outspoken, stubborn, unwilling to be led or manipulated. Waller found that he wanted desperately to possess her.

And he would. Of that he was convinced.

CHAPTER

55

REGGIE ROSE early and swam in the pool before first light had broken. It was usually this way with her on the final day of a mission. She always did something pleasurable, as it might be the last day of her life. The water felt cool against her skin as she sliced through it, counting her strokes, taking her practiced breaths. She didn't bother to see if anyone was spying on her from the villa next door. It didn't matter anymore.

She finished, went inside, up the corkscrew stairs to her bathroom, and stripped off her bikini. The next instant she whirled to stare at the far corner of the space.

She was sure she'd heard something, seen a shadow lingering . . . But there was nothing.

She locked the door and took a shower, letting the hot water slide over her, seeing if it could overwhelm the chills. She was nervous before the end of every mission, when the person she planned to kill would discover who she really was.

She thought now of Bill Young. She knew she shouldn't have gone to see him. Yet something inside her, perhaps deeper than she had cared to delve for a long time, had forced her to do so. It wouldn't matter now. After today, none of it would matter. What she felt. Or what he felt. They would never see each other again. She caught her gaze in the mirror as she recalled the spark between them when their hands touched. How he looked at her. How she had to work so hard to control herself around him.

Stop it, Reggie. Just stop it now.

She dried her hair and dressed in slacks, sneakers, and a loose-fitting shirt over a tank top with a bandanna in her hair. The shoes were a practical choice in case she had to run. The bandanna conceivably could be used as a garrote. Yet if it came to that desperate recourse, her chances of survival were very low. The mental images of Fedir Kuchin's victims, housed in her brain for weeks now, paraded past her.

Today is for all of you, she thought.

She looked out her window onto the cobbled path below. People on foot were already starting up the hill to the market. They looked happy, eager, excited. She was all those things too; well, perhaps not happy, not yet. Small cars and vans moved slowly past, their wares crammed into the tiny spaces. As she stood there, first Whit and then Dom trudged past carrying large duffels. Neither man looked up at her. In a few moments they were gone from her sight. The new wrinkle Whit had added was a brilliant one, she thought. Now all she had to do was execute it properly.

She closed the window, went downstairs, and made her coffee. She lingered over the cup and the toast and fried eggs she'd made. She kept taking steady breaths, willing away any nerves, going over the plan again and again both for reassurance and also as a way to minimize any potential mistakes. She had met one final time with Whit and Dom and they had taken her through the revised plan. The equipment Dom had purchased in Avignon would work perfectly. Everything was loaded and ready to go. Each man complimented her on the idea.

"Makes for a right fitting show for old Kuchin," Whit had said.

"A right fitting show," repeated Reggie now as she washed her cup and dishes and set them back in the cabinet.

She walked to the terrace and watched as the sun marched upward, firing the sky. The ridge of mountains and the plain of the valley came alive as though administered a transfusion of fresh blood. Reggie's nerves faded, her breathing returned to normal, and her features became determined and finally set in stone. It was time.

If today was to be her final day, Reggie swore that no matter what else happened it would be Fedir Kuchin's last as well. Some things were just worth the price.

* * *

Back at Harrowsfield, Miles Mallory was on the telephone. The call was from just a few kilometers outside of Gordes, and the caller was not Whit or Dom. It was Niles Jansen, and he was telling Mallory things he did not want to hear.

"She actually went to see this man?" Mallory snapped into the phone. "He knows we're going after Kuchin?"

Jansen answered. Mallory exclaimed, "And he's with some law enforcement organization?" Jansen said something in response.

"Wait for my phone call back," ordered Mallory. "I need to think this through."

He replaced the receiver and sat back in his chair. It had been unbelievably reckless of Whit to tell Reggie that they had Bill Young captive. The plan had been to let the man go after the mission was finished. But Mallory wasn't certain that was an option any longer. If people ever found out about what they were doing . . . He absently pulled his pipe from his pocket, looked at it, and then threw it across the room where its stem cracked against the mantel.

He called Jansen back. His message was terse. "Whether the mission succeeds or not, he cannot live. Do it now." He put the phone down, sat forward, and put his face in his hands.

"Miles?"

He looked up to see Liza staring at him. "What's wrong?" she said.

He shook his head, started to speak, but then lowered his eyes and stared at the floor, his hands dangling uselessly in front of him like he'd just suffered a stroke.

"Miles!"

"Not now, Liza, please, not now."

56

Niles Jansen checked the Glock 17's magazine, which carried nineteen bullets in an extended double-column box configuration. He'd worked as support on three missions with Whit and Reggie, but he'd never been ordered to do something like this before. He was nervous but determined. He chambered a round and drew from his pocket a capped syringe that was marked with a poison label. Jansen was alone, so the plan was to have the prisoner handcuff himself to the chair and then he would administer the poison. The prisoner, he believed, would just assume it was another sleeping solution. It would be easy. It turned out not to be.

He walked slowly down the hallway and then stopped, unable to believe what he was seeing. Water was pouring out from under the locked door and also through the food slot.

He rushed forward calling out, "What the hell happened?"

"The pipe on the toilet broke and the whole damn room is flooding. I'm up to my ass in water," Shaw yelled back. "Where's the water cutoff?"

"Step away from the door."

"Step away from the door? I'm crunched against a wall. The whole building's going to come down. I've been screaming for somebody for an hour."

Jansen reached the door and pulled out his keys. His plan was to open the door and then quickly step aside as the water rushed out. Things did not go according to plan, however.

The door being knocked off its hinges was the first indication of things going awry. The door landing on top of Jansen was the second. Shaw dropped the heavy toilet he had used to bash his way to freedom, grabbed the man's gun, and pulled the stunned Jansen up. When the object fell to the floor Shaw stooped and picked it up. It was the syringe. He looked at the man.

"Was this meant for me?"

Jansen said nothing. Shaw shook him. "I'm about a second from putting a round in your brain. Was this meant for me?" He placed the muzzle against the man's forehead. "Now."

Jansen said, "I was just following orders."

"Whose? One of the other guys here? The woman?"

"No. They don't know."

Shaw knocked Jansen unconscious with a blistering left hand that carried about as much pure anger as Shaw had felt in a while. He laid him back down, pocketed the syringe, rushed back into the room, turned the water off where the commode used to be, and then ran back out. The water hadn't been up to his butt, of course, but just high enough to reach the level of the door slot and start pouring out. Shaw had used a plastic water bottle to stop up the hole in the floor revealed after he'd worked the commode loose using his nifty homemade tools.

He carried Jansen over his shoulder, the gun held out in front of him just in case anyone else was around who wanted a piece of him. He used a lamp cord to tie him up, lifted his cell phone and his car keys, kicked open the front door, leapt off the short stack of steps, and climbed into a two-door gray hatchback parked in front of the house.

Ten seconds later he was flying down the road. The car had GPS and he inputted his destination with jabs of his finger.

Gordes.

He checked the clock on the dash that also had the current date.

Market day.

He might still have time. He floored the little car and reached a main road. He punched in a number. Frank's voice came on. When he heard Shaw he started yelling.

"Shut up, Frank, and listen."

"Me listen! Shaw, I will have your ass — "

"They're going to hit Waller."

That caught Frank's attention. "What? Who is?"

Shaw filled Frank in on all that had happened. "I'm pretty sure it's going down today. I need some backup."

"There is none. We pulled all our assets from the area."

"There's nobody?"

"I've been spending all my time covering for your ass with my bosses. They think you went nutso over this chick. They are pissed."

"I can't do this by myself. I need some help. Waller has a lot of muscle."

Frank was silent.

"Hey," Shaw cried out, "talk to me."

"There is one asset in the area."

"Who?"

"Me."

"Why are you still here?"

"Forget it, I just am."

"Why, Frank?"

"Because I've been looking for you, that's why. Happy? Now how do you want to play this?"

"Here's how." Shaw started talking fast.

When he was done Frank said, "Do you really trust this woman?"

"To the extent I trust anybody, yeah, I trust her."

"Well, I hope to hell you're right."

Shaw clicked off and floored it. The hatchback's engine whined to near its breaking point as the Provençal countryside whizzed by.

He reached the turnoff to Gordes, saw the traffic backup, ditched the car, and sprinted up the winding road. Reaching and clearing the side street leading to the twin villas, he saw no guard in front of Waller's place, which meant he was probably not there. He looked around at the groups heading up to the market and the line of cars and vans filled with goods for sale. Walking up to one slow-moving truck that had racks of clothing and hats piled in the back, he pulled out some euros, and a minute later Shaw was covered up with a colorful poncho, a wide-brimmed canvas hat, and a cheap pair of sunglasses that the driver had thrown in from his own pocket for free.

He jumped in the back of the truck and got a ride up to town. There he moved quickly through the crowds, slouching to disguise his height. His gaze darted to all corners, looking for Reggie, Waller, or anyone else of interest. Finally his observation paid off when he passed by a side alley, glanced down it, and then drew back. He waited for a few moments, then pulled out his phone and made the call to Frank, telling him what to do.

That done, he checked the gun he'd stolen. You never went into possible combat without doing something that basic. The Glock 17 had been designed in the 1980s by its namesake Gaston Glock, an Austrian who had never built a gun before. What he did have was a lot of knowledge about advanced synthetic polymers. So he made, basically, the world's first plastic handgun. It beat out H&K, SIG Sauer, the Italians' Beretta, the Browning, and the top-notch Steyr favored by special forces personnel in a competition to arm the Austrian army. Its success around the world had been immediate and immense. Seven out of ten cops in America carried it in their holster. And yet with all that, just like any other weapon it wasn't infallible. Shaw was stunned he hadn't noticed it before.

The muzzle was cracked. It must've happened from the collision of the heavy door and heavier toilet against the weapon's polymer frame. Thank God he hadn't had to fire the pistol. It probably would've exploded in his hand. A Glock could fire wet all day. No gun, however, could fire safely with a damaged barrel. Now he had no weapon and no way to get one. Frank was at least thirty minutes away and Shaw was out of time.

The only way to move was forward. So he did.

57

THIS MARKET is certainly well-attended," said Waller as he walked next to Reggie along the crowded and narrow streets of Gordes. "But one could become quite claustrophobic." Waller glanced behind him. His two beefy guards were pushing past vendors and customers, struggling to keep up with the pair. Reggie had her market basket in her right hand and her walking pace was brisk. She'd already purchased some things, including six hand-stitched table napkins from a man with his wares housed in an ancient van with ratty tires. He'd given her a good price and even a bonus item that rested at the bottom of the basket but still within easy reach: a Beretta pistol.

"Well, the Saturday market is the big one."

"I can see that. Would you like me to carry your basket?" offered Waller.

"Never ask a woman that when she's in a shopping frenzy," said Reggie, drawing a laugh from the man. He held up his hands. "I defer to the consumer expertise of the fairer sex."

"Thank you."

Reggie glanced over Waller's shoulder and saw the sign. On cue, a car started to putter through the crowds and the mass of people slowly moved out of the way to allow the vehicle to pass. Reggie counted off the seconds along with her footsteps. She had to hit her marks precisely.

"That's strange," she said, as she stopped to look at a pair of sandals hanging from a rack at one vendor's spot.

"What?" asked Waller.

She pointed over his shoulder. "I've never seen any Muslims here before."

Waller jerked around and stared across the road, where two bearded men in starched robes and turbans were climbing out of the dented car that had been puttering along.

"Oh my God, are those guns?" exclaimed Reggie.

Waller looked for his guards, but then several loud bangs sounded and the street became filled with dense smoke. People screamed and ran blindly, crashing into racks of goods as well as each other. Waller called out for his guards. He couldn't see them anywhere. That was because they were both on the ground, having received well-placed blows to the back of the head. A young woman raced past them shouting, the items in her market basket cascading into the street. Everywhere there were screams and sounds of people running. Two more twin bangs occurred and the smoke in the street grew thicker. From out of the haze the two men in robes and turbans appeared with guns out and protective masks over their faces. They had the street completely blocked.

"Shit!" exclaimed Waller as he saw them approaching.

"Evan, do you know those men?"

"We need to get out of here. Now!"

She grabbed his hand. "Quick. I know a way."

They raced down a side street off the main courtyard. The street dead-ended here. Waller looked up and saw the church's bell tower.

"There is no way out," Waller screamed in fury.

"There is, but we have to go through the church. It'll put us on the other side of the village. Remember the way I showed you before? It's the only escape route."

That was why she'd shown him the route earlier. So he would know it was a way to safety. It was risky but otherwise she could not have counted on his following her. Only this time she would not be leading him to safety.

To give urgency to their flight, a well-timed bullet whizzed over their heads. Waller turned back to see one of the Muslims rushing after them.

"Oh my God, they're shooting at us," screamed Reggie.

"Just keep moving," urged Waller, grabbing her by the shoulder and thrusting her forward. "To the damn church, quickly."

Reggie pushed open the door and Waller followed her in. He slid a heavy credenza against the door before turning toward the altar.

"Who are those men?" gasped Reggie.

"Not now. Move!"

Reggie and Waller raced down the set of steps next to the altar. They passed through a door, which he locked behind them. Running down another set of stairs, they came out into an open but darkened area. Here was the critical moment, Reggie knew. The passage they'd gone down previously to exit the church was to the left. She was counting on the fact that under the extreme circumstances Waller wouldn't remember that. She turned to the right. Waller glanced back up the stairs as something crashed overhead.

"They've gotten in the church," he exclaimed.

"Come on, Evan." She pulled him down the passage to the right and into the room.

The walls, ceiling, and floor burst with light. Waller shielded his face against this brilliance. When he looked at her Reggie was pointing her pistol at him.

"Welcome to hell, Fedir Kuchin," she said.

CHAPTER

58

Strong hands grabbed Kuchin, pulled him over to a crypt, and tied him down on top of it. Kuchin looked slowly around. Whit, Dom, and Reggie had surrounded him.

"Who are you?" Kuchin said calmly.

Whit said, "I'm a bit disappointed the man's not more impressed."

"We're people who know who you really are," answered Reggie, her eyes on the Ukrainian. By her tone and attitude she was no longer role-playing as the naïve American Janie Collins. She was Reggie Campion and fully in the zone to finish this man.

"Fedir Kuchin," added Dominic. "The real butcher of Ukraine."

"And we brought back some of your victims," said Reggie.

"Before we do to you what you did to them," added Whit. "Although we're normally very nice people, we're working really hard to be cruel and evil for your benefit."

Whit spread his arm wide. Kuchin looked up at the ceiling and over at the walls that were awash in light as Dominic's projection equipment continued operating. Nothing Goya could have conceived would have equaled the horror captured in these images. The pictures of the dead or dying men, women, and children stared back at them. On one wall was the photo of the mass grave with the exposed small bones of the children buried there.

"One atrocity after another," said Reggie. "Take your time. We want you to relive the past."

"Who are you?" asked Kuchin again.

"Why does it matter?" retorted Whit.

"Because I want to know who I'm going to kill in the future. The near future."

"I don't see that happening," said Whit.

"Then you are blind."

Reggie pointed to one wall depicting a stack of bodies piled up like cords of wood. "The slaughter in Sevastopol." She indicated another image on the ceiling where gaunt near-death faces peered out from behind barbed wire. "The torture camp in Ivano-Frankivsk Oblast in western Ukraine."

A third image was of the skull-like countenances of women and children lying in the dirt. "Kotsuri in Volyn Oblast," said Dominic. "You took a page from the Holodomor with that one, didn't you? Starving rural farmers?"

Kuchin stared up at the pictures as they glimmered across the stone ceiling, like heat rising from a desert floor. When he looked back at them his face held no trace of remorse. "There is no need to show me any of this. I remember it quite well." He smiled. "Down to the last skeleton, in fact."

Whit snapped, "Okay, screw the pics. Let's just do it right now and throw him in the bone box." He pointed to a crypt along the side of the wall with its top off. "That's where your skeleton's going to be, Fed. Hope you'll enjoy rotting in old Gordes for all eternity."

Fedir ignored this and continued to stare at Reggie. "I should have been more cautious. Never trust a beautiful woman when she plays, how do you say, hard to get?"

"Look at the pictures," said Reggie. "And if you really are as religious as you claim, make peace with your God."

"And how will the fatal blow come. Gun, knife?" Kuchin cocked his head. "Will you strangle me with your bare hands? But do you dare get that close to me now? I can smell the fear you have of me. No, you will keep your distance, I think."

"You're not the first monster and you certainly won't be the last."

"Never lump me in with others," barked Kuchin. "I stand alone."

Whit looked over at the open crypt. "Well you won't be *lying* alone. There's another set of bones in there. I actually feel bad some poor bloke has to share it with the likes of you."

The click of multiple gun hammers made Whit freeze and mutter a curse.

Reggie slowly turned to see the men standing there, pointing weapons at them. She recognized two of them as Kuchin's other bodyguards.

Reggie's forehead was lined up on Pascal's front pistol sight. "Gun down. Now."

Reggie bent down and placed it on the floor.

"Kick it away."

She did so.

Alan Rice stepped out from behind his hiding place. He stared inscrutably at Reggie before saying, "Untie him. Now."

As she started to move forward Whit said, "No, I'll do it."

He took the straps off Kuchin, who rose slowly, rubbing his wrists and ankles. When he stood fully upright he nodded at Whit and then drove a fist into his gut, doubling him over. A kick against Whit's head slammed him against the crypt, where his blood mixed with centuries-old bone dust. Dominic and Reggie darted forward, but Pascal fired a bullet in front of them and they froze.

Kuchin put out his hand and Pascal tossed him a spare pistol. He turned to Reggie. "You seem to know a lot about me. Enough to send two *Muslim terrorists* after me. I assume they were imposters whose sole purpose was to funnel me here."

Reggie said nothing. Her breathing was shallow, all in her throat, but controlled.

"You don't wish to answer?" Kuchin motioned to the images on the wall. "You bring me here under false pretenses, to show me all this? And then to kill me? And yet you don't wish to explain yourself?" His easy smile disappeared as he grabbed her neck and squeezed on a point near the left jugular vein. Reggie bit her lip but made no sound. He increased the pressure and she felt the blood and oxygen supply disappearing from her brain. She finally grabbed his arm and hit a nerve point that made his hand weaken. He let go and she gasped and fell back. She planted a hand against a wall and righted herself, her gaze holding on him.

He said, "Impressive. But if you couldn't endure such a *small* measure of pain I suppose you would not be in this line of work." He looked at Dominic. "You mentioned a butcher: You think I'm dangerous? The second coming of the Holodomor? I actually like that description."

He placed the muzzle of his pistol against Dominic's forehead and pulled the trigger. Reggie screamed and Dominic flinched but then opened his eyes. There was no entry wound. The front and back of his head were still intact. No blood. No death. He looked bewildered by his survival.

Kuchin looked furious. "*Never* hand me a pistol, Pascal, without a round in the chamber."

Kuchin corrected the omission and started to line up his shot again, taking his time, completely in control. This turned out to be a very significant miscalculation.

The blur of motion to his right made Kuchin look away for a vital second from Dominic. Shaw catapulted out of hiding, both elbows raised horizontally to the top of his delts. An arced jab of hard bone against soft face threw one of the guards with such force against the stone wall that he crumpled to the floor, the fight and his senses driven completely from him. The element of surprise distinctly his, Shaw kept moving forward and caught Pascal in the throat with a strike that left the smaller man flat on his face gasping and gagging for air, his gun bouncing across the floor. He stopped gagging when Shaw slammed his foot on the back of Pascal's head, ricocheting it off the stone and knocking him out.

Alan Rice made the mistake of following the effect of the attack rather than the source. He screamed and fired his weapon; his wild round barely missed Kuchin's head and unfortunately embedded itself in Dominic's forearm, shattering bone and burning tissue. Dominic grunted and fell to the floor.

Whit launched and caught Kuchin in the sternum, sending him heels over ass, the Ukrainian's weapon sailing away.

Shaw pounced on Rice, swung him around, and slammed him against a crypt. He slid to the floor unconscious as blood streamed out of his smashed nose.

Kuchin got to his feet as everyone scrambled for weapons or cover in the ongoing shimmer of the images on the wall. With the added human movement the entire spectacle took on the aspect of some bizarre performance art. Reggie lunged for her pistol but Kuchin kicked her in the face, slashing her cheek with the heel of his shoe. When Whit hurled himself at the man a second time, Kuchin was prepared. He deftly sidestepped the thrust and, taking a page from Shaw's attack method, slammed a bony elbow into Whit's face, dropping the Irishman in his tracks.

Kuchin snatched up Reggie's Beretta, turned, aimed, and would have fired a bullet into the fallen woman's brain from inches away if Shaw hadn't connected with such a massive uppercut to the chin that it lifted the two-hundred-and-thirty-pound Ukrainian completely off his feet. He crumbled backward and hit the floor, spit out a tooth and tried to rise, but he was too dazed by the terrific shot he'd taken.

Shaw jammed one gun in his belt and grabbed another pistol off the floor and tossed it to Whit, who'd staggered to his feet holding his face. Shaw stooped, snagged Reggie's arm, and pulled her up. With his other hand he hauled Dom to his feet. "We have to get out of here. Now!"

"Not before we kill that bastard!" screamed Whit.

At that instant Kuchin managed to get to his feet, and he ran out of the catacombs.

"Hey!" yelled Whit. He ran after Kuchin, followed by the others.

"Stop!" barked Shaw, and he grabbed Whit, who was lining up a shot. "He's got other muscle, and they're probably on their way right now."

As soon as Shaw had finished speaking, three more armed men clattered down the stairs and saw them. They opened fire. The sleepy hamlet of Gordes probably hadn't seen such aggression since the Romans had been in town two millennia before.

"This way," yelled Reggie. She led them to the passage that would carry them to the doorway near the villa.

Kuchin ran toward his men and screamed, "Get them, but don't kill the woman!"

Shaw turned and fired at the men. As the bullets ricocheted off the stone walls Kuchin's guards scrambled for cover. Whit pulled a slender canister from his pocket, popped a tab, and tossed it into the room. Dense smoke formed a wall between them and their pursuers.

They turned and fled down the passage, steel-jacketed rounds chasing them every step of the way.

Fittingly for a church, they all mouthed silent prayers as they fled.

CHAPTER

59

DOWN THIS WAY," Reggie told Shaw. "There's another exit."

"The one that lets out down by the villas?" said Shaw.

Reggie stared at him as they rushed along. "How did you know?"

"I can recon. But that door opens onto a public street."

"And Kuchin knows about it," said Reggie. "I had to show him that route earlier to convince him to go to the church today. Then I led him to the catacombs instead."

Shaw said, "Then it's no good for two reasons." He looked over at Dominic, who ran bent over, clutching his injured arm. "Are you going to make it?"

Reggie took off her bandanna and wrapped it around the wound.

"I can make it," Dominic said, grimacing.

Whit eyed Shaw. "What then? We can't go back unless we want to shoot our way out, and those guys have a lot more bullets than we do."

Shaw pointed to his left. "That way."

Whit grabbed his arm. "There's nothing down there. I checked."

"At the end of the hall is a hidden door built into the stone. The passage there leads to the old fort."

"How do you know that?" demanded Whit.

"Through a little history reading."

"What?"

"Catholic priests often had to run for their lives. Just like we are. Now let's go!"

They reached the end of the hall, Shaw pulled on a stone set in the lower half of the wall, and a slight gap appeared. He tugged on the section and old hinges creaked as the door swung open. They fled through and Shaw clicked the door shut behind them.

As he led them down a dark, musty passageway Shaw hit some keys on his cell phone and the electronic message flew off. They passed through another door and reached a hall through which sunlight eased in via slits in the stone block far above their heads. They were now in the old fort.

He reached one more door, tugged it open, and they entered a courtyard. The car screeched to a stop in front of them and Whit aimed his gun at the driver.

"He's with me," said Shaw, putting a hand on Whit's arm.

Frank rolled down the passenger-side window and said, "The whole town is going nuts."

Shaw and Reggie helped Dominic into the backseat and then slid in next to him. Whit jumped in next to Frank, who gunned it, and the car sped off laying black tread down on ancient cobblestone.

"Okay, Shaw, start talking," said Frank as he maneuvered the car through the narrow streets and down the hill toward where the villas were located.

"Your name is Shaw?" said Reggie, looking at him.

He glanced in the rearview mirror to see Frank staring at him. "They snagged Waller, but his men ambushed them. I was there to help out."

"Help out?" exclaimed Whit. "We'd all be dead but for you."

"Well, we still might be," snapped Frank.

As he finished speaking one of Waller's men ran out from the doorway that led from the church; it was the same passageway out that Reggie and Kuchin had taken when they'd visited the church the first time. The gunman spotted them and fired. Everyone ducked as the windshield cracked. There was a bump, the man was catapulted into the air by the collision with the car, and dropped to the ground. Frank looked up.

"Hey, Shaw?"

"Yeah?"

"Can you drive?"

"Why?"

"Because the son of a bitch just shot me!"

Shaw saw the blood seeping from Frank's jacket, pushed the man to the side, climbed over the seat, and took over the wheel. He floored it and then checked Frank, who was slumped over next to Whit.

"How bad?"

Frank fumbled with his shirt and looked. "Missed the belly, think it went through me. Hard to say."

Whit checked the seatback. "It did. Here's the slug." He held it up.

"Hang on, Frank, and tell me where to go," said Shaw.

"Private strip sixty kilometers south of here. Wings waiting." He gave Shaw the specific directions and then fell silent, his breathing labored and his face turning gray.

Reggie and Whit took off Frank's jacket, tore open his shirt, and checked the wound more carefully. Reggie said, "Look in the glove compartment for a first-aid kit."

There wasn't one but there was a box of sterilized wipes. She used those to clean the wound and then used strips of Frank's shirt to help stop the bleeding and to bandage the wound. She sat back. "That's all I can do for now. He needs medical attention."

"There's a doc on the plane," mumbled Frank. Shaw glanced at him to see the other man's gaze on him. "Knowing you I figured it was a good idea." Shaw grabbed an antiseptic pack and tossed it to Reggie. "For your face. Waller got you good with his shoe."

She cleaned up her face as best she could and then worked on Dominic's injured arm.

The siren made them all jerk around.

"Cop car right behind us," said Whit as he stared in the side mirror.

"Shit, there is no way we can stop and explain this," said Shaw. He floored it.

Five miles later as the sounds of the siren faded into the Provençal countryside Whit said, "You're a right good wheel man."

"Let's just be thankful they didn't have the resources out here to do a call-ahead roadblock. Then I'd just be a 'right good' prisoner."

They finally reached the private airstrip. Parked next to the plane was a shimmering black Range Rover. The physician on board the jet cleaned up Frank's wound and reset Dominic's bone, holding it in place with two small pieces of wood and lots of medical tape.

"He'll need a cast," said the doctor. "I don't have the materials to do one here."

Shaw helped Reggie bandage her face while Whit watched stonily from a corner of the luxurious cabin. The copilot came back to them. "We're ready to go wheels up whenever you give the word," he told Frank as the man slowly sat up, rubbing his arm where the doctor had given him an injection of painkiller.

"That won't be happening,"

Everyone turned to see Whit standing there pointing a gun. "You two can go," he said, indicating Shaw and Frank. "But the three of us are gonna take those fresh wheels out there and head on."

"That's not a good idea," said Shaw.

"For us it is," shot back Whit. "I don't know who you blokes are, and I don't want to know. Thanks for the assist, but you go your way and we'll go ours. No hard feelings, I promise."

"You guys will never get away," said Frank, attempting to stand before Shaw put a restraining hand on his shoulder.

"I actually like our odds."

"You'll need a hostage," said Shaw. "Because without that, you really have no chance against this guy here." Shaw pointed at Frank. "He's got more resources than you can deal with. But he also doesn't want to lose me. That gives you leverage."

Whit looked skeptical. "So you want us to take *you* hostage? That ain't happening."

"Then you have no chance," snapped Shaw.

Whit poked a finger into Shaw's chest. "Bugger off."

Reggie stepped between Whit and Shaw. "He's right, Whit."

"I'm not taking your lover boy along for the ride just because you—"

Shaw moved Reggie to the side and took a step toward Whit. "You couldn't even recon a site properly. You let them ambush you and would be dead if it weren't for me. You said so yourself. Now we have to get out of the country. Without wings we'll have to go another way. I can do that because I've done it a hundred times. Can you?"

Now Whit looked uneasily at Reggie.

Dominic said, "He's right, Whit, we're not prepared for this."

Whit fumed inwardly for a few seconds. "All right, but the first time you try anything . . ."

"Right, whatever." Shaw brushed past him heading for the aircraft's exit door.

"Shaw!" shouted Frank. "You can't do this. You don't even know who they are."

"I'll be in touch, Frank. Hope you heal fast."

The others followed him off the plane.

As they climbed into the Range Rover, Whit asked Shaw, "Hey, how did you get away in the first place?"

"With a toilet, a little water, and some elbow grease. And you might want to call somebody to untie your guy after they wake him up."

"Bloody hell," said an impressed Whit.

CHAPTER

60

FEDIR KUCHIN's villa was empty. No SUVs out front, no windows open, no cigar-smoking in the rear grounds. The bags had been packed, battered men gathered up, and they were gone. A phone call had been placed and his private jet had picked him up not at the commercial airport in Avignon but at a corporate jet park. He now looked down at the French landscape from twenty thousand feet as his private plane worked its way up plateaus of calm air to its cruising altitude.

Next to him sat Alan Rice holding an ice pack against his face with another strapped to his right knee. Pascal, and two of the other guards who'd been attacked by the Muslim impersonators, were nursing their own injuries. The man who'd been hit by the car had a broken leg. Kuchin's mouth and jaw were badly swollen from Shaw's blow and there were two new empty spots in his gums. He had refused any medical attention, not even Advil. He simply sat in his seat and stared down at the quickly vanishing French terrain.

They are down there somewhere. And they know who I really am.

He flicked a gaze at Rice. "In all the excitement you have not explained how you were able to rescue me, Alan," he said, his damaged mouth moving slowly.

Rice gingerly removed the ice pack and glanced at his boss. "I followed the woman to the church one night."

"Why?"

"Because I didn't trust her," he said simply. "That's why I tested her."

"Tested her?"

"When I pretended to warn her off. I lied to her and said that you had become infatuated with women in the past. I wanted to see if she would do the rational thing and leave you alone. She didn't. That, coupled with her late-night excursion, made me even more suspicious. I also didn't like the way she was playing you off against that other man."

"So you followed her? But how is it that you were in those catacombs waiting for us?"

"I also saw who she was meeting with that night. I had him followed."

"You did all this without telling me?"

"I wanted to be sure, Evan. I didn't want to turn out to be wrong. I am a smart man, meaning I am terrified of you."

Kuchin leaned back into the leather of his seat. "And then?"

"And then we saw them go into the church and down to the catacombs. When they came back out to get something, we snuck down there and took up position. I was very afraid because they had guns, and I have never even fired one. Witness my poor shot today."

"You saved my life."

"I'm glad I could be there for you. Had I known what this was all about I never would have let you go with her to the market today. By the time I realized what was happening it was too late. They were cunning. I assumed the two guards with you would be sufficient, but I was obviously wrong."

"So I struck you in error earlier?"

"You had every right. I *appeared* to have overstepped my bounds."

"I was surprised by that."

"I'm sure. But I was just trying to protect you."

Kuchin turned away, stared out at a cloud. "I'm sorry, Alan. I misjudged you. I saved your life, now we are even on that."

"Well, thank God it ended all right."

"End? No. This has not *ended*."

"You're going after them?"

"You had doubts?"

"No, no doubts," Rice said nervously.

"The tall man? Why do I think he was not with them?"

"But he was there."

Kuchin said, "I think he followed *you* into the church."

"Me?"

Kuchin ran a finger along his battered jaw. Talking was painful but he was focused on something else. "You heard what they called me?"

"The name?"

"Fedir Kuchin."

"Yes. I heard." Rice put the bag of ice back on his face and tried to breathe normally.

"Do you know who that is?"

"No. I don't."

Kuchin was both pleased and disappointed by this. He bent down and removed an object from his briefcase. It was a bag wrapped in plastic. Inside was a gun.

"This is the woman's pistol that she left in the church. I want it checked for prints but I doubt we'll be successful there. When I picked it up I probably smudged any that were there. But it's a relatively new model and we can check for serial numbers on the slider, barrel, and breech face."

"They probably sterilized it. Used acid or a drill to remove the numbers."

"You know more about guns than you let on, Alan. Yes, that is true, but there is a thing called microstamping. It uses a laser to imprint the numbers microscopically on the breech face and the firing pin among other places. They are not so easy to remove. If we can trace the gun perhaps we can trace the woman."

"You really want her, don't you?"

"The background check we ran on her was obviously flawed. I want you to find out all you can about who she really is."

Kuchin stopped rubbing his jaw and took out the laptop computer they had found in the catacombs that was the source of the picture show down there. He turned it on and pushed some keys. A few moments later he was staring at graphic images of his work in Ukraine. He turned to see Rice glancing over his shoulder. The younger man quickly looked away. Kuchin finally eased his gaze from the images on the computer and put it away. He retrieved a small book from his bag and opened it. On one page were the beginnings of a sketch. Holding a bit of charcoal, Kuchin's hand moved across the paper. As he did so Janie Collins's face began to more fully appear.

61

So FIRST, where do you want to go?"

Shaw was driving with Whit next to him. Reggie and Dominic were in the backseat of the Range Rover. Dominic had dozed off from the painkillers the doctor had given him.

Reggie and Whit looked at each other.

"It's a valid question," said Shaw as he patted the steering wheel. "It sort of tells me which way to point the ride."

"North," answered Reggie as Whit glared at her.

"North?" said Shaw. "Paris? Normandy? Calais?"

"Farther north."

Shaw eyed Whit. "The Channel? The North Sea? Do you live on a boat?"

"Funny."

"You mean you're Brits?" Shaw added sarcastically, "Bloody hell."

"I'm Irish, remember, *Paddy*? *Not* British," retorted Whit. "But I'll let it pass. This time. So you got an idea how to get across the Channel? Hey, maybe this Rover's amphibious."

"Do you have passports?"

Whit pointed behind them. "Back there. But we can make some calls and get them quick enough. In fact, I don't know what we need you for, actually."

"Because I know what I'm doing. And don't underestimate the French police."

Whit slowly nodded. "I don't underestimate anybody, least of all *you*."

"Make the call. Tell him we'll meet at Reims in four hours. When we get close we'll call and pick the place."

"So you know France?" asked Whit.

"Even speak the language passably," replied Shaw.

"Goody for you."

Whit made arrangements to meet one of their people who had the fake documents they would need to get out of the country.

"Okay, that's done. Now what?"

"Just sit back and relax."

Whit kept his gun in his hand. "And after Reims?"

"Since we can't risk an airport, the Chunnel train to St. Pancras is the most direct route. That's why we need passports. If that doesn't pan out we head east and work our way across the Channel by boat. Maybe from Belgium or Amsterdam."

"Passport Control is pretty tight at Gare du Nord," pointed out Reggie.

"It is, but airport security is a lot tighter. And there're fewer ways out of an airport if things go bad. And most of them take you through lots of armed guys in uniforms."

"Okay, the train. And after that?"

"We'll play it by ear."

"Who are you with?" asked Reggie as she leaned forward from the rear seat.

"I'm with Frank back there on the plane. That's pretty much all you need to know."

"So you're cops," said Whit.

"I wouldn't describe it that way, no."

"Spies."

"No comment."

"What's left?"

"Me."

Whit grinned and looked at Reggie. "The big guy is growing on me, Reg. He really is. Now here's the deal, Shaw army of one. If we get to England safe and sound you're going to go your way and we're going ours."

"Who's going to protect you against, what was his name, Kuchin?"

"You obviously don't know who that is," said Reggie.

"Should I?"

"There was a man named Mykola Shevchenko. KGB. He's known as the Butcher of Kiev, but Kuchin was his top assistant, and he was the man who slaughtered hundreds of thousands of innocent people in the most brutal ways possible. Shevchenko was executed by firing squad after the Wall fell, but Kuchin got away."

"I guess history only remembers the top guy, not the ones running around pulling the triggers," said Shaw. "So you were going after the guy for that. What's your connection? Some of you Ukrainian?"

"Yeah, on my mother's side," said Whit with a smirk. "And to answer your other question, we can protect ourselves."

Shaw eyed him skeptically. "You've done a hell of a job of it so far."

"Sometimes plans go awry, things don't work, the unexpected occurs."

"Come on! It was a cock-up from start to finish," fired back Shaw.

Whit snapped, "Well, you blokes were here to nail him too and then you pulled out without even taking a shot. At least we tried."

"Not my call."

"Where were you going to hit him?" asked Reggie.

Shaw hesitated. "Les Baux, the caves."

She considered this. "Probably a better place than the one we chose."

"Hey," barked Whit. "We did the best we could with what we had. And you coming into the equation didn't help matters," he added, glowering at Shaw. "We might not have fancy jets but we usually get the job done."

"I'll have to take your word for that. But if you think you can protect yourselves against this guy without help, you're wrong. You can ask some dead Muslims about it."

"I don't care if he snuffed a couple of those guys," declared Whit. "And you know what else? I'm going after his ass again. And this time we'll get him."

"The only thing you'll *get* is dead."

"Why don't you just shut up and drive?" Whit turned to stare moodily out the windshield.

Shaw glanced in the rearview mirror and saw Reggie staring at him.

He mouthed, *It'll be okay.*

But even as he said it Shaw knew he was lying to the woman.

He turned his gaze back to the road.

CHAPTER

62

K<small>UCHIN'S PLANE</small> was halfway across the Atlantic. Rice had accessed the Internet to check on the Facebook page that had been set up for Reggie posing as Jane Collins and also the other background information they had found there. It had all been deleted.

He fearfully told Kuchin of this while the man rested in his seat.

"We didn't print copies out either," Rice said, his voice trembling. "So we don't even have her photo."

"*I* have her photo," said Kuchin surprisingly. "I took it when you both were out on the terrace talking before dinner."

"You had suspicions?"

"No, I wanted a picture of a beautiful woman. But now, now I have suspicions," Kuchin added sarcastically.

"We have nothing on Bill Young."

By now Kuchin had drawn sketches of Reggie, Shaw, Whit, and Dominic. His eye and memory for detail were astonishing. He showed them to Rice, who nodded approvingly. "Spot-on, Evan. You're quite an artist."

"I want the three sketches of the men transferred into a digital format or whatever it is called. Can this be done in a way that would allow a search through a photo database?"

"I believe so, yes."

"Then make it happen. Along with the photo of the woman, of course. On every database we can buy our way onto."

"Understood. But if you have a picture of the woman why did you sketch her too?"

Kuchin didn't answer this. Instead he said, "I do not like leaving

Europe. The accents from the men were unmistakable, particularly the Irishman."

"But not the lobbyist?"

"No. He is different." Kuchin rubbed his battered jaw. "I have been hit before in my life. I have never been hit that hard. I am stunned my jaw isn't broken. A strong man. A dangerous man."

Rice added, "He knocked out Manuel like he was nothing. And then took out Pascal like he was cardboard, and you know how good Pascal is. And he lifted me up like I was a child. I felt his arm, it was like iron."

"It was not so much his strength that impressed me," said Kuchin. "There are many strong men, stronger even than he is. It was the speed, and the skill. Three armed men, four counting you, Alan. But three armed men who are good with weapons, and still he managed to do it."

"There was some luck involved, surely."

"There is always an element of luck. The question becomes, did it happen on its own, or did he create it himself? I tend to think the latter. He came out with his elbows raised horizontally, a classic close-quarters combat technique. It allowed him to strike fast on a pivot and with maximum power since he could use his weight and the leverage of his torso and hips. And bent-elbow strikes are preferable over a fist. There are many small bones in the hand that can break on contact. Any one of them snaps, that limb is useless. An elbow, on the other hand, is comprised of only three bones at a pivotal juncture, and they're all relatively large. The elbow is at its greatest risk of breaking when it's extended. You fall, reach out palm down, arm straight, and the part of the anatomy that takes the brunt of the fall is the elbow. It snaps." Kuchin made a V with his arm. "But if you bend the arm those stress points vanish and the resulting durability and striking power are formidable."

"You know a lot about these things."

"I know enough. And he kept moving, always moving, making it very difficult to line up a shot."

"If he's that good, maybe we should give it a pass."

Kuchin looked at him, clearly disappointed. "They strapped me to a crypt. They were going to put me in a grave with old bones.

They defiled consecrated ground in a Catholic church. And I must now hit them back far harder than they hit me. So from this point forward it is the only thing I will focus on."

"But the business."

"That is why I have you." He put an arm around the other man's narrow shoulders and squeezed. Rice moaned slightly, since his entire body was sore from his brief but painful encounter with Shaw. "You will do a good job. And if I see any indication of you overstepping your authority or trying to replace me at the top, just keep in mind that the dogs I used on Abdul-Majeed are still available."

Rice said nervously, "Evan, about the name they called you?"

"I would not think of it ever again if I were you."

The plane did not land in Montreal. Kuchin had ordered a change in the flight plan. They put down on a long strip of level asphalt that he'd built in far eastern Canada on the Labrador side of the province of Labrador and Newfoundland.

Rice looked out the window as the plane taxied to a stop. "Evan, what's going on? Why are we landing at your place here?"

"I'm not going on to Montreal. The plane will." He rose and slipped on a long coat.

"But why here?"

"And you won't be leaving on this plane."

Rice looked pale. "I don't understand."

"Unfortunately it can't be helped. My jet is too easily followed."

"You mean I'm driving all the way to Montreal? That's a long way."

"Over a thousand miles, actually. But you'll be driven and you won't have to go the whole way. In Goose Bay, I will engage another plane that will fly you the rest of the way to Montreal. You'll be there in time for a late dinner. But you will not go to your home or the office. You will stay at the safe house outside of the city. You will conduct your business from there. And two of my men will be with you at all times. Understood?"

"Certainly, yes. You think these precautions are actually necessary?"

"Considering that I was almost dumped into a crypt in the basement of a church in Gordes, yes, I do." He laid a hand on his assistant's shoulder. "I will be monitoring your progress closely. You can stay on the plane. I will send transportation out to you."

The jet door and gangway descended and Kuchin stepped off, climbed in a waiting Escalade, and was driven off.

Kuchin did not look back at his jet but kept his gaze resolutely ahead. If they knew he was Fedir Kuchin, what would be their next step? They were prepared to kill him, so he didn't believe they were tied to an official organization like Interpol, or America's FBI. Or even the successor to the old KGB, the Russian Federal Security Service. It had been known in the past to round up old Soviet targets and imprison or execute them after a very public trial for the global goodwill it would inspire. They did that, Kuchin thought with contempt, while a former KGB officer was now leading the country. It was disgusting what democracy could inspire.

Yet if he were wrong and they were official? They could come swooping in and dismantle his entire organization. They might be waiting for the jet to land in Montreal. Well, they would find it empty, and he trusted his pilots not to reveal his location. This was not simply an act of faith on his part. They had both been with him many years, and they knew that Kuchin knew where their families lived.

He had built a compound in a remote location nearly forty kilometers from here. He had over the years accumulated thousands of acres and put his house in the middle of some of the most rugged, glaciated tundra outside of Siberia. It was unforgiving terrain and yet Kuchin found solace and familiarity here. He and Rice had devised many successful business models here over the last four years. He could think here, deeply. And he would do so now as he planned his counterattack.

63

We're screwed," muttered Shaw as he stared at the interior of the train station. Wearing a hat, tinted sunglasses, and, despite the warm air, a bulky sweatshirt, he'd entered the immense bustle of Gare du Nord in Paris only to find that numerous police officers were walking the floor holding pictures of him. Reggie, Whit, and Dominic, similarly disguised, had followed him in separately and just seen what he had.

Then he pointed to a policewoman walking near an entrance door. In her hand was a color image of a second person.

Reggie recognized her image immediately. "Shit."

After confirming that these were the only pictures being distributed, Shaw turned and left the station. The others joined him outside near a rack of luggage carts.

"Now what?" asked Dominic.

Whit answered. "I say the three of us take our chances and you"—he pointed at Shaw—"can take your chances somewhere else."

Shaw said, "I disagree."

"I don't care if you bloody disagree."

"Use your brain, Whit. Four together is easier to catch. They've got my and Reggie's pictures in there, not you two. You get on the train and get back to London. Reggie and I will get there another way."

"I don't think so," Whit shot back.

"He's right, Whit," said Reggie. "It's better to split up. If they catch us, so be it. But it would be stupid to let them catch all of us at once."

Whit was unmoved by her arguments. "You seem to be trying awfully hard to think of reasons to stay with this guy."

Shaw leaned against the wall of the station and said, "Why don't you let the lady make up her own mind, Whit, or is that against company policy?"

"Why don't you shut the hell up? You don't know anything about us."

"Not for lack of interest or trying."

"If we go on the train, how are you getting back to England?" Whit asked Reggie.

Shaw answered, "Amsterdam. We can grab a ferry there. I know somebody. They don't ask questions and I doubt the police will be covering it."

Reggie said, "Whit, you and Dom get on the damn train. He needs to get his arm looked after as soon as possible. A little over two hours on a train is a lot better than pitching on the Channel in a boat for days."

"You're really serious, aren't you? You're going with this bloke even though you don't know who the hell he is?"

"I know he saved our lives. I know he disobeyed orders to come with us. Do I need to know more?"

Whit eyed her and then Shaw and finally looked at Dominic for support. The young man's gaze, however, went directly to the pavement.

"Fine," said Whit. "You two just go off doing whatever. Maybe I'll see you back in England and maybe I won't. I'll drop you a line when I finish off Kuchin." He turned and stalked back into the station, Dominic scuttling after him.

Shaw looked at Reggie. "Is he always this good-natured?"

"He's a bloody man, isn't he? It's not part of their psychology to be good-natured *when they don't get their bloody way!*" She yelled these last words after Whit, but he and Dominic had already disappeared into Gare du Nord. Reggie stalked off in the opposite direction.

Five minutes later she and Shaw were driving off in a dark blue Ford compact Shaw had snatched because the driver had helpfully left the keys on the front seat. After driving three blocks Shaw had pulled over. He'd taken the plates off the Range Rover before ditch-ing it. Now he switched out the Ford's license plates with those.

"The cops will match the make and model before they check the plates," he told Reggie. "Range Rover, not Ford. And the guy whose car we stole—"

"It'll be the reverse. Plates before make and model. So on to Holland?"

"Right. Get some sleep."

"What if you get drowsy?"

"I don't," said Shaw.

64

WHIT HAD just finished speaking. Dominic sat next to him, his wounded arm in a fresh cast. Professor Mallory and Liza sat opposite them in the library at Harrowsfield. Mallory tapped his new pipe stem idly against the old table while Liza, her mouth screwed up in concentration, stared down at her hands.

"You're sure that this tall fellow, what was his real name again?" began Mallory.

"Shaw," said Whit.

"Yes, this Shaw fellow. He could not have been the one who set you up?"

"He saved us, Professor. I don't know why he would have sabotaged the hit only to later come in and pull our asses out of the fire."

"It appears he may be exactly what he says he is," said Liza. "An agent for another organization that was on Kuchin's trail for another reason."

"The nuclear trafficking," said Mallory. "Yes, I suppose that is the most logical explanation. Damn inconvenient coincidence, going after the same scoundrel at the same time but for different reasons."

Liza responded, "Not so much of a coincidence. They undoubtedly had the same thinking we did. Attack the man on his holiday because they might not get another chance."

"And no word from Regina?" asked Mallory.

Whit shook his head. "Not yet, no. They're probably on a boat right now chugging across the water to here. At least I hope they are."

"But not to Harrowsfield," said Mallory, looking alarmed. "She wouldn't bring him here?"

"She's not daft," said Whit, but he looked away when he said it.

"You have to contact her, Whit, and tell her to come in alone," said Mallory. "She cannot bring this man with her."

"I've been *trying* to contact her but she's not answering her damn phone."

"Then you need to try harder. You need to go out there and find her." Mallory waved his hand toward the window.

Whit looked enraged. "Out there? Where out there? Are you talking the grounds at Harrowsfield or the bleeding world? And she got herself into this bloody mess so she can sure as hell get herself out, can't she?"

"I don't think that attitude is helping," admonished Mallory.

"Well, right this minute, I don't really care what you think," Whit shot back.

"I believe we all need to calm down," said Liza. "Perhaps some tea."

Whit snorted. "Tea? Hell, Liza, give me a bottle of Locke's eight-year-old single malt and then maybe I'll calm down enough to listen to this doddering old bloke again."

Dominic spoke up. "I think we need to trust Reggie to do the right thing." He looked around at the others, who now all stared back at him. "I know I trust her." He sat back and rubbed his bad arm, seemingly exhausted after his little speech.

"I think Dominic is right," said Liza.

"Do you really want to take that chance?" asked Mallory. "Sacrifice everything we've worked for here? You remember the concerns you had about her and this Shaw chap," he added, looking at Whit. "She could be persuaded, perhaps. Blinded by, well, you get my point, surely."

The Irishman looked uncomfortable now. "She pretty well explained that away. And the fact is we had the bastard in our crosshairs. The mission should have succeeded."

"And then you were ambushed?" said Mallory.

Whit said, "The fact is, Prof, those blokes knew right where we were. They got the clear jump on us. I want to know how that happened. No, I *need* to know how that happened."

"You might have made a mistake," said Liza. "They could have grown suspicious and followed one of you. Learned about it that way."

"No one would've known me and Dom were involved until D-day. Whenever Reggie came to visit us at the cottage there was no way she was followed."

"You met at the church at night," Dominic pointed out.

"That might be a hole," Whit admitted. "But we have to know for sure."

"And Kuchin is still out there," said Mallory.

"It's not done, Prof. I can't keep breathing knowing he's still alive."

"And I'm sure Fedir Kuchin is thinking the same thing about us," responded Liza.

"That's what Shaw said," added Dominic. "He wanted to help protect us against Kuchin."

"And I told him we didn't need his protection," said Whit sharply. "And we don't."

"And no clue as to who he's with?" said Liza.

"They have their own wings, so they're not operating on a shoe-string like us," Whit told her with a touch of envy in his voice.

"I don't like this at all," said Mallory after a long silence. "I don't know whether I'm more worried about Fedir Kuchin or this man Shaw."

"Know what? I say we worry about them *both*," retorted Whit.

CHAPTER

65

REGGIE, clutching her stomach, stepped onto the wharf, knelt down, and kissed the grimy boards as the ferry pulled back from the dock and began its drift out to sea in heavy swells. It was piloted by a Dutchman whom Shaw had known for years, for reasons he would not divulge to Reggie. The drop-off point was actually a long-forgotten World War II–era naval landing spot technically in the middle of nowhere. It had taken nearly three days for Shaw and Reggie to get back into England, much of it spent on the vessel as it slowly made its way through turbulent waters.

"Thank you, Jesus," moaned Reggie.

"The boat ride *was* a little rough," Shaw remarked as he helped her back up.

"A little rough?" Reggie's throat convulsed and she looked ready to throw up again, but finally she stood straight and let out a long breath, putting an arm on his shoulder to steady herself. "I thought the only place we were going to reach was the bottom of the bloody sea."

"Last boat ride I took was across the Irish Sea. It was pretty choppy then too. The woman I was with kept throwing up, just like you. Must be a girl thing."

"Who was that?" Reggie asked while eagerly if gingerly walking next to Shaw toward solid earth.

"*That* was a long time ago."

"How did you know about this place?"

"It's come in handy a couple of times in the past."

"Quite a hole in our border security."

"Every country has at least one."

When they reached the grassy area next to the pier, Reggie checked her cell phone. It only had a sliver of juice left and no bars. She hadn't been able to contact anyone about her status and still couldn't. "Damn it. This is just great."

"I've got bars and juice. Give me the number and I'll make the call."

"I don't think so. Then you'll have the number on your phone."

"This isn't my phone. It belongs to one of your guys. The one I knocked out with a toilet."

"Did you look at any of the contact information on it?"

"No."

"You're lying."

"Maybe I am," he said.

"Can I have it? I need a phone."

"Maybe later."

Since he had nearly a foot in height and over a hundred pounds on her, she didn't push it, but looked around at the dark surroundings. "Where are we?"

"A few hours outside of London. I've arranged for wheels. Where do you want to head now?"

"I think our separate ways."

"That is not a good idea. Kuchin can—"

"He can do a lot of things, but catching us is not one of them. In fact, Whit was right. We'll go back after him."

Shaw took her by the arm like he wanted to shake her. "What part of the memo didn't you get? He almost killed you all when he didn't know you were coming. Now that he's warned you've got no chance of taking him."

"We almost got him before."

"Did you ever stop and think why you didn't?"

"What?"

"How did those guys end up ambushing you?"

Reggie pulled away from him. "How should I know that?"

"You *need* to know that. They had inside information. They were waiting for you. You've got a mole somewhere."

"That's impossible."

"Then give me another explanation that fits."

"We screwed up in the field somehow and they got onto us that way. I went to the church before to meet with Whit to go over the plan. Someone could have followed me then."

"Why would they even suspect you?"

"You're the one who's trumpeting how good Kuchin is. He probably suspects everybody."

"I listened to him when he was tied to that crypt, and so did you. He tried to bluster about killing you, but that was a man who expected to die that day. And if he suspected you, why would he have come with you to the church in the first place?"

"We used the Muslim information you gave us to work an angle to herd him that way."

"Just like that?"

"Just like that," she said defensively. "And it worked."

"If someone had followed you to the church earlier and knew what was up, why would they let it play out? Why not blow the whistle? That way Kuchin is never in danger at all."

After staring at the dark, rolling sea for a bit, she said, "I can't answer that. I don't know why."

"But the answer, whatever it is, is not good for you. If you do have a traitor in your ranks it'll make it pretty easy for Kuchin to come after you."

She closed her eyes for a moment and wearily rubbed her temples. "Look, you said you made arrangements for some wheels. Can you just get me to London? It's the middle of the night and I'm too tired and dirty and still way too nauseous to think clearly about this right now."

He stared at her before shrugging. "Sure, the wheels are just up there."

"Just up there" turned out to be a half-mile walk through uneven terrain in the pitch dark to a road. A motorbike was near the tree line, keys under the seat. He tossed her the spare helmet. "It's not the Vespa but it'll do."

She clung to him on the way back to town. When they reached London, lines of smoky pink were beginning to burn against the sky, and early morning commuters were making their way along the still mostly empty streets. A few cabs and one bendy-bus puttered along the roads.

She tapped him on the shoulder and pointed to one corner. He slowed the bike and then stopped near the entrance to the Tube. She got off and handed him back the spare helmet.

"Sure you don't want to hang with me?" he said.

"First stop we made for petrol I'd just sneak out of the bathroom window. Why not save time and cut to the chase?"

He pulled the phone from his jacket pocket and tossed it to her. "*Bonne chance.*"

"So that's it? No more trying to convince me? Just wish me good luck?" It seemed clear to Shaw that part of her wanted to stay with him. But he wasn't feeling conciliatory right now.

"Just another job."

He throttled the bike.

"Thanks for saving our butts, Shaw," she said, a bit guiltily.

"Like I said, just another job. *Reg.*"

He popped the gear changer with his heel, released the clutch, and pulled away, leaving her to trudge on to the Underground alone.

CHAPTER

66

REGGIE LOOKED AROUND the small footprint of her dingy flat in London. There was a lumpy four-poster bed, an old chest that had belonged to her mother, a square of frayed carpet, a table with two straight-backed chairs, a hotplate, a small under-the-counter fridge, a four-foot-high shelf crammed with books, and two dirty windows that looked out on the back of another grimy building. Her single potted plant was quite dead because a freak heat wave that had hit London while she was gone had baked her room, which sat defenseless without the benefit of central air-conditioning. The toilet and shower were down the hall. The folks in her building were early risers and if she wanted to bathe with even moderately hot water she had to get there by 6 a.m.

I'm twenty-eight and still live like I'm at university.

She'd showered in cold water since she'd arrived home late, and then changed into the only clean clothes she had left in her closet. She bagged up her dirty laundry with the intent of washing it later in the facilities downstairs. Since she'd been gone awhile, her fridge held nothing edible. She ate breakfast at a café down the street, taking her time over eggs, coffee, and a buttery croissant. She'd charged her phone and sent a text to Whit. She'd received an immediate reply. All their people had gotten out safely. One had even gone to the villa and retrieved her personal things and brought them back to England. In his message Whit wanted to know where Shaw was. He wrote, "Make sure he can't find Harrowsfield." She emailed him back and told him that Shaw was no longer with her and that she would make sure she wasn't followed.

Walking down the street Reggie stretched her arms and worked the kinks out of her legs. The boat ride had been horrible, pitching and swaying nonstop. Shaw had taken the ordeal easily in stride. He'd never once become sick. He just sat at a table, reading a book and even eating, and would hand her towels and a bucket when she needed it, which was frequently.

When she would glance up at him for sympathy she didn't receive any. Then she felt guilty for even seeking it. It was an unforgiving business and one had to tough it out. He certainly had. She, on the other hand, had come up a little short with her sea legs. At least she was safely back in England, as was her entire team. While it was true they had missed Kuchin, things could be far worse.

She rode the Tube to Knightsbridge. She was heading out to Harrowsfield later to brief the others but had something to do first. She had a sixty-millimeter-size safe deposit box housed at a company that specialized in storing people's valuables. It had all the latest technological security devices—biometric scanners, access cards, and each box wired directly to the closest police station while closed-circuit cameras monitored the vault. This level of security cost nearly a hundred pounds a year and was worth every penny to her.

She entered the building and successfully passed through the various layers of security. Alone in the vault room, she accessed her box and slid out the contents. Making sure her back was between the camera overhead and the items she was looking at, Reggie sat down at the table and began to read through things she knew by heart.

This was her ritual. After every mission she came and did this. All other times she had been successful. This was her first miss, her first loss, her first ass-kicking. But still here she was. It was important.

The newspaper articles were old and yellowed. Over time the paper would fully disintegrate, but the information contained in the pages would never be erased from her mind. Some days she wished that it would disappear.

Robert O'Donnell, age thirty-six. The photo of the man was a faded black-and-white, but Reggie had no trouble recognizing him. He was her father, after all. He'd died on her seventh birthday. The headline from the *Daily Mail* had covered all the basic points and added in its typical dash of hyperbole:

London's Most Notorious Serial Killer Since Jack the Ripper Dead!

It was not exactly what a little girl wanted to read about her dad on her birthday.

Twenty-four victims, all female and all in their teens and twenties, had died at her father's sadistic hands. At least those were the ones that were known. People had even compared him to the American serial killer Ted Bundy, who'd been executed around that time. A charming, good-looking man who'd lured young women to their deaths. Except Bundy had not been married with children. He'd been a loner. Reggie's father had a good job, a loving wife, and a boy and a girl. And yet somehow over the years he'd managed to slaughter at least two dozen human beings with such ferocity and depravity that veteran constables who'd discovered some of the bodies had spent time afterwards in therapy to help them through the horrors they'd witnessed.

Even now, once the truth had been established past all doubt, she still couldn't quite bring herself to accept that the man who had helped create her was the same man in these horrible stories. She looked at another newspaper, one written on the fourth anniversary of her father's death. It had a full-page picture of him in his last days. In the face Reggie could see a man possessed by something not human at all. But she also saw something else that terrified her even more.

My eyes. My nose. My mouth. My chin.

Physically she was far more her father than her mother. Physically.

The end of her father's violent life had been crushing because it also marked the end of the other two lives she cared most about. Her mother's. And her beloved older brother's.

It was her brother who had been the hero. At age twelve and having figured out what his father had done, Lionel O'Donnell had gone to the police. At first they had not believed the ramblings of a child. They were swamped with leads, most of them false, and under enormous pressure to catch the worst serial killer any of them could remember.

It was only afterwards that they realized he was right. By then it was too late. Her entire family had perished on a single day. Her enraged father had discovered his son's betrayal and killed them. He would've killed Reggie too if the police hadn't arrived when they did. She still had nightmares about it. She supposed she would always have nightmares.

Reggie turned to another article and started trembling as soon as she saw the photo and caption underneath. The girl's hair was done in pigtails. The eyes were vacant. The small mouth was set in a thin, unemotional line. No joy, no sadness, no feelings at all. More than twenty years later Reggie struggled to remember what it felt like to be photographed that day. Where she was, what she'd been thinking.

Her gaze drifted to the caption underneath: *Only surviving family member Jane Regina O'Donnell, age seven.*

The next weeks, months, even years were a frantic whirl of events. Her mother's family took her in. They left the country. New lives were set up. Nothing was ever said about the past—not her mother, her brother, and certainly not the monster of a father. And yet Reggie, armed with her mother's maiden name instead of her father's, had eventually come back to the city where he'd committed his atrocities. Her identity had been buried deep. She was no longer seven and vacant. She was Reggie Campion, a grown woman on a mission rebuilding a life from the catastrophic ruins of her past.

And yet she now wondered, and not for the first time, whether Professor Miles Mallory knew who she really was. And if that was why he'd approached her. He had never given any indication that he did know her true history, but he was also the sort of man who wouldn't have let on if he did.

There were other items in the box, yet she decided to look at only two more. One was a photo of her mother, a petite blonde woman whom Reggie remembered as innocent if not overly intelligent or curious, and yet someone who loved her children unconditionally. The second item was a photo of her brother, Lionel, who had gone to the police and ended the monster's reign in London, though it had cost him his life. Even at age twelve, he was tall, like his father, who had been six-four and well over two hundred pounds. Lionel took after their mother, not in stature, but in looks. The hair was light, the eyes a dim blue, the mouth usually curled into a smile. But not in this picture. This was a photo of her brother lying dead in his coffin. Reggie didn't know where it had come from, only that she'd discovered it years ago and now found herself unable to part with it. It was sick, macabre, she realized that. But it was also a reminder of her brother's ultimate sacrifice to save all of them from evil.

She put the items back in the box, locked it up, and slid it back into the wall vault receptacle. Reggie returned to her flat, packed a bag, climbed in her little car, and drove to Harrowsfield.

On the way there she thought of nothing else other than how to get one more chance at Fedir Kuchin. Well, that was not entirely true. Another tall man with dark hair kept uncomfortably intruding on those thoughts too.

Where was Shaw now?

CHAPTER

67

Almost as soon as Reggie passed the town of Leavesden and started making her way along the winding roads to the estate, the sun disappeared behind darkening clouds. At least the meteorological conditions matched her mood. She passed the entry gates, parked her car, took a long breath, and walked inside.

She'd phoned ahead with her expected time of arrival and they were waiting for her in the library. The professor, Whit, Liza, and Dominic. As she passed down the hall she saw Niles Jansen, the colleague that Shaw had steamrolled back at the cottage in Provence. She tossed him back his cell phone that Shaw had taken.

"How is it?" she asked, indicating the large bruise on his face.

"Like a bloody tank hit me," said Jansen.

"Actually, I think it did."

She drew a calming breath and opened the door to the library. Taking a seat on one side of the long table with all the rest aligned on the other, she painstakingly went through everything she recalled from her time in Gordes and then briefed them on the days spent with Shaw.

"And you learned nothing more about him than that?" asked Mallory, who did not bother to hide his incredulity.

"It's hard to be a competent interrogator when you're vomiting your brains out," she answered. "And he's not the sort to volunteer much information. He's obviously an experienced hand. Other than that, it's all speculation."

"But his organization is obviously official whilst ours is not," pointed out Mallory.

"Meaning that we could all be charged with attempted murder

for all the good we've done," said Whit. "Hell, Kuchin could sue us for what we did and probably win. Maybe we should all retain solicitors."

"This isn't funny, Whit," snapped Liza. "Our entire operation could be jeopardized."

"Shaw doesn't know where we are," said Reggie. "It wasn't like I was going to bring him here."

"See, I told you that," noted Whit. He looked at Reggie. "And Dom here reminded all of us that you'd earned the right to be trusted."

Reggie gave Dominic a grateful look before turning back to Mallory. "But that's not a real solution. With their resources, they may be able to track us down. They certainly know what the three of us look like."

"I suggest that all of you stay at Harrowsfield until further notice," said Mallory.

Both Whit and Dominic slowly nodded in agreement.

But Reggie said, "I've got some things to take care of, but then I'll be back here to stay."

Mallory nodded. "Good, that's settled. Now let's move on to more important issues, namely Fedir Kuchin and his unfortunate survival."

"We'll go after him again, like we talked about yesterday," said Whit.

"I actually agree, after much deliberation, with your Mr. Shaw," said Mallory, surprisingly.

Reggie, having not been privy to this conversation, said, "Agree with him in what way?"

Whit spoke up. "He's talking about your buddy's assessment that Kuchin will be coming after us. So instead of going after him we have to guard our own flanks."

"We talked about that too, right before we parted company," said Reggie.

Mallory rose, walked over to the empty fireplace, and knocked out the dregs from a new pipe into the hearth. "I'm sure you did. Indeed, it seems that this other organization might be more aptly suited to take Mr. Kuchin down than we are."

Whit burst out, "But they're not going to do it. I told you that. They were pulling out. Apparently they don't care that he's selling girls as whores. Once he dropped the nuke angle it was all copacetic as far as those blokes were concerned."

"That was before they knew who he was." He looked at Reggie. "You told him, correct? That Waller was Fedir Kuchin?"

"Yes. But he didn't know who that was."

Mallory took a few moments to puff his pipe to life. "No matter. He will look into it now, and then there you are. When he knows the real Butcher of Kiev is out there, chances are very good that either they'll go after him or they'll notify another appropriate agency to do so."

"So we just fob off on them the job we set out to do?" said Reggie. "Why should they have to deal with him?"

Mallory eyed her with interest. "Are you really thinking why should this *Shaw* fellow have to deal with him?"

Reggie's face reddened. "That is not what I said, Professor."

"And there's no guarantee they will go after him," protested Whit. "They might have other things on their agenda."

Mallory turned to him. "There are no guarantees about anything we do, Whit. And I believe this is the best we can do. At least currently."

"Well, I disagree."

"I don't mind disagreement so long as you do not turn it into unilateral action."

"Well, what if Kuchin ends up walking free?"

"There are many men like him out there. I will not jeopardize catching all of them in order to take one down."

Whit snapped, "But we've already shown him the shit from his past. Now all we need to do is kill the bastard. A rifle shot from long distance. Poison in his morning coffee. Stick the prick in the street with an umbrella tipped with poison, like they did that Bulgarian fellow."

Mallory shook his head. "But since the authorities presumably will know who he is, they will investigate his death and past and publicize their results to the world—that he is indeed the Butcher of Kiev. And all others will be warned."

"All others?" scoffed Whit. "You think these assholes send out newsletters to each other? Look out, fellow scum, the good guys are gunning for you? I've never bought that rationale before, Prof, and I sure as hell don't buy it now. You're saying we as good as let him go free forever."

"No, I said we can let others handle it for now."

Reggie spoke up. "I think I side with Whit on this, but the problem is that Kuchin will dig in so deep now we'll never be able to find him. He probably has safe houses all over the world."

"Since we have limited resources, that makes all the more reason to move on to someone else. But for now, I think all of you should relax and regroup. Dominic needs to heal physically." Mallory looked at Reggie and then at Whit. "And you need to do so in other ways."

"My head is on as straight as ever," muttered Whit.

"I wasn't necessarily talking about you," replied Mallory.

"So me then?" exclaimed Reggie. She looked darkly at the man.

"Just everyone please take a rest," said Mallory a trifle wearily.

"Even if the Ukrainian psychopath has us in his gunsights?" asked Whit.

"Yes, even then," said the professor sharply. Mallory then rose and left the room.

"He's under a lot of pressure," said Liza defensively.

"We're all under a lot of pressure, Liza," rejoined Reggie.

"The operation in Provence cost a lot of money," Liza continued. "And funds are getting harder and harder to come by. Miles spends a great deal of his time finding benefactors."

Whit scowled at her. "Great, fine. I'll cut my salary. Oh, that's right, I don't really get paid a bleeding quid to risk life and limb, now do I?"

"I didn't mean it that way, Whit," she said.

"I don't think any of us mean anything we're saying right now," said Dominic.

Whit rose. "Speak for yourself, Dom. I meant it all."

Before anyone could say anything he'd slammed the library door behind him.

CHAPTER

68

Reggie decided against seeking refuge in the underground shooting range. This was principally because she didn't think her still queasy stomach could take the pungent smells created by the weapon's discharge in close quarters. Yet she didn't want to remain inside the distinctly chilly atmosphere at Harrowsfield, so she settled on wandering the grounds. That of course led her to the graveyard and then to the gravesite of Laura R. Campion. She'd visited her mother's and brother's graves only once, years ago, and her father's never. And yet here she was, for the hundredth time standing in front of what was almost certainly a stranger's final resting place.

Are you going mad, Reg? Is this what it feels like? . . . Is this what happened to my . . . dad?

She had long ago convinced herself that her father had become insane, because that was the only way to explain what he'd done. But at a certain level she knew that might not be true. And it terrified her.

She said out loud, "Do you just go mad? Or are you simply born evil? Or do you simply slaughter because history gives you the chance?"

"Yes to all three," said a voice.

Reggie nearly toppled over as she spun around, her mind recognizing the voice but also at the same instant wondering how it could possibly be.

Shaw stood at the edge of the yew hedge that nearly surrounded the cemetery.

"How?" she began, before Shaw put a finger to his lips as he came forward.

He stood beside her. "Good to see you again too."

"How the hell did you get here?"

"The phone I gave back to you? GPS."

"That's impossible. We disable all GPS chips in our phones when we're on mission to prevent just this sort of thing."

"I know. That's why I had to put one in it on the boat ride over."

Reggie groaned and put a hand to her forehead. "I can't believe I was that incredibly stupid."

"You're not stupid, you're really good. But I'm pretty good at what I do too."

Reggie looked around nervously. "If they find you here?"

"What? They'll kill me?"

"We don't do that," she said sternly.

"Oh really?" He reached in his jacket pocket and slipped out the syringe he'd taken from Niles Jansen at the cottage where he had been held captive. He held it up.

Reggie looked from the syringe to Shaw. "What are you doing with that?"

"They were going to kill me with it, Reggie."

"That's impossible. We never told anyone—"

"The guy I knocked out said the order came from someone else." He looked in the direction of the mansion. "Maybe somebody in the big house I passed?"

"Shaw, that is just not possible."

"So do you guys just carry this stuff around with you?"

"That poison was intended for Kuchin. But we already had a syringe with us."

"So why a second one?"

"In case something happened to the first, I imagine," she said lamely.

"Or in case someone got in the way. Like me."

"This is absurd. He actually said that somebody ordered him to kill you?"

"I'm not really in the habit of making stuff like that up. I mean, what would be the point?"

Reggie slowly moved away from him and slumped down on a weathered stone bench on the edge of the small cemetery. Shaw joined her there, drawing up his collar against the chilly air and cloudy skies that had come back to England with a vengeance as if to make up for the rare heat and sunshine.

"The plan was to let you go once we'd finished with Kuchin."

"Plans change if the right person wants them to. Who here has that kind of clout?"

Reggie involuntarily glanced toward the mansion.

"So I was right. They're in there. You got a name?"

"Why? Are you going to go in there and arrest him?"

"So it's a he? Trouble is, I don't actually have any authority to arrest anyone."

"Then what? Kill him? You go after him you'll have a lot of other people you'll have to kill too."

"Including you?"

"Yes," she said without hesitation.

"Well, then I find my options limited." He handed her the syringe. "Just make sure whoever you stick with that really needs killing. No second chances there."

Reggie held the capped needle in her open palm while gazing up at Shaw. "Why did you come here?"

"Wanted to see for myself the competition, I guess. Nice digs. My office is either at forty thousand feet or right at ground level with lots of excitement going on all around me."

"Is that all?"

"Oh, there was something else. I wanted to make sure you weren't still puking your guts out. See, I feel a little responsible for that. And I guess I wasn't as sympathetic to you as I should have been while we were bouncing across the water."

This drew a meager smile from Reggie. "Well, truthfully, I'm still a bit wobbly, but my bearings are slowly returning." She paused while carefully pocketing the syringe. "Does your boss know that you're here?"

"We're not always in sync."

She glanced once more in the direction of the old mansion. "Actually, I can relate to that. How long will you be in England?"

"That depends."

"On what?"

"On whether you'll agree to have dinner with me tonight. If yes, I'll be here at least another day. If not, I'm out of here right now."

Reggie glanced down.

"Problem getting away?" said Shaw.

"Actually we've all been given a spot of time off. But if anyone sees you. Whit or—"

"No one's going to see me. I'll go back out the way I came in. I kind of make a living sneaking around. But to be on the safe side let's meet in London around eight tonight." He gave her the name of a side street off Trafalgar Square. "We can pick a place to go after that."

"Can I let you know?"

"Yeah, right now, or I'm flying out tonight. And I doubt I'll be back, Reggie."

"You don't give a girl much time to make up her mind."

"No, I really don't."

"All right. But what are we going to talk about at dinner?"

"Oh, I'm sure we'll find something of mutual interest. And if we're lucky, it might even be entertaining too." He looked over her shoulder at the sunken ground of the cemetery. "And it might cheer you up a bit. Looks like you need it."

"I guess it seems weird to you, my staring at graves."

"No."

"Why not?"

"Because I do it too."

CHAPTER

69

FEDIR KUCHIN had nothing, and because he had nothing the man was growing increasingly frustrated. In ninety-degree angles he paced the three-thousand-square-foot cabin perched near an ocean whose water temperature never got much above fifty degrees even in August. Kuchin's mood was tied directly to his underling's failure. Alan Rice had purchased access to a dozen databases and yet there had not been one hit on any of the digital images made from his drawings or the photo. Every other avenue of investigation he'd pursued had ended with a similar lack of progress. Kuchin's large hands clenched and then loosened as his nimble mind galloped along trying to envision some way to move forward.

Finally, Kuchin drew on a parka and walked outside. He had taken with him a rifle and scope and some cartridges. It was summer but one wouldn't know it by the weather. It wasn't cold enough to snow, but as he looked around the terrain reminded him starkly of his birthplace in the Ukraine. Perhaps that's why he'd built a home here with nothing else around for miles. He had two guards with him who stayed in another building five hundred meters from his house. Yet there wasn't much danger out here. Other than the threat of being gored or trampled by a moose or a caribou, Kuchin felt fairly secure.

He trudged over ground that brought back memories of a little boy trailing his burly father as he went off to work. Work was fishing on a commercial trawler in the Sea of Azov. Forty thousand square kilometers in area, the Azov's deepest point was surprisingly less than fifteen meters. It was in fact the shallowest sea in the world. Because of that its waters were turned over quickly. This did not keep it fresh, however. When Kuchin was a child the pollutants from factories and oil and gas exploration were already pouring into the sea's meager depths.

By the 1970s dead and mutated fish by the thousands were piling up on the shores, clearly victims of man-made toxins and radioactive poisons. To swim in the waters today would be suicidal. Yet all the children in Kuchin's village had spent their summers in waters whose temperatures would soar toward thirty degrees Celsius in July. In winter the sea would be frozen solid for months and the children would take their homemade skates and have races until their mothers would call out to them from shore to come eat their dinners. Kuchin could even remember lying facedown on the ice and licking it with his seven-year-old tongue.

Now Kuchin had heard that the Azov was in danger of becoming a dead sea and that commercial fishing should be banned for twenty years. This was not as draconian as it sounded. For forty years fishing yields had been reduced to nearly zero simply because all the sea life was dead. And yet he could recall vividly his father cleaning the fish he'd caught for their personal table with his big gutting knife, efficiently slicing up perch, sturgeon, and mackerel that his mother would then fry up in her big iron skillet with secret spices and ingredients that Frenchwomen seemed to naturally possess.

South of here was the Strait of Belle Isle, across from which was the region of Newfoundland. Kuchin had hiked there often and watched the cargo ships pass through the narrow channel. Indeed, some of his human cargo passed through these same waters. Before he reached adulthood Kuchin's life had been inextricably tied to water, polluted water as it turned out. He realized it was probably a miracle he was not dead from some horrible cancer rising from the shallow depths of the Azov. Yet there could be tumors right now growing in his body, wrapping silently but lethally around essential organs, crushing blood vessels or invading his brain.

However, despite the environmental dangers of his childhood, growing up there had provided him with an ambition to succeed that had been inexhaustible. Everything he'd ever set out to do he'd achieved, which made this present situation unacceptable.

He made the trek to the Belle Strait and stared out at seawater that represented the most direct route to Europe for ships coming from either the St. Lawrence Seaway or Great Lakes ports. Yet fogs, gales, and ice-choked seas for ten months of the year made navigation here some of the most treacherous in the world. The strait could hold wondrous sights too, however. These included humpback whales doing spectacular flips and wandering icebergs calved from glaciers in Greenland and bundled south by the Labrador Current before starting to come apart, with massive crashes, into the warmer waters off the coast. And *Belle Isle*, after which the strait was named, meant "Beautiful Island." It sat at the eastern tip of the waterway and was roughly halfway between Labrador and Newfoundland, which together formed the Canadian province of the same name.

Beauty in the midst of nothing, thought Kuchin. He believed, however briefly, that he'd found beauty in Provence. A woman who intrigued him, bewitched him, even; one whom he thought he might like to possibly entertain for longer than one night without a bloody mess to clean up afterward. And yet the beauty had almost killed him. It was a sense of betrayal—even though realistically the woman owed him no measure of loyalty—that fueled Kuchin's smoldering rage.

He walked up to the top of a small knoll, the strait behind him and the land in front of him flat for as far as the eye could see. Newfoundland was known as "the Rock." Its eastern region used to be part of northern Africa. The last glaciation had scraped almost all the soil off the southeastern coast, leaving it with more rock than anything else, hence the nickname. Labrador, the easternmost section of the Canadian Shield, had roughly three times the landmass of Newfoundland but with approximately five percent of its population. Its climate was technically classified as polar tundra, and polar bears indeed prowled the coastal areas and caribou outnumbered people by over twenty to one. Here, Kuchin had his pick of massive mountains to hike, isolated bays in which to fish, barren tundra to ski across, and breathtaking and brutal fjords cut into bedrock by glacier saws to view. The slopes were often sheer and the current in the water deceptively fast.

Kuchin drew a bead with his rifle, sighting through a scope man-

ufactured by Zeiss, the same outfit that had supplied the Third
Reich. It had everything an experienced shooter would expect in a
high-end sighting device, including O-ring seals and nitrogen fill
for fogproofing, all in a lightweight package with enhanced field of
vision.

When hunting large game it was generally agreed that a minimum
of a thousand foot-pounds of force from the round was necessary.
For the biggest game like moose that requirement ratcheted up to
roughly fifteen hundred foot-pounds at about five hundred yards.
He was using pointed boat-tailed 140-grain rounds that would
drop just about anything on four hooves and certainly anyone on
two feet.

Kuchin had had this rifle custom built. It was lightweight for
ease of carrying and maneuverability and he had fought his ego
and opted for somewhat less power because that translated to less
recoil, which resulted invariably in greater accuracy. He had
splurged on a premium barrel because that played a major factor
in the only thing that mattered: whether you hit your intended
target or not.

The small coyote was wandering along about two hundred yards
away from him, its agile gait carrying the animal along rapidly over
the flat terrain. It was early for the beast to be searching for food,
thought Kuchin, but here one never knew. Kill when you can was
probably a good motto for such a desolate place. It was probably a
female, Kuchin noted as he examined through the glass the small
chest and frame of the animal.

He lay prone on the ground, carrying the weight of the weapon
on his elbows. He steadied himself, fixing his grip around the stock
and underbelly of the gun, but relaxing his muscles. This was the
magic recipe of the successful sniper and long-range hunter, firm
but loose, heartbeat and breaths mellow, unhurried but with any
possible vibration removed. The butt of the weapon hard to his bicep, his index finger dropped to the trigger guard and from there to
the slender bit of curved metal. With one pull the immediately
heated round would burst from the elongated barrel, lands and
grooves branded into its metal hide from the force of the rapid ex-
pulsion. The quarter-gram metal missile would cover the distance

between man and beast roughly six times faster than if it had been perched in a seat on a commercial jet aircraft.

And yet with the coyote dead in his sights Kuchin did not pull the trigger. He lowered the weapon. The beast, unaware of how close it had come to annihilation at the hands of a far more dangerous predator, scampered along until it was nearly out of sight. Kuchin trudged the solitary miles back to his cabin. He had never enjoyed killing wildlife. Fishing held little interest for him either despite having been his father's trade.

It was only living things that looked like him that had ever motivated Fedir Kuchin to pull the trigger, light the match to the gas-filled pits, kick out the stool from under the noosed victim, or plunge the knife into someone's chest. It was just who and what he was.

He returned to his cabin, slid the parka on a hook by the door, locked his rifle back up in his gun safe, and returned to his desk. There was a blinking light on his phone. The message on the recording dispelled all the bad thoughts Kuchin had been harboring for most of the day.

It was Alan Rice.

"We found him."

CHAPTER

70

REGGIE LOVED Trafalgar Square. For her it seemed to define all things British in one sparkling geographic footprint. One had Lord Nelson on his forty-six-meter-high granite column, the savior of the British Empire honored for all time for his heroic death at the Battle of Trafalgar. And even if every school-aged child no longer knew exactly who Nelson was or what he'd done, his statue still stood as a memorial to the indomitability of the British people.

And yet there were also the great beastly pigeons. Though Nelson had been scrubbed clean several years ago and the city had taken steps to rid the area of the cooing winged creatures, the birds were simply an unstoppable force, such that the poor admiral was routinely covered in pigeon shit. Down below every make, model, and manner of human being walked, sat, danced, cried, ate, drank, performed, snapped pictures, read, flirted with their neighbor, and occasionally had sex late at night. This all went on while colorful cabs covered in advertisements and red elongated bendy-buses sped by with the intensity necessary to survive in one of the world's great metropolises. It was the perfect blend of the staid historical and the radical new and Reggie took it all in, forgetting for the moment that she was going to meet a man who could possibly destroy her.

Although it seemed a bit absurd considering all she had to think about, Reggie had been most nervous about what to wear. She had washed all her clothes and selected a pale green dress of simple design that tapered at the waist, showed off her tan, and stopped several inches above her knees. Its front was scooped but not too much. She had pulled out and then discarded the one push-up bra she owned, selecting a more modest one instead. She had decided against wearing a sweater over the dress because the weather in London had not matched that in Leavesden, which was often the case. The skies had cleared, the temperature had cracked seventy, which was cause for celebration across the city, and the slight breeze from the south was even more warming. Her heels were high, taking her to within eight inches of the man with whom she would shortly be having dinner. She had packed her hair up high, letting a few strands drizzle down her long neck. Chunky aquamarine earrings and a matching necklace she'd purchased years ago in Thailand completed the ensemble.

As she walked down the side street where he had arranged to meet her, Reggie surreptitiously checked her makeup in the side mirror of a parked motorbike while pretending to admire the machine. With his height he would be easy to spot even with all the people around. Yet the street also had many places of hidden observation. He was probably watching her right now, in fact.

She thought for a moment and then just decided what the hell. She pirouetted in a tight circle, one heel spike firmly planted against the pavement, while slowly waving in all directions like a beauty queen on display. This action made her briefly forget her troubles on a rare gorgeous summer's eve in the city she adored above all others.

The touch on her shoulder made her jump. She stopped spinning and faced him. Her first observation was that he'd also dressed carefully for the evening, in pressed gray slacks with a sharp crease, white polo shirt, and a navy blazer. His short hair had the shine of shampoo and he was freshly shaved. His scent reminded her of the luxurious beach in Thailand where she'd bought the necklace and earrings from a pale-skinned man carrying a shabby briefcase full of trinkets and wearing a Speedo. Shaw's smell was balmy, sand, ocean, the sway of exotic trees; it settled just firmly enough in her nostrils to make her feel a bit unsteady on her feet.

"You look great," he said.

"No more seasickness. I promise." She tapped the ground with her spike heels. "Firmly on terra firma."

Shaw glanced around before returning his gaze to her. Reggie could sense in that one motion that he had assessed all potential threats and filed them away in some neat data bank in his mind.

"You like seafood?" he said.

"That's actually my absolute favorite."

"I know a place in Mayfair."

"Sounds brilliant."

He looked hesitant for a moment and then held out his arm. She quickly slipped her hand through it before he could reconsider the offer. His hesitation had made Reggie inwardly smile. Uncertainty humanized a person so wonderfully, she thought. Reggie slightly increased the pressure on his arm to show him he'd made the right decision.

"It's not too far from here," he said. "It's a nice night, we can walk." He glanced down at her shoes. "Can you manage in those things? We can cab it if you want."

"I can walk over in these heels. I just might not be able to walk back."

"I can always carry you."

They walked down Haymarket Street, cut through Piccadilly Circus, and over to Mayfair.

"It's only a few more blocks," said Shaw as they ambled slowly along. "Just off Grosvenor."

"I'm good."

He glanced down at her. "You do seem good."

She interpreted his remark as she glanced around at other couples doing exactly what they were doing. "It's just nice to *pretend* to be normal. I guess that seems weird."

"No it doesn't. In our professions those moments are few and far between."

The restaurant was set midblock, and had a green awning out front partially obscuring a pair of formidable mahogany doors. Inside, the ceilings were high, the wood dark, the booths leather-backed, the linens starched, and the napkins poofed up in cut crystal water glasses. Topping chest-high wood cabinets were iced platters of lobster tails, shrimp, black-shelled mussels, and spidery crab legs arranged in concentric circles. Shaw had made a reservation and a curvy young Indian woman in a black dress tight enough to reveal her choice of thong underwear led them to their table. It was situated in the back diagonally across from the entrance.

Shaw took the seat opposite the mahogany doors.

This had not been lost on Reggie. "Firing lines sufficiently established?" she asked impishly.

"They'll do. Unless that platter of steamed squid fouls the shot."

"Why do I think you're not joking?"

He picked up his menu.

She did the same. "Any recommendations?"

"Pretty much anything that has a fin, gills, and/or a shell is a safe bet to be classified as an aphrodisiac."

She dropped the menu. "Then why don't you pick for me?"

Shaw's gaze topped his menu. "Indecisive?"

"Actually, cautious enough to defer to another's *enhanced* expertise."

"There's a lot that can be interpreted from that remark," he said candidly.

"There is. But for now, let's limit it to the food."

He put his menu aside. "Then we'll double down on the Primavera Frutti di Mare."

They ordered their food and a white wine to go with it. The waiter drew out the cork and poured the small taster portion, which Shaw approved with a sip and a nod. The waiter filled their glasses, set a basket of bread and a bottle of olive oil between them, placed the wine in a chiller sleeve, and left them alone.

Shaw held up his glass and Reggie dinked it with hers.

"Is the pretending to be normal period almost over?" she said resignedly.

"Almost, but not quite."

"I love London," Reggie said, looking around.

"There's a lot to love," agreed Shaw.

"Can I ask you a question?" she said.

He remained silent but stared at her expectantly.

"You mentioned back in the cemetery at Harrowsfield that you stare at graves too. What did you mean by that?"

"Not graves, *grave*, singular."

"Whose?"

"It's in Germany, an hour's ride outside of Frankfurt, a small village."

"That's where, but *whose* grave do you look at there?"

"A woman's." The strain on Shaw's face was perceptible.

"I take it you two were close?"

"Close enough."

"Can you tell me her name?"

"Anna. And now I think the pretending to be normal period *is* over."

CHAPTER

71

FEDIR KUCHIN was impatient, which meant he was irritable, which meant he was once more pacing in his precise ninety-degree grids. A leased jet had just touched down forty kilometers from here. He envisioned Alan Rice climbing in an SUV and setting off to come and meet with him. In his possession was information that Kuchin now craved more than he had anything in his life.

But he had to wait. Forty kilometers over mediocre roads. An hour, perhaps more if the weather continued to deteriorate as it had threatened to do all day.

"Everything okay, Mr. Waller?"

He stopped pacing and looked up to find Pascal standing in the doorway. He wore jeans, boots, flannel shirt, and a leather jacket. Always a jacket and always a gun underneath the jacket, Kuchin knew. His mother had been small, spare, and Pascal had taken after her instead of his tall father. The facial features too were hers. Greek had trumped Ukrainian in this genetic instance. Those features were now marred by yellow and purplish bruises, thanks to the tall man who'd beaten them both in the catacombs of Gordes.

"Just thinking, Pascal. The others will be here in about an hour."

"Yes sir."

"How are you feeling?"

"Not bad."

The little man was tough, Kuchin could not deny that. His arm could be dangling by a sliver of skin and he would probably only ask for aspirin or more likely nothing at all.

He is tough, like his father.

The affair had been brief but memorable. Kuchin had taken a

holiday in Greece as reward for his good work in Ukraine. Under brilliant sunlight that did not seem to exist in the Soviet Union, at least that he'd experienced, Fedir Kuchin had bedded a woman and together they'd made a baby. Kuchin had not been there for the birth but he had named his son. Pascal was a Francophone given name for a male. In Latin it meant relating to Easter and in Hebrew to be born or associated with Passover. Kuchin had named the boy in honor of his French mother, who was also a Jew, though she'd converted to Catholicism when still a young girl. He'd never told anyone about her ethnicity, nor of her and his religious beliefs. In the power circles of the Soviet Union, that would not have been looked on in a positive way.

"You do good work, Pascal," said Kuchin. Searching the other man's features, as he sometimes did, Kuchin would imagine he saw a glimmer of himself there. He had sent his son off to various skirmishes across the world as a mercenary. Pascal had been trained by some of the best military minds around. He'd fought in places like Kosovo and Slovakia, Bosnia and Honduras, Colombia and Somalia. He'd always returned to his father with a smile on his face and more experience grafted into his DNA. Kuchin had taught him some old tricks of the trade as well, taking some fatherly pride in doing so, but not too much. He was a bastard child after all. But he was also all Kuchin had in the way of descendants. Not smart enough to run the business, but smart enough to protect those who did.

"Thank you, sir, you need anything, you just let me know."

Pascal moved off and Kuchin rubbed the scars on his wrist. They'd been caused by ten-pound fishing line that had cut into his skin so deeply as a child that the marks had become permanent. This was his father's way of teaching his son to obey. These lessons were usually accompanied by drunken screams and thundering fists. He would be strung up like one of his father's catches, his toes barely touching the icy floor. This would go on for hours until Kuchin thought his hamstrings would collapse, his Achilles tendons dissolve.

His back too held the marks of violent intrusion. A belt, a strap, a fishing reel whose metal guides had bitten into his prepubescent skin and stung like the blitzkrieg of a thousand-wasp army. These were his father's choices, his father's life lessons to his only child.

His good mother would always fight for him and even attack her far larger husband, whose height and girth eventually had been passed on to his son. And for her loyalty to her child the woman had been dealt with more cruelly. For hours afterwards they would lie on the floor and cradle each other, nursing wounds, sharing tears, speaking in French in low voices so the father and husband could not hear, for it would undoubtedly drive him into another rage.

Kuchin had lied to Alan Rice and later to Janie Collins or whatever her real name was. His father had not died from a fall at the cottage in Roussillon. Kuchin's father had never been to Roussillon or even France at all. A poor family from rural Ukraine during that time would never have had the money nor the permission to travel abroad. They would never even have made it to the border. No proper papers, no reason to be leaving the Soviet empire. They would have been executed on the spot, their bodies left where they fell like trash flung from a truck as a message to others contemplating disobedience. And Kuchin had to admit, that message could be very effective. He'd later conveyed such messages himself.

It was only after he'd risen to his post in the KGB that out-of-country travel was possible for the most loyal, which included him of course. He had gotten special permission to take his mother to the town of her birth. By now she was clearly old before her time, and the years left to her were few. The cottage had been empty, and Kuchin, though he did not have much money back then, had found a way to purchase it for her. She lived there for five happy years until her death. Kuchin visited her when he could. She would call him by a French name that in her diminished mental state she believed to be his real one. A Soviet to the core, Kuchin would have killed any man who called him that, but when his old, failing mother did so he would merely nod and shed a tear or two and hold her withered hand, answering her queries like a nice little Frenchman looking to appease his beloved mama.

Kuchin stared out the window of his cabin, toward the not too distant coast. Yet his hearing was attuned to the swirl of rubber over crushed gravel that lay on the opposite side of the house. He checked his watch. Alan Rice should be here in no more than twenty minutes. His gaze returned to the nearby waters and another memory entered his thoughts. This time it was a happy one.

The Sea of Azov was far too shallow for his plan, of course. That was why one moonless night in October several decades ago, a grown-up and very strong Kuchin, now a valued member of the deeply feared Komitet Gosudarstvennoy Bezopasnosti, or KGB, had dragged his father from his shack, loaded him on a boat, and set off to deep water. Through the Strait of Kerch they had entered the Black Sea, which had an area over ten times the size of the adjacent Azov. More importantly, the deepest point there was over two thousand meters.

Kuchin had anchored down and he and three of his comrades who had come to help him had used the strongest fishing line they could find to tie up the old man. The senior Kuchin's eyes bulged with the terror of what was happening to him. Attached to the line and the heavy metal cables that they'd draped over his head and shoulders were two fifty-gallon metal drums filled with sand. It was a favored disposal technique for the Soviet security forces. Indeed, some of the KGB officers had started terming this pairing the "golden slippers."

Kuchin had looked into his father's eyes one last time. The roles were reversed now. The large was now small and the young child was now a strong man more than capable of defeating the monster that had punished him relentlessly for so long. He spoke to him in two languages. First he said the words in French, which he knew the old man could understand, however grudgingly. And then in Ukrainian, which he knew would be crystal clear to the bastard.

Then over the gunwale the drums went and seconds later the cables drew taut and the old man sailed overboard too, screaming in terror. In a few seconds it was finished. Kuchin took the helm and steered them back to where they had come. He looked back only once at the spot where the man who had plagued him would carry out the last few seconds of his life. And then he turned back and thought no more of him.

The SUV came into view. Alan Rice was here with the promised intelligence.

For Fedir Kuchin it was time to track down and catch another adversary who would dare seek to harm him.

72

Yᴏᴜ ᴅɪᴅ ɴᴏᴛ use the company jet, correct?" asked Kuchin.

"No. Like you said to, I rented a private plane under one of the corporate shells we have. Untraceable to you or me."

"And you have stayed outside of the city in the safe house?"

"Yes. Just as you instructed. I've conducted business through secure phone and computer lines." He paused. "You think people are after me?"

"No, they're after me, but they can use you to help in that search. I could have killed you or kept you under wraps. I chose the latter."

Rice looked like he might be sick.

Kuchin gripped his arm. "Now your report."

"It was quite fascinating how we were able to crack this. The technology is really remarkable. We started with using—"

Kuchin raised a cautioning hand. "Alan, get to the point."

"We found nothing on the data banks we could get into. No doubt if we had access to some of the Americans' files or even Interpol's it would have been a different story. But we don't and thus we had to turn to other things. Now, in these alternative venues the data streams were immense and the server access protocols were complex, but—"

"The point," snapped Kuchin.

Rice hurried on. "The thing we turned to was aftermarket surveillance feeds."

"Aftermarket surveillance feeds? Explain this."

"These days there are observational cameras everywhere. I'm not talking about people running around with their cell phones snapping away when a celebrity does something stupid and it gets posted online. I mean cameras at ATM sites, along streets, office buildings, courthouses, airports, train stations, and millions of other places. Hell, London is one big camera, particularly with the congestion charge enforcement requirements. The result is there are literally trillions of bytes of images out there and it ends up on enormous servers. It's made the cops' job easier. With just about any crime, at least in a public area, there's a decent chance it was captured on film somewhere."

"But how does that help us? Were there such cameras in the ancient town of Gordes?" Kuchin said skeptically.

Rice opened up his laptop and set it on a wooden coffee table. "No, we went at it from a different angle. You have to understand that a lot of this data is not locally stored. The capacity just isn't there, particularly for smaller firms and average-size municipalities, and it's hugely expensive to store and maintain even for megafirms and large cities. So what do folks do when confronted with a need that they are not equipped to handle or is too capital-intensive to take on alone?"

"They outsource it to firms who specialize in that area."

"Exactly. So much of this data is stored centrally at gigantic server complexes around the world. Think of it as massive file cabinets organized by countries, states, cities, towns, suburbs, or divided tactically into government buildings, banks, commercial office properties, even military facilities, and dozens of other subcategories. The images are typically saved for years, or even in perpetuity. It's not like you've got billions of photos stacked somewhere. It's all digital. The storage footprint is relatively small."

"And you never know when some of this data might have value?"

"Exactly. Let's say there's an image of an employee meeting outside a building with the same person for weeks. It might not mean anything then, but two years from now when business secrets are stolen it might very well aid in building a corporate espionage case against that employee."

"I see. Go on."

"Years ago entrepreneurs saw opportunities in this fledgling field and took advantage to build substantial global businesses from the fact that we really have become a Big Brother society. Now, here is the key for our purposes. Certain people within some of these companies quickly realized that the stored images had value to many others besides the original client. This is so because a camera captures many things outside of the original intent of why it was placed in a certain location. For example, aside from anything to do with the client who put the camera there, if you know someone was at a certain place at a certain time and you want a compromising picture of that person, chances are very good there was an electronic eye there and that the feed exists on some server."

"So in effect employees of these companies are selling the images to people who want them for reasons unrelated to why the surveillance was conducted in the first place?"

"Exactly. They let it be known discreetly that they can run checks for the right price and the picture is delivered for a fee. Some have gone a step further and the actual companies that collect this data and store it are also selling images to third parties. Apparently the law is vague in some countries, or at least inconsistent enough about the uses that can be made of the stored information to allow sufficient wiggle room for the companies to do this. And the original clients either don't care or more likely are unaware of these additional uses of the data.

"And that's where we came in. We sent one well-known server platform covering a number of countries in Europe the digitized images taken from your drawings and the photo of the woman. They ran it through every file they had. We didn't get a hit the first go-round, but we did the second."

"And the *hit*?"

Rice keyed in some commands on his computer and turned the screen around for Kuchin to see. "It was only one hit, but it was better than nothing. Zurich. Outside a hotel, seven months ago," Rice explained.

Kuchin sat forward and studied the picture. That was the tall man all right.

"But *who* is he?"

"We don't know yet."

Kuchin slapped the table with his palm. "Then this is *useless* to me."

"Wait, Evan, please, there's more. Look at the woman beside him."

Kuchin did. She was tall, slender, and blonde. Then he noted that the woman's arm was touching Shaw's hand. He shot a glance at Rice. "They are together?"

"Apparently so, yes. We checked with the hotel. They would give out no information on either of them, so we next ran her photo through the image data banks."

"And you got a hit?"

"More than that." Rice handed him a file. "I know you prefer paper to digital."

Kuchin took the file, but did not open it. "Her name?"

"Katie James."

CAN'T WE at least eat our meal before the pretend time is over?" said Reggie earnestly.

"Does it mean that much to you?"

"Actually it does."

Shaw rifled a glance at the waiter hovering nearby. "Okay, this is probably not the best place to do it anyway."

Their food came and they talked about things other people would normally talk about over a meal out. Another bottle of wine, this one a red, was ordered and fully drunk. Coffees followed and they shared a dessert that had coconut and ribbons of white icing on top. Shaw paid the bill with a credit card.

"A. Shaw?" said Reggie as she spied the name on the plastic. "What's the A stand for?"

"Absolutely nothing."

He signed on the dotted line and they rose and left. The evening was still warm, at least by London standards, though now Reggie wished she had brought the sweater. Noticing her chill bumps, Shaw took off his jacket and draped it around her shoulders. It hung down like a dress.

"Forty-six extra long?" she said, gripping the material.

"Something like that. How're the feet?"

"Depends on where we're headed."

"My hotel's in that direction. Ten-minute cab ride."

She looked startled. "Your hotel?"

"Or we can go to your place."

"Why does it have to be either one?"

"Or we can just go to another public place and talk about it and hope nobody overhears us."

Reggie thought of the sex-crazed couple in the rooms above her. "My place is not that quiet," she said.

"Mine is."

"Where exactly is it?"

"The Savoy. It recently reopened. Excellent river views. Very nice."

"What did you tell me before about being forward? Going to your hotel room this late at night seems to fall into that category."

"That was before, this is now. We can cab it. It's down in the Strand."

"I know where the damn Savoy is."

"Then let's go."

An efficient cabbie with "the knowledge," as Londoners referred to the mental map cabdrivers were required to learn over several years, whisked them along Piccadilly, over to Haymarket, around Lord Nelson and his army of pigeons, and onto the Strand.

"It's always puzzled me why the only place one drives on the right in all of Britain is down the little street to the Savoy entrance," said Shaw.

"It's because the hotel's forecourt was too narrow for coachmen to pull up to the front doors if they had to hug the left side." Shaw stared at her in mild amusement. She said sharply, "What? I *am* English, after all."

They walked through the lobby, up a flight of stairs, and rode an elevator car up to Shaw's room. He closed the door behind them, dropped his keys on the table, and pointed to a chair for Reggie to take while he sat on the edge of the bed.

"Wretched heels." She slipped off her shoes and rubbed her aching feet. "Now what?"

"Now we talk survival."

"Yours or mine?"

"Both, if we're lucky."

"Maybe it was just me, but your boss didn't seem all that keen on working with us. It was more like he wanted to arrest us."

"*Should* he want to do that?"

Reggie's features stiffened a bit. "I'm not going to think for him."

Shaw opened the room safe housed in a cabinet and pulled out a paper file. He flicked through some pages. "Fedir Kuchin. I read up on him."

"I could have saved you the trouble. We have lots of paper on him."

"People believed he was dead; killed in an uprising in Ukraine years before the Wall fell."

"Carefully orchestrated escape strategy. A number of them did that."

Shaw looked over the top of the file at her. "A number of them? Interesting word choice. What exactly is it that you and your comrades in arms do at Harrowsfield?"

"Something that I can't tell you about. Ever."

"You're going to have to tell somebody."

"Why? Have you already told your boss about the place?"

"I haven't told him anything about anything. What I'm telling you is that you might need a friend on this."

"And you're that friend?" she scoffed.

"I didn't say I was that friend. I don't know enough to know whether I want to be your friend or not."

"Meaning you might end up against us?"

"Just talk to me."

Reggie rose and paced in her bare feet, scrunching her toes against the soft carpet, working out the cramps. "It's not that simple. Nothing about this is simple, Shaw."

"It's only as hard as you make it."

"Oh come on, that's bullshit logic and you know it."

"Maybe it is, but I'm finding the words hard to come by to convince you to trust me. I thought maybe I'd earned some of that back in Gordes."

"That was then, this is now," she said, throwing Shaw's own words back at him.

"I guess risking life and limb doesn't mean as much as it used to."

Reggie stopped pacing and sat down next to him on the bed. She looked down at the floor and sighed. "No, it actually does."

"So what's the problem? I know Kuchin is a bad guy."

"But you know what we were going to do to him."

"Seemed pretty obvious."

"I take it you don't play by those rules?"

"Not unless it's either them or me. Then I'll do what I have to, to walk away."

"That's not exactly splitting hairs. It's a big difference in philosophy."

"Like I said before, I don't have the authority to arrest anyone."

"Right, sure." She stood and drew over to the window and opened the drapes.

"Nicest views in London," said Shaw, who joined her there.

Grateful for this momentary change in the discussion, Reggie pointed to a lighted structure in the distance and said, "Have you been on the Eye?"

It looked like a Ferris wheel on growth hormones.

"Once, but only because a guy I was trailing decided to take a ride."

Reggie pointed at another structure. "Did you know Claude Monet painted a picture of Waterloo Bridge from a balcony here? And that Fred Astaire danced on the Savoy's roof?"

"No, I didn't know that."

She closed the drape and turned to him. "But the oddest story I ever heard about the Savoy has to do with a cat named Kaspar."

"Kaspar the cat?"

"Yes. He's the oldest resident here, actually. Whenever there's a dinner party at the Savoy where the number of guests is thirteen Kaspar comes out and fills a fourteenth seat."

"That's because superstition has it that the first person who gets up from a party of thirteen will die?"

"Precisely. I believe Agatha Christie even wrote a mystery about it."

"But eating with a cat?"

"Kaspar is carved out of wood, which makes him invaluable as a dinner partner, if only for the 'quiet' companionship he provides."

"Nice story," Shaw said.

"Yes, isn't it?" Reggie replied quietly.

"How many other Kuchins have there been?" Shaw asked.

"You deduce that from my vague phraseology? Big assumption on your part."

"Not really."

"What then?"

"You don't get that good your first time out."

"I'm not sure how good we really are. Gordes was a major cock-up all around, as you said."

"Things happen in the field, no matter how well you plan it out. But the way I see it you have two major problems and they may be connected."

She sat back down on the bed and looked up at him. "Okay. What are they?"

"First, you guys got ambushed. That means you either let somebody sneak up on you or you have a mole."

"And the second?"

"Kuchin is still out there." He patted the file he'd pulled from the safe. "And unless the guy in these pages has really mellowed over the years he's not going to just walk away from this. And if he did take out those Muslim terrorists he's apparently still got his killing mojo. Now, if he also has a plant inside your place that makes it even more problematic."

"But if he did have a mole, how could we have gotten him down to the catacombs?"

"Not sure. But regardless, the issue becomes, what are you going to do about it?"

"Quite frankly, this is a little bit of new territory for us."

"I'd like to help you with this."

"You would have no idea what you were getting into, trust me."

"That's all I'm asking you to do, trust *me*."

"I've never really trusted anyone. Perhaps not even myself at times," she added in a strained voice.

He perched next to her on the bed. "How did you get mixed up in something like this?"

She said angrily, "How did you get mixed up in what *you* do?"

"It was pretty much against my will, actually."

"Yeah, well, I went voluntarily down my road."

"Then I'll voluntarily go down that same road with you."

"Why? Why help me?"

"I don't get to help many people. When the chance comes I try not to miss it."

Reggie's anger faded and she touched his cheek. "Who was Anna?"

"A woman I cared for. I told you."

"I'm sorry."

"So am I."

"I'm not Anna, Shaw."

His eyes glimmered. "I know that. No one can be Anna." He started to say something else but she covered his mouth with her hand.

She said, "Please. Don't."

He looked at her as Reggie's hand slid from his mouth to his cheek.

"Reggie?"

She shook her head, stood, unzipped her dress, and stepped out of it. Reggie stood there in front of him in panties and bra. It was as though she was waiting for him to tell her to stop. Shaw said nothing, just looked at her. He finally put his hand on her hip, squeezed lightly. She pushed him flat on the bed and straddled him.

Reggie attacked his mouth, biting his lower lip and then kissing him on the neck and face before hungrily returning to his mouth, as they hastily worked their clothes off. There was energy and anger and desperation and even violence barely restrained as they went at one another.

Sweat dripped off them both as the Savoy's new HVAC system largely failed to keep up with the mingled heat thrown from their energized coupling. They eventually collapsed into a crazy tangle, her hair in his eyes, his knee between her legs, her arm curved around his head. She gently rubbed his face, kissed it.

Shaw's eyes were closed, his breathing slowly returning to normal.

"Seems like it was as long in between for you as it was for me," she said, her lungs still heaving.

He disengaged from her and sat against the headboard.

"Did I say something wrong?"

"It was nothing you did, Reggie."

She wrapped her body against him, curling one of his chest hairs with her finger. "Wouldn't it be nice if we could just stay like this for a bit? Maybe a few years?"

"It would get old, don't you think?"

"Actually, I'd really like to see for myself."

I just don't see that happening, thought Shaw.

CHAPTER

74

AFTER FALLING deeply asleep they rose late the next morning and showered together, taking turns soaping the other. Five minutes into it they had sex again while the hot water poured over them. Later, Reggie dressed and sat on the bed next to Shaw, who wore only a robe.

"So where does all this leave us?" she asked, her gaze searching his face.

"I'm not sure. We still haven't resolved Kuchin. And you still haven't told me enough to help you."

"I was talking about the sex, actually."

He looked at her, a bit perplexed.

"I guess it's a girl thing to want to know about that. I suppose you blokes just take it at face value."

"It was terrific, but I still need to understand your operation."

"Very sensitive of you. But if I tell you, you have to tell others. I can't let that happen."

"And the trust thing?"

"Like I said, I don't trust easily."

"Neither do I. But I think I trust you."

"Think?"

"Well, I'm apparently further along the trust road than you are."

"So you believe Kuchin will come after us and that we might have a mole in our midst?"

"Even if you don't have a traitor he can still come after you."

"I wouldn't be too sure about that. Our cover was excellent."

"You don't know how good your cover is because it hasn't been tested yet. And this guy *will* test it. And you didn't leave the area clean. You had to rush. Things might've gotten left behind. People might've heard or seen something. Now he's out there planning how to get to you. He's doing it 24/7."

"How do you know that?"

"Because it's what I would be doing."

"Comforting to know that you and he think alike. And he'll be coming after you too."

"Right. So we work together. Then maybe we get the guy before he gets us."

"Your shop isn't interested anymore. Are you saying you'll go outside your people to make this happen?"

"If necessary, yes."

"That Frank guy didn't seem the lenient or understanding type to me."

"He's not."

"Then why do it at all?"

"Because I don't want to keep looking over my shoulder for this guy."

Reggie looked at him questioningly. "Only reason?"

"Let's just take it one step at a time."

"But you think someone on my side was prepared to kill you. How is that going to play out? I'm not going to help you take your revenge against my colleagues."

"Even if they *were* going to kill me?"

"Like you said, let's take it one step at a time," she said coolly.

"Harrowsfield."

"What about it?"

"Take me there."

Reggie looked startled. "What?"

"Take me there."

"Have you gone mental? You want me to waltz right in and say, 'Hello, everyone, here's Shaw. I don't know really who the hell he is, but let's all have a spot of tea and play nice'?"

"I'll leave the explanation up to you."

"You can't be serious."

"I'm very serious."

"And what if I refuse?"

"Then I make a phone call and it's out of my hands. All of you go down."

She slowly stood and glared down at him. "You'd really do that to me? After what just happened on this bed? And in that damn shower?"

"First rule in the line of work we loosely call a job? Personal gets checked at the door. Only amateurs forget that rule, or maybe they never understood it in the first place."

"So you just banged me for the hell of it? And then dropped this threat on me? You bastard." She moved to slap him, but he caught her hand.

"What you don't seem to get, Reggie, is that I'm putting my life entirely on the line to help *you*. The odds are much greater he'll get to you and your people first. I'm offering to do all I can to stop him. But in order to do that you have to trust me. What happened between us in this room I don't take lightly. If that explanation isn't good enough for you, then go ahead and hit me. But make it as hard as you can. It'll be the only shot you get."

He let go of her hand and waited.

They stared eye to eye in silence for several long seconds.

Finally, Reggie said, "Get dressed. I need to go to my place to change clothes. And you're going to at least feed me a proper English breakfast before I go down in flames at *bloody* Harrowsfield."

CHAPTER

75

Shaw had three cups of coffee while Reggie ate probably the biggest breakfast of her life.

"Sex gives you an appetite?" said Shaw.

"It wasn't the sex."

"What then?"

"Guilt."

"Nothing to feel guilty about."

"Maybe for you. Me, I've got plenty to feel shitty about."

They took the Tube to her flat, where Shaw waited downstairs while she changed into white jeans, a denim shirt, and flats. They picked up the City-Coupé from her garage and drove out to Leavesden. Shaw's head touched the top of the car's interior and his knees were crunched against the dash. Reggie looked pleased at his obvious discomfort.

As they passed down the lane heading toward the aged twin columns she said, "Shaw, I'm really not sure about this."

"Just take a deep breath and keep driving straight."

They parked in front of the house and got out. Shaw could feel eyes on them as they walked to the front door. It opened before Reggie could put a hand on the knob.

Whit looked ready to shoot both of them.

"I can't believe you'd bring this bloke here. Are you out of your bleeding mind?"

Shaw answered. "She didn't have an option. It was either me or the cops."

"How did you even know about this place?" Whit demanded.

"It's hard to keep secrets anymore."

"Whit," began Reggie, "we all need to sit down and talk this out."

"You've absolutely gone over the edge." He pointed a finger at Shaw. "This guy is going to bring us all down."

"Use your brain, Whit," said Shaw. "If I were going to do that why would I even need to be here? I could've just sent the police."

Whit looked at him, then Reggie, then back at Shaw. "Then what the hell do you want?"

"To help."

"Oh, right, you're the bloody good fairy what brings all sorts of pixie sprinkles to nice little boys and girls?"

"I don't really care what you think. I came here to talk to the people running this 'operation,' and I know it's not you. So either get out of the way or try and stop me."

Whit looked up at the six-six broad-shouldered Shaw, his ropy muscles clearly visible under his shirt.

"All right, Paddy, come on in. But don't say I didn't warn you."

As soon as Shaw moved forward, Whit pulled his gun or tried to. Shaw jammed him against the wall with his shoulder, ripped the gun out of his hand, kicked out the Irishman's legs, and pressed a size thirteen shoe to the side of his head. Shaw released the mag, racked back the slider, cleared the seated round, and put the mag and round in his pocket before tossing the empty pistol back to Whit. He reached down, grabbed the man by the shoulder, and jerked him to his feet.

"If you want to get Kuchin then we need to get this op rolling."

"What op?"

Reggie said fiercely, "The one we're apparently going to be planning with *him*."

"You don't sound too happy about this whole thing," remarked Whit as he rubbed his sore shoulder.

Reggie looked at Shaw. "Like the man said, I didn't really have a choice. Where's the professor?"

"Right here."

They all looked down the hall. Professor Miles Mallory was holding a pistol pointed at Shaw.

"Would you care to step this way, Mr. Shaw?" said Mallory. "I think we need a word. And for the record, this weapon is fully loaded and I'm a fairly decent shot."

Shaw didn't hesitate. He moved through the front door. "I'd like that, *Professor.* And hopefully I can find out why you thought it was necessary to order one of your foot soldiers to inject me with enough botulinum to put a rhino down for good."

CHAPTER

76

KUCHIN HAD SPENT a full day going over the collected file on Katie James. When he turned the final page he called Rice into the room. "A lot of information but very little that might tell us where she is currently."

"She had an apartment in New York, but she lost her job, couldn't pay the rent, and she got kicked out. She left no forwarding address. From what I've learned she has a habit of using the homes of former colleagues around the world to crash for a few days or weeks at a time."

"I remember the story of course that she worked on most recently," said Kuchin.

"Katie James was a key player in bringing that whole conspiracy to light. Even now the whole truth isn't known."

"Buried," said Kuchin knowingly. "Because the truth would embarrass important people. It's always that way."

Rice tapped the mound of pages. "Well, I'm thinking that as good a journalist as she undoubtedly is, I don't believe she navigated that whole episode alone."

"Bill Young the lobbyist, you mean? And that was why they were together soon after in Zurich?"

"That's one theory, anyway."

Kuchin said, "There might be other more plausible ones. But I don't really care what they are. We have to find her."

"I can get some people working on it. Check plane records, charge card transactions."

"No, I will handle it."

"But—"

Kuchin rose, hefting the file in his right hand. "I told you, Alan, you're to concentrate on the business. I will be preoccupied with this until the matter is resolved." He looked down at his assistant. "Now, there has been no unusual activity around the office, I take it?"

"Unusual activity?"

"Any extraordinary interest in my whereabouts by any parties, official or otherwise?"

"Not that I've personally seen or heard from anyone. It's been business as usual."

"Then it is possible that I will return on the jet." Kuchin seemed to be talking more to himself than Rice.

"All right, Evan, certainly. You're paying for the plane after all."

"I *know* that. I'll be ready to leave in one hour. Alert the pilots."

Kuchin packed a small bag. Among the many perks of flying via private wings was that you could bring anything on board with you. Weapons, explosives, victims. He had transported all three.

After closing his bag Kuchin picked up a phone and hit a button. "Pascal?"

"Yes, Mr. Waller?"

"I'm going to Montreal. I want you with me."

"Yes sir. I'm ready to go."

"How did you know?"

"Just my job, sir."

The faithful little servant.

"Five minutes."

"Yes sir."

Rice was waiting by the door when Kuchin came out with his bag and briefcase. "Jet's all ready. The flight to Montreal isn't much longer than the car ride from the landing strip to here."

"Excellent. I will call you when I touch down."

"Call me?" said a startled Rice.

"Yes, you will be staying here."

"But I thought . . . The business."

"Computer access, a cell tower not that far away so phone service is very good. You can operate from here, can you not?"

"Yes, but—"

"I'll be in touch." Kuchin brushed past him with Pascal right behind.

They were wheels up a little over an hour after that. As the Gulf-stream knifed into the sky Kuchin settled at his desk and spread the file on Katie James in front of him. In his career with the KGB he had been tasked with finding lots of people. These targets never wanted to be found, because if they were they would be tortured, killed, or most likely both. Because of that Kuchin had learned many of the ploys used by people who wanted to remain "lost." But that was decades ago. Things had changed. There were new ways to cover one's tracks. Yet Kuchin figured he had at least one advantage. Katie James might not know that anyone was after her. If so, she might not be hiding at all.

Seven months ago in Zurich. Last known address in New York. If she went from New York to Switzerland she would have gone by plane. After that Kuchin did not know where she might have traveled, or how she might have traveled there. But the means by which she might have done so would be limited. Plane. Train. Car. And then the payment method, of course. Credit card transactions, email activity. There would be records of that in each instance.

They landed, and on the drive into the city Kuchin made a phone call to a man whom he trusted as much as he did anyone. He was not going to his penthouse in case that was being watched. He had another hideaway in the city. After the call was finished he turned to Pascal.

"I will need your help with this, Pascal," said Kuchin.

"Anything you need done, Mr. Waller, I'll take care of it."

"The tall man?"

"Yes sir, I apologize for him getting the best of me. I should've seen that coming, but we really didn't have much time to put it all together."

"Yes, that is interesting. I would like you to tell me exactly how it was all *put together*, as you said."

"A couple hours before you left to go to the market with the lady Mr. Rice came and got me and Manuel. He said there might be a problem and he wanted to make sure things were okay."

"Did he say why he thought there might be a problem?"

"Just that he had a suspicion about the woman. I told him if that was the case we should tell you."

"And his response?"

"That he wanted to make sure. He knew, well, that you liked the lady and he didn't want to mess things up in case he was wrong. He didn't want you to get mad at him. Said you'd already shown your displeasure with him on that score."

"All right, I can see that. Go on."

"We went to the church. Checked out the altar and stuff like that. Then Mr. Rice said we needed to check out the basement."

"The catacombs?"

"I guess so. Anyway, we got there and didn't find anything at first, but Mr. Rice noticed that one of the tops was off I guess a crypt thing. And then we saw some equipment set up down there. A battery generator and some lights and stuff. Mr. Rice said we were going to park there and see if something happened."

"And it did."

"Oh, yeah. Never saw the big guy, though. He came out of no-where." Pascal rubbed his head. "Packs a punch. I'm looking for-ward to paying him back."

"But we have to find him first." Kuchin held up a photo of Katie James. "This woman is really the only link we have to him. She's a journalist. A very famous one, and yet no one has seen her recently. But if we can find her, we might be able to find him."

"You want me to start looking?"

"I'm going to make some inquiries first. Narrow the search down. Then I'll put you on it."

"Yes sir."

Kuchin looked down at the photo. She was a very lovely woman. Too old and too white to be one of his sex units, but still attractive. He wondered how close she was to this man. He hoped it was close enough. Close enough to use her to get to him.

CHAPTER

77

Shaw eased into a chair in the library. There was no fire in the fireplace; the day was warm, the skies tensing for a thunderstorm later. Reggie and Whit stood by the door. Professor Mallory, still holding the gun, sat down across from Shaw. Liza stood with one hand on the long table. Dominic and his injured arm leaned against a far wall. All their gazes were solely on Shaw.

"If you could keep that muzzle down until you intend to use it, I'd appreciate it," said Shaw. "That gun has a grip safety and is known for having a touchy trigger pull."

Mallory edged the muzzle down slightly.

Whit looked at Mallory. "What the hell does he mean about botulinum?"

Before Mallory could answer Reggie came forward, drew the syringe from her purse, and placed it on the table next to the professor.

As she stepped back Mallory looked down at it. "Long considered to be the most toxic poison in the world," he said in a pedantic tone. "Though it has infinite medical uses, including cosmetic under the name Botox, of course."

"You die fast, but in excruciating pain," said Shaw, his gaze never wavering from the other man's face.

"You would not have," declared the professor. "You will note that that syringe has two solutions in separate compartments but with a semipermeable barrier. The additional element was a potent anesthesia. You would have been unconscious. Would have felt nothing."

"As I died."

"Well, yes," conceded Mallory. "That *was* the point after all."

"Miles!" exclaimed Liza. "What were you thinking? We don't do that to innocent people."

"Well, the easy answer to that is I didn't know how *innocent* Mr. Shaw was, or, frankly, *is*. What I did know was that he had been told of our operation and plan with Fedir Kuchin. Allowing him to go free after that seemed problematic at best."

"But to order his death?" said Reggie in an icy tone. "We're not murderers—" She stopped, paled, and glanced away. Whit, Dominic, and Liza could not meet one another's eyes. By their expressions they seemed to all be thinking the same thing.

Technically, we are murderers.

"It was a judgment call I made in the heat of battle," snapped Mallory. "I did not make it lightly or without some misgivings."

"Well, that makes me feel better," said Shaw sarcastically. "But here I am alive and well."

"Yes, well, sometimes plans go awry."

"But let me tell you what'll make me feel even better."

Mallory and the others looked at one another. "What?" he said.

"Your putting that gun down. Before I have to do something about it."

The two men stared at each other. As Reggie watched, she felt like what she was witnessing was two rams about to smack horns. Yet finally Mallory set the gun on the table next to him, its muzzle pointed harmlessly at a wall.

"Kuchin," said Shaw. "He's alive, and on the hunt."

"Our cover was very good," said Mallory.

"Very good won't cut it. I read the report on the guy. A mental makeup like that often houses an obsession factor that goes far beyond all reason or predictability. We need to simply assume that he is looking for all of us and that he will find us at some point. When he does, what are you prepared to do about it?"

"Kill him," answered Whit. "Which is what we should have done in the first place. In fact I could've put a bullet right in his brain if you hadn't stopped me."

"In all fairness, we also would've died if he hadn't been there," Reggie reminded him.

Whit looked darkly at her. "That's part of the risk. I was willing to accept it. I assumed you were as well."

"Talking about the past doesn't deal with the future," said Shaw. He kept staring at Mallory. "Are you prepared to deal with the future?"

Mallory sat back. "What do you suggest?"

"I need all the intel you have on Kuchin. If we can get to him first, I'll take it from there."

"Meaning what exactly?" said Whit.

"I'm assuming you have proof that he is Fedir Kuchin and he committed all those crimes?"

"We do."

"Then the guy will be tried and convicted."

"That's not exactly how we do things here, Mr. Shaw," said Mallory.

"Yeah, well I do things a little differently. But I imagine there's a court in Ukraine that would be very interested in dealing with the man. I doubt he would walk out of that country alive."

"That may be true, although quite frankly I don't know if our evidence would stand up in a court of law. I know it would morally, but the law doesn't seem to care about such things anymore. But more to the point, if he is tried and convicted does our involvement have to come out?"

Shaw glanced at Reggie. "I don't see a reason for that, no."

"Then it comes down to whether we can trust you or not."

"Oh for God's sake, Miles," said Liza. "If the man wanted to bury us, he certainly has had the opportunity to do so by now."

"She's right," said Reggie. "He didn't have to come here with me. He'd already found the place."

Mallory looked interested by this. "May I ask why you wish to help us?"

"Pretty simple, actually. Kuchin deserves whatever's coming to him," said Shaw. "If I can help you bring him in, I'm more than happy to do it."

"And the people you work with are okay with that?"

"I didn't ask their permission."

"And that isn't a problem?"

"Not unless you make it one." Shaw stood. "Now we've reached the point of wasting time. Do we have a deal? We get Kuchin and he gets tried in a court?"

Mallory eyed the others. "Unless anyone objects, I think we can welcome you to our team then."

Shaw took Whit's mag out of his pocket and tossed it to him. Then he eyed Reggie. "Actually, I prefer to think of it as a temporary assignment."

CHAPTER

78

THANK YOU for helping me, my friend," said Kuchin as he shook the other man's hand and gripped his shoulder. They were meeting in Kuchin's hideaway place on the outskirts of Montreal. The other fellow had the build and the confident manner of someone who probably walked alone and unafraid down dark streets in unfamiliar cities. Fifteen years ago he had held the position that Pascal now did before going on to start his own business.

"Urgency in your voice, Evan. We do go back."

Kuchin poured out a drink for him and slid it across the table. The man took a sip, cradled the glass, and said, "She left a trail. Not a particularly clean one, but there are things there to lean on."

Kuchin sat and looked expectant.

The man drained his glass, wiped his mouth, and opened a file. "Credit card and travel records. From Zurich she traveled by Swissair to Frankfurt. In Frankfurt she rented a car. The mileage shows she went no farther than one hour outside of Frankfurt. Still, that constitutes a large radius. She stayed at a small hotel in Wisbach. Why she was there and what she did is not revealed. I will need to put assets on the ground in order to build that information."

"Let's hear the rest first."

"From Frankfurt she traveled to Paris. She stayed there for four days. From Paris she took the Chunnel to London. It is unclear where she stayed in London. There are no credit card records for that time."

"She stays at friends' homes from time to time, apparently while they're not there."

"Then that makes sense. There would be no record in that case.

She returned to the States. New York, D.C., San Francisco. If she worked for anyone during that time we could find no record of such."

"What about her cell phone? They can be tracked via GPS now."

"We tried that route. She has apparently disabled her GPS chip. And cell tower triangulation in circumstances such as this can be unreliable. If I had the resources of the FBI or the NSA, not so difficult, but I do not. She is a woman who does not want to be found, I think."

"What do you have most recently?" asked Kuchin.

"I can tell you that several weeks ago she was in Paris."

Kuchin sat forward. "What else?"

"There is nothing else. No hotel. No credit card purchases for food. She either uses cash only or eats like a bird out of trash cans. She didn't stay long. She left Paris the next day and returned to the States. I have seen the flight reservation and accompanying documentation myself. And she appeared on the security camera at de Gaulle on that day."

"So she returned to San Francisco?"

"No. Washington, D.C. I've checked the airlines, the trains, the buses, and the rental car companies outgoing from that city and found nothing. Now, she could have used fake documents under an assumed name, but she might still be there."

"But again, no hotel?"

"No. Perhaps she has another friend who accommodates her there."

"Perhaps," said Kuchin thoughtfully.

"Relatively speaking Washington is not that big. I can send in some of my people, beat the bushes, see if she pops out."

Kuchin was already shaking his head. "No. That won't be necessary. I will take up the hunt from here."

The other man rose. "I will continue to feed you any additional information that comes along. I have markers in place in the system. If she buys a plane ticket, rents a car, uses her credit or ATM card, or engages her GPS chip I will know about it, and then so will you."

After the man left Kuchin sat in his chair thinking. He actually had several matters on his plate that demanded attention. He was used to this, though he was a man who liked focus and compartmentalization. Yet sometimes one did not get what one wished for.

Still, his focus had to be Katie James. She was the only link they had. He had to find the woman.

79

Two days had passed. Shaw had been over every inch of Harrowsfield, observing the personnel tracking down the next target, and having long, detailed conversations with Professor Mallory, Liza, Reggie, Whit, and Dominic. He'd even ventured to the underground firing range with Reggie. There he'd watched her nail the target over ninety percent of the time even with a wall of smoke between her and the silhouette at which she was firing.

"I'm impressed," he said as they moved back to fresher air. "How do you do it?"

"I remember where the target is under the smoke."

"Well, in real life targets almost never stay still."

They passed the cemetery on their way back to the house. Shaw paused in front of Laura R. Campion's grave.

"Related?" he said. Reggie had told him her last name.

"I doubt it."

"You come here often?"

"More often than I probably should," she admitted.

She sat down on the old bench. He stood next to her. "So you come and stare at a grave of someone you may or may not be related to and call it, what, mental health time?"

"Don't be a git. Everyone has quirks."

"Okay, what about your *known* family?"

"What about them?" she said a bit too defensively.

"Are they living?"

"No. How're your kids doing? Fix that problem with your son back in the States, did you?"

"My first memories were of a fat old nun in an orphanage. And I never married. No kids."

"The truth this time?"

"Yes."

"But a grave outside of Frankfurt. Anna?"

Shaw inclined his head at the sunken trough of earth. "But I *knew* the woman in that grave."

Reggie looked in that direction. "Like I said, quirks. But I would like to know more about her."

"Who? The woman in my grave or yours?"

"Both."

Shaw stared off, eyeing a bird riding a breeze across the sky. "So what happened to your family?"

"They died," she said sharply. "They just died," she added more quietly. She looked over at him. "People do, you know. Every second of every day." Her expression changed. "So what have you learned about us so far?"

"That you're lucky to be alive."

Reggie frowned. "How do you mean?"

"You might be good in the field, though I've only witnessed the debacle in Gordes. But this place has no perimeter security, little internal safeguards, and most of the people I've met would never pass a basic security clearance check. Whit, for example, is a wreck just waiting for a train to come by. And your fearless leader Professor Mallory looks like a reincarnation of C. S. Lewis only with a homicidal edge to him."

"Actually, I believe he's partial to Tolkien."

"Doesn't really change the equation. You guys are skating on thin ice."

Reggie stood. "Well, you know what? We've gotten by just fine. Until you showed up."

"If I hadn't shown up, you'd be dead," he reminded her.

"Fine. You want me to get down on my knees and attest to your superiority? We don't have big budgets and planes and all that crap, but we get the job done."

"*Most* of the time you get the job done," he corrected.

Now she looked away, her face reddening. When she stared back,

Reggie said, "Any other insults you want to send my way while you're in such rare form?"

"They're not insults. They're critiques. You asked me what I thought and I told you. If you didn't want to know, then you shouldn't have asked."

"You really are something," she said heatedly.

"Is there a problem I'm not seeing? Because your attitude is a little hostile."

"No problems. Like you said before, it's just a job. That's all you're here for. A bloody job. Right? 'Temporary assignment,' I believe were also your words, with emphasis on the temporary, I reckon."

"And I also told you I don't fall into bed with someone lightly."

"Yeah, that is what you *told* me."

"And I meant it."

"Right. I'm sure you did."

"I'm here to help you. Doesn't that count for something?"

"I think you're also here to nail Kuchin and make sure you don't have to look over your shoulder for the rest of your life. Don't pretend it's all about altruism."

"Frankly, I already have to look over my shoulder anyway. And he's actually not the worst scum I've had to track down."

"And have *you* always been successful?"

Shaw snatched a glance at the grave. "Not always, no."

A minute of silence passed and Reggie's expression finally softened. "Look, I guess I'm a bit out of line. I'm also confused, and to put it bluntly I'm a bit knock-kneed about this whole damn thing." She looked around. "Harrowsfield and what we do here, it's all I've really got, Shaw. Probably seems pretty pathetic to you, but that's just the way it is with me. And if I lose this, then I'm not quite sure what'll be left."

"Then I guess we'll have to make sure you don't lose it."

"I suppose I'll find out soon enough, won't I?"

"Actually, we both will."

CHAPTER

80

FEDIR KUCHIN stared out the window of his hotel room into the wash of streetlights. He was dissecting the city in his mind. Washington, D.C., was separated into four quadrants. The sector tourists were most familiar with was northwest D.C., where most of the major monuments and the White House were located. This area was relatively safe. Yet there were narrow but consistent pockets of violence throughout the rest of the city. He had learned that three percent of the zip codes here accounted for over seventy percent of the violent crime. Much of it was drug- and gang-related and kept the police chief deploying more and more resources in those areas.

Kuchin sat back down and studied his map of the city, breaking it down as he had in other battles. D.C. had a fairly large footprint, but was certainly not the most populous metropolis in the country. Still, nearly six hundred thousand people called it home and far more than that commuted into the city every day from the suburbs. He did not think Katie James would be staying in any of the high-crime sections, so that somewhat limited his search. In the business district were mostly hotels. To stay there she would need to use a credit card, so he could reasonably rule that out. Around the U.S. Capitol Building where the four quadrants converged were residential neighborhoods where she conceivably might be staying. There were also high-dollar areas in Georgetown to the west and up along Massachusetts Avenue, or Embassy Row as it was known, and on Connecticut Avenue and Sixteenth Street heading toward the Maryland state line. He had a finite amount of manpower with him and did not intend on deploying it inefficiently.

He was staying at the Hay-Adams Hotel, on the back side of

Lafayette Park, which was across Pennsylvania Avenue from the White House. He was here with six men including Pascal to conduct his hunt for the elusive journalist. And that was the key for him. She was a journalist. What did journalists do? They traveled, wrote stories, interviewed people, and checked in with their employers from time to time. The problem was, it seemed that James was not currently employed.

He stared down at his list. Still, she might be working at some point. If so, there were a few possibilities.

The *Washington Post* was the city's best-known newspaper. James had worked for them years ago and had since done freelance jobs for them, though not for several years. Its offices were on Fifteenth Street northwest. Kuchin had a man posted there with a picture of James. Another man was watching the bureau offices of the *New York Tribune*, which was two blocks over from the *Post*. James had won two Pulitzers while at the *Trib*, but Kuchin had learned that the reporter and the paper had had a falling-out. Still, it was a base he had to cover.

The *New York Times* had its bureau headquarters at First Street, also in the northwest quadrant. CNN, while not a print publication, was also located on First Street, but in the northeast. Both the *Times* and CNN were in sight of the Capitol. According to her file, James had also worked for the *Times* and had done both on- and off-camera reporting for CNN during the first years of the Afghan war. There were many other news organizations in the city, but these, at least in Kuchin's mind, were the most likely to attract the attention of a journalist with the hefty reputation of Katie James.

Kuchin paced his hotel room. He would give this strategy a few days to see if anything came of it. He would also hope that Katie James used a credit or ATM card, or perhaps enabled her GPS chip in her phone. If she did Kuchin was confident his "friend" would alert him. He also had another list from this same source. It contained four names, all friends of James, who were also in the news business and lived in the D.C. area. Two, Roberta McCormick and Erin Rhodes, were stateside and thus it was doubtful that James would be encamping in their homes. The other two were out of the country. Thus Kuchin had sent his remaining men to those locations.

He thought things over. His chess pieces were in place as best he could employ them. It was a waiting game now, and despite his combat experience, Kuchin had never been comfortable waiting. He took a walk. He passed the White House, stopped and stared through the wrought iron fence. Thirty years ago Kuchin and his fellow Soviets had done everything in their power to bring down the person occupying this house. Capitalism was evil, personal liberties were even more counterproductive. Marx had it right; Lenin had it even more right; and Stalin and his progeny had perfected the system. Yet they all had been wrong, of course. The wall of communism had toppled, Kuchin had fled, and now he lived like a king in the land of his former nemesis employing the same free-market tools he had long fought against. Well, one adapted or one died, he reasoned.

He eyed a uniformed Secret Service agent who seemed to be taking an unhealthy interest in him. He backed away from the fence and walked toward Fifteenth Street, drawing in the fresh, hot air and showing a middling interest in the gaggles of tourists and their stupid cameras.

His phone buzzed.

"Yes?"

"She just used her ATM card," said his friend. "Corner of M and Thirty-first in Georgetown. I'm awaiting photo confirmation from the ATM camera."

Kuchin immediately phoned his man closest to this location and then jogged back to the hotel. In five minutes he was in a rental SUV driving himself west to Georgetown. The traffic was bad, the intersections snarled. Kuchin anxiously tapped his fingers against the glass. His phone rang again. He was still at least ten minutes away.

"Yes?"

"No sign of her, sir," said Manuel.

"Call in the rest of the teams. Set a ten-block perimeter outward from the ATM. Four men walk every square inch of it starting at that point. Two men in cars ride a circuit on the outside of the perimeter, one clockwise and the other in the opposite direction. I'll be there as soon as I can. She just got cash so it's a reasonable bet she's going to spend it on something, so check any shops or restaurants you think appropriate."

He slipped the phone back in his jacket. He had been convinced they would not find her on this go-round. That would be too easy, too lucky. Those things happened in movies, not in real life. But now they had a perimeter. And Kuchin knew how to work a perimeter like few people in the world.

CHAPTER

81

TELL ME about Kuchin's friend," said Shaw.

"Which friend?" asked Reggie.

"The skinny one with white hair who shot Dominic in the arm."

It was late at night and they were sitting in a small room on the second floor at Harrowsfield that Reggie shared with Whit as an office of sorts. It was cramped and cluttered. Reggie sat on the only chair and Shaw was perched uncomfortably on a small cardboard box. Outside a light rain fell.

"Alan Rice. He's a business associate of Kuchin."

"What else?"

"I only spoke with him a few times. Although there was one odd thing."

Shaw sat up straighter. "Word for word."

"Well, I can't remember it word for word, but he was warning me. About Kuchin. Well, of course he used the name Evan Waller."

"Warning you how?"

"He said that his boss could get a bit weird around women. That he'd done so in the past. Become obsessed. He was basically telling me to shove off for my own good."

"So he was concerned for your safety?"

"Apparently so, yes, although he said he was doing it to protect his boss."

"That's interesting."

"Why is it interesting?"

"Because I think Rice tried to kill his boss in the catacombs back in Gordes."

Reggie looked over at him in shock. "What? Why do you think that?"

"In a crisis you fire your weapon at primary threats, Reggie, not at secondary targets."

"I'm not following."

"Rice had his gun pointed at Whit, who was not near Kuchin. On the other hand, Dominic was maybe a foot to the right of Kuchin. When I hit the first guy, Rice wheeled around and saw me. A second later I hit the second guy, the smaller one. Rice could have taken me out then. He was only five feet away with a clear line of fire. Instead he turned and fired at his boss."

"But he hit Dominic."

"He hit Dominic probably because he was a bad shot. It's a lot harder to nail someone from even ten feet away than it looks. But that round did come within a hair of impacting Kuchin's brain. So he doesn't take me out when he could but instead tries to kill his boss."

"But that makes no sense. Why try to kill Kuchin? He was there to rescue him."

"Or make it look that way."

"What would it matter how it looked if Kuchin ended up dead?"

"Think it through. Kuchin's guys would still be alive. They might not take too kindly to the second banana blatantly offing the boss in front of them. It has to look like an accident. And on the other hand, what if Kuchin survived the shooting?"

"Do you think he knew you were there? And would try to stop Kuchin from killing us?"

"Highly doubtful. He might've gone in thinking he was indeed going to save his boss. Maybe he saw you coming out of the church one night and got onto you that way. Then he's in the catacombs, sees me burst out of hiding, and he hits on a second plan in a matter of seconds. In the confusion of me coming on the scene he fires his gun, everyone scrambles, shots go off, Kuchin/Waller ends up dead. Then he inherits the business."

"I guess that could be possible."

"Now, you tracked Kuchin down. How?"

"This building is full of people who do that. Researchers, linguists, academics."

"No, I didn't mean following the trail that showed Evan Waller was really Fedir Kuchin. I mean how did you know he would be in Gordes and when?"

"Our people got those details and they passed them along to us for the mission. That's how we operate. I don't know how they came by the intelligence. An inside source perhaps?"

"Let me ask you this. Could Alan Rice be your inside guy?"

"I just told you I don't know how we got that information. How did *you* know he would be in Gordes? Do you have someone on the inside?"

"No. All our intel came from satellite surveillance of phone calls, electronic credit card receipts, and other high-tech gadgetry."

Reggie looked envious. "Must be nice."

"They're only nice if they work. Would Mallory know who the inside source was?"

She looked doubtful. "I suppose, but I don't think he'll divulge that sort of thing to you. He likes to keep things very close to the vest."

"He may have to reveal them if he wants to continue doing what he's doing."

"You mean you'll shut us down? Put us in the dock?"

"I just keep going back to my original point. If we don't get him first, Kuchin will get all of you."

"Then why don't we go ask the professor?"

Shaw checked his watch. "It's nearly one in the morning. Do you think he'll be up?"

"The professor sleeps even less than I do. We'll probably find him in the library."

"Is he an insomniac?"

"No, an enlarged prostate actually."

Shaw could only shake his head.

82

As it turned out Mallory was not in the library. They found him in his office. The professor was fully dressed, sitting behind his desk, his hands forming a confident steeple; yet his gaze kept twitching from Reggie to Shaw when Shaw asked the question.

"I don't know the person's identity," said Mallory tersely.

"But there was someone?" said Shaw.

"Yes. We sometimes have to rely on informants."

"But if you didn't know who, how were you sure you could trust the source?"

"I was confident enough to follow through. And this would probably be our only opportunity to get to the man."

"Confident enough?" exclaimed Reggie. "To risk our lives in case you were wrong?"

"I told you this would come back to bite you, Miles."

They all turned to see Liza standing at the door. She wore slacks and a long sweater. Obviously she had not gone to bed either. She leveled a withering gaze on the professor before settling down in a chair across from him. She looked up at Shaw and Reggie. "Miles and I had words about this a number of times, didn't we?"

"You expressed your opinion thoroughly," he noted diplomatically.

"My opinion was that it was rubbish sending out a team based on intelligence from an anonymous source."

"But that anonymous source proved to be correct in Kuchin's movements," pointed out the professor. "He did travel to Gordes, to that villa, and with the exact security team that was provided to us."

"But still to trust the person—"

"What motive would the person have to double-cross us?" interrupted Mallory.

"How about to kill you before you killed his boss once this informant found out you were gunning for him?" said Shaw.

"It didn't work that way. The person approached us."

"How did he know to approach us?" asked Reggie.

"There are avenues to do that," answered Mallory.

"Constructed by whom?" asked Shaw.

"Me."

"And you never thought to tell us about these avenues?" Reggie wanted to know.

"It didn't seem relevant. It's never backfired against us yet. You work with the model that provides results. And finding out the history of someone is only part of the equation. We then have to get to them. And to do that one needs intelligence."

"Well, after what happened in Gordes it seems that it might've finally backfired, Miles," said Liza.

"There is no conclusive proof of that yet," he countered.

"Someone knew we were going to be in the catacombs with Kuchin."

"If you recall, that was a suggestion you made to me, Reggie, because of Kuchin's religious faith. But the selection of the exact location, the catacombs, was done while you were in Gordes. Our anonymous source would not have known of that."

"But they could have followed us there," said Reggie. "If they knew we were going after Kuchin and wanted to stop us."

"Again, I fail to see, logically, why the person would help us get to the man and then at the last instant try and stop us."

"Maybe it was neither," said Shaw. This comment made all the others look at him in surprise.

"Explain yourself," said Mallory.

"Alan Rice could be your source. He wants Kuchin dead, but for his own reasons, namely to take over the man's criminal empire. I theorized to Reggie before that he might've attempted to kill his boss on the spur of the moment when I appeared on the scene and threw a monkey wrench in the works. But now I'm not so sure."

"If that was his intent why wouldn't he just let us kill him, then?" said Liza curiously. "Why show up and try and stop it?"

"You kill him and stuff him in some crypt, no one knows what happened to the guy. That creates uncertainty. The enterprise can't go forward under new leadership because everyone's waiting for the boss to come back. Or other guys make a grab for it. It's not clean. If Rice is there and tries to save his boss, he earns big creds from the troops. And then you have closure. The king is dead. Rice can step in as the logical successor."

"That hardly sounds logical," sniffed Mallory.

"I was in those catacombs," rejoined Shaw. "I saw Rice take a shot at Kuchin. He was trying to kill his boss."

"*Could* your informant be Rice?" said Reggie.

The professor shrugged. "It's possible, I suppose. As I said, he remained *anonymous*."

Liza spoke up. "And if what you say is true, Shaw, how does that further our goal of getting to Kuchin?"

"If Rice is the inside guy we can use that against him to get to the boss. He's got to be a little nervous already. Kuchin is alive, after all." He looked at Reggie. "You guys said his real name that night. Rice had to hear it. I doubt Kuchin is thrilled about that. Rice may think his days are numbered anyway."

"But how do we get to Alan Rice?"

"Kuchin has a string of legit businesses. Presumably Rice has a hand in running them. Kuchin's headquarters are in Montreal. He has a downtown penthouse there. I say I go to Canada and start pushing some buttons."

"You?" asked Reggie.

He looked at her. "Yeah, me."

Reggie automatically glanced at the professor. "What do you think?"

"What about Whit going too?" he said, but Shaw was already shaking his head.

"We don't play well together. And he's a hothead who probably won't follow my lead."

"I'll go," said Reggie.

"Not a good idea," shot back Shaw.

"Why?"

"Just not, trust me."

"I disagree," said Mallory. "I think she should go."

"I don't think you're calling the shots," said Shaw. "I am."

"We have a vested interest in bringing this all together," said Mallory. "And more to the point, keep in mind that while I concede that you can bring us down, that sword can cut both ways."

"Meaning?"

"Meaning, it seems, that you also work for a highly secret organization. If our existence comes to public light, I can assure you that so will yours."

Shaw considered this, keeping his true feelings behind a mask of inscrutability. "I'll think about it."

"Don't think too long," said Mallory. "As you said, Kuchin is coming for us."

Shaw and Reggie drove back to London. She dropped him off at the Savoy.

"Do you want me to come up?" she asked. "Just to talk," she added quickly.

"Not tonight. I've got a lot to think about. Maybe another night."

Clearly disappointed, she drove off.

Shaw rode the elevator to his room. He opened the door, flicked on the light.

"How's it going, Shaw?"

Frank sat at the desk, the bulge of the bandages wound around his middle visible through his shirt.

Shaw was clearly not surprised to see him. He took off his jacket and laid it on the bed. "We might be screwed, Frank."

"Things not going according to our little plan?"

Shaw slumped on the bed. "Definitely not."

CHAPTER

83

Katie James ate a few forkfuls of her Chinese takeout before losing her appetite. That had been a waste of twenty bucks from the ATM. She tossed the containers in the trash, put her fork in the dishwasher, rinsed her hands off, and wandered into the living room. The house was dark, which was how she seemed to like things these days.

These days? More like these months.

She sat in a chair and stared moodily at the wall opposite where photos of her friend and the woman's family were hanging. She rose, went over to them, touching each one, running her finger along the heads of the kids. In the progression of the photos, they evolved from infants to squirrel-cheeked kindergartners to tall high schoolers and then on to adulthood with their own children, judging by the recent photos of little kids on the wall.

Katie had never been married, except to her career. Never had kids, never come close, actually. She had two Pulitzers and an ugly bullet wound tacked permanently on her upper arm. She had seen the world on someone else's dime. She would be remembered perhaps for a long time for her reporting. She had excelled professionally and failed miserably on the personal side. It was an old story with her hardly the only victim, if she was a victim at all. And yet when she'd been thirteen the only thing she had wanted in life was to be a mother with a little house with a green lawn and a tree, preferably an apple tree because she had always loved apples.

Instead, somewhere along the way she had chosen documenting one world crisis after another and racking up millions of airline miles in this single-minded pursuit. She suddenly felt chilled, though outside was a typical Washington summer's evening, meaning warm and humid enough to push sweat through one's pores with only a brisk walking pace. She slipped a sweater around her shoulders and just stood there in the dark.

She had stopped drinking, at least. Not one drop for months. Not even on the morning Shaw had left her in Zurich without a word. She had surprised herself. If she were going to fall off the proverbial wagon it would've been then, she assumed. She had stayed two extra days, called him repeatedly, and then phoned Frank a dozen times until the man had finally answered her.

"He's hurting," Frank had told her. "Give him some time."

And so Katie had given him time. Weeks. And then two months. And she'd tried to call again, but now his number had been changed.

Then it was back to Frank, who said he would help. And he had, giving her information about Shaw, including the fact that he was back at work, meaning he was risking his life in impossibly dangerous situations all over the world. Every time the phone rang Katie would assume it was Frank calling to report Shaw's death. She assumed this because she had stopped believing that Shaw would ever call her back.

And then Frank had come to her aid again. He'd given Shaw her number on a special phone Frank had provided her. He'd called and hung up when he heard her voice. This hadn't entirely surprised her, but she had been slightly disappointed. Yet he'd called back and the conversation had been brief, but at least they had talked.

And then she'd traveled to Paris. On Frank's tip. When she saw Shaw sitting alone at that table, she just stood there. He hadn't seen her yet and so she watched him. The way he divided the room into grids, looking for possible dangers, just how he lived his life. The only way he could now, of course. They had never had sex, though they'd once shared a bedroom. Never even kissed. Never really come close, at least on his part, she assumed again. She wasn't sure on her end. Well, maybe she was. It was all very confusing actually.

In truth, Katie wasn't sure when she had fallen in love with him. It was clearly before he'd left her in Zurich. It might have been that final night in Wisbach, Germany, outside the graveyard where

Anna was buried. He was not capable of loving her back, not then. Maybe never.

She stared at the photos on the wall again. If she hadn't left the restaurant so abruptly? But he hadn't tried to stop her, bring her back to the table. If he had just followed her out, she would have come back, desperately wanted to come and talk to him. But she had walked down the street and he hadn't come for her.

She drifted to the window and looked out. There were a few passersby, couples mostly, walking hand in hand. Laughter filtered in from out there. A car roared by, going too fast for the narrow streets in the residential area. Katie had no idea how long she would stay here. Or where she would go from here.

She slipped her cell phone from her pocket, thought of calling Frank again, to see if he had news about Shaw. Her finger poised over the keypad, but didn't descend.

What really was the point, she thought. Packing misery on top of improbability did not seem like a viable long-term solution. She instead went to bed with the reasonable assurance that tomorrow would not be any better than today.

84

"THINGS SEEMED pretty straightforward to me," Frank was saying. "Well, other than me getting shot. I posted your and the lady's photos at the train station, like we discussed. That caused the four of you to split up like we wanted, since the Irishman was one loose cannon. You put the GPS chip in the phone you took, rode the boat over, worked her for more information, then gave her the phone back from one of their people. We let her get settled, you followed her to her headquarters, and infiltrated the place. Simple."

"I did all that, and reported it back to you."

"I know. And you've been there for a couple days now. So report again."

Shaw filled him in on what he'd seen and heard over the last forty-eight hours.

"So they really have been doing this awhile." Frank brushed some lint off his rumpled suit jacket. "You know, we suspected something like this was going down."

"How?" asked Shaw.

Frank took a moment to pop open the room's minibar concealed in a cabinet and pulled out a Coke. He uncapped it and took a swallow. "Dead Nazis," he said.

"What?"

"Well, their being Nazis was never confirmed on our side, but we had a string of ninety-year-old guys making mysterious exits from life at various points around the world over the last five or six years. A couple in South America where those Third Reich higher-ups tended to migrate after Hitler offed himself in that bunker."

"Why was that even on your radar?"

"Because some of them were later involved in stuff that came damn close to being in our bailiwick. On two occasions we traced them back to their Berlin days. But the guys were already dead and there didn't seem to be much point in pursuing it after that. But if that's the case more power to these guys for taking those assholes down."

"You mean being vigilantes?"

"I mean working out justice where there wasn't any before. That is sort of what we do here, Shaw."

"We've never been ordered to murder anybody."

"No, but do you think all the guys we find and turn over get a jury of their peers?"

"I know they don't."

"Then let's get back to the matter at hand. So what's the issue now?"

Shaw told him of Mallory's ultimatum. "Either Reggie comes with me while I'm hunting Kuchin or they expose us too."

Frank finished his Coke. "Is that all? Then I don't see the problem, really. Take her with you."

Shaw's jaw went slack. "I don't want to go after this bastard with her tagging along. It's too dangerous."

"But the flip side is if you leave her alone, maybe Kuchin catches up to her while you're looking for him. Then this time he finishes the job." Frank tossed the empty Coke bottle in the trash and fished out a package of salted almonds from his pocket and started popping them into his mouth, crunching down hard with his back molars.

Shaw looked uncomfortable.

Frank said, "You disagree?"

"Not necessarily, but what's the ultimate goal here?"

"You tell me what you think it is and I'll tell you if you're right or not."

"Get Kuchin? But I thought the expensive suits didn't care about that anymore. He's just back to making kids into whores for profit. No more mushroom clouds. That's what you said."

Frank finished the almonds before answering. "Well, I truthfully can't say their attitude has changed on that. But what they are interested in is this new angle in England."

"Why?"

"Why?" Frank said incredulously. "Another organization doing stuff that might have global repercussions? Hmmm, let's think about that."

"It really has nothing to do with us," Shaw said a bit lamely.

"You think so, Shaw? Then let me enlighten you. The part that really interested us was the fact that these guys are not only going after past 'monsters,' but current ones too. You said they were researching stuff right now in Africa, Asia, and South America, although they wouldn't tell you who."

"So what?"

Frank tossed the empty packet of nuts in the trash and wiped off his hands on his pants. "I'll tell you so what. Deposed scumballs sometimes come back to power. These Brits kill a recently deposed dictator, then in geopolitical terms things can get hairy fast."

"Who cares if they go after people like that? Didn't you just say it was a good thing as far as you were concerned?"

"I was talking about the Nazis. They aren't coming back to power."

"I don't understand the difference."

"Don't be a virgin. If you want black and white, go watch a Bogie and Bacall flick. These guys take out a monster in the Middle East or South America we could have revolutions going on in places we don't need them, you see what I'm saying?"

"No, I really don't. Because if they've already been deposed?"

"Like I said, they sometimes come back. And depending on who deposed them, it might be in our interests to make sure they *do* come back because the asshole that knocked them off their perch is even worse. I can give you about a dozen historical examples of that if you want. But we don't have that option if they're dead."

"Jesus, this is insane."

Frank rose. "Maybe I don't disagree with you. But it doesn't really matter what the hell we think. We're just grunts on the ground. So go after Kuchin and take the chick with you. That way you can work on the inside with them and learn even more about their operation. We'll give you primary support, whatever you need."

"And when and if we catch him?" Shaw asked dubiously.

"Then he'll get what's coming to him."

"And Reggie and her people?"

Frank slid on his hat and walked to the door. "And they'll get what's coming to them."

"Frank, there has to be another way."

Frank eyed him intently. "Tell me something."

"What?"

"You already slept with her, didn't you?"

"What?" Shaw said with a stunned look on his face.

"We were watching this place, genius. You two came in that night all touchy-feely and didn't show again until breakfast." He added bitterly, "You didn't deserve Anna. Or Katie James for that matter, you son of a bitch."

"Frank—"

"I've cut you enough slack. Now just do your damn job, Shaw."

Frank slammed the door on his way out.

CHAPTER

85

SHAW AND REGGIE were private wings up eight hours later heading to Montreal. At thirty-nine thousand feet Shaw pulled out some documents and spread them over the dining table and motioned Reggie to sit opposite him.

They were both dressed casually, she in jeans and a long-sleeved T-shirt and Shaw in khakis and a dark short-sleeved shirt.

"Nice way to travel," she said, admiring the interior of the Gulfstream V.

"We've got a lot of work to do and not a lot of time, so let's get to it," he said in a tone that could only fairly be described as a bark.

She sat. "What the hell is your problem?"

"I've got too many to list right now. So let's just focus on this one."

He indicated the architectural plans in front of him. "Kuchin's penthouse in downtown Montreal."

"What, are we going to break into it?" she said jokingly.

"Do you have a problem with that?"

She looked at him incredulously. "I thought we were going to find Alan Rice and hold his feet to the fire about him being the informant. And then use him to get to Kuchin."

"That's one possibility. But what if he isn't the inside guy? What then?"

"But he has to be."

"No he doesn't. And if we make all our plans contingent on that we're idiots. No, we're *dead* idiots. Now, we have Rice's address too. The problem is if we go to him first and he isn't the guy, then Kuchin will be warned."

"Wait a minute, isn't he already warned? I thought the little en-counter in the catacombs would've been enough to put the man on his guard for the rest of his life."

"You're not analyzing the picture deeply enough, Reggie," Shaw said in a clearly condescending tone.

"Well, then, *Professor*, why don't you spell it out for me since I can't get my poor brain to do it."

"The fact that Interpol hasn't knocked on his door yet tells Kuchin that you guys were totally unofficial. He probably thinks the same about me. Interpol or the FBI comes in with badges and overwhelming force. We had neither. So, for now, he's not feeling that his liberty is at risk, just his life. That will impact how he acts from here on. He'll go underground, but not as deeply as if it were the FBI or an officially sanctioned hit squad on his butt."

"Okay, I guess I see that."

"Good. But we still have to tread cautiously. While he's plotting against us, he has to assume that we'll likely come after him again."

"Do you really think so?"

"A guy like that didn't survive in the KGB all those years with-out knowing how to anticipate his adversary's next moves. In the Soviet Union at that time you were far more likely to get popped not by the West, but by a guy in your own office who wanted your job, your flat, and your car, even if it was always breaking down. So he'll definitely plan for a second strike on our part."

Reggie glanced down at the documents. "So what are we going to do?"

"Two-pronged attack, with Kuchin first."

"How?"

"We get into his penthouse, search the place, and hopefully dig up some intel on where he is right now."

"How do we know he's not in his penthouse?"

"Because we have people posted there. He hasn't been there since leaving for France."

"Wait a minute, if you guys knew where he was all along, why didn't you just nail him in Montreal? Why go after him in Gordes?"

"That's classified."

"That's bullshit. You talk about trust, but it's apparently all one-sided."

Shaw sat back. Her request, under the circumstances, wasn't all that unreasonable. "He had more guards in Montreal. And a shoot-out on the street there was not an option. We've also had some issues with the Canadians before and they are not our best friends. A holiday in Provence where we could get him in a cave was a far better option."

Mollified, Reggie looked down at the drawings. "He must have a fairly sophisticated security system in place at his home."

"He does, but we've broken better."

"So what's my role?"

"To do exactly what I say."

"Okay, I'll just be in the back of the plane. You let me know when you want to bite my head off again. I'll come running like a good little mate."

Shaw grabbed her arm. She was whirling to slug him when he said, "I'm sorry."

She froze with her fist only a few inches from his chin. She lowered her hand. "Okay." But her tone was one of bewilderment rather than conciliation.

Shaw seemed to sense what she was thinking. "Look, I didn't want you to come on this thing. I just thought it was too risky. Kuchin almost got you once."

"I volunteered. But if you didn't want me to come, why am I here?"

"You heard Mallory. You don't come then he goes public."

"Oh come off it, there's no way you believed that. He was bluffing." She watched him closely. "But you knew that, didn't you? You knew it was an empty threat. You just didn't want me to get hurt."

"People around me tend to get hurt, Reggie. Really hurt."

"Then, again, why am I here?"

"I guess Frank took the threat seriously. He insisted that you come along."

She eyed the plans on the table. "I won't be dead weight, Shaw. I'll do everything I can to be an asset."

"I appreciate that. But—"

"You see, I don't want you to get hurt either."

"My safety shouldn't be your concern."

"But it is. I've got your back. Do you have mine?"

"Yes."

"Then please understand this. If it comes down to me living or Kuchin dying, tell the monster I'll see him in hell. Do not miss him, Shaw. Do not. Even if it means I don't make it back. Will you promise me that?"

Shaw didn't answer.

86

THE TRUCK backed into the loading dock behind the high-rise building. Work orders were duly scanned and proper signatures obtained. The two big boxes were offloaded and placed inside the dock's storage area. The manifest said that inside were some antiques belonging to a resident in the building who was away for the summer. The crates were to be stored and opened only when the owner returned.

A few hours later the loading dock was locked up and the supervisor and his crew left. Thirty more minutes passed before a side of one of the crates collapsed outward and Shaw emerged. Using a small focused beam light he went over to the second crate and helped Reggie out of her hiding place.

They were both dressed in black and had various pieces of equipment hanging off their belts.

"You ready to hit it?" Shaw whispered.

She nodded.

He clipped on a headset, powered it up, and said, "You there, Frank?"

"Copy that. Have your partner give us the video feed."

Frank had flown in separately from England to set up the support they needed to break into Kuchin's penthouse.

Shaw nodded at Reggie and she slipped a strap around her chest at the center of which was a round dial roughly three inches across with a glass lens. She flipped a switch on its side and a red light popped on.

Shaw said into the headset, "You good?"

"Roger that. Video is live. Proceed to target area."

The elevator security was defeated by a cloned card Shaw inserted in the slot.

Frank's voice once more came over the headset. "The building's video surveillance is on a monitored loop but we've remotely frozen the security cameras in the delivery elevator and outside Kuchin's penthouse. The elevator isn't typically used after hours and the guards won't expect any change on that camera or outside Kuchin's place since he's out of town. But they do make periodic rounds. The next one is sixty minutes from now. After that you're on your own."

They took the elevator to the top floor. The doors opened to reveal a small entry foyer with a steel door and a security pad mounted on the wall next to this portal. Shaw looked in the corner at the surveillance camera and waved, though he muttered under his breath a little prayer that Frank had indeed managed to freeze the feed. He motioned Reggie to video the security pad.

"Got the picture?" asked Shaw into his headset. "It's a retina recognition system like our research said."

"Got it. Have her stand closer so we can get a better look and confirm the manufacturer."

Shaw motioned for Reggie to stand immediately in front of the retina-reader bubble.

"Okay, we're good," said Frank. "Get the laser ready, Shaw. We cut the juice to the building in five seconds. There's a backup battery for the security system, but we're sending a calibrated power spike right behind the power cut that'll burn that backup out. But we have to turn the power back on quickly or it'll trigger an emergency response."

"Understood."

Shaw pulled the laser from a holder on his belt and pointed it straight at the retina reader.

"On my mark," said Frank. "Five . . . four . . . three . . ."

Right after the count of one the power to the building vanished and they were in complete darkness inside the enclosed foyer. The red power light on the retina reader went out. Shaw powered up the laser and pointed it right at the reader. The red beam shot into the glass disc, filling it with a reflected crimson color. A moment later the power came back on.

The door clicked open.

Reggie looked at Shaw as he put the laser away. He said, "Little flaw in this particular system we discovered awhile back. Power off, power on, and in that millisecond of start-up it'll read a laser point set at a specific frequency as if it were an authorized retina."

"Pretty cool," she said with admiration.

"Well, it's not really a flaw."

"What do you mean?"

"I mean we have a good working relationship with some major security hardware firms. We do some stuff for them from time to time and they leave back doors like this for us."

Reggie shook her head while Shaw pulled the steel door all the way open. "Fifty-nine minutes and counting. Let's get to it."

Shaw slipped a miniaturized laminated set of floor plans from his pocket and looked at them using a low-power penlight. "Keep away from the windows," he advised. "Just in case Kuchin has real eyeballs on the place from another building. Even without any lights on we could be seen with the right surveillance equipment."

"Too bad."

"Why?"

"I wanted to check out the views."

They searched quickly but methodically, and on their bellies when they had to get close to the window line. After thirty minutes they had found nothing helpful.

They stood in the middle of Kuchin's bedroom. Reggie looked disappointed, but Shaw seemed curious.

"What is it?" she finally asked, noting his puzzled look.

"I used the laser to mark out the square footage of the place as we went along, but according to these plans we're about fifteen hundred square feet short."

"How can that be?"

Shaw spent five minutes pacing off parameters. "Center core is off," he finally said.

"What does that mean?"

"That means there's some hidden space in the interior block of this penthouse and it's too big just to be the HVAC equipment. That's usually in the ceiling in places like this anyway."

After some more searching they reached the end of the hall and stared at the elaborate built-in cabinet there. "Why do I think that thing's set on a pivot?" said Shaw to Reggie. "You see it, Frank?" he said into his headset.

"Yeah. I'm with you. We got less than thirty minutes. Start poking around."

Four minutes later, a twist of a knob in a counterclockwise motion by Reggie made the entry code panel pop out. Shaw pulled a spray canister from his belt and shot it over the panel. Then he hit it with a blue light, which revealed fingerprints on certain number keys. "Got the four digits," he said. He attached a small device to the panel's wiring and turned it on. He looked up at Reggie. "Knowing which four digits are part of the code cuts the combination possibilities way down."

"Yeah, that I know. Then you just have to find out the order of the numbers," she said. "And you manage that with a full numbers assault."

The numbers 4-6-9-7 froze on the screen and the wall cabinet clicked open, revealing a darkened space beyond.

"So let's go see what Mr. Kuchin is hiding in here," he said.

CHAPTER

87

Kuchin was sitting in a chair in his hotel room. His strategy had not worked. His men had searched the perimeter from the inside out and there was no trace of Katie James. They were all still posted at these positions, but Pascal's last communication had been discouraging. They had simply run out of places to look. The woman had either gone underground in the city somewhere or else she had left. Nether possibility was palatable to the Ukrainian.

He took out a small kit, filled a syringe with his special concoction, and shot it into one of his veins. Normally this would give him at least a momentary rush of euphoria, of invincibility. He swore it made him think more clearly too, which he desperately needed at this moment.

Yet nothing happened. Well, something did occur. He felt even more depressed. He threw the empty syringe across the room, where it struck a wall and broke. The last time Fedir Kuchin had suffered defeat was back in the Ukraine, when he had been forced to fake his death and flee his homeland one step ahead of the masses that would take their revenge on his years of terror. At least they would call it terror. He would call it something else. His duty. His job. Perhaps his destiny.

Though he lived the good life of a successful westernized capitalist now, where personal liberties were highly prized, Kuchin, in his heart, would forever believe that only a select few should rule all others. And the way one accomplished that was with selectively and effectively used power. Most people were only capable of being followers. Even in the West only a few ever rose to riches and leadership positions. In his command back in Ukraine Kuchin could pick out, within five minutes of meeting them, those of his men who would forever be sheep and those few who would be the shepherds. And he had never been wrong.

Yes, the West was the part of the world where there was opportunity for all. Kuchin could only sneer at this. He had been a leader in his homeland and he had become a leader here. A follower over there would be merely a follower over here. Sheep didn't change because they were given *opportunities*.

And yet will I now be defeated again?

He could not stay here indefinitely. He could not keep his men here much longer without arousing suspicion. Washington, D.C., was perhaps the world's most closely guarded city. There were policemen, spies, federal agents—probing, peering eyes everywhere. If they were looking for Kuchin he might be playing right into their hands. And yet if he left this city without Katie James he had nothing. He would be beaten. It was a guaranteed fate.

He grabbed a remote and turned on the TV. The news was on. The lead story was trouble in Afghanistan for the Americans and their allies. This both made him smile and also conjured up bitter memories of his own country's devastating defeat in that ancient land.

The woman reporting on this story, he noted, was around fifty. Not the young, long-legged, and often bottle blondes who typically read off the teleprompter and had never been near the war zones they were "reporting" on. Her statements were succinct, informed, and told Kuchin in a short few moments that she knew what she was talking about. He assumed that Katie James, though she was younger and prettier than this woman, had these same attributes. From what he'd read of her background she had certainly been to every global hot spot in the last fifteen years. No teleprompter for her.

He refocused on the TV. Kuchin was anxious to see in more detail what sort of trouble the Americans were in. At least it would take him away from his own problems for a few moments. He had no inkling it would lead to the solution of at least one of those problems.

"This is Roberta McCormick reporting live from Kabul," said the woman on the screen as she closed out her segment.

The name froze for an instant in Kuchin's mind.

Roberta McCormick?

He leapt from his chair and raced across the room to where his soft-sided briefcase lay on the desk. He flipped it open and found the list.

On here were the names and addresses of the people who lived in D.C. who were known colleagues of Katie James. Kuchin had his men covering two of the residences because their owners were out of the country. The other two were supposedly in town and thus Kuchin had not allocated any surveillance at those places. He ran his eye down to the last name.

Roberta McCormick. She was supposed to be home but she was in Kabul, thousands of miles away. He had just seen that for himself. She lived in Georgetown, up near R Street, which was just outside the perimeter that Kuchin had set for his men. Her husband had passed away, her children were grown. She lived alone.

But perhaps her home was not empty right now.

88

"My God," exclaimed Reggie as she and Shaw looked at the interior of the room.

Shaw said, "I feel like I just stepped back in time to the middle of the cold war."

The lights had come on automatically when they walked into the room.

"Holy shit!" said Frank over the headset. He had seen what they were seeing through the feed from the camera strapped to Reggie's chest. "This guy has issues."

"You think?" said Shaw as he looked around at the Soviet flag, the old lockers, the battered desk, and the file cabinets. "Reggie, sweep the room so Frank can record it all on the camera."

She did so, getting as close to as many objects as she could.

Shaw opened one of the lockers and saw the uniform that Kuchin had worn while with the KGB. He next searched the file cabinets and took out documents showing some of the atrocities that the man had exacted on innocent men, women, and children. Reggie captured all of this with her camera.

And then they found the film reel and projector. It took a few minutes to set up. As the film ran Shaw and Reggie said nothing. Not even Frank muttered a word. Finally, Reggie hit the off switch. "I can't watch anymore," she said as the face of the dead child faded on the screen.

When Shaw looked over at her he saw the tears in the woman's eyes. He put the projector away but slipped the film reel in his bag.

"We need to see anything else, Frank?" he said.

When Frank answered his voice was strained. "No, good to go."

* * *

A couple of minutes later, Shaw and Reggie were walking down the streets of Montreal. A car picked them up and took them to a low-rise office building about a half mile away. Frank was waiting for them there.

They all sat in silence for a few moments, staring down at their hands.

Shaw looked up. "Okay, this confirms a lot. The guy is a psycho—not that we ever doubted that."

"But what did we find that might help us get to him?" asked Reggie.

Shaw looked over at Frank. "Alan Rice?"

"The plane came back from France. That we know. It landed at the airport in Montreal. Neither Rice nor Kuchin were on it. And Rice is not at his home or office or any other place we can find. He's either dead or more likely laying low. To go any further than that we would have to involve the local authorities, and we don't want to go there. At least not yet. Might actually make matters worse."

"So we can't use Rice as leverage?" asked Reggie.

"It's Kuchin or nothing, it seems."

"But where is he?" she asked. "We took a risk in breaking into his place and really came away with nothing that'll help us find him."

Shaw and Frank exchanged glances.

"There's been no sign of him since France," said Frank. "You know it was private wings so it's conceivable he never actually left France, or the plane made an unscheduled stop en route to Canada. The wings have been on the ground here ever since. But he could easily hire another plane under a fake name."

"So he could be anywhere," said Reggie.

"But now we have evidence of his involvement with the KGB in Ukraine," pointed out Frank.

"We already knew that," shot back Reggie. "And I'm no solicitor, but I hardly think the courts will allow in the evidence we got because I'm pretty certain our burglary wasn't authorized."

Shaw said, "She's right about that."

Frank didn't look convinced. "Maybe, maybe not. As far as I'm concerned this bastard qualifies for war crimes treatment at the

Hague, and their rules of evidence are a little different. And the stuff is still there in his penthouse. Maybe we tip the Canadian cops or Interpol and they go get it with nice official search warrants."

"Fine, then he'll be tried in bloody absentia," snapped Reggie.

"Nobody said this would be easy," remarked Frank. "Did you think you were going to waltz in there and find the secret key that would take us right to the guy?"

"No, but I was hoping for something to help us. But since there wasn't anything, what's our next step?" She looked expectantly between Shaw and Frank.

"We beat the bushes some more," said Frank vaguely.

"Wonderful. You know, you guys have all this really cool, whiz-bang technology with your lasers and your being able to knock out power to an entire skyscraper with a push of a little button, but sometimes I think our tin-can-and-string approach is more effective."

"It wasn't more effective in Gordes," pointed out Frank.

"Well, at least we didn't give up like you blokes did," barked Reggie as she got up and stormed out.

After the door slammed behind her Frank looked at Shaw. "Damn, I thought Brits were more laid-back than that."

"There is nothing laid-back about her," said Shaw. "But she's also right. We're no closer to finding Kuchin."

"Well, he's also probably no closer to finding her or you."

"I wouldn't count on that," Shaw said slowly.

"You know something?"

Shaw didn't answer. He didn't know anything, not for sure. But what he did have was an instinct that almost never led him down the wrong path. And every inner warning signal he had was blaring away.

CHAPTER

89

KATIE JAMES kept waking up. It was nothing unusual; it was just how she was. A noise here, an internal thought there, a nightmare that seemed so real she could touch it, kept hammering away. She finally rose, got some water and settled in an armchair, flicked on a reading light, and picked up the latest Lee Child thriller.

The phone ringing startled her. She automatically checked her watch. It was nearly midnight. She debated whether to answer it. This wasn't her home after all. But it might be Roberta calling. She looked at the caller ID on the readout screen. Nothing. She hesitated again, but then picked up the phone.

"Yes?"

"Is Roberta in?"

"Who's calling?"

"Is this Roberta?"

That was odd. If they knew Roberta they should know it was not Roberta's voice. "Who's calling?" she asked again, but the line went dead.

Unnerved, she quickly went to check that the front and back doors were locked. With that secured she grabbed a poker from the fireplace and went back into the bedroom and closed the door behind her. She eyed her cell phone. She could call Shaw if she simply hit redial. But he was probably thousands of miles away and in no position to come watch over her. And he might not want to anyway.

The hand was around her mouth before she could scream. The poker was ripped from her grip along with her cell phone. The smell was awful, making her nostrils clench.

A moment later Katie collapsed.

* * *

The pounding in her head was fierce. Her eyes opened and quickly closed when they encountered the bright lights overhead. She groaned, felt sick to her stomach. She opened her eyes again and this time they stayed that way. She sat up and then froze as she saw the man standing there watching her.

He held out a hand. "I hope you are feeling better," said Kuchin.

She didn't take his hand, but remained where she was. Katie looked around. Except for the light on her the area beyond was dark. She felt a bump under her, and then another. She looked down. She was on a chair that had folded down to a bed. Another bump, and then her ears dialed in to the familiar hum. How many millions of miles had she heard that?

She was on a plane.

She sat up, swung her legs out into the aisle. The man backed up slightly to accommodate this movement.

"Can I ask the obvious?" she said.

He sat down in a chair across from her. "Please."

"Who are you and why am I here?"

"Both good questions. Who I am is irrelevant to you. Why you are here may be of interest."

He held out a glossy piece of square-shaped paper.

Katie took it, looked at the photo. Her and Shaw in Zurich. She eyed her hand on top of his arm. As intimate as they'd gotten.

Shaw. That's why I'm here.

She glanced up and handed it back. "I still don't understand."

"Your mouth says that, your eyes do not. It is too late for such tactics. You know him, he knows you. And I would like to get to know him too."

I bet.

"Why?"

"He is an interesting man."

"I don't know where he is."

Kuchin let out a sigh. The next moment Katie was lying on the floor of the plane cabin, blood running down her face from where he'd struck her. Her brain was still trying to process this event when she was wrenched up by her hair and thrown back in her seat.

She slumped there holding her face and trying to stop the blood running from her nose.

She felt something brush against her face.

Kuchin was handing her a towel.

"Forgive me for that. I am impulsive. You see, I desperately need to meet with your friend. He owes me something."

"What," Katie said slowly through her busted mouth.

"Again, not relevant to you."

"I don't know where he is. I'm telling you the truth."

"But you can get in touch with him."

"No, I can't. I—" She froze again when he held up her cell phone.

"It is interesting that we found two cell phones. One you were holding and another in your purse. The one in your purse was much like any other phone, the usual contacts, emails, calendar. But this one, this phone, had none of that. In fact, according to the phone list you have only received two calls on this phone. Now, this man I am seeking, your friend? Why do I think he is a man who would give you such a phone?"

"He didn't," said Katie as she wiped off her face.

"Then you have no trouble with my calling back this number? Just to see who answers?"

Katie looked down for a moment, trying to get her breath and her nerves under control.

What the hell has Shaw done to get a guy like this ticked off at him?

"I will take your silence as an affirmation."

"He won't come."

"I think he will."

"Why?" Katie said miserably.

Kuchin looked at the photo of Shaw and Katie. "I think you know why."

CHAPTER

90

SHAW WAS lying on the couch when it happened. He looked at the caller ID screen. He recognized the number. It was the phone Frank had given Katie. She was calling him again. He slumped back on the couch. He wasn't going to answer. What would be the point? He was absorbed with guilt over sleeping with Reggie. Frank had accused him of disrespecting Anna's memory, and maybe he was right. Shaw still wasn't sure how it had all happened. But he did know that he had wanted it to happen. He had wanted the woman in a way that he had wanted no other. Perhaps even Anna. He couldn't explain it and didn't have the energy to even try.

The phone stopped ringing. He sat up, rubbed his head, now feeling even guiltier for not answering the call. The phone started ringing again. Okay, now he had another chance to at least make this right.

"Hello?"

"Bill Young?"

The voice from the catacombs, so close then, seemed right in his face now. Shaw almost never felt afraid anymore. It wasn't that he was careless or considered himself invulnerable. Paralyzing fear simply had been eradicated from his psyche through an accelerated process of evolution. He spent much of his time in dangerous situations. If he continually froze up, he'd be dead. The ones who didn't let fear get the best of them tended to live to fight another day. He was one such man.

Now Shaw felt fear like he hadn't in a long time. But it wasn't for himself.

"How did you get this number?" He already knew the answer and yet he was hoping beyond all reason that he was wrong.

The next voice he heard destroyed this possibility. "Shaw, stay away. Do *not* do what this guy says. Just stay away."

Katie sounded scared but also resolute. In those few words Shaw was reminded starkly of how courageous the lady was. She was sitting next to one of the great psychopaths of the ages and she was telling him to just let her die. Frank had been right; he didn't deserve her.

"Mr. *Shaw*?" said Kuchin.

"How did you get to her?"

"It doesn't matter," said Kuchin. "I have her. Now I want you and the woman."

"I can only speak for myself."

"You and the woman," repeated Kuchin.

"And you'll let Katie go? Right, sure. I'll come. Just me."

"If it's just you, don't bother. Your friend here will not be alive to greet you."

"I'm telling you I don't know where she is."

"Then I suggest you try very hard to find her."

"And if I can't?"

"I have a box, Mr. Shaw. It's from my days in my home country. In that box are some very persuasive tools that I employ from time to time. Indeed, I just used them on another acquaintance of mine. I have to tell you that he did not seem to enjoy it. I do not often pull out my little box, but I will for your friend if you do not do as I say. I will videotape my work and send it to you."

"What if I can find her? What then?"

"I will call you back on this number in two hours."

"That's not enough time."

"In two hours," repeated Kuchin. "Then I will tell you exactly how and when this will happen. And I would advise you strongly not to let this conversation go beyond you and 'Janie.' Such a tactic would be fruitless and will ensure your friend's death in the most painful way I can possibly achieve. You saw the pretty pictures on the wall beneath that church. You know what I'm capable of."

"Listen to me—"

But Kuchin was gone. Shaw stared down at the phone like it was a live grenade that he needed to throw himself on to save everyone else. But it wasn't a grenade, it was a phone. And he apparently couldn't save anyone. And Reggie? He couldn't ask her to do it. He wouldn't ask her to do it.

He would tell Kuchin when he called back that he had found Reggie. They would arrange the meeting. He would go alone, make an excuse, and do his best to get Katie out alive. That was all he could think of.

He looked up when something thumped against his door.

"Yeah?" His voice broke on the simple word.

"It's Reggie. Can we talk?"

Shit.

"I was just getting ready to crash," he called out.

"Please."

He hesitated, but finally opened the door and motioned her in. She eyed him curiously.

"Are you okay? You look like you're about to vomit."

"I'm fine."

She sat in a chair, he on the couch.

"What's up?"

Reggie started talking, but he wasn't listening. Shaw knew that Kuchin was too smart for something as simple as his plan. He would want proof that Reggie was coming. He would ask to speak with her. Shaw would never get the chance to save Katie unless . . .

"Shaw? Shaw?"

He looked up to see Reggie standing next to him, poking him in the shoulder.

"Yeah?" he said in a bewildered tone.

"You haven't listened to one bloody word I've been saying."

"I'm sorry. Look, this is just bad timing."

She eyed the phone still clutched in his hand and looked at him suspiciously. "What's going on?" she demanded.

"Nothing is going on."

She knelt in front of him, her hands on his knees. "Something is going on and you're going to tell me what it is."

Shaw could barely form words. Indelibly painted on his brain were the images of Katie and Kuchin. "It's nothing. I'll handle it."

She pounced. "Handle what?"

"Will you please let it alone?"

"It's him, isn't it?"

"Who?"

She grabbed his thick shoulders and shook them. "Oh for God's sake. Talk to me."

He stood abruptly, causing her to fall on her backside, and walked away. "I said I'll handle it."

She rose, followed him. "How?"

"I'll think of something."

"He has someone, doesn't he? Someone you care about?"

He whirled, terrible suspicions running through his own mind now, but none of them made sense. "How did you—"

"I guessed," she said. "I don't think you'd ever be scared for yourself. So it had to be somebody else. How did he get to them?"

Shaw sank down on the edge of the bed. "I don't know."

"Who is it?"

"Her name is Katie James."

"I've heard of her."

"Journalist."

"Right, that's right. He's got her? You're sure?"

"Too sure."

"And what does he want?"

"Me." He hesitated, licked his lips. "And you."

"The package?"

"I told him I didn't know where you were."

"But that wasn't good enough, was it?"

"What do you think?"

"So where and when?"

"Reggie, don't even go there."

"I'm already *there*, Shaw."

"I'm not going to let you do this."

"Are you kidding? This is the best thing that could've happened."

"What?" he said in a shocked voice.

"I don't mean for your friend. I'm very sorry about that," she added quickly. "But we were never going to find Kuchin. And now the guy is inviting us to come to him. This is our opportunity. Our shot."

"It's hardly an invitation, Reggie. He's going to kill us."

"No, he's going to *try* and kill us," she corrected. "And we're going to do the same to him."

"Well, given the circumstances, I think the odds lie with him."

"It's still our only chance."

"Do you understand that if you come with me you're most likely going to be murdered in some sadistic, painful way? Do you get that loud and clear?" He pointed to the door. "Just walk out and keep going."

Instead Reggie sat down next to him. "I guess I could say something cute or flippant to show that I'm not scared, even though I am, but I think I'll try the truth."

This got Shaw's attention. He stared over at her.

"Part of me never wants to see Kuchin again, Shaw, never again. I see the man in my head all the time. I wake up with him in my brain. I see him over my shoulder. I came one instant from dying that night. I saw his eyes. There was nothing there. I might as well have been a gnat. He didn't give a shit. There's no way for a normal, sane person to match something like that."

"And you still want to go?"

"I can't live while that guy is still breathing. That's the bottom line. I want him as badly as anything I've ever wanted in my life. I will kill him with my own hands, if I have to. He'll have to kill me, because I will never stop going for him."

"The guy is the monster."

"No, he's *a* monster. He's not the first, and he's not the last. And he has to be dealt with."

"Why the hell do you do this?"

She stood. "Just tell me when it's time to go. I'll be ready."

The two hours came and on the dot the phone rang. Shaw was correct in his thinking. Kuchin asked to speak to Reggie.

"Hello, little Janie," he said after she had confirmed she was on the line. "Our last meeting was cut short. I look forward to visiting with you again."

Reggie said nothing else and simply handed the phone back to Shaw.

Arrangements were made. They would leave the following day. They were to say nothing to anyone. "She will be dead long before you reach her if you disobey," Kuchin had warned.

"But if you plan to kill her anyway?" Shaw had countered.

"I give you my word that if you follow my instructions to the letter, I will release the woman unharmed."

"Your word?" Shaw had said incredulously.

"As a former officer of the KGB."

"That really does nothing for me."

"On my mother's grave, then. I swear it. I have no fight against your friend. My issue is with you and the woman."

"Where and when?"

"That depends on where you are currently."

"In your own backyard. Montreal."

Shaw thought he could hear a small gasp from the other man and it gave him some pleasure at having startled him.

"Then that simplifies matters," said Kuchin. He explained the details.

When he was done Shaw clicked off and looked at Reggie. "You still game for this?"

"Even more so now. His arrogance pisses me off. He takes it as a foregone conclusion that we're just sheep blithely going to the slaughter."

Well, aren't we? thought Shaw.

CHAPTER

91

THE NEXT AFTERNOON Reggie and Shaw met at a café down the street from the hotel where they were staying. Shaw checked his watch.

"One hour," he said. "The address we're supposed to meet at is a five-minute cab ride from here."

"Good, then we can catch up, Paddy."

Shaw jerked around when he heard the voice.

Whit was standing there next to the table, with Dominic behind him.

"What the hell are you two doing here?"

"I'll take that as an invitation to sit down," said Whit, who did. Dominic sat across from him, resting his arm cast on the table.

Shaw looked at Reggie. "You arranged this?"

"I called and told them what was up. They were the ones who insisted on flying over."

"Slept all the way," said Whit as he stretched out his back. "Nice and rested for our little trip."

"You aren't going," snapped Shaw.

"Why not?"

"Because he's not expecting four, only two. And he said if I didn't follow his instructions to the letter Katie is dead."

"We thought about that," said Reggie. "So when we go to meet if they say no, Whit and Dominic will back off."

"Back off? More likely they'll be killed."

"My life," said Whit cavalierly. "I can do what I want with it."

Dominic simply nodded in agreement.

"But if you're really concerned," said Reggie, "then call Kuchin back and ask his permission. You just have to hit last number received."

Shaw pulled the phone out of his pocket and stared at it for a moment before looking up at Whit. "You do realize if he approves this you probably won't be coming back alive?"

Whit glanced at his friend. "You okay with that, Dom?"

"I wouldn't be here if I wasn't."

"There's your answer," said Whit.

Shaw made the call. The answer was a little surprising. Kuchin seemed happy to add two more to his list.

"I welcome you all," he said before Shaw clicked off, shaking his head.

"Everything good?" asked Reggie.

"Oh yeah, now we got four funerals instead of two. Break out the champagne."

They rode in a cab to the rendezvous spot. It was a warehouse, which didn't surprise Shaw.

"It's *usually* a damn warehouse," he said to Reggie.

The door was unlocked. They went inside. There was no one there, just a tan GMC Yukon XL with the keys on the front seat and a set of directions under the visor.

That did surprise Shaw, at least until he thought about it.

"If we were going to set up an ambush they just took that opportunity away. But this leaves us in control, so I'm not getting it fully."

They drove out of Montreal heading northeast. Two hours later, following the directions, they turned off onto a one-lane road in an area covered with forest and not a sign of human life anywhere. Two hundred yards down this strip of gravel the truck suddenly cut off. Shaw tried to restart it but the engine never even turned over.

"We've got a half tank of gas," Reggie said, pointing to the gauge on the dash. "Everything else looks normal."

"It's a new truck too," said Whit from the backseat.

Shaw looked up at the button above the rearview mirror. "It's also got an OnStar system."

"So?" said Reggie.

"So they can take remote control of the car in case of an emergency or you lock yourself out. Or cut off the engine in case it's been stolen. If someone overrode that system or piggybacked on it, they can pull the power to the engine and there's nothing I can do about it."

"I think you're right," said Reggie as she looked out the window at the two trucks pulling up to their vehicle, one in front and one behind.

Six men climbed out with SIGs, Glocks, and MP5s pointed at them.

Twenty minutes later they were standing naked in a circle inside a small concrete-block building. They had been searched first by hand and then via a scanner, and then hosed down with a jet stream of water. After that the men repeatedly dragged hard metal combs through their hair and across their arms and legs, leaving long red marks on their limbs. They had also cut off Dominic's cast and thrown it away. They'd given him a sling in replacement.

After they dried off they were given clean clothes to wear consisting of bright yellow jumpsuits, underwear, and sneakers with white socks.

"What the hell was that all about?" fumed Whit as he pulled on his shoes. "They almost drowned us."

Reggie was dressing behind a door propped open for privacy, though everyone had already seen the others naked.

Shaw buttoned up his jumpsuit; it was several inches too short for him in the arms and legs. The sneakers were tight on his long feet. "Surveillance devices. These days they have trackers built into fake hair follicles, fake skin patches. They scanned and searched us for the obvious and did the hose-comb treatment for the sophisticated stuff."

Whit smelled his skin. "There was something else mixed in that water. Probably causes cancer," he said irritably.

"You should hope to live that long," replied Shaw.

Reggie joined them after zipping up her jumpsuit. "Well, I can see you're still Mr. Optimistic."

"I'm just being realistic."

"Why do you think the yellow jumpsuits?" asked Dominic.

"If I had to guess," said Shaw, "the harder it will be to lose us."

"Lose us?" exclaimed Whit. "How the hell could they possibly lose us?"

"I guess that depends on us, doesn't it?" said Reggie.

CHAPTER

92

More hours passed, and then with hands cuffed, feet shackled, mouths taped, and hoods over their heads they were stuffed in an SUV with blacked-out windows and driven for a long time. Shaw had been counting off the seconds in his head. And while they were not on major highways, at least that he could tell, their speed had been pretty consistent and at least sixty miles an hour from the sound of the engine and the whine of the wind outside the truck.

When the vehicle finally pulled to a stop he had a rough gauge. Nine hours. In which direction he wasn't certain, though he didn't think it likely it had been back west toward Montreal or south to the United States. Security between the U.S. and Canada wasn't that tight, but four hooded and trussed-up figures in an SUV would have raised at least modest curiosity along the way. If not, there was no hope ever of border security.

That left the direction they'd gone in as north or east. Nine hours due east in Canada at sixty miles an hour would also have taken them through Maine in the United States, in order to reach New Brunswick or farther along to Nova Scotia. And when the Yukon had cut off, the largest city they had been near was Quebec. From there to Halifax in Nova Scotia was far longer than the approximate distance they'd driven. For those reasons Shaw concluded they'd been heading more north than east, skirting the border with America but not crossing it. They had been allowed one bathroom break along the side of the road, and then they were off again.

Later, the vehicle's doors opened and they were forced to lie face-down partially on top of each other in the back cargo area. For one terrible moment Shaw thought this was it. Execution time. From

the quick breathing of his companions, he deduced they were thinking the same thing.

Instead, a heavy tarp was thrown over them and a voice said,
"Not a sound or your friend is dead."

Truck doors closed and the vehicle drove on. Then it stopped.
Doors popped open again. There was talk. The doors closed again
and the vehicle pulled forward haltingly, and then stopped. Whatever they were on now, it was not solid ground, Shaw could tell.
The truck was moving though the engine was off. Only it was moving slightly up and down and side to side. Or at least whatever it
was on was doing that.

A few minutes passed and Shaw heard more noises, including the
clanging of a bell and feet moving fast. There was a lurch and the
sensation of something sliding away, like a train leaving a station
platform. The first real jolt he felt answered the question.

We're on a boat. Probably a car ferry.

The water was rough, the ride uncomfortable, particularly lying
facedown while wedged in the back of a truck. Shaw could hear
Reggie moaning next to him and he thought she might become sick
again, as she had on the ferry crossing from Amsterdam. And then
it was over. They drove for more hours and then the truck stopped
again. They were pulled from the back and made to march, still
hooded and shackled, in single file. They were maneuvered roughly
into seats in a confined space. Shaw actually hit his head on the top
of whatever they were inside. When the engine engaged, the sound
of the prop wash started, and the stomach lurch occurred when the
vertical lift happened, he knew they were on a chopper.

Shaw continued to count the seconds even as he tried to calibrate
their speed. When they began their descent at least eighteen thousand seconds, or five hours, had elapsed. If they'd been traveling in
excess of two hundred knots north or east they would have covered
over a thousand kilometers. That put New Brunswick or even Nova
Scotia in play, though much farther than a thousand kilometers east
and they would've been in the Atlantic. But Shaw didn't think they
had traveled directly east, because of the ferry.

While in the truck coming from Montreal and then Quebec they
had been on the southern tip of the strip of water that cut through

that part of Canada and that employed ferry service to cross it. He knew that because he had been on one of those ferries. No one would bother to take a boat north only to chopper back across that slice of water to head south or east. If New Brunswick or Nova Scotia was the destination, they would've gotten on the chopper on the southern side and not used the ferry at all. One would use the ferry if one were going due north, toward Hudson Bay or even the Arctic Circle, or to the east to Newfoundland and Labrador.

When the chopper set down and they climbed out, Shaw knew they were not in the Arctic Circle; they hadn't flown long enough or stopped for refueling. He didn't know what sort of chopper they were on but figured for most models five hours of flight with that many people on board bumped right up against the limits of the fuel load. And it was too warm. If he had to guess, they were more east than north. When the chopper engine quieted down and he heard the ocean slamming against the shore he concluded they were on the coast of either Newfoundland or Labrador, which still covered a lot of territory. And how knowing all this helped their current situation he didn't quite have a handle on yet.

The hoods and mouth tape were finally removed and they all looked around, their eyes adjusting to the new light levels. They had left Montreal in the late afternoon and now dusk was giving over to dark. An entire day had passed and then some, Shaw calculated. His grumbling stomach confirmed this.

They were driven in a truck on a route away from the ocean.

"Any idea where we are?" Reggie whispered to Shaw.

"Shut up!" said the man riding next to the driver.

Ten minutes later lights came into view.

The house was built from sturdy logs with a covered front porch and a cedar shake roof. Trucks were parked out front. Several hundred meters away Shaw saw another building that was dark. In the distance he could see the shadows of mountains. The extreme northern extension of the Appalachians, he figured. He had been to this area a couple of times in the past, as part of his work. It was foreboding, desolate, and there was no possibility of a handy policeman lurking on a street corner. The law was whatever someone with a gun or at least the upper hand said it was.

The truck stopped. They were offloaded and marched into the house, still shackled and cuffed. The first man they saw was Pascal; his grin threatened to split his face in half. The second man was Alan Rice. The third face was why they were all here.

Fedir Kuchin walked into the room. He was dressed casually in jeans and a corduroy shirt with thick work boots on his feet. He was not smiling in triumph, nor did he look angry. His features were inscrutable. This made Shaw more uneasy than if the man had started attacking him. It showed self-control, careful preparation. But for what?

The next person he saw made him forget about Fedir Kuchin.

A battered-looking Katie James smiled weakly at him.

CHAPTER

93

No matter what else happens, thought Shaw as he looked at Katie, *I will kill him before this is over.*

"Are you all right, Katie?" he asked, as she started to move toward him, before Pascal blocked her way.

"Yes. I'm sorry."

"Sorry? I'm the only reason you're involved in this—"

The explosion was so unexpected that Rice ducked and even Pascal jumped.

A bullet passed by so close to Shaw's ear that it seemed a miracle he still had it. Kuchin lowered the weapon, his gaze first on Reggie and then Shaw.

"Thank you for your attention," Kuchin said. "The matter is a simple one." He pointed the gun at Katie. "She was the bait I used to bring you here. Now you are here." He ran his gaze over Whit and Dominic. "All four of you, including the Irishman who was so anxious to put me in a box of bones."

"Still looking forward to it," said Whit, managing a grin.

Kuchin turned to Reggie and placed his gun against her head. "And the lovely one. The one who made me so careless, so eager to please. You made me two things I believed I was not, old and a fool."

"Pleasure," said Reggie, staring right back at him, the cold touch of the gun metal not seeming to faze her at all.

Kuchin next placed the muzzle against her forehead, even as Shaw tensed for a leap. But Kuchin removed the weapon just as abruptly. "Not that easy," he said. "You made me experience your little ritual. I intend to have an equal opportunity."

Kuchin turned his attention to Dominic. "And the lucky one.

The man who survived a point-blank shot to the forehead with a large-caliber semiautomatic pistol because my faithful colleague Pascal handed me an unloaded weapon."

Kuchin raised his gun, placed it against Dominic's forehead as he had done with Reggie. Only this time he pulled the trigger. The back of the young man's head exploded outward as blood, tissue, and bone were propelled in front of the release of kinetic energy.

"Dominic!" screamed Reggie as he toppled backwards to the hardwood floor, his eyes wide and his lips slightly parted.

Whit struggled mightily to reach Kuchin, but chained as he was all he did was fall awkwardly over. Kuchin put a foot on his head and pinned him to the spot as he would have done to a bug.

Shaw simply stood there. His gaze flicked to dead Dominic then to Reggie, whose face was wet with tears, and finally came to rest on Katie.

I'm sorry, he mouthed to her.

Her look said that she understood, but how could she really? How could anyone really?

Kuchin slipped the heated gun into a belt holster he wore. His expression hadn't changed at all. From blowing out a man's brains to talking about the weather, it apparently didn't matter to him.

"No one is that lucky the second time around," he said. He took his foot off Whit's face and flicked a signal at his men. The Irishman was pulled up by two of the guards while he screamed obscenities at Kuchin.

After Whit finally grew silent and stood there trembling and staring down at the body of his friend, Kuchin said, "You could not have possibly expected anything differently. You knew if you came you would die. It will not be complex. I like simple. I always have."

"Like your office back in your apartment?" said Shaw. "That was simple enough. Desk, file cabinets, locker with your old uniform. And your little film archives."

Kuchin turned to face him. The pistol came out of the holster. He placed the muzzle against Shaw's forehead. "I have a plan," he said. "A well-thought-out one. But I can alter that plan at any time." He cocked the hammer back.

A hand was on his arm before anyone else could move. "Please," begged Katie James. "Please don't."

Kuchin looked at her and then back at Shaw. "I promised you that if you followed my instructions she would be released unharmed."

"I'm holding you to that," said Shaw.

"A funny remark to make when I have a gun against your brain."

"On your mother's grave? Just because I went to your apartment doesn't change that."

Kuchin hesitated a few moments but finally put the gun away. He pointed at Katie. "She will remain here. You four will be out there." He pointed out the window into the darkness.

"You got your math wrong," said Shaw. "There're only three of us left."

"You misunderstand me. That is why I killed him. Because I only wanted there to be four of you, and he was the odd man out."

Shaw stared at him in confusion. Kuchin snapped his fingers. One of his men brought a yellow jumpsuit and sneakers forward. Kuchin took them and turned to Alan Rice.

"Alan, please put these on."

Rice took a step back, his face turning first red as the blood rushed there and then white as the reality of the man's words hit him and the blood drained right back out.

"Evan?"

Kuchin tossed the jumpsuit and shoes at Rice, who managed to snare the suit but the shoes clunked to the floor.

"Evan?" he said again as he began to totter on his feet, his lips trembling.

"You should have aimed better in the church, Alan." He touched his ear. "Still, it was close. Singed my skin a bit, actually."

"But that was an accident. I was aiming at him." He pointed at the dead Dominic. "I shot him."

"Shooting him was the accident. Missing me was an unforgivable sin."

"I . . . I'm no good with guns, you know that."

"You have been taking shooting lessons for the last six months. Pascal here followed you on my orders. And your knowledge of guns, you let that slip out too. Your only fault was that you believed since you could hit a paper target at twenty-five yards that you could kill a man in the middle of confusion at twenty feet. You couldn't. And thus I lived."

"You're mistaken, Evan. I took the lessons so I wouldn't disappoint you, in case something came up. I didn't want to disappoint you. You saved my life."

"I told you I would be monitoring the business."

Rice seemed to gain new life. "But I've done nothing against your interests. Your monitoring would show nothing."

"Every dime was accounted for."

"So then I don't understand what this is all about."

"Freight charges haven't gone up, Alan. The price of gas has actually fallen sixty percent from a year ago. Cargo ships still run on fuel, do they not? It took some digging, but we found the account with the fuel money in it."

"No, you're wrong. It was that way because the shipments come in on two boats. I told you that."

"But they weren't coming in on two ships, only one, but you were double-billing for the fuel. I know this because right before Pascal cut his tongue out, your colleague down at the docks confessed. And then you try to kill me so you can take over the business completely."

"No, Evan, no, I—"

"Put the clothes and shoes on, Alan. Now. Or you'll get the next bullet to the brain right here. I will allow you to make the choice."

Sobbing, Alan Rice slowly slipped them on, but Pascal had to help him because the man was shaking so badly.

Kuchin turned to the others. "You will have an hour's head start. I would advise you not to run toward the ocean and dive in as the water is around ten degrees Celsius even in the summer." He pointed out the window to his left. "That is the way to go. But keep in mind that this was once a glacier. There are many fjords, ruts deep enough to be lost forever in, water that moves very fast, and slopes that quickly turn into precipices. Also, there are animals out there that will hurt you at night."

"Including you?" said Reggie.

"Including me most of all."

"So is this some sort of hunt?" asked Shaw.

"Not some sort," answered Kuchin. "It *is* a hunt."

"So us unarmed against you and all your men? Some hunt."

"No, all of you against only me."

"But you'll have weapons."

"Of course I will."

"And what, if we get away, that's it?"

"You will not get away. I own the land for miles. And the land that I don't own, no one else does either. There is nothing out there. Nothing. Except you and me."

"And Katie?" asked Shaw.

"So long as you follow my instructions, she will be released unharmed."

"I want to go with Shaw," said Katie.

Kuchin ignored her and instead looked at his watch. "You now have fifty-nine minutes." He nodded to his men, who freed the three from their bindings.

Shaw looked at Katie for what would be the last time, he assumed. He tried to say something, but what was there to say? She seemed to be having the same problem. They finally simply exchanged a brief if earnest smile.

Reggie finally pulled Whit away from staring at Dominic's body and they followed Shaw out the door, where they set off at a fast trot.

Alan Rice had not moved.

"Alan?" said Kuchin.

"Please, Evan, please don't do this," the younger man moaned.

"You said it yourself. I pay them thousands and yet they want millions. You wanted more, it's that simple. And do not beg. Men do not beg." He fired a round into the floor next to Rice, who leapt to his feet and raced out the door. Katie James was taken away and locked in another room.

It was then that Kuchin turned to Pascal. "Get the dogs ready."

ALAN RICE sprinted past them but quickly fell back, tugging at a painful stitch in his side. He was obviously not in good physical shape. He would be a drag on the rest of them, making it easier for Kuchin to catch them. Because of that Shaw's first inclination was to leave him, but then another thought occurred to him. He fell back and put his hand under Rice's arm, helping him along.

"Just pace yourself. Not too fast or slow."

"Okay, okay," gasped Rice, and his stride became more measured.

Reggie, seeming to sense what Shaw was doing, dropped back to join them. Whit ran on ahead, his head bowed, his focus no doubt still on Dominic.

"What can you tell us about this place?" asked Reggie. "Anything that'll give us an edge."

"Like what?" said Rice.

Shaw said, "I figure we're in Newfoundland or Labrador."

"It's Labrador, right on the edge of the coast."

"How did you know that?" Reggie asked Shaw.

"I had a lot of time to count seconds," he answered.

Rice snapped, "There's nothing out here. We're screwed. We're dead."

They passed a small pond of scummy water. Before Shaw could react, Reggie had grabbed Rice, hauled him over to the pond, and pushed him in. He went under and then came up sputtering. She pushed him under again and held him there for several seconds.

When he came up again he screamed, "What the hell are you doing?"

"Just in case you have an electronic tracker on you," she said. "Water and electronics don't play well with each other."

Shaw glanced over at her. "Nice catch. I should've thought of it."

"Figured it wouldn't be past Kuchin to plant a spy with us under the pretense of punishing his guy."

"Let's keep moving," said Shaw.

As they jogged along Shaw said, "What else can you tell us?"

"He has hunting dogs too, follow any scent."

"That's another reason they took our clothes," Shaw said. "For the dogs."

"Has he done this before? Hunted people?"

"Well, I know he doesn't hunt animals. He told me once he hated it."

Reggie grimaced. "Well, there's your answer. He has hunting dogs but doesn't hunt animals."

"At least not animals on four legs," said Shaw.

"He's cruel and unpredictable," added Rice.

"The cruel part I get. It's the unpredictable part I'm worried about." Shaw looked around. "Are we heading towards the way someone would drive in here?"

"It's hard to tell in the dark, but I think so."

"What's close?"

"Nothing. Well, there's an airstrip about forty kilometers in the direction we're heading, but the last time I looked we don't have a plane. Goose Bay is maybe the closest town, but it's a long way. Hours by car, days on foot."

"Does he have weapons here?"

"You're kidding, right? He has a gun safe in the house full of them."

"You know the combination to that safe?"

"Oh yeah, I've got it right here in my pocket."

Shaw jerked hard on the man's arm and stopped, nearly throwing Rice to the ground. "We can just leave your ass back there for Kuchin to chew on first. You want that? Or do you want to stop with the wiseass cracks and try to help us here?"

"I don't know anything that can help you. I've been here before lots of times, but I just fly in and out. I almost never leave the house. Waller, Kuchin, whatever the hell his real name is, he knows this area better than anyone."

"That's reassuring," said Reggie grimly.

"If he has dogs," Shaw said, "we have to address that."

They started jogging again.

"How?" asked Reggie.

"Change our scent."

"How do we do that?" asked Rice as he puffed along beside them. "I thought dogs couldn't be fooled."

"Anything can be fooled, even scent dogs. And we have an advantage."

"What?" asked Reggie.

"Take a whiff."

"What?"

"Take a deep breath."

Both she and Rice drew in heavy breaths. Rice almost gagged while Reggie wrinkled her nose. "Rotten eggs," she said.

"Sulfur dioxide," amended Shaw. "There's probably a lot of metamorphic rock around here. That means a lot of sulfur. Probably some sulfur pools too."

"So you mean?" Reggie began slowly.

"We cover ourselves in the smell. That way we smell like everything around here. It's not perfect, but we may confuse the dogs just enough. And we don't have a lot of options. And we need to turn our jumpsuits inside out. The lining color stands out a lot less than the neon yellow."

He ran ahead to tell Whit this. They reversed their jumpsuits and twenty minutes later, following a stronger odor, they found a shallow pool of water that reeked of the naturally occurring mineral.

"We have to go in that?" exclaimed Rice.

"If you want to live a little longer, yeah," said Shaw. "Just don't drink it."

Drenched, chilled, and smelling horribly, they continued on west for a bit longer before Shaw brought them to a stop, looking frustrated. "This is all wrong."

"What the hell are you talking about?" demanded Whit, his wet hair down in his eyes. "We're trying to stay ahead of the guy. He's back there coming this way. So we have to go that way." He pointed straight ahead.

"And that's exactly what he wants. He *told* us to go this way, Whit. Why do you think that is?"

Reggie answered, "Ambush? Driving us to a perimeter?"

"That's what I'm thinking. I didn't actually believe the guy when he said it was just him against us."

"And so what do we do about it?" asked Whit.

"I've always taken it as a good tactic that when your opponent expects you to go left you go right."

"Meaning?"

Shaw said, "Meaning we skirt the ground we just covered and head back to the house."

"What if he thought we'd do that and plans to ambush us that way?"

"Then he probably deserves to win."

"He *will* win," whined Rice.

Before Shaw could react, Reggie grabbed Rice by the neck and squeezed. "Tell me something, you bloody piece of shit. *Were* you cheating him on the shipping costs?"

Rice said nothing. She squeezed harder. "Were you!"

"Yes."

"And you *did* try to shoot him?"

Rice nodded, looking miserable.

"Then damn you for missing the bastard. Now let's go."

95

Kᴜᴄʜɪɴ ᴡᴀʟᴋᴇᴅ ᴀʟᴏɴᴇ, his rifle in his right hand, muzzle down. Up ahead he could hear the baying of the hounds. It really wouldn't matter, though, whether the animals were able to get on the track or not. Scents up here were problematic because of the terrain and the composition of the underlying rock. He felt certain that a man like Shaw would have experience in dodging even experienced scent hounds. This was a chess match and one had to think of the current and at least four future moves. Kuchin had followed traitors through the muck, mud, ice, and waters of Ukraine as part of his duties with the KGB. He had almost always succeeded, aided by an internal desire never to concede defeat. It was the same attribute that had fueled his swift rise up the security agency's ladder. Superiors loved men like Kuchin, because they made them look good to *their* superiors.

He had long debated how to do this. Part of him strongly wanted to tie each of them naked to a table and then pull out his little metal suitcase. He wanted to peel off their skin, cut out their intestines, and put them through torture that Abdul-Majeed, mutilated as he was, could never have imagined. But he had finally decided against that. He had done so principally because unlike Abdul-Majeed they had shown courage. They had confronted him directly, risking their lives. They had not hidden like the Muslim and let a drugged-out lackey attempt to do the killing. For that Kuchin had grudging respect for the group. Rice was another matter. He would die either way, but Kuchin had placed him with the others solely as a matter of convenience. He did not intend on wasting too much time with Alan Rice. The man did not deserve it.

That left only the hunt. Here, on his home turf, Kuchin had given them a sporting chance, if a poor sporting chance. He was not a fool. He would survive this, they would not. But at least they had an opportunity to postpone their deaths a bit. And it wasn't as though Kuchin would escape either. In a way he'd come full circle. They knew about his little room at his penthouse. Others undoubtedly knew of it too. They were probably there right now gathering all the evidence they needed to send him to Ukraine to stand trial, with his execution the inevitable outcome.

My fellow countrymen will probably tear me limb from limb.

His days of hiding were over. Evan Waller was dead. The Canadian businessman was a pale imitation of the man Fedir Kuchin really was. When it was over, he would not run. He was through with hiding. They would have to take him here, at his last stand. They eventually would win, through superior numbers, but he would take many with him. It was a fitting way for an old warrior to go out. On his terms.

He smiled. And perhaps this would result in his finally being written into history. The true Butcher of Kiev. But that would come later. He had four lives to extinguish tonight. He did not expect them to die easily, especially Shaw and the woman. They would fight hard. They were survivors. Well, so was he. And he intended to save the woman for last. He had special plans for her. She would take the longest to die.

He stopped, raised his rifle, and drew a bead through his electronic scope on a caribou a few hundred yards distant. The Soviets had excelled at killing via long range in Afghanistan with their snipers and attack choppers. They might have won the war if the Americans hadn't equipped the mujahideen with handheld rocket launchers and a mountain of RPG rounds. Kuchin could take some solace in the fact that some of these same weapons were now being used against the Americans. But only some solace. The simple Afghans had brought down the mighty Red Army and with it a superpower.

If he pulled the trigger on his rifle he could have killed the large animal that was wandering over the ground in front of him searching for food. But, as before, he had no interest in extinguishing that life. He trudged on, his eyes alert, all his senses heightened.

Alan Rice had been a disappointment, but at bottom Kuchin really should have expected it. He had taken over the business of his mentor by violent ways, so why should he expect any different treatment? Ambitious men who wanted something took it. The chief difference was that Kuchin was the sort of man who could achieve that goal. He had nerve and skill. Rice had failed on both counts. His skill was not good enough and his nerve had been nowhere near where it needed to be to topple a man like him. Which was why Kuchin had hired him in the first place. Never bring in a man more ruthless than yourself.

He knew they were up ahead of him, jogging, trying to pace themselves. They would reach a point where they would question their own tactics, perhaps argue among themselves. That would waste time, diminish the lead he had given them. They might change directions on him, believe that he was herding them in a particular direction for some purpose. He had put that into his calculations too, along with several other factors.

He checked his illuminated watch. Because it was summer and they were at a high latitude the nighttime would not last much beyond six hours. Kuchin expected it to be all over by then. The remains would be taken to the ocean, weighted down, and dumped in, never to be seen again except by the sea life that would devour them.

He lifted the rifle to his shoulder once more and checked the reticle, which most people would know simply as a "crosshairs." Kuchin for years had used the SVD Type model favored by Russian snipers. Two years ago though he had managed to obtain the American military's widely deployed Advanced Combat Optical Gunsight, or ACOG. It was an illuminated telescopic reflex sight. The shooter used the ACOG with both eyes open instead of closing one because the brain would automatically graft the image in the reticle from the dominant eye to the other pupil. This ensured normal depth perception and a complete field of view. A lot of fancy terminology, but the result was that Kuchin could acquire and terminate a target much faster than before. And since he had four targets that needed acquiring and terminating, a few seconds saved would be invaluable on the battlefield.

Kuchin was carrying a weapon that would kill with one shot

whatever it hit. But he didn't want that. Slow was the key here. Timing was everything. He had every right to be angry, furious with people who had done their best to kill him. But he was too wily to let this become too personal. When emotions dominated your mind you almost always lost. He would let his skill and reason rule the hunt. The emotion, the joy, could come later, when it was done and four more people lay dead by his hand.

CHAPTER

96

AFTER DOUBLING BACK and keeping to the far fringes of the route they had taken, Shaw and the others had managed to reach the house, which was now dark. They had first heard the baying of the hounds nearly an hour ago, but then the sounds had receded. Reggie had fallen into a large rut cut by some ancient glacier's retreat, but they had managed to pull her out. Rice was exhausted and Shaw had had to help him the last mile or so.

The four stared at the darkened space. There were no trucks parked in front.

Reggie whispered, "Do you think they're all out helping Kuchin look for us?"

"The guy was in the KGB. It would be crazy not to leave a rear guard," replied Shaw.

"So how do we do this?"

"Element of surprise. All we have. We have to get some weapons."

"Is that all?" asked Reggie. "What about your friend?"

"If she's here we're taking her." He turned to Whit. "You take the rear. I'll work my way towards the front. See anyone, just give a low whistle."

"That'll give us away," said Reggie.

"Well, what's the option?" snapped Shaw. "I left my walkie-talkie with my machine gun."

"A whistle will have to do," agreed Whit.

"What about us?" Reggie said, indicating her and Rice.

"If things go to hell, get away from here. Go in the direction of the water and try to signal a ship from the coastline."

Reggie did not look pleased by this, but kept silent. It was clear she did not enjoy letting Shaw run the show, but he obviously had more experience in this than she did. And Whit was deferring to him too.

A few minutes later Shaw reached the back door and peered through the glass. He stiffened when he saw her. Katie James was sitting in a chair bound tightly. She appeared to be dozing. He tried the knob on the door. It was locked. No surprise there. What did surprise him was seeing Whit crawling on his belly into the room. He saw Shaw at the window, rose, crab-walked across the room, and opened the door.

"Got in through a window," he said. "The place looks empty."

They quickly woke and then untied Katie.

"Where the hell is everybody?" Shaw asked as they exchanged a brief but fierce hug.

"All out looking for you, I guess. They had dogs too."

"We heard."

Whit glanced around, his face creased with emotion. "Where's Dominic's body?"

"They took it away. I don't know where. I'm sorry."

"Yeah," Whit said.

"I don't think he anticipated you doubling back and getting past them," she said.

"Apparently not."

"What now?" asked Whit.

"Gun safe."

They found it and spent twenty precious minutes trying to break into it with no luck. Shaw finally threw down the crowbar he'd found in the garage. On the other side of that three-inch door was probably enough firepower to get them out of this safely, and he couldn't get to any of it.

"Well, it looks like they did anticipate we might come back this way," he said.

"You think this is an ambush?" asked Whit. "Make it seem like they pulled everybody? Let us get in, get Katie, and then hit us on the way out?"

"Nothing would surprise me at this point," said Shaw. "But they could have killed us easily enough when we first got here too."

They searched the rest of the house, but Shaw only came away with two serrated knives from the kitchen. He handed one to Whit.

"Knife against guns?" said Whit.

"Best we can do. Now let's see if we can find a phone or anything that'll let us call for help."

They didn't. No land line, no cell phone, not even a walkie-talkie or a computer.

"Shaw!"

It was Reggie standing just inside the front door; Rice was next to her.

She said, "Trucks are coming. We have to get out of here."

They ran to the back of the house and outside. Beams of headlights cut through the darkness. One truck, no idea how many men were inside. Shaw thought quickly. "We need wheels," he said.

Reggie looked around and pointed to her left. "Whit can take Rice and Katie off that way and hide behind that berm. You and I can double back, grab the wheels, and take whatever weapons if any they have in there. Then we pick the others up and get the hell out of here."

"Okay," agreed Shaw.

Whit led Katie and Rice to the raised mound of earth behind the house. Shaw went around one side of the cabin and Reggie the other. Four men climbed out of the truck and headed to the house. Shaw knew they only had at best thirty seconds before they discovered Katie was not there.

He raced toward the truck. Reggie did the same on the other side.

"Shit," Shaw muttered. They'd locked the doors. He peered inside the window. No keys dangling conveniently in the ignition. He saw no guns either. Reggie joined him.

"Even if I can break the glass, it's not like you can easily hot-wire cars these days. And—"

They both heard it at the same time. Shouts from inside the house. They'd found out Katie was gone.

"Come on, Shaw!" Reggie exclaimed. "We have to run for it."

"Go, go," he said, pushing her off into a sprint.

She looked back once and then was gone around the side of the cabin.

"If we don't have wheels neither will you," Shaw said. He used the knife to slash the two right-side tires before running off. Seconds later the front door flew open and the men poured out, guns ready. Some ran to opposite sides of the cabin and fired out into the darkness with their submachine guns. Bullets whizzed over Shaw's head but he kept going. He doubted they could actually see him. And there was little chance that their MP5s could intentionally hit him at this distance, but they could get lucky. He reached the others and they ran as hard as they could away from the cabin. But they clearly heard the frustrated curses of the men when the truck started and then wobbled forward on the trashed tires.

Shaw leading the way, they made a wide circle around the property and headed back west. Within five minutes the lights from the cabin had disappeared from their vision.

"Close," said Shaw as they finally stopped running. "Too close and we got zip for our troubles."

"Where to now?" Rice said.

Shaw answered. "Now we're behind them. They won't expect that."

"Yes they will. They'll know we've been there because she's gone," Reggie shot back as she hooked a thumb in Katie's direction.

Shaw stared first at Reggie, then at Katie, and then back at Reggie. "What, do you want us to take her back?"

Reggie blanched. "Of course not!"

"Then we'll just have to make the best of it."

Whit cut in, "And how the hell do we do that? Sneak up and attack them with kitchenware?"

"I thought you'd figured that out. Our goal is not to engage them. It's to get away and find help. We didn't get the wheels so now we have to look for an alternate. If I have my bearings right and the coast is over that way, then if we head due south we'll run into the Belle Strait. This time of year there will be ships coming through that channel going to and from Europe. If we can survive until daylight we may be able to attract the crew on one of them. They can send out a boat for us."

"Sounds reasonable," said Reggie.

Katie looked at Shaw. "I expect at some point you'll tell me what all this is about?"

"At some point, but not now." He gripped her arm. "But at some point, yeah. I certainly owe you that."

Reggie watched as Katie placed her hand overtop of Shaw's. Then she looked away.

They had gone nearly a mile when the sound shattered the silence and all their plans ended up for naught.

CHAPTER

97

Alan Rice screamed and grabbed his leg where the heavy-caliber round had ripped into his flesh and shattered his femur. He fell hard, rolled, and came to a stop against a small boulder. Shaw grabbed Katie and threw her facedown behind an elevated stretch of ground. Whit and Reggie took cover too. Shaw peered over the top of the mound.

"Anybody see the muzzle flash?" he called out.

Nobody had.

"Rice," he shouted. "Get behind that chunk of rock."

"My damn leg is broken," he screamed back.

"You'll have more broken if you don't get behind that rock."

Crawling on his belly, Rice had almost made it to the rock when another round slammed into his shoulder.

"Shit!" Shaw jumped up and ran in zigzags to Rice and pulled him behind the rock. The man was bleeding heavily from both wounds and drifting in and out of consciousness from the pain. The break was a compound one, the pale snapped bone sticking out of his thigh. If it had ripped the femoral artery on the way out, Rice was dead, Shaw knew. Using his knife he tore a length of cloth off his jumpsuit and made a crude tourniquet for Rice's leg, cranking it down just above the thigh. The blood flow ebbed a bit. But only a bit.

"Am I going to die?" gasped Rice as he came to.

"Look, I'm going to try and get you out of here. Can you stand?"

"He'll just shoot us," yelled Rice. "He'll just shoot us both dead."

Shaw looked down at him. The man was going into shock and there was nothing he could do to stop it. He froze with the sound of the dogs. Only this time it wasn't baying. It was snarls and paralyzing growls that made every hair on the back of Shaw's neck go vertical. He eased his head over the top of the boulder to see.

"Shaw!" screamed Katie and Reggie together.

Two of the largest, fiercest dogs Shaw had ever seen were bearing down on his location at speed. They bounded over the rough terrain like it was level high-pile carpet.

"Shaw, run!" yelled Reggie.

Shaw held his knife tightly, processing through the possible scenarios as fast as he could. He stood but kept in a squat because he didn't know if the dogs were a ploy to get him in range for a killing round. He looked over the rock again in time to see the first dog leap. Shaw slashed with the knife, catching the two-hundred-pound beast across its massive chest and opening a gaping but unfortunately largely superficial wound. He used his free hand to lever the airborne animal into a tight arc, and it hit the ground hard, but didn't stay down.

With a speed and agility that no human could match, the dog rolled, gained purchase on the rocky dirt, turned in a split second, accelerated on its four legs, and collided with Shaw, chest to chest. He went down, his own blood from one of the dog's canines ripping into his arm mingled with the blood from the dog's chest wound. Shaw was up again in an instant because lying on the ground he had no chance. His fist collided with the animal's snout once and then twice, momentarily stunning it. The impacts sent stingers all the way up Shaw's arm and into the tight mass of muscles on his shoulder. He cut with the knife one more time, the beast let out a whine, and then Shaw jumped over the boulder and ran, his feet slipping in the loose dirt.

He tensed for the rifle round hitting him in the back or else the dog attacking him from behind. In his mind he saw it pulling him down, the jaws, the stench of breath in his face as the dog bit into his neck, following an ages-old instinctual tactic it knew would rip the big blood vessels and kill the prey. None of it would be less than a nightmare.

But it didn't happen. He understood a second later why.

Rice screamed louder than Shaw had ever heard anyone do before. It was like he had ripped his lungs from his chest and inflated them with a ton of oxygen, producing a sound that froze Shaw to his core. He looked back and wished he hadn't. Shaw had seen a lot of violence in his life, more than most people. But he had never seen anything like this.

One dog had Rice's arm in its mouth. The other had just torn through most of the doomed man's chest as freed blood sprayed everywhere. Shaw had a fleeting image of the Goya painting he'd seen of the monster eating the man. Nothing as feeble as oils and canvas, even powered by the imagination of a genius, could match the horror of the real spectacle. It was only at this point, his body perhaps more gone than not, that Alan Rice finally died.

Shaw reached the others and they ran as fast and as far as they could. Shaw half-carried Katie as they slipped and slid and rolled across ground that, at best, should have been traveled over at a measured, cautious pace.

Two miles later they collapsed, flat on the ground, their breaths coming so hard that it sounded like they were sucking on their last bits of oxygen.

"How?" Whit finally said as he sat up, his chest still heaving.

"I don't know how," answered Shaw. "He outmaneuvered us."

Reggie slowly sat up. "We have to keep going. If we have to jump in the Belle Strait and swim to a boat, that's what we have to do. We stay here we die."

Whit punched his knife into the dirt. "Get a clue. We are dead. It'll be the dogs on us next. We've got no chance, Reggie."

Shaw stood, helping Katie up with him. "Reggie's right. We have to keep moving."

Whit looked up at him. "You really think that will make any difference?"

"No, but I'm going to make that son of a bitch work a little bit more for it. How about you?"

Reinvigorated, Whit slipped the knife in his pocket and jumped to his feet. They ran as hard as they could to the water.

WHAT WAS LEFT of Alan Rice was swept into plastic trash bags and carried off. The gorged dogs, blood running down their jowls, were corralled with the long metal control poles and their muzzles were once more attached. Sitting on his haunches, his rifle lying across his thighs, Kuchin watched this work even as he muddled over his next maneuver.

He looked off into the distance. Water. It was a requirement of life. They would be heading there now. It was logical. Indeed, it was their only option. He could kill them all easily right now, but that wasn't the point. Kuchin could have shot Shaw when he went to Rice's aid or after Shaw fled the dogs. Yet again, it wasn't when they were going to die. It was *how*. And he would dictate those terms. And they had done one thing that he assumed they would. He rose, and as he did so he smiled. They would not understand the significance of their action now, of course. But he intended to point it out moments before it was all going to end.

One down, three to go. Well, two down if he counted the man back at the house, but Kuchin didn't really care about that. He already had the order of deaths planned out. The woman would go last. Kuchin had not forgotten his earlier desire. He would possess her and then finish her. He could think of no better revenge. And her death would be by far the most painful of any of them. In his backpack he had his skin peeler. He would see if he could beat his record of under one hour. He felt that he could. He could already hear her screams in his mind.

"Pascal?" he said, and the small man appeared next to him almost immediately.

"Yes, Mr. Waller?"

"It is time to move on, I think." He looked to the sky. The darkest moment of night had come and gone. Above him now was the very earliest appearance of the tipping point of night passing to dawn. "They will be heading to the strait. The ships."

Pascal nodded in agreement. "The channel is wider than they probably think. And there was an ice floe reported there yesterday, hugging the Labrador side. All the ships will stay well to the south of that. They will see no ships."

"I believe they will realize that when they arrive there. It will be lighter then. They will wait and they will try to signal in the hope that there is something out there. The gun safe was intact?"

"Yes sir. We checked after they left. We'd emptied it of all the weapons and ammo just in case they were successful in breaking into it. They only took knives. The big man used his on one of the dogs, but he seems fine."

Kuchin stroked the barrel of his custom-built rifle. "A knife. A poor weapon against this."

"I can take the shortcut and turn them back towards you. Tactically, they will have nowhere else to go except into the strait."

"Do that, Pascal. Drive them to me." He pulled out a pocket map and Pascal shone a light on it. "Drive them there." He indicated a spot on the map.

"It's a good choice," said Pascal, nodding his head approvingly. He looked back at one of the trucks where they were loading the trash bags with the remains of Alan Rice.

"He was a stupid man."

"He was actually a very smart man, which can make someone do very stupid things. In intelligence there is ambition. And in ambition there is peril."

"If you say so, Mr. Waller."

"Drive them to me, Pascal."

CHAPTER

99

THERE WAS nothing. No ships visible certainly, but not even a light on the water that would indicate one was close by. And to impede matters more, a fog was rolling in from off the strait. Shaw stood and looked over at the others and then at the rocks below. "We can climb down there, hide until something comes along."

The other three looked wearily up at him. "Postpone the inevitable?" said Whit.

"I like to think of it as securing a defensive position. At least then he has to come down and try and take us."

"Or stand up here on the high ground and pick us off one by one," pointed out Reggie. "We never even saw from where he shot Rice. But it was a hell of a long way away."

"You have a better idea?" asked Katie.

Reggie toed the rock with her sneaker. "Not really, no."

Shaw looked back at where they had come from. "What are you thinking?" asked Reggie.

"He outmaneuvered us once. I'd like to return the favor this time."

"How? He has every tactical and strategic advantage."

Whit added, "And he has guns and *dogs* that would make the Hound of the Baskervilles seem like a bleeding Pekinese."

Shaw squatted down, thought about this. He looked at the lightening sky. "The fog could help us hide."

Reggie nodded. "It could, but chances are pretty good the sun will burn it off and then we're exposed again. And while we can probably make our way down those rocks, I don't see us making our way back up. And there's not a lot of cover down there. We could be halfway down and he could stand up here and pick us off."

"Only good thing about that," said Whit, "is that the dogs won't be able to get down there to have a nice dinner."

Katie stood. "Jesus, people, Shaw is trying to think of a way to get us out of here and all you can do is — "

Shaw put a hand over her mouth and looked around. They all heard it. Something was moving to the right and above them. Shaw motioned to the others to follow him. They set off to the left, away from the noise.

"Look, Shaw!" said Reggie, pointing back.

They all stood still, watching as it snaked down the cliff. A rope with a bag attached. It reached the bottom and the rope went slack, the plastic bag fell over on its side.

"Take it," said a voice.

They all looked up.

Pascal was standing at the top of the cliff.

Shaw and Whit automatically held up their knives.

Pascal grinned and shook his head. The fog was rolling in faster now, almost obscuring him. "Take it. It will help you."

Watching him closely, Shaw moved cautiously toward the bag. When he reached it and saw what was inside it, his jaw slackened in amazement. He pulled out the gun and the cell phone.

Pascal said, "The phone is fully juiced. You have full bars. There is a cell tower that Mr. Waller had put in a mile from here. Call whoever you need to. And its GPS chip is activated."

"Why are you doing this?" Shaw asked.

"He wants me to drive you that way," said Pascal, pointing back the way they had come. "About a mile from here where the two trails converge. There is high ground to the west. If I had to guess, he will be there waiting."

"You haven't answered my question." Shaw automatically checked the gun to make sure the mag was loaded and all critical elements were in working order.

Surprisingly, Pascal looked over at Reggie and Whit. "I hoped you would've killed him in Gordes. The information I passed on to your colleagues I thought was sufficient. But Rice got in the way. He followed you," Pascal said, pointing at Reggie. "To the church."

"*You* were our inside contact?" asked Reggie in amazement.

"Damn," added Whit, shaking his head in disbelief.

"I didn't know what Rice had discovered until it was too late. I went with him to the church thinking I might be able to help you somehow." He looked at Shaw. "Then he showed up and you no longer needed help from me."

"You wanted Waller dead?" asked Reggie.

"He was Fedir Kuchin when my mother knew him. I'm Greek and he visited us there on holiday from Ukraine when I was little."

"You knew him when you were a boy?" asked Katie.

"You could say that. He was my father, though he was never much of a father. And he left my mother to die with nothing. We Greeks do not forgive or forget that. He believes I do not know who he really is. He does not think I am smart enough to figure it all out. He thinks I believe he simply came to Greece and rescued a poor orphaned boy. It's true he gave me food and shelter and trained me. But he still is the reason my mother died, and so nothing he did could ever make up for that."

Shaw looked down at the gun. "What is this for?"

"So you will have a chance."

Whit called out, "Why don't you just kill him yourself?"

"I have my reasons. And he *is* my father. I will take care of the others. And the dogs too. You take care of him. Good luck," he added curtly.

The next moment Pascal was gone.

They all eyed each other.

"What do you think?" said Katie. "Do you believe this is legit?"

Shaw fingered the gun. "Legit enough for him to give us a real weapon and a communication line. And let's just take care of that right now." He punched in a number. Frank's sleepy voice answered.

"I've got one minute to explain, Frank, and then I need you to move like you've never moved in your whole damn life."

Shaw told Frank what he needed to hear and then clicked off. He fingered the gun and glanced at Katie. "You and Reggie stay here with Whit. I'll take the gun and kill the guy. Then I'll come back for you."

"It's not just him, Shaw, he has other people," said Reggie. "You may need help."

"You heard Pascal, he'll take care of the others."

Whit shook his head. "Yeah, but he's only one guy. They might kill him. And then there's the bleeding dogs. I can go with you. The ladies can stay here and wait for us to come back."

Reggie said, "We've been together this whole time. I don't see any reason to break us up now."

"I agree," said Katie. "All or none."

"Tactically, that makes no sense," retorted Shaw. "If we're all together it just makes his job that much easier."

"Or harder," said Reggie. "Depending on your perspective."

"Okay, why can't we all stay here and wait for Frank to come?" asked Whit.

"Because if we do Kuchin will just come to us. Even by plane or chopper it'll take Frank awhile to get here."

"We can ambush him here."

"The ground here is not good. We're sitting ducks. Look how easily that guy snuck up on us. If I go back there where he's expecting us, but hit it from a different angle, I may be able to get the jump on him. And he's not expecting me to have a gun."

"We're not staying behind, Shaw," said Katie. "I finally found you, so I'm not letting you go that easily."

Reggie looked at Shaw and added, "I'm coming too."

Shaw eyed Whit for support, but the Irishman merely shrugged helplessly. "I've never won an argument with a woman in my life. And I don't think I'm going to start a winning streak with these two."

Shaw sighed deeply and, holding the gun ready, he set off. The others followed right behind.

CHAPTER

100

KUCHIN HAD chosen the ground, but not in the location one would have expected, not even Pascal. High ground was almost always good ground when it came to a conflict. Almost always. He aimed his rifle, sighting through the scope, and used a gloved hand to rub a bit of dirt off the glass. He pulled up his glove and eyed his watch. Then he lay back and waited, counting off seconds in his head to keep alert.

When the sounds first came he didn't move. As the footfalls came closer he timed their impact with the ground and moved when they struck to disguise any noise he might make. The barrel came up; his dominant right eye leaned to the glass. The reticle did its job. Target acquired, there was no reason to wait. He fired.

"Shit!" screamed Whit, clutching his leg and falling to the ground immediately behind Shaw.

"Everyone down," yelled Shaw.

They all flattened to the ground. Reggie slid over to Whit to see how bad the hit was. He was already pulling open his jumpsuit to try to stop the bleeding. "It went through," he grunted. "Don't think it hit the bone, but Jesus it hurts like hell."

Reggie said, "We'll get you out of this."

Whit shook his head, his face growing pale. "It's just like Rice. The bastard has his method, Reg. Leg first, then the torso." He grunted in anguish, his whole body shaking with pain. His mouth quivering, he added, "And then the damn dogs."

"I won't let that happen."

He grabbed her with his good arm and thrust the knife into her hand. "If you hear those dogs coming just finish me off before they get to me. Promise me!" She couldn't answer him, but stared back at him helplessly. He shook her. "Damn it, Reggie, promise me. Don't let them do to me what they did to Rice."

Reggie looked down at the knife as tears formed in her eyes. "Whit, I can't. I can't do that."

Whit seemed to gather his strength to make one more plea. "If you don't then Kuchin wins. And we can't let the bloody monster win, Reg, can we?" He lay back gasping.

Reggie clenched the knife tighter, brushed the tears away, and said, "All right, I will. If I *have* to."

From where he crouched Shaw surveyed the landscape ahead. The fog was still rolling in, heavier now, covering everything with a gauzy haze. The shapes of things began to alter and transform, playing tricks on one's eyes. The direction Whit had been shot from meant that Kuchin was somewhere in front of him, but that left a lot of degrees of the compass to account for. They might only get one chance at this. He told Katie to stay where she was and crawled over to Reggie and Whit. After checking on the wounded man, he handed her the gun. She looked at him questioningly.

Shaw said, "This is our last chance, Reggie. The only way we get out of this is to smoke him out."

"How?"

"Muzzle flash. We haven't seen one yet, but it's still dark enough for the light to be clearly visible when it comes."

"How are you going to manage that?"

"By making him fire again."

"I know that, but how!" she said fiercely.

He pointed up ahead. "I'm going to run in a straight line directly in front of you from right to left. You keep your eyes up there. The flash will come from that direction. He's close. I could tell from the sound of the discharge. It wasn't fired from a distance."

"Shaw, you—"

He looked over at Whit moaning on the ground. "When the muzzle flash comes—"

"Shaw, I can't—"

He slapped her in the face so hard it left her cheek red and raw. "Don't tell me what you can't do. You *will* do this."

She looked stunned from his strike but her eyes didn't water. They appeared to harden. He seemed to notice this and his voice softened a notch. "You can make this shot, Reggie. I've seen you do it on the firing range. Six inches below the muzzle flash. Place a triple tap right there, grouped close. He won't be wearing body armor because he doesn't know we have a gun. As soon as you do it, you and Katie help Whit back to the coastline, and wait for Frank there." He handed her the cell phone. "Keep calling him to check his progress and that way he should be able to link on the GPS chip in the phone."

Reggie licked her lips. "Shaw?" she began.

"Just do it, Reggie. Just finish it. For me."

She finally nodded dumbly and he immediately turned from her and stood half bent over.

"Shaw," screamed Katie as she rose from the dirt and moved toward him. "Look out."

Shaw glanced to his left. The son of a bitch had changed positions somehow, with the silence of a ghost. And he looked ghostly too, through the cover of fog. There was Kuchin, rifle already raised and ready to fire. With a weapon like that it was really point-blank. He couldn't miss.

Shaw threw out his arms a split second before the shot. He felt the bullet burn across the surface of his right limb. As he lowered his arms, he wondered how the man could have missed that badly at this range. Then, like an avalanche, the truth came and crushed him.

"Katie!"

He turned in time to see Katie James toppling backward from the force of the ordnance that had just blown through her. The wisps of her blonde hair flew outward as the round exited her back and splattered into a rock behind her. She hit the ground, bounced slightly, and lay still.

Kuchin stood there, barely forty feet away. He looked down at the fallen woman and then up at Shaw, who could not draw his gaze from her.

Kuchin said, "I told you if you followed my instructions *to the letter* she would be released unharmed. Instead, you disobeyed me. You went back to the house and took her. You broke our compact. You are actually the reason for her death, my friend."

By millimeter increments Shaw pulled his gaze from Katie to Kuchin. From the look in the man's eyes, he realized that this had all been planned. No guards at the house, Katie all alone. A truck coming in at the end and a handful of shots fired to make it look good. It hadn't been a planned ambush. He'd wanted Shaw to rescue Katie. Break the agreement. And he'd walked right into the trap. Fallen for it like the greenest sucker on earth.

With a blur of motion fueled by a level of rage he'd only felt one other time in his life, Shaw exploded forward and within four seconds had covered nearly all the ground between him and Kuchin, his knife raised in a killing position. But it had taken Kuchin less time than that to raise his rifle once more and take careful aim. Shaw's brain was sighted clearly on his American-made reticle that had never missed its target. Right before he fired a swirl of fog covered Kuchin completely.

The shot came. Then another. And then a final one.

Kuchin lowered the rifle even as Shaw leapt. Then the rifle fell to the dirt as the Ukrainian's grip weakened and blood started to spurt out of the three holes in his chest. The shots were so closely grouped that all three bullets had smashed into his heart.

Reggie lowered the pistol. The smoky firing range had paid off. She had just memorized where he was behind the fog. And this time the target hadn't moved.

Kuchin dropped to his knees, his eyes wide with disbelief about what had just happened. This was so even though the man was already medically dead. Scientists sometimes referred to this as the "technical soul," the last synaptic firing from a dead brain that left some trace of reason despite physical life already having come to an end.

An instant later, Shaw collided with Kuchin and drove the knife right through his skull with such force that it broke off at the handle. Fedir Kuchin fell backwards with Shaw on top of him. And he hit him, once, twice, the blows accelerating, raining down on the dead man until there was no face left, only tissue that had been turned to pulp as Shaw's knuckles cracked and his hands bled.

"Shaw! He's dead. He's *dead*."

Reggie tried to pull him off, but he used one big arm to knock her off her feet. Then, seeming to realize what had happened, Shaw jumped up and raced to Katie. He checked her pulse but couldn't find one. He straddled her, pumped her chest, then pinched her nose and blew air into her mouth. He pumped and blew. Pushing down on her chest, forcing air into lungs that refused to expand. But then she finally gave a moan, her body jerked, and she took an enormous breath.

Shaw looked up at Reggie, who'd raced over next to him. "Help me. Please."

While Shaw cradled Katie's head in his arms, Reggie opened her shirt and checked the wound.

"It went through her," she said. "But it entered very close to her heart." She dressed the wound and stopped the bleeding as best as she could. Shaw called Frank and told him what had happened. They were bringing a medical team with them, he told Shaw.

As Katie slowly breathed in and out, Reggie sat back on her haunches, looked over at Whit, who lay on the dirt clutching his leg and quietly moaning. Next, she stared over at Kuchin's battered body and she remembered something. "May God understand why I do this," she mumbled, then crossed herself.

When Reggie noticed that Shaw's arm was bleeding she pulled up his sleeve, saw the bullet track scored into his skin.

"You fouled his shot," she said.

"What?" said Shaw.

"His shot hit your arm before it hit her. You screwed the trajectory. He was probably aiming for her head. From what he said, he thought it was a kill shot for certain."

Shaw looked at Katie, clearly not interested in this. "I'm the reason she got shot in the first place."

"Shaw, you saved her life."

"Not yet," he said, a sob escaping his lips. "Not yet." He held Katie as tightly as he could, as though that would prevent life from leaving her. And from the woman leaving him.

101

KATIE AND WHIT were treated on the plane by a medical team Frank had brought. When they landed in Boston they were both rushed to a trauma hospital. Shaw, Reggie, and Frank sat in the waiting room for hours, Frank drinking cup after cup of bad vending-machine coffee while Shaw just stared at the floor. The doctors came out to tell them that Whit was fine and would fully recover. Then more hours passed.

Shaw stirred when a tall man and woman walked past the waiting room. It was Katie's parents. He recognized them from a photo she'd once shown him. They looked both exhausted and frantic. They were with their daughter for an hour before they came back out and into the waiting room.

Shaw remembered that Katie had told him her father was an English professor. He was tall and spare, his hair mostly gray. Katie's mother looked like her daughter, slim and blonde, same eyes, same way of walking.

Katie's father said, "They told us that you helped our daughter." He directed this at Shaw. Shaw could barely lift his head to look at the man. He tried to speak, but couldn't. He looked back down, his guilt paralyzing him.

"Thank you," said Katie's mother.

Shaw still couldn't look at them.

Sensing what he was going through, Frank rose and escorted the Jameses out of the room, talking to them in a low voice. He came back in later and sat next to Shaw. "I put them in another waiting room. They're calling the rest of the family."

Reggie glanced over at him. "How is Katie?"

Frank said, "Still touch and go apparently. They still don't know the extent of the damage."

More hours passed. Frank had gotten some food from the cafeteria for them, but only he and Reggie ate any of it. Shaw just kept staring at the floor. Then they saw Katie's parents come out of the intensive care unit again.

From the looks on their faces the news was good. Katie's mother came over to Shaw. This time he rose and she hugged him. "She's going to make it," the woman said. "She's out of danger." This came out in a gush of relief. Her husband shook Shaw's hand. "I don't know what really happened, but I do want to thank you with all my heart for helping to save her life."

After a few more minutes they left to call Katie's siblings and give them the good news.

Shaw just stood there staring at his feet.

"You did help save her, Shaw," said Frank.

Shaw waved off his comment with a short thrust of his hand.

Reggie said, "Shaw, you need to go in and see her."

He shook his head. "No."

"Why not?"

"I don't have that right," he said between gritted teeth. He clenched and unclenched his hands, looked like he wanted to put both fists through the wall. "She almost died because of me. And her parents are thanking me for saving her. It's not right. None of that is right."

Reggie gripped his face and turned it so he was forced to look at her. "You *need* to go and see her."

"Why?" he said fiercely.

"Because *she* deserves that."

Their gazes locked for what seemed like forever. Reggie slowly released him and stepped back.

Shaw moved silently past her and left the waiting room. A few minutes later he was standing next to Katie's bed. Tubes covered her; machines surrounded her. The nurse told Shaw he only had a minute, then she retreated, leaving them alone. He picked up Katie's hand, holding it gently.

"I'm sorry, Katie. About a lot of things."

He knew she was full of pain meds and wasn't conscious, but he had to say these things. If he didn't he felt he would combust.

"I shouldn't have left you in Zurich. I should have come after you sooner in Paris. I . . ." He faltered, fell silent. "I really, really care about you. And . . ." The tears started to trickle down his cheeks and he drew a ragged breath, felt sick to his stomach. He bent down and kissed her hand. As soon as he did, he felt her fingers tighten slightly around his hand. He looked at her face. She was still unconscious, but she had squeezed his hand.

He saw the nurse staring at him from the doorway.

"Good-bye, Katie," he said, finally letting her go.

102

Sure you don't want me to drive?" Frank said. He'd just climbed in the passenger seat of their rental.

"Yeah, I'm sure." Shaw drove faster than he should have to the airport.

Frank looked over nervously from time to time, but seemed loath to break the silence. Finally, he said, "We found the rest of Kuchin's boys, all dead, all except for this Pascal guy. He was nowhere to be found."

"Good for him." Shaw's gaze never veered from the road ahead.

"You sure you don't want to stay around here? I can get you the time off. You can be there when Katie leaves the hospital."

"The only thing I'm going to do is get as far away from her as I possibly can."

"But Shaw—"

Shaw slammed on the brakes, bringing the car to a rubber-burning stop as horns blared all around them and cars whizzed past on either side.

"What the hell are you doing?" exclaimed a stunned Frank.

Shaw's face was red; his big body shook like he was suffering from meth withdrawal. "She almost died because of me. And it wasn't the first time. So I am never going near her because this is never going to happen again, Frank. Do you understand me?"

"Yeah, yeah, I got it." Frank had seen Shaw under virtually every situation imaginable, but he had never seen him like this.

Later that night Shaw and Frank boarded a British Airways 777 at Boston's Logan Airport that would take them to London by the next morning. During the flight Frank watched a movie, had some drinks and dinner, did some work and napped.

Shaw spent the entire six-hour-and-twenty-minute flight staring out the window. When they landed the men cleared customs at Heathrow and walked toward the exits.

"Shaw, I've got a car. You want a lift into town?"

"Just get me another assignment, the sooner the better." Shaw kept walking, head down, bag swinging at his side.

Frank stared at him for a bit, then found his ride and was driven off.

Shaw got into London an hour later on a bus. He didn't go to the Savoy. He wasn't working. He couldn't afford the place on his own dime. He checked into a far more modestly priced room in a far less desirable part of town. He had just thrown his bag down in a chair when his phone rang.

He didn't even bother to look at the caller ID. He wasn't talking to anyone right now. He went out, bought some beer, came back, popped one, drank it down and then another, crumpling the empty cans in one hand and throwing them into the trash.

The phone rang again. He had another beer, went to the window, gazed out on the street, and saw a bunch of people pass by who had never personally known Katie James and might not even know how close she had come to dying.

"She's a terrific person," Shaw said to the window. "I don't deserve her. And she sure as hell doesn't deserve me." He held up his beer can, tapped it against the glass, thinking of her hand squeezing his. It had felt wonderful and yet he knew he would never feel it again.

At midnight his phone stopped ringing even as he finished off the last beer, which was now warm. He couldn't sleep and rose in the middle of the night to throw up all that he had drunk into the toilet. He showered, shaved, dressed in fresh clothes, and headed out to find some breakfast at 4 a.m. This being London, he was successful after only a two-block search. He sat in the back of the mostly empty café and ordered the biggest platter they had. When it came he just stared at the food and instead drank down two cups of black

coffee before dropping a pile of British notes on the checkered ta-
blecloth and leaving.

He walked along the Thames and found the spot where he and
Katie had stood when a shot had rung out and a man had fallen dead
into the river. Then he ventured to another street where if he'd been
a second later Katie would have been murdered by a man wielding a
syringe. He passed a shop where they had had dinner together. And
finally the hotel where he had thrown her breakfast cart against a wall
and she'd responded by calmly pouring him a cup of coffee. This
memory drew a smile from him that quickly collapsed into a sob. At
that same encounter she'd shown him the bullet wound on her upper
arm. And shared with him the story of the Afghan boy who had died,
she said, as a result of Katie's reaching too far, too hard for a story.

She'd flown across the Atlantic on a moment's notice to be with
Shaw when he needed her. She had always been there when he'd
needed her. And now she was lying in a hospital with a hole in her
chest because of him. Shaw staggered into an alleyway, leaned
against a dirty brick building, and wept so hard he finally got the
dry heaves.

Later, at Trafalgar Square, he sat red-eyed with the pigeons, staring up at Lord Nelson until his neck hurt because he didn't know
where else to look. London was coming to life now, the pace of feet
and vehicles picking up. As the sun rose, the air warmed. After all
that had happened, it was hard to believe that it was still summer.
Gordes, even Canada, seemed an eternity ago to him.

He rose, looked around, debating where next to go, then stopped.
Across the square Reggie was staring back at him. He started to
walk in the opposite direction, but something made him reverse his
path and cross the space toward her.

"How'd you know?"

"Lucky guess," she said. "And I called Frank. He told me you
were back in London."

"How's Whit?"

"Leg's stiff but he'll be fine. I'm glad Katie will be okay too."

Shaw absently nodded.

Reggie wore the white jeans she'd had in Gordes, black flats, and
a blue cotton blouse. Her hair hung limp to her shoulders. She

looked older, thought Shaw. Hell, they all looked older. He felt like he was a hundred.

"Tried to call you, but you didn't answer."

"I think my service was turned off," he said.

He started walking and she fell in beside him.

He said, "Thanks for taking out Kuchin. It was a hell of a shot."

"I should've been faster. If I had, Katie—"

He moved slightly away from her. "Don't, Reggie, just don't."

She fell silent as they walked farther into the Strand.

"Did they ever find Dominic's body?" he asked.

"No. And the worst part is his parents will never really know what happened to him."

"I'm sorry about that."

She looked down, seeming to search for the right words. "Frank is talking to us about working with you."

Shaw stopped and looked down coldly at her. "With *me*?"

"No, I meant with him. With *his* organization," she said hurriedly.

Shaw started walking again. "I don't see how that could be possible."

She started speaking rapidly. "We would have to change some of the ways we operate. I mean we can't, well, finish the jobs like we used to. But he said the information network and research support we have could prove useful if we were to combine certain—"

Shaw held up a hand indicating for her to stop. "I don't really care, okay?"

She looked crushed by this but said, "Sure. Okay. I can understand that."

They came to a park and Shaw sat down on a bench. Reggie hesitated, seeming unsure whether he wanted her to join him or not. She finally just sat down, but kept a healthy space between them, which was difficult since Shaw was so big.

"I don't think I ever thanked you for saving my life."

"Shaw, you don't have to thank me. I wouldn't be here if it weren't for you."

"I needed to say it."

"Fine, you said it. That's enough." She crossed her legs, drew an exaggerated breath. "It's none of my business, but—"

He cut her off. "Then drop it."

A minute of silence passed.

"We weren't more than friends," Shaw said, breaking the quiet. "Not yet anyway. But we *were* friends. And she meant . . . she *means* a lot to me. More than I realized."

"Okay." A tear slid down Reggie's cheek.

"And whether we ever would be more than friends is something that . . ." He shook his head, stared over at a little boy with his mother, and then dropped his gaze to the grass.

"But, Shaw, she's going to be okay. You can go and—"

"That won't be happening," he said firmly.

Another few moments of silence passed.

"What are you going to do now?" she asked.

"Few days off wandering around here until Frank puts me back to work."

"You could come out to Harrowsfield. In fact, I believe Frank is traveling there tomorrow to go over some things. And we could—" She stopped talking when he abruptly stood.

"No, Reggie, I really don't think we could."

He turned to leave.

"Please, Shaw."

He looked over his shoulder at her. "I'm sorry."

"But if we can just take it slow." Tears were starting to cluster in her eyes and this seemed to anger her. She brushed them away.

He turned to face her as she stood to do the same. "I buried the one woman who meant more to me than anyone else. And I nearly lost another woman who I care about deeply." He paused and drew a short breath. "I'm not going to make it three. Take care of yourself, Reggie."

She stared after him until even his tall figure disappeared into the growing crowds as London came to life.

Reggie finally walked off in the opposite direction. She could not bring herself to look back.

If she had glanced back, however, she would have seen Shaw stop and stare back at her for a long moment. Then he slowly turned around and kept walking.

ACKNOWLEDGMENTS

To MICHELLE, who makes all our lives work.

To Mitch Hoffman, editor extraordinaire.

To David Young, Jamie Raab, Emi Battaglia, Jennifer Romanello, Tom Maciag, Martha Otis, Bob Castillo, Anthony Goff, Kim Hoffman, and everyone at Grand Central Publishing, for all you do.

To Aaron and Arleen Priest, Lucy Childs, Lisa Erbach Vance, Nicole Kenealy, Frances Jalet-Miller, and John Richmond, for helping me every step of the way.

To Roland Ottewell, for your keen eye.

To Maria Rejt and Katie James at Pan Macmillan, for their well-timed support from across the pond.

To Grace McQuade and Lynn Goldberg, for wonderful publicity.

To Bob Schule, for world-class consultant services.

To Lynette, Deborah, and Natasha, for being a great team.